Also by Suzanne Lazear
Innocent Darkness
Charmed Vengeance
(Books 1 and 2 of the Aether Chronicles)

FRAGILE DESTINY

The Aether Chronicles • Book 3

SUZANNE LAZEAR

flux
®

First Edition
First Printing, 2014

Book design by Bob Gaul
Cover design by Kevin R. Brown
Cover image: iStockphoto.com/11473356/©Alexey Ivanov
Cover illustration by John Kicksee/The July Group

Flux, an imprint of Llewellyn Worldwide Ltd.

Library of Congress Cataloging-in-Publication Data
Lazear, Suzanne.
    Fragile destiny/Suzanne Lazear.—First edition.
        pages cm.—(The aether chronicles; book 3)
    Summary: To prevent the Realm of Faerie from falling under the sway of the dark king, seventeen-year-old Noli and her friends rush to find and protect the pieces of a powerful artifact.
    ISBN 978-0-7387-3986-1
    [1. Fantasy. 2. Fairies—Fiction. 3. Magic—Fiction.] I. Title.
    PZ7.L4494Fr 2014
    [Fic]—dc23

                                                            2014011458

Flux
Llewellyn Worldwide Ltd.
2143 Wooddale Drive
Woodbury, MN 55125-2989
www.fluxnow.com

Printed in the United States of America

Dad, this one's for you.
And for Erika.
Miss you both.

'Twas brillig, and the slithy toves,
Did gyre and gimble in the wabe;
All the mimsy were the borogoves,
  And the mome raths outgrabe.
—Lewis Carroll, "Jabberwocky"

Fight and Flight

"Where are we going, Quinn? Where are James and Steven?" Elise gripped Quinn's large hand tightly with her small one as they hurried through the darkness. Something was wrong, and had been wrong ever since Quinn had retrieved her from dance class yesterday, shoved a valise into her hands, and hauled her onto an airship with no explanation whatsoever.

She wished someone would tell her what was happening.

"I told you, we're going to meet Mathias in the park," Quinn shushed, walking even faster through a giant place that he called "Central Park."

"Then you'll tell me what's going on?" Cold chilled her to the bone, and hunger and fear gnawed at her belly. She pulled her cape closer. Fatigue made each footfall a chore. "I want Dadaí." Elise hadn't called her father that in a long time, but that's what she wanted right now. Her daddy. Even if he was often irritable—when he was around.

"Hush. Head down, walk fast, don't make eye contact," Quinn whispered as he put an arm around her, bringing her close as they hurried down the dark path. The sun still hadn't awoken, and the chill in the air made her shiver.

A humming under her skin sent prickles up her spine. Magic. Her heart beat faster as her small legs struggled to match Quinn's much longer stride.

"Quinn the Fair, halt," someone yelled from behind them.

Quinn the Fair? Certainly her tutor was fair, with his near-white hair and pale skin. But she'd never heard him called that before.

"Run." Quinn half-dragged her down the path. They ran until her chest ached and she could barely breathe. The magic closed in on them like a net. Fear crept through her, twining around her limbs like morning fog. She tried to push it away. Quinn was here, he'd protect her.

When they ducked behind a tree, he pressed a card into her hand. "Run until you find a policeman. Tell him that you're lost and men are chasing you. Give him this and say that your dadaí is at that address."

"Dadaí's there?" The idea of running *more* made her want to collapse. However, the urgency in his voice made her heart skip a beat.

"No, it's Mathias. Pretend that he's your dadaí. He'll keep you safe until we can find your brothers. I give you permission to use magic to defend yourself—any kind of magic you like." His blue eyes sliced through her like a knife through bread.

"What?" The words only cemented the fact that something was dreadfully wrong. Usually she wasn't allowed to use magic unless it was a lesson, and then only earth magic.

Someone yelled from down the path, "There they are!"

Quinn kissed her forehead. "Be good. Now, *run*. Don't let them catch you, *no matter what*. Go." He pushed her. "Run—and don't look back."

Nodding, Elise barreled down the path, as fast as her feet could take her, valise thumping across her back. Quinn wouldn't tell her to do such a thing unless it was important.

"Ah, I caught you." A man in a strange green outfit grabbed her around the waist.

Don't let them catch you no matter what. Quinn's words rang in her ears.

"No." Squishing her eyes shut, she launched a little ball of fire at her pursuer. He yelped, and she kicked him in the shins and took off.

Elise sprinted until her legs burned and sweat dripped down her back. She didn't slow down, not even to look behind her to see if she was still being followed. A policeman. She needed a policeman. Not that she saw one. Maybe it was too early? An ornate gate caught her eye, a garden behind it. Yes, she'd be safe there. She'd catch her breath, then find a policeman.

She sent out a hint of magic to make the gate open. Looking both ways to see if anyone watched, she slipped inside. As she took in the beautiful garden surrounding her, she meandered through an arch of ivy and came to a little pond. Not a soul was in sight. Good. What she needed was a tree to hide her while she rested.

Were there any wood faeries about? A garden like this *must* have wood faeries. Holding out her hand, she gave them a silent call. A moment later, a green ball of light landed on her finger. The ball of light resembled a tiny man with translucent wings and clothes made of leaves, but she recognized it as a wood faery.

"Hello, I'm lost and tired. Is there a tree that will hide me while I rest?" Elise cocked her head to hear the tiny faery's answer. "There's a magic tree that can take me home?" She tried to imagine such a thing. "That would be even better." Yes, home to Dadaí, Steven, and James. "I'd love it if you'd take me there."

The little faery led her through the garden to a tree. It glowed with balls of light—pink, yellow, blue, even purple, as tiny faces peered at her.

"Hello there, I'm Elise." She bobbed a curtsey. "How do I make the tree work? I've never traveled by tree before. Usually we just take an auto—or an airship." Magic thrummed under her fingertips as they brushed the tree's trunk.

Several faeries attempted to speak at once.

"One at a time, please." If only she had something in the pocket of her pinafore to feed them. If only she had something in her pocket to feed herself. "All I have to do is tell the tree where I'd like to go?"

They kept using the word *portal* and she had no idea what that meant. Oh, a portal was probably another tree.

Yes, magic travel from tree to tree—brilliant! Certainly, not every tree was magic. But Noli had a faery tree. No faeries lived in it, but it was next door to her house. She could climb through the fence and be home. Perfect.

Elise pictured Noli's tree in her mind and put both hands on the trunk, glad Noli's tree was so distinctive with its J-shaped trunk and tree house. "I'd like to go there please, to the tree with the house in it."

Her arms and hands grew tingly. The little green wood faery perched on her shoulder. His presence comforted her. The garden began to spin faster and faster, as if she were on a carousel. Elise gripped the trunk with all her might. Then everything faded away.

· · · · · · · ·

"Come out, come out, wherever you are," Kevighn muttered as he wandered through Central Park. Why would Quinn and the girl come here? And *so* early. He yawned. Prickles shot up his spine. Quinn and the girl were close. Extremely close.

"You'll never get her," someone yelled in the distance.

Magic swirled around him so thick he could practically hold it in his hands. He sprinted toward the clamor. Several men in earth court guardsman's uniforms flew at a man in mortal clothing—a tall, thin man with pale hair. There was no sign of anyone else. Not even a girl.

Quinn the Fair hurled balls of light at the earth court guards. One of the guards stamped the ground, his earth magic making the path ripple under Quinn's feet. As Quinn tumbled to the ground, he lobbed more balls of light at the guards.

Kevighn ran faster, fueled by both triumph and anger. He'd found Quinn. No one got to kill Quinn the Fair but *him*. Taking his bow out of his rucksack, he fired fire arrows into all three of the guards. Not stowing his bow, he breathed a sigh of relief as the guards fell, and then he approached Quinn.

"I never thought I'd be saved by the likes of you." Quinn lay on the ground, his wiry form crumpled and bleeding.

Kevighn whipped an arrow out of his quiver on his back, the one with Quinn's name carved into it, and loaded it. "Three on one isn't fair. Even for someone like you."

Quinn stood up, his injuries obviously causing him pain. He was hunched over and bleeding, a hand over one of the wounds. "I suppose you mean to kill me, Kevighn?"

His voice was composed. He didn't tremble, and his calmness angered Kevighn. Quinn should be scared. He should be begging for his life. Anger at Quinn's lack of reaction swirled within Kevighn.

"Where's the girl?" Kevighn pointed the bow at Quinn as he cast his eyes about the area searching for a sign of her. Nothing.

"She's safe. Safe from Tiana, safe from Brogan. She's a *girl*, not a pawn," Quinn spat, his expression challenging, and although the man couldn't even stand up straight, Kevighn could sense his pride, his strength.

He tightened his lips and resolved to still make Quinn

pay. "I don't work for Tiana anymore," he retorted, the need for revenge coursing through him. "Also, I've always thought Brogan was a prat."

"Brogan *is* a prat," Quinn agreed, color draining out of his pale face. "But Dom... Dom regretted doing what he did, as do I. We..." His entire being crumpled as the life drained out of him and he sank to the ground. "Creideamh and I could have been happy in exile. Ahh, everything is clearer in hindsight."

"You killed my sister." Kevighn prepared to fire at him. Why couldn't Quinn flinch like a normal man, beg for his life?

"I did. My pride and arrogance killed her." His blue eyes went misty. "I loved your sister so much. Kill me, Kevighn. Kill me now. At least then I'll be with her once again." His body moved slightly to make it a clean and clear shot to the heart.

Of course the bastard would beg to be killed. Fury boiled in Kevighn's veins. *No, no, no.* This wasn't how revenge was supposed to be.

"No, you won't. She's in the place where the good and kind people go. You said you were my friend. You promised to protect her. You *knew* what bringing her into the earth court would do to someone like her." Kevighn kept his bow trained on Quinn, face and voice burning with a rage so fierce he expected something to ignite at any time.

Only those of the high queen's line were allowed to possess the talent of more than one court. To have an affinity for *both* earth and fire was blasphemous, considering those courts were bitter enemies. Even Kevighn's tiny amount of earth manipulation ability could get him killed. Cre-ideamh's gift, on the other hand, had grown too great to hide among the proper elemental courts. So they'd lurked in the dark court, where no one cared.

Until she'd fallen in love with Quinn.

Quinn's chin rose slightly, eyes brimming with angst that would soften a lesser man's heart. "I thought that I could protect her. At least…" His head dropped.

"At least what?" Kevighn demanded, taking a step closer. Why did Quinn always have to be so damn civil?

His voice quieted. "Please, let him know I love him. It's too little, too late, I know, but it was all we could do."

"What are you talking about?" Kevighn yelled, anger roaring in his ears.

Quinn didn't answer, eyes closed, breath fading.

No, Quinn couldn't die, not unless it was at his hand. Kevighn unleashed the arrow, the arrow he'd carved by hand, pouring all his anger and frustration into it. It zoomed through the air, piercing Quinn in the heart. Blood pooled at the arrow's entrance. Quinn didn't move.

"Creideamh, you have been avenged." Kevighn's head tilted upward to the grey sky, fist to his heart, bow dangling in his free hand.

Police whistles echoed in the background. Kevighn touched the arrow in Quinn's chest, reducing it to ash. He drew a glyph in the air, which turned red, erasing his presence for a good hundred yards. His rucksack went over his shoulder and he ducked behind the nearest building, pulling the magic with him to cover his tracks both physically and magically.

He should feel elated, but instead he felt...empty. Unsatisfied. Like he needed to get very drunk and go to bed with a room full of beautiful women.

For so many years, he'd yearned to avenge Creideamh's death. Now he had. What now?

And what *had* Quinn been babbling about?

He shook it off. First, he needed to find Ailís.

It matters not how strait the gate,
How charged with punishments the scroll,
I am the master of my fate;
I am the captain of my soul.
—William Ernest Henley, "Invictus"

Return to Los Angeles

Noli glanced from her dilapidated house to the neatly kept Darrow residence next door. Her belly rolled with a million different emotions. Between her mother moving to Boston and the shock of finding V and James' father murdered in his own home by earth court guards, she thought they'd never return to Los Angeles again.

Yet here they were.

"I still can't believe Uncle Brogan wasn't home," James Darrow said, pouting as they stood in front of their houses, the winter sun streaming down onto their backs.

Steven Darrow, whom Noli always called "V," put his fist to his chest. "Believe me. Father will be avenged. *And thus the whirligig of time brings in his revenges.*"

"I know. Though I really wish you would stop quoting Chaucer." James ran a hand through his messy, dark blond curls. Even though he was younger than V, he was taller and broader. But V was catching up.

"It's *Shakespeare*," V grumbled, taking Noli's hand. "Truly, I should get you his complete works for Christmas."

Noli had a feeling that James knew very well it was Shakespeare. Riling V could be amusing.

They'd come straight from the earth court palace, after failing to find Brogan to challenge him to a duel. As luck would have it, their uncle was away on earth court business, so V had suggested they return to the Darrow house in Los Angeles to see if any of Quinn's journals and research materials were still there. They'd already buried Mr. Darrow at the big house, the family's home in the Otherworld, and now their main task was to find information about the mysterious artifact Brogan was trying to assemble.

All three were still in Otherworld dress. The boys' green and brown velvet outfits were heavy with embroidery, their swords on their backs. They both looked so handsome. So…adult. Even Noli still wore an embroidered, green velvet gown with a drop waist and a brown corset on top, with no bustle or crinoline, and her green cloak instead of a cape.

"I think I should sleep at my house." She shot another sidelong glance at V's house as a car flew overhead. The idea of staying overnight in the place where V and James' father had been murdered sent chills up her spine.

"I think we should *all* sleep at your house, Noli." James shivered a little, as if echoing her own thoughts. "The last thing I want is to be haunted by Father. I'm sure he'll find some reason to scold us in our sleep."

V shoved his brother, a frown tugging at his lips. "How could you say something so disrespectful?"

James shoved him back, his jaw set. "It's true."

Actually, Noli *could* see the dour Mr. Darrow doing just that. However, V had a point about disrespecting the dead.

"I'll go to the market and buy a few things so we have something to eat. I have a little money," she told them, partially to escape having to enter the house, partially out of practicality. There'd be nothing edible in either house, she was sure.

Cake, I want cake! the sprite interjected mentally.

Thanks to an ill-worded bargain with High Queen Tiana, Noli currently shared head-space with an earth sprite, and every day it got increasingly difficult to keep her from taking over. V promised to help her fix it. Somehow.

Cake? Perhaps. Actually, Noli liked that idea.

Also, she still felt odd, like she hadn't fully recovered from the illness Brogan had given her back on her brother's airship, the Vixen's Revenge, when she'd refused to hand over the piece of artifact that she'd kept. Her brother Jeff's crew, hired by Brogan, had stolen fragments of the artifact from museums across the country. But instead of letting Jeff deliver the pieces to Brogan—since Noli knew Brogan was up to no good—she'd given them to Kevighn Silver, who'd promised to hide them once again.

Yet, on an impulse, she'd kept a piece of the artifact for herself. As insurance.

This she hadn't mentioned to V, since he had other things to deal with—like Brogan, his father's death, and the

3

fact that Quinn, their tutor, and Elise, their little sister, had gone missing and had yet to be found.

The artifact. All the pieces made up one single, powerful artifact so dangerous it had been expelled to the mortal realm long ago. However, she had a feeling there was something else she was supposed to remember about it. But every time she almost did, it slipped away like a will-o'-the-wisp.

V's voice cut through her thoughts, bringing her back to the present. "You don't wish to stay and help us look through journals?" His green eyes went wide with disappointment.

No. Not particularly. Really she should assist him, since he was trying to figure out what the artifact *was*. If only she could remember.

You think too much, the sprite chided.

"I don't blame you. The house is creepy now." James' face screwed up in distaste. "We need to eat. Besides, while Noli's out she can check and see if we've received any aethergraphs. Perhaps Quinn's trying to get in touch with us."

"That's a good idea. I'm very worried about them since we haven't gotten word." V looked from his brother to his house and back again, his lips pressing tight, then releasing. His blond hair didn't quite lie flat, a lock hanging in eyes, which were green like oak leaves. "You know where to find us. James and I should get started."

James made a barf-face. "Could you get us something good for supper? Please?"

Noli laughed. "Like what, cake?"

His green eyes lit up like a basket of wood faeries. "Yes, chocolate cake."

4

"We can't—" Wait. Why *couldn't* they have cake for supper? There were no parents here. Not anymore. It would also make the sprite happy.

Cake, cake, cake, cake, the sprite chanted.

Fine, we'll have cake for supper, she laughed. "We can't have cake without tea, so if I'm to make it to the shops before they close, I should be going." Not that she wanted to go back into town, to have to explain her reappearance, but James was right, they needed to eat.

Crossing the space between them, V straightened her hat. "Could you please get us more than cake and tea, please? I'll give you money. Will you be all right shopping by yourself?"

"Why wouldn't I? I've spent my entire life running around this town alone." Well, not quite, but she was used to being independent and his lack of confidence in her made her bristle.

"I know." He gave her a lopsided grin in apology. "See you soon."

Before she could answer, his lips met hers. His arm snaked around her waist, bringing her chest to his. She deepened their kiss, holding on to him as if any moment he might float away.

"I'll be inside," James muttered behind them.

V touched his forehead to hers as he broke off their kiss. "Hurry back."

"I'll probably be at my house, cleaning up so we have places to sleep." Her finger traced his cheekbone. She let go of him and watched as V entered his house, then climbed up the familiar front stairs of her own home and turned the doorknob. Locked.

Walking around the house, she tried the back door, which was never locked. But the door didn't open. *Hmm.* Grandfather Montgomery must have locked it when he'd helped her mother move to Boston. Noli hoped her mother was finding happiness there, since she hadn't found much in Los Angeles after her husband vanished.

Seven years ago, Noli's father had disappeared while in San Francisco, helping to rebuild the city after a devastating earthquake. Even though there'd been no word all these years, Noli still clung to the idea that her father was alive and would someday return to them.

She gazed up at her bedroom window, which was on the second floor. She'd scaled it before.

Why don't we use magic? the sprite supplied.

Oh, I could do that, couldn't I? I just put my hand on it and ask it to open? That's what V always did. The idea of using magic was still so strange to her.

I think so, the sprite replied.

Noli put her hand on the metal knob. She envisioned an invisible key turning inside the mechanism. *Open.* The lock clicked. When she turned the knob, the door opened without resistance.

She entered the dark kitchen and put her valise on the table. On a scrap of paper she jotted down what they needed: *Food. Tea. Cake. Milk. Sugar. Candles.*

Then she gazed around the sparkling clean kitchen. It hadn't been this way when she'd left. She opened the cupboards—the everyday dishes were there, but the china and silver were gone. Startled, she ran into her mother's sewing room. The only thing that remained was a box half-filled with odds and ends and the steam-powered sewing machine she'd built. The sitting room, also clean, lacked the portraits on the walls and Mama's special keepsakes—and the piano.

Noli plopped down in a worn floral chair, the familiar musty scent wafting around her. Oh. Grandfather probably had someone pack up Mama's things and take them to Boston. The clock struck and she stood. She should get the market basket and be off. There'd be time to explore the house later.

....

Pulling her green cloak closer, Noli hurried down the street, basket on her arm. She wished she could hoverboard, since it would be much faster. It was probably early December by now…she'd lost track of time. V and James had put her in a tree for a while, to heal her from the illness Brogan had given her, and time between the mortal realm and the faerie realm ran a little differently in general—and not in a way that made sense. At least to her.

A display of gloves caught her eye as she walked past the milliner's shop.

Can we go inside? Please? the sprite pleaded. She liked pretty gloves.

We can—but only for a few moments. Perhaps they had net gloves, like the ones she'd gotten on the Vixen's Revenge.

She'd like to get some in colors other than black to match her different dresses.

A bell tinkled when she entered. The store wasn't empty and the shop girl seemed busy. Noli looked at the gloves on display—silk, kidskin, lace, ones covered in pearls or embroidery. None were net. Pity.

"Noli, is that you? Noli Braddock?" a voice screeched from behind her.

Noli winced. Of course *she'd* be here. Turning around, Noli plastered on a fake smile, greeting the two women she least wanted to see. "Why hello, Missy, Mrs. Sassafras."

Missy Sassafras' dull brown eyes widened and a smirk twitched on her lips. "My, what an unusual dress you have on."

"I think it's rather lovely. Your mother's work? It looks quite comfortable. Green looks so nice on you." Mrs. Sassafras smiled kindly at Noli. She always reminded Noli of an apple dumpling—round and ordinary. The fact that Mrs. Sassafras preferred to dress in mousy brown to match her hair and eyes never helped. Missy, on the other hand, always reminded Noli of a peacock. Loud, proud, and full of bright colors. Also, some girls weren't meant to wear bustles. Missy was one of them.

"I think it looks like a peasant's dress," Missy continued. "But isn't that what you are, really? Is that a *corset* on the *outside* of your dress?" Her thin lips curved into a sneer.

Peasant? What century was Missy living in? Noli looked at Mrs. Sassafras, who turned pink but didn't scold her daughter. She never did.

Bristling, Noli placed her hands on the corset. "It's a popular fashion in court."

"Court where?" Missy tossed her head as if she were a horse.

Noli stopped mid-breath. It wasn't as if she could tell Missy it was all the rage in the Otherworld, since most mortals had no idea that faeries—and the realm of Faerie—existed. Or that what they called *aether* was actually magic leaking into their realm from the Otherworld.

"France," Noli replied instead. That's what her mother always said when trying to coerce a customer at her dress shop into trying something new. She itched to get away from Missy.

Missy rolled her eyes. "I haven't seen it in any magazines."

"It's too new," Noli returned, feeling as if she were playing verbal Mintonette. "V's aunt was telling me all about it when we had tea with her earlier today." Lies. Aunt Dinessa had been telling them about gardening. Even though Brogan hadn't been home when they'd gone to the earth palace, his sister had insisted they stay for tea.

"Oh, Steven Darrow is back in town?" Missy took out her fan and fluttered it. The sparkle in her eyes turned accusing as her fan snapped shut. "Aren't you supposed to be in Boston with your mother?"

Mrs. Sassafras waved her gloved hand. "Oh, are you in town for the ball? Do you think your mother would have time to make some alterations to Missy's dress? Perhaps you should come to call; Missy has developed a new recipe for scones."

Missy and her blasted perfect scones. Did she have no other hobbies?

"The Christmas ball?" Noli blinked. Surely that much time hadn't passed.

Ball? I want to go. We're supposed to go, right? The sprite bounced around the inside of her head.

"I don't think Noli would be invited to the museum's ball," Missy simpered before she had a chance to silently answer the sprite.

I don't like her, she's mean, the sprite replied.

That Missy was. The Sassafrases weren't *that* rich and the money they had was recent. In Boston they'd be looked down upon as *nouveau riche.*

Missy, however, enjoyed putting on airs. Yes, Boston society would eat her alive. If Noli were a lesser person, she'd get Missy sponsored for the season there, just so she could watch her squirm. However, that would mean enduring it herself. She'd rather eat gears.

"I'm sure your Steven has an invitation." Mrs. Sassafras patted her arm. "Besides, you look as if you're doing well."

"Mama's fine. She's remaining in Boston; I'm still here to take care of some…unfinished business." Yes, that sounded acceptable. Noli tried to capture the shop girl's attention so she could *leave.*

Missy touched the tip of Noli's ear and giggled. "You really should visit that doctor in Europe."

Noli flinched as if burned. Being a sprite had given her ears a slight point. Usually she was able to cover them with her hair.

"May I help you?" The shop girl finally hustled over.

Thank goodness. One more moment and she'd smack Missy with her market basket. "Yes, do you have any net gloves?"

"Do you mean lace, miss?" The shop girl's face contorted in confusion.

"No, I mean net, like, well ... a net, only it's finer and softer." She should have brought a pair so she could show the shop girl what she meant.

The shop girl shook her head, lips puckering. "No, miss. We have nothing like that here. I'm not even sure where you'd look..."

Missy tittered in the background as she tried on a hat with a birdhouse on it. "Net gloves, truly?"

"Well, I do appreciate your help." Noli smiled at the girl. She gave the other ladies a curt nod. "Mrs. Sassafras, Missy," and left the shop and hustled down the street, waving at a car flying overhead, simply because.

Ugh. Missy was such a social-climbing dollymop.

Noli strode into the bakery. "I need a really large chocolate cake."

Mr. Benson, the baker, smiled at her from behind the glass counter as he wiped his hands on his white apron. "Did you have that bad of a day, Noli?"

"I just ran into Missy Sassafras." She eyed the trays of colorful confections. "I'd like the big chocolate cake in the front, the one with the candied cherries on top."

Yes, that one, the sprite agreed.

Noli's favorite cake wasn't found here in the mortal realm, but chocolate was just fine with her—and the sprite.

Her eyes traveled from the cakes and pastries to the cookies. "I'd also like a dozen—"

"Cookies with chocolate on top, of course." He laughed. "For your mother?"

Mama had always kept them in her dress shop for her customers. The shop wasn't far. Noli should check on it—if it was even still there.

"Mama's in Boston, I'm going to eat these all by myself." Noli's mouth watered at the thought as he packaged up the cookies and cake.

Cake, cake, cake, the sprite got excited.

Yes, cake. Noli did like cake, but those cookies were her favorites and had been such a rare indulgence. She couldn't wait to eat every single one herself. Perhaps she'd share with the boys. Maybe.

"I'd heard you'd moved back east," the baker replied as he packed up the pastries. "Are you here getting the last few things out of your house before the new owners take over?"

Noli nearly dropped her basket in shock. "Yes, of course," she lied.

Her heart thumped in her chest. Grandfather had sold their house?

The bag of cookies went in the basket, but the cake box didn't quite fit. Perhaps she should have gone there last. A hoverboard would be useful—or asking James to drive her, since Mr. Darrow owned an auto. Oh well. She'd just have to balance carefully.

As she bought tea, tinned milk, sugar, crackers, and tins of food at the greengrocer, all she could think of was that soon some other family would move into *her* house. Other children would play in her tree house. Sleep in her room.

When Papa finally came home, he'd find some other family living there.

She walked past her mother's dress shop, which was closed and dusty, as if no one had been inside in ages. A faded note said *closed until further notice*.

Sniffing, Noli made her final stop at Mr. Thompson's General Store.

"Are there any aethergraphs for Magnolia Braddock, or Steven or James Darrow?" she asked Mr. Thompson as she bought some candles.

He shook his head and handed her the parcel. "No, I'm sorry, Noli."

"Oh." She stuffed it in the basket and shuffled back to the house, shoulders rounded in defeat.

Are we going to the ball? the sprite asked. *We should go and be prettier than Missy. We're always prettier than Missy, but now we can be especially prettier.*

Part of her wanted to, even though she'd normally rather do homework than attend a ball. *I don't think we'll have time* she answered. The sprite pouted, but didn't reply.

Noli walked through the back door into the kitchen, set the cake on the counter, and unpacked her basket. Through the window over the sink she could see pinks and oranges streaking the sky as darkness fell.

Sold. The house had been *sold*. Had her mother packed

13

up her room? Noli put the kettle on to boil, took down the old teapot since the nice one was gone, grabbed her valise, and trudged upstairs to see what state the rest of the house was in.

Her room looked exactly the same as when she'd left, complete with the discarded pile of clothes on the bed. She set her valise on the desk and fingered the half-finished ball gown her mother had been making for her to wear to the Christmas Ball.

We could wear that, the sprite said. *I think we can finish it.*

Perhaps, if we were going, but I don't think we are. Right now we have work to do. She needed to tidy up so everyone had a place to sleep. Noli put away the dresses and everything else she'd left behind the night she'd fled with Jeff. She had joined the crew of the Vixen's Revenge instead of going to Boston with her mother and grandfather like a good little society girl. Really, she had everything she needed from here. Perhaps. At least her valise was magic and she could tuck plenty inside if necessary.

She changed the linens on her bed, then went into Jeff's room to freshen those. James could stay in there. The room was barren of personality, more a guest room than her brother's, though they had a guest room too. One day after Jeff had left to become an aeronaut—well, an air pirate—their mother had stormed in and thrown out most of his things, leaving only the furniture and a few books.

Had her mother's things all been packed up? Noli peeked into her mother's room. That, too, seemed empty of everything personal. Her forehead furrowed as she spied an open suitcase lying on the inexpertly made bed. A suitcase filled with clothes that didn't look like her mother's. A cup sat on the nightstand. Was someone *here*?

A hand touched her shoulder and she jumped.

"Noli, I'm so glad you haven't left yet. When we arrived this morning, we thought we'd missed you and you'd already returned to fairyland." Jeff stood behind her, a large grin on his face, chin scraggly with whiskers as usual. Her older brother looked even more like her father than he did just a few days—or was that weeks—ago, right down to the cleft in his chin.

"Vix needs to make you shave. Air pirates don't need to be unkempt." Standing on tiptoe, she gave her brother a kiss on the cheek, wrapping her arms around him. Vix was Jeff's fiancée. She was also a fearsome air pirate and captain of the Vixen's Revenge. Jeff was her pilot.

"What fun is that?" Jeff teased.

"You must have received my aethergraph," Noli said. The last time they'd come to the mortal realm—when they'd found Mr. Darrow's body—she'd aethergraphed her mother and brother to let them know she was all right.

"I did. I'm glad it's you knocking about the house and not some very polite burglars. Tea and cake for supper?" Jeff grinned, goggles still on his forehead.

"Why not?" She grinned back. "It's not as if Mama's here to tell us we can't. Oh." The smile slid off her face. "Did Grandfather really sell the house?"

"He did—to us. You were ill when we discussed it, so we didn't have the chance to tell you." Vix joined them in the hallway. "We..." Her cheeks pinked. "We thought it might be nice to have a place to call home besides the ship."

"Hello, Vix." Noli gave her sister-in-law-to-be a hug, her heart lightening at the idea that strange children *wouldn't* be playing in her tree house. "I think that's a wonderful idea. I'm glad he sold it to you. Now when Papa returns, you can tell him where Mama is."

A sad look flitted through Jeff's blue eyes as he patted her on the shoulder. "Of course, Noli. We won't be home most of the time, but we'll leave him a note."

"You're the best. You're staying in there?" Noli glanced at their mother's bedroom.

"Is that all right?" Vix shifted from foot to foot. Tall, thin, and built like a boy, she often wore men's clothes, which clashed slightly with her Southern drawl. Today she wore the same sort of trousers and loose shirt Jeff did, only he also wore his usual vest, filled with pockets and loops, while hers resembled a waistcoat. Her black hair was boyishly short and a blue lock hung in her slightly angled dark eyes.

"That's fine. It's just that... well," Noli tried not to fidget, since their presence actually presented a different dilemma. "I told James and V they could stay here too. They weren't fond of the idea of sleeping at their house."

Jeff's brow furrowed in dismay. "They *live* there."

Noli took a deep breath, chest shuddering slightly. "Someone murdered Mr. Darrow. We're pretty sure Brogan did it... he said he'd get V and me for not giving him the artifacts."

"Someone did *what*?" Horror streaked Jeff's face and

Vix let out a gasp, probably remembering how Brogan had attacked them on the ship back in San Francisco.

"Did you summon the police? What did they say? Mr. Darrow was such a quiet chap." Jeff's look went solemn.

"Why would we contact the police? This is Otherworld business," Noli replied, trying to understand what the police had to do with any of this. "We already took care of the body. We'll take care of Brogan later. But that's not why we're here."

"Why are you here?" Jeff pulled her to him, concern dancing in his eyes. "Though you're welcome here *anytime*; we'll even keep your room for you."

Vix nodded in agreement. "If you're … coming and going … you might need a base, too."

"I appreciate that." That might have its uses. Also, Vix and Jeff were far more understanding than her mother, not to mention they knew about the Otherworld. "Do you remember the artifact? We're doing some research on it." Well, trying.

"If you need help, I might be able to put you in touch with some people." Vix's voice went soft. "People I trust with my life. We did a little asking around, and Kyran has hired more people than us to steal strange things."

Noli's eyes opened and she nodded. "I appreciate that. I'll let you know."

Kyran was the alias Brogan had used when hiring Jeff, Vix, and their crew to steal the artifact pieces. It was also the name of someone else in the Otherworld, but she wasn't sure who.

"How are you feeling?" Jeff ushered her down the back stairs. "You weren't in good sorts when you left us."

"I'm fine," she replied, though that wasn't the entire truth. She didn't want him fussing over her—or sending her back to their mother. They entered the kitchen and her eyes fell on the pot. "Oh, I forgot about the water." Noli rushed over and saw that someone had already put the tea to steep. Two hoverboards, one brown, one blue, sat propped up by the back door. A pair of goggles hung from the blue board.

Jeff flipped a switch on the wall near the door and the gaslights flickered on. She blinked. It had been a long time since they'd used the gaslights in the kitchen, since they were so expensive. Would they fire up the boiler next?

Noli retrieved some cups from the cupboard. They didn't match, but it would do. "I suppose Mama had her things sent over?"

"Yes. Grandfather hired someone to take away what she wanted; she told me while we were in Boston. She wasn't sure whether or not to bring your things, so she'd left them here for now. Since we own the place, it doesn't matter." He took a seat at the wooden kitchen table, clean and clear of its usual clutter but the surface still marred with wax. Jeff didn't remove his goggles from his forehead; he'd probably forgotten they were there.

Noli brought over cups of tea, fixed the way everyone liked, and set them on the table.

"Thank you." Vix took a seat next to Jeff. "We'll be staying here a few days then taking off again. Will you come with us?"

Noli took down some plates and sliced the cake. She was glad she'd gotten chocolate since it was Vix's favorite. "You *want* me to come aboard?" She and Vix hadn't been the best of friends in the brief time she'd been the ship's engineer, but she respected Vix immensely.

"You're an ace engineer," Vix replied, sipping her tea. "Odd, but an ace engineer. If you'd like your place back aboard the Vixen's Revenge, it's yours."

"I ... I can't tell you how good that makes me feel." It was high praise, coming from the likes of Vix. Noli set slices of cake in front of Jeff and Vix. She returned to the counter to get her own tea and cake, then took a seat on Jeff's other side. "I appreciate it. However, right now I'm going to help V and James."

"And then what?" Jeff took a bite of chocolate cake.

"We'll take back the earth court and live happily ever after." Her mouth snapped shut as words she hadn't meant to say slipped out. She'd be so relieved when V finally found a way to get rid of the sprite so she'd have full control of her body again.

Don't you like me? Hurt dripped through the sprite's mental voice.

I do. It's just very difficult sharing the body, Noli assured her.

Oh. It is hard, especially since you never let me have a turn. I think I'd like my own body. Then I can pick what we wear every day and have the body whenever I want. The sprite preened.

Noli had no idea what would happen to the sprite when they finally found a way to make her normal again. In fact, she hadn't thought of anything but simply getting rid of her, so she could have full control of her being again. Now that the sprite, of all people, had brought it up, it made sense.

Yes, if it was possible, the sprite deserved a body of her very own.

Vix's eyebrows rose. "I thought you wanted to go university and study botany?"

"It will be a while before V can take back the earth court," she replied. That was partly because V wasn't of age yet, but also he genuinely disliked the idea of having to kill his uncle and was hoping to find another way. "Perhaps we'll apply to university for next fall, like we'd planned."

Jeff gave her arm a squeeze. "Let me know and I'll help get you set up." His eyes twinkled in the way that meant he had an idea. "How much do you bet I can discover where Mother hid the money I sent her?"

Noli paused, fork of cake halfway to her mouth. "Really?"

If anyone could locate it, he could. When Jeff had left to seek his fortune as an air pirate, he'd sent money home to support them. However, her mother disapproved of air piracy, and even though they'd desperately needed the money, she'd hidden most of it away. Noli had never discovered it.

"I haven't found it yet. But I will." Those eyes continued to sparkle. "It should be enough to set you up at a university for a little while—especially if you wish to go off on your own, *without* Darrow." He glowered as he said that.

"V and I have worked everything out," she assured him, not wanting them to be at odds.

"If he ever hurts you again..." Vix stabbed her cake with her fork for emphasis.

It wasn't V's fault. He'd just been obeying the high queen's orders—not that she expected them to understand.

The back door flew open. "Flying figs, you're actually having cake for dinner?" James strode in, bringing the cold air with him. "Vix, Jeff, what are you doing here?"

Noli shut the door behind him and got James cake and tea. "They bought the house."

"You're not retiring from being air pirates, are you?" James plopped down in the wooden chair next to Vix.

"Never." Vix squared her shoulders. "But we could use a base, and Jeff didn't wish for his home to be sold to strangers."

Noli carried the cake and tea back to the table and set it before James, along with a fork.

"Noli, please aethergraph your mother if you don't plan on returning to Boston or staying with us. She's nothing but a giant ball of worry and the last thing I need is her blaming me because you ran off to fairyland without telling anyone," Vix told her.

Noli sat and took a sip of tea. "What exactly *did* you tell Mama so she'd permit me to return to the Otherworld with V and James?"

It wasn't as if they could tell her the truth. Her mother knew nothing about the Otherworld, faeries, or that the Darrows weren't mortal.

"Um..." A flush rose on Jeff's cheeks. "We told her that V and James took you to a special hospital."

"I see." Noli glanced out the window at the Darrow house, where a single light was burning. "V's still at it. Should

I bring him some supper?" Not that she wanted to venture into that house, especially after dark.

"I should get everyone some supper." Jeff stood. "Cake isn't supper."

Vix's dark eyebrows rose as she speared the last bite of cake on her plate. "Why not?"

Jeff shook his head and held out his hand to Vix. "Let's find some takeaway."

Noli finished her cake as Jeff and Vix grabbed their hoverboards and left.

"That was interesting." James shot the back door a long look.

She cleared away the plates. "I fixed Jeff's room for you." Noli started up the stairs.

"Where are you going?" James shoved more cake in his mouth.

"I'm going to freshen up the guest room for V." Since Jeff and Vix were staying at the house, V couldn't sleep in her room. They might be more liberal than her mother, but Jeff was still, first and foremost, her elder brother.

....

After she finished, Noli returned to her room. The light was still on at V's house. Had he found out anything?

With a sigh, she took the piece of the artifact out of her valise—the fragment she'd hidden from Kevighn and refused to give to Brogan. It was one of the pieces Jeff had stolen from the museum in Denver. Sitting on her bed, she traced the partial design on it: five interlocking rings, the high queen's symbol.

Noli. A voice brushed her ears, soft as feathers.

She looked around. There was no one in here but her, and it wasn't the sprite. The same thing had happened when they'd gone to the earth court palace that morning to find Brogan.

Perhaps she *was* going mad. Also, what *was* she supposed to remember?

I think it's the shinies, the sprite said. *They're talking to you. There were lots of shinies in the palace today. Next time we go there, we should take them. They're not for him.*

Shinies? Noli looked at the piece in her hand. *These are the shinies?* It made sense that Brogan would have some in the earth palace, since he'd been collecting them. How many pieces did he have? How close was he to assembling the artifact? *You're right. Brogan shouldn't have them. We have to keep them safe.*

The last thing she wanted was for Brogan to assemble it … whatever *it* was.

It came back to whatever it was she needed to remember.

Squinting in the lamplight, she held the piece tight. *What are you, little piece?*

The force of the images playing across her mind knocked her backward onto the bed. Magic and memories pulsed under her skin—including a glimpse of what the legendary artifact looked like. Fully assembled, it was a staff.

Noli's chest shook as she exhaled. "James, James!" She

pulled herself into a sitting position, urgency coursing through her.

Footsteps echoed down the hall and James appeared in her doorway, a concerned look on his face. "What's wrong, Noli?"

She held up the piece of the artifact. "Will you come with me to find V? I think I know what Brogan is trying to do."

TW⊕

Into the Otherworld

Elise opened her eyes. An ominous wood straight out of a scary story surrounded her, and she was leaning against a dead-looking tree. Her stomach lurched. This wasn't Noli's tree house—or any place she recognized.

"Where are we?" she asked the green wood faery, who still perched on her shoulder. "You said this would take me to the tree with the tree house."

The wood faery left her shoulder and flew ahead, urging her on.

She didn't have any choice other than to follow. Carefully, she picked her way through the gloomy wood, branches grabbing at her dress and stockings. Suddenly, the air sizzled. When it stopped, they came to a grove of magnificent trees. A tantalizing scent made her nose twitch and she could make out a dusky pink and purple sky through the treetops as they entered a grove.

"Now *that's* a tree house," she breathed. In the center of the grove stood a tree and in its branches sat a house *formed* of the tree itself. Pink and blue star-shaped flowers surrounded the base of the tree. Little balls of light flitted around her.

A purple wood faery flew over and sat on her other shoulder, pulling her hair.

Elise giggled. "Hey."

Another, this one blue, landed on her nose, and she went cross-eyed. The faery flew off and hovered near the green one.

"I'm very lost," Elise told them. "I was trying to get to a different tree house. The one in my friend Noli's backyard." She sent them a mental picture of the tree and Noli. "This one's quite nice, but it's not next to my home, like hers. The other tree must have misunderstood me."

They spoke all at once. Wood faeries weren't very patient.

"Wait." Elise held up a hand. "What do you mean? This isn't Noli's tree house." Concentrating, she tried to understand what they were telling her. "Oh, Noli comes here?" She gave the tree house an appreciative glance. "I can see why." It was so grand.

The faeries showed her a mental picture of Noli, along with a dark-haired man she'd never seen before.

"Will Noli return soon?" she asked them, hope bubbling inside her. Perhaps things would work out after all.

The faeries nodded, tiny heads bobbing furiously as they assured her that Noli, or the man with her, would return soon.

"I'll wait in the tree house until someone comes." If

not Noli, then the man with the dark hair. He could take her to Noli—and she'd bring her to Steven or James.

Her stomach rumbled. Would it be too much to hope for something to eat?

Several faeries led her into the grand tree house. It was much larger than Noli's. Noli could probably stand up in it. This one even had a table and chairs. Elise sat her valise on the table and poked about the one-room house. A few moments later, several faeries flew through the open window, each with a small piece of fruit in their hands.

"Oh, I appreciate that so much." Elise devoured the sweet-as-sugar fruit as the faeries darted in and out the window carrying grass. If only there were more fruit—and something to drink. She yawned, fatigue pressing down on her.

The purple faery pulled her over to the corner opposite the window.

"You made me a bed?" Grass didn't sound very comfortable, but exhaustion consumed her. "Please wake me when Noli comes." Elise curled up in the little bed and went to sleep.

• • • • • • • •

Kevighn couldn't shake the feeling that killing Quinn should have been less … anticlimactic.

But it had to be done. For his sister. For himself.

Now, to find the girl.

The place the portal left him reminded him vaguely of the wildwood by the palace. It wasn't, but it still seemed familiar. His eyes cast about the eerie wood as he tried to discern his whereabouts. He'd tracked the little girl to a garden with a portal. Odd that she'd headed there. It was a dark court portal and most would fear to use it. The faery tree took him to wherever she'd gone. Considering who Ailís was, he'd expected to end up near the House of Oak, the earth court palace, or the high palace.

He peered at the half-dead tree. His skin prickled. It resembled the old portal at his parents' home. But then the house should be...

No, the house was gone, taken by the high queen when he was exiled. The grounds remained, yet they looked wilder, fiercer, waiting for someone to tame them with their magic.

Why had the girl come *here*? Where did she go?

He made his way through the rift in the magic that brought him to Creideamh's grove. Darkness surrounded him and he made a small light in the palm of his hand.

Wood faeries accosted him, pulling his hair and tugging at his clothing.

"She's waiting for *me*?" Kevighn blinked in surprise at their words. The Bright Lady seemed to enjoy toying with him. He climbed into the tree house. There, in a bed of grass, lay a sleeping blond girl in a pink dress and a white pinafore, both streaked with dirt.

"Ailís?" he whispered.

She sat up with a start, a frown on her pink lips. "Who are you?"

"Shhh, it's all right. I'm Kevighn Silver. Why are you

in my tree house?" He kept his voice gentle, not wishing to spook the tiny thing.

"I'm so sorry. I'm Elise Darrow. I was trying to take the magic tree to Noli's tree house, but I've never traveled by tree before and it brought me here instead. But the faeries said Noli came here and that you were her friend. Will you take me to her? Please?" Giant blue eyes, Queen Tiana's eyes, shone in the darkness.

Ah, yes, the portal didn't take Ailís to Magnolia's tree because that tree wasn't a portal. By the Bright Lady, this could work.

"Yes, Noli was very worried about you and asked me to keep you safe until she could get here," he lied, needing the girl to trust him. Magnolia was probably still on her brother's airship back in the mortal realm.

"Oh, I'm so glad." Elise looked visibly relieved. "Everyone is always off having adventures and I'm afraid they'll forget me."

My, how naïve she was.

"Will you come with me?" Kevighn held out his hand. "You must be hungry. We'll find you something hot to eat and a much more comfortable place to sleep."

She eyed him, lips pursing slightly, head cocked to one side. "How will Noli know where I am? Is she there?"

Kevighn flashed her his most disarming smile. "Noli's not there, *but* that's where I told her to find me. We'll send word so she won't worry about you." He motioned for the purple wood faery, the one that loved Magnolia best. "Find

Magnolia and tell her to come to the Thirsty Pooka as soon as possible."

The faery nodded and flew out the window. Odds were the faery wouldn't find Magnolia, but the little girl sat back on her heels and gave him a satisfied nod. Good.

If the faery did actually bring his fair blossom, well, that would be even better.

"All right, Elise." He noted that she said her name differently. A mortal name like her brothers, no doubt. "Why don't we go before it gets too late?"

She stood, smoothed her dirty dress with her smudged hand, then picked her valise up off the table. "Where are we going?"

He took her hand. "Why, to a wondrous place. It's called the Thirsty Pooka."

THREE

The Staff of Eris

Surrounded by books, Steven sat on the floor of Quinn's office. Opening another journal, he flipped through the pages, trying to find anything helpful. Quinn had spent much of his life researching rare and odd artifacts in the Otherworld. If anyone knew what Brogan was trying to assemble, it would be Quinn. Unfortunately, Quinn wasn't here, so these journals would have to suffice. Not that Steven was finding anything.

A word on the page caught his eye:

Every day I mourn Creideamh more and more, and further regret the role I played in her death. Even Dom wishes he didn't do what he did. But it's the law. I should have told her to accept exile and promised to go with her. We could have been happy in the mortal realm—or even among the dark court with her family and friends. No.

I allowed my pride to blind me. In the end, I will never forgive myself. All that I've done to atone for my sins will never be enough. I lost the greatest gift I'd ever had without realizing what I'd done until it was too late. One day her brother will track me down and kill me. When he does, I'll allow it. Then my love and I will be together once again.

Steven marked the page with his finger. *Creideamh.* Where had he heard that name before? Never had he known Quinn to have a wife or girlfriend. *Dom* would be Steven's father. A sigh escaped his lips. If only he knew what information might be relevant—or where to look.

Noli burst into the room, James with her. He looked up. They didn't look as if they'd brought supper.

"V, V, I remember. I know what Brogan's trying to do. We have to protect the pieces. We have to keep them safe." Noli's steel-colored eyes danced like a mad woman's, her expression frantic. She no longer wore her hat, and chestnut waves escaped her coif, adding to the effect.

"Wait, what?" He blinked. She *remembered*? From where?

She plopped down on the floor next to him, spreading her skirts around her. "I know what it is."

James took a seat in Quinn's chair.

Steven traced a glyph in the air with his finger, the design glowing green, then fading.

"What's that?" A lock of dark hair fell in Noli's eyes as she peered up at him.

"A soundproofing spell. We need to be cautious." The three of them appearing at the earth court palace this morning to challenge his uncle had cost them the element of surprise. They had to be wary of earth court spies.

"Can I do that kind of spell?" Noli asked.

Steven thought for a moment. "I have no idea. I know nothing of sprite magic."

"The sprite says we have lots of magic." Noli closed her eyes. "We deflected cannonballs when the cannon ship was after the Vixen's Revenge."

"What?" He knew little of what had happened when she was aboard her brother's airship while he and James were off on a fool's errand for his mother. An errand he'd owed her for his poorly worded bargain to free Noli, which had enabled his mother to turn Noli into a sprite in the first place. An errand that had caused him to be far from home when Brogan sent earth court guards to kill his father.

Noli's eyes snapped open, boring into him. "If the cannons hit the ship, we'd be dead. I had to use magic to keep us alive."

"I understand. I'd do the same. But you need to be very cautious about using magic in the mortal realm." Steven's heart thundered so hard it roared in his ears. She'd done *what*? That sounded complicated, considering she'd never had a single magic lesson.

He *had* promised to teach her how to defend herself with magic.

But Noli's behavior was worrying him. She'd been odd ever since the sprite had taken up residence in her head, and now it seemed to be getting worse.

James let out an impatient huff, legs waggling as he

draped them over the side of the chair. "Noli, you said you know what the artifact is?"

"Oh, yes. It's a staff of great power." Her eyes closed again. "When it was in one piece, the land didn't need a mortal girl with the Spark to be sacrificed every seven years. She had enough nourishment from the staff…" Noli sighed, eyes opening, a frustrated look on her face. "I'm having trouble recalling everything. But the staff was also terrible. So terrible that the Bright Lady herself tore it apart and flung it into the mortal realm. If Brogan reassembles it, it could be disastrous."

Steven racked his memory, trying to recall any stories about a staff. "There's no staff in the story Father tells…I…I mean told…about why we have the sacrifice."

The very idea crawled under his skin, making him want to recoil in dismay. A staff powerful enough that it fed the magic composing the Otherworld itself. A staff misused so badly that the Bright Lady herself tore it apart and cast it into another realm.

"She said no one remembered the real story—especially the monarchs." Noli frowned.

"Who?" James rubbed his chin, frowning. "I've never heard anything about a staff."

"Me neither. I wish we could find Quinn," Steven replied. So far there'd been no word and he was beginning to worry. "Noli, who told you all this? Kevighn?"

Not that he'd believe the likes of Kevighn Silver.

"Kevighn knows what it is, but he didn't tell me." Noli's lower lip stuck out in a petulant pout. "You don't believe me."

Steven put an arm around her, bringing her to him.

"How can I believe you when I have no idea what you're talking about? It makes sense, and we know the pieces compose a powerful artifact. However, this staff isn't something I've ever heard of. Who told you about it?"

"I..." Her face contorted in puzzlement. "I'm not sure. I think it was the Bright Lady."

His heart fell. Yes, it seemed as if the sprite's grip on Noli was increasing once again.

James looked over from his perch, legs still dangling over the chair. "Why?"

Noli leaned forward, elbows on her knees. "A voice—and not the sprite—spoke to me when Brogan came onboard the airship to retrieve the artifacts from Vix and Jeff. She said I couldn't permit Brogan to have it. I...I stole a piece. The voice also spoke to me in the tree. Well, I believe it was the same voice. She told me about the staff and directed me to keep it safe."

A noise of disbelief escaped his lips. The Bright Lady spoke to Noli while she was inside a tree? Yes, they needed to reverse what Tiana had done to her before it was too late.

Her face crumpled like a discarded handkerchief. "Why don't you believe me?"

"It's...it's a lot to believe. You said that you have a piece of the artifact. May I see it?" They knew it was something, but to be an item that could change the fate of his realm?

"Here. I asked it for information just now, and it showed me things." She shuddered, then put the piece in his hand. "But we can't let Brogan have it. In fact, I really should steal the pieces he has. He can't be permitted to assemble it." Panic tinged her voice.

"No, he can't," he soothed. No matter what the artifact became when assembled, Uncle Brogan would use it for evil.

"Why don't you believe me?" Noli glared at Steven. She popped up off the floor and marched out of the library. He just sat there, watching her. What had just happened?

"Why *don't* you believe her?" James sat up and leaned forward, brows furrowing. "Noli's no liar."

Steven sighed. "Even though I've never heard of this staff, and it's different from the stories we've been told, I could believe it. Also, if the piece showed her things, that, too, I could believe, even though it's advanced magic. It's the Bright Lady speaking to her that I doubt. The Bright Lady doesn't speak often, and Noli's not even truly one of us."

James' arms crossed over his chest. "You're an elitist snob."

"I am not." He shot his brother a dirty look. "I'm supposed to believe a goddess spoke to her while she was in a tree?"

"Noli said she *thought* it could be the Bright Lady. It could be something else. We know all sorts of creatures lurk in the Otherworld. Perhaps when we put her in the tree to heal her it made her vulnerable," James replied. "We shouldn't discount any of this yet—even the crazy bits—until we finish researching."

Steven shook his head. "You as the voice of reason continues to disturb me. But you're right. This is Noli. Still, I'm worried about her. Something's more not right than usual."

"That's why you're going to reverse what Tiana did."

James blew a lock of hair out of his face. "In the meantime, you can teach Noli magic. I'll take over her sword lessons."

"Noli in her current state with a sword unnerves me," Steven observed truthfully.

James shook his head in dismay. "She's still Noli. Don't forget that."

He got up and followed Noli out of the room.

"Why are girls so maddening?" Steven muttered. He examined the small gold piece in his hand. It looked like a bit of junk. Closing his eyes, he tried to convince the piece to reveal its secrets to him. Trees and plants, not metal, were his specialty, but he should be able to get something from it.

He mentally reached out to the piece in his hand. *Tell me your secrets.*

A blast of fire spread through his mind. *No, this isn't the staff of power,* a female voice yelled as he watched the chaos play across his mind's eye like a moving picture. *This is the Staff of Eris and I expel it from this realm. You shall bear the cost as atonement for your sins.*

Steven ripped himself from the memory ingrained in the piece. The Staff of Eris? Eris was the Greek goddess of discord. Considering the Greek Pantheon meant nothing in the Otherworld, it was probably more figurative than literal. Still, it gave him a place to start.

Besides, anything that could cause discord had no place in the hands of his uncle.

He continued to flip though Quinn's journals. Staff of Eris. Staff of Eris. Was there even such a thing?

Exile in the mortal realm suits me. However, I seem to have lost some of my research. Considering it concerns the Staff of Eris, I'm a little worried. At least I never kept all of my research in one place. Still, once I realized the truth about it, it was a folly to keep anything beyond recollections of the basic lore. If anyone should ever get ahold of some of my more sensitive findings, it could be the end of this realm.

Steven scanned the pages for anything else regarding the staff, but found no further mentions. The journal dropped to his lap. The Staff of Eris was real, dangerous, and Quinn had indeed known about it.

....

Steven's fingers traced the sketch on the page. He'd gone back to Quinn's earlier journals, from long before he'd come to the mortal realm in exile with his father. It did look as if some of the research was missing, or hidden, but he had found something of interest—a drawing.

According to my research, the staff may look something like this, Quinn had scrawled. It was just a regular staff, like something a monarch might carry but lacking in decoration or opulence. Looks could be deceiving, especially in objects originating in the Otherworld.

If one needed all the pieces for it to work, it would make sense that if even one piece were destroyed, then the staff would be useless for eternity.

On the other hand…

Over and over, he'd thought that there had to be a better way to nourish the magic than tricking mortal girls with the Spark into becoming the sacrifice. The Spark, that extra bit of "something" in some mortals, fed the very magic that made the Otherworld exist. When Noli had been mortal, she'd possessed it in spades. So had her friend Charlotte, who'd volunteered to be the sacrifice in order to save Noli. An act that James was still recovering from, since he'd been in love with Charlotte.

Steven had hoped they could find more volunteers like Charlotte, rather than trapping the girls, but now the staff—if reassembled—seemed to offer a third option. No sacrifice at all. No need to hunt down girls and drain them of their blood just to keep the Otherworld alive. He hadn't finished reading all of Quinn's notes, but it appeared as if the staff wasn't wicked in and of itself—in the hands of the pure of heart, it could be an advantageous tool. Something that could usher in a new age for the Otherworld.

His mother and Uncle Brogan weren't pure of heart in the slightest.

Also, since it had been broken into pieces and scattered in the mortal realm, rather than destroyed, it seemed as if it were meant to be reassembled at another point in time.

Could *he* wield such a thing? The idea of becoming supreme ruler of the Otherworld was certainly tempting. No one would *ever* be able to hurt him or those he loved if he were in charge and armed with such a weapon.

Steven shook his head, expelling such an idea. He was no

queen. A queen had *always* ruled the High Court. A queen with the ability to command all four elements. Someone like his mother ... or Elise.

His belly lurched. If Queen Tiana, or anyone else, knew Elise had the abilities of a high queen, two things could happen. Someone would kill her. Or someone would steal her away and use her.

Bright Lady bless, he hoped Quinn and Elise were safe.

"V?" Noli called from down the hall. "Are you still here?"

"I'm in Quinn's study." He looked at his pocket watch. Goodness, it was late. His belly squawked in agreement. But Noli had stormed out hours ago. Would it be too much to hope that this time she'd brought supper?

A moment later, Noli appeared. "Always with the books."

He couldn't help but return her smile, since she no longer looked angry. "Please tell me that you've come bearing supper."

"It's back at the house. Jeff and Vix are visiting; they brought it."

"They're here?" Steven looked up at her in surprise. That wasn't expected.

"Yes. They bought the house." Noli peered at the books on the floor. "Did you find anything useful?"

"Perhaps. I haven't examined everything yet, but I did find something that might be helpful." He held up the journal.

"You believe me." Her entire face lit up.

"I do," he replied. About the staff, at least. "Quinn was a noted scholar. This was one of his projects. But he lost some of his research when he joined my father in exile. Considering my uncle was sending people to steal pieces, I'm of the mind that Brogan found it."

"Are we going to sneak into the palace and steal it back? Eris ... why does that sound familiar?" Noli plopped down on the floor next to him in a flurry of skirts.

"*The Iliad.* Eris is the goddess of strife," he explained. They'd read it together, once.

"There are Greek gods in the Otherworld?" She picked up another journal from the pile and paged through it.

"I think it's figurative." That also meant that during the mortal time of the Greeks—or shortly thereafter—the staff was still in use. Interesting. Had the Bright Lady used a spell to cause her people to forget? Whose idea had it been to use the blood of a young mortal girl with the Spark to nourish the magic?

Noli sucked in a breath and looked up at him, the book in her hand, eyes glassy. "You never told me Quinn was with Creideamh. But Creideamh was with an earth court prince. Quinn's not a prince, is he?"

Steven wiped away the tear on her face with his finger. "Who's Creideamh?"

"She's Kevighn's sister. The one who died." She closed the journal and set it aside.

"Oh." That explained a lot. "Quinn's quite wellborn, but I'm not sure how. I never knew him to be involved with anyone—just like I don't know why he followed Father into exile. Anyway ... " He handed the journal to her, open to the sketch. "This is what Quinn thinks the staff looks like."

Noli took the book into her hands and frowned. "Not

quite." Her finger traced the image. "When I asked the piece to show me things, I saw what it looked like. There are designs on it. The high court symbol—the one with the five circles." At the top of the staff she tapped the page with her finger. "There's something right there. Something that holds the key to the entire artifact." She closed one eye and squinted. "It's purple and large, maybe the size of my fist?"

"Do you mean a jewel?" When the piece of the staff "spoke" to him, he hadn't seen an actual image of the assembled staff.

"Exactly. Somehow it's the *jewel* that provides what the land needs," Noli agreed, still frowning over the sketch.

"Why don't we return to your house? We can research more in the morning." The idea of a powerful jewel as the centerpiece made sense; there were plenty of magical gems in the Otherworld. Still, before jumping to conclusions, he wanted to see if Quinn had anything about it in his research.

Noli's eyes widened and she sat straight up. "I ... I might know where to find it."

"We're not even sure there *is* a jewel." He gathered a few books and stood.

A mischievous grin played at her lips and her eyes grew alight with a look that usually ended with them being in *big* trouble. "Remember the new museum? Well, it opened— that was why my grandfather was in Los Angeles. He told me they had an exhibit on faeries, which included a gem rumored to have once belonged to a faery queen."

"Odds are it's a fake. Most things in this realm said to belong to faeries are," he replied. Her face fell. "I suppose it wouldn't hurt to look. I did want to see their exhibit of Dutch Golden Age painters," he added hastily, not wishing to hurt her feelings, but still unsure about the jewel.

"Good. If it's the gem, we'll steal it back." Her grin returned, illuminating her entire face.

"We don't know anything about stealing gems." What was she thinking? This was much worse than the time they'd tried to steal pieces for the tree house from an abandoned building. That had ended with a visit from the fire department and a trip to the doctor. This could end in being hauled off to jail—and Quinn wasn't around to send aethergraphs so he could bail them out.

"We'll ask Jeff and Vix. After all, they steal things for a living." She waved her hand as if this were nothing.

"We can't involve them. Also, we can't simply waltz into the museum and take something." His hand raked his hair. Noli often had outrageous ideas, but this topped them all.

She waved a paper under his nose. "Why not? The museum is having a very exclusive ball … and *you* have an invitation. Now, come along. I'll warm up supper." Noli dragged him out of the room, flipping off the light in the process. "I even set up the guest room for you."

"You did?" Hurt leaked through his voice. He thought they'd share her room.

They closed the back door behind them and crossed his backyard. "I told you. Jeff and Vix are staying at the house. *Please* be nice." They ducked through the loose board in the fence between their houses, into her yard.

Noli moved so that she was in front of him. "Don't you want to take me to the ball?" she pouted.

Girls were so odd. "I didn't think you liked balls."

"I don't, but you wanted to see the museum. At the very least we could investigate the gem, and I could be prettier than blasted Missy Sassafras." Her mouth snapped shut, but not before she swished her skirts a little.

Oh. "Did you run into her while shopping? I don't know why you let her bother you. She's not pretty, she's not that rich, and she has no class. Truly, she's beneath people like us."

"People like us?" she laughed. "Do you hear what you're saying?"

"You're from a fine old family." Steven held her the best he could with books in his hands. "I'm a prince. And I love *you.*" He pushed her forehead up with his and kissed her. How he missed her when they were apart. She was such a part of his life, of him.

A pistol clicked. He jumped back from Noli, dropping the books in the process.

"Vix, I *told* you, V and I are fine now. We've worked everything out. He's even standing up to his mother for our right to be together." Noli's voice firmed.

Steven turned around to see Vix aiming a pistol at him.

"It's fun to see pretty boy squirm." Vix tucked her pistol away and strode inside.

Noli shook her head and picked up the fallen books. "I always wanted a sister, but I never thought I'd get one quite like Vix."

"It is a bit terrifying." Steven stared at Noli's place. Perhaps he should sleep at his house.

"Next time she does that, pull out your sword. Now, let's get you some supper."

FOUR

Aodhan

The little girl clutched Kevighn's hand tightly as he led her through the Blackwoods. Dark and ominous in an entirely different way than the place they'd been before, this forest was one of the oldest in the Otherworld, filled with strange plants and even stranger creatures. It was also deep within dark court territory, and home to many dark fae.

"These woods are very dangerous," he warned. "You must not wander about them by yourself."

Elise made an annoyed noise. "I get tired of everyone telling me what to do."

"I suppose you do," he replied. Certainly, he had as a boy. A light emerged from the trees and he steered her into the clearing where the Thirsty Pooka sat. He could feel the eyes of Ciarán's guards watching them from the distance, determining if they were friend or foe.

"Stay close." Kevighn opened the door of the pub; the usual cacophony greeted him as they entered the large main room. He walked Elise past some gambling goblins and brownies screeching dirty songs around the piano, and over to the bar. He sat her on a tall stool and took the one next to her. Behind the bar sat a staircase that led to the rooms where the dark king conducted court business.

The comely leprechaun bartender's lips curved into a sneer as she peered at them from her perch on a box behind the bar. "She's young even for you, Silver."

He rolled his eyes at her comment. "Deidre, this is Elise, she's hungry—"

"Kevighn, has anyone ever told you that you can't bring children into a pub?" Ciarán teased from behind him.

"You can't?" He frowned. "Where else was I supposed to bring her?"

Elise's lower lip jutted out and she turned to face him. "I'm not a child."

"No, you're a little lady, aren't you." Ciarán's hood stayed up and she leaned toward Kevighn, eyeing the dark king warily.

"Elise, this is Kyran," Kevighn said, using the dark king's alias. "He's my friend."

Elise curtseyed the best she could while sitting on a stool. "How do you do?"

Ciarán smiled. "Really, Kevighn, this isn't the place for a lady. Why don't you both come with me? Deidre, have Luce send supper up."

They followed him up the stairs behind the bar, past

Ciarán's office, down a hall, and through a door hidden by a bookcase. They entered Ciarán's private living quarters and walked into a simple but clean and cheerful sitting area. It had been a *long* time since he'd been up here.

A boy, roughly Elise's age, ran up to Ciarán. He stopped in his tracks and eyed them. His hair was such a pale blond it was near white. Yellow eyes gleamed with curiosity.

No. It couldn't be. All the air escaped Kevighn's body. He'd been told the child had perished with his sister.

"Breathe, old friend." Ciarán's large hand clapped his shoulder. "Look who I brought to see you, Aodhan. I finally got your Uncle Kevighn to stand still for a moment and visit us."

"It's Uncle Kevighn? Truly?" The boy bounced on the soles of his bare feet. "And he'll teach me to shoot a bow and tell me about all his adventures?"

Uncle Kevighn? He had no words, literally. Anything he could, should, or would say leaked out his ears, pooling around his feet on the wooden floor of Ciarán's sitting room.

"Yes, he will. But right now, I need you to stay with Elise and keep her company while she has the nice supper Grandma Luce is bringing up for her." Ciarán smiled at the boy. "Perhaps if you ask nicely, she'll bring dessert for the *both* of you."

"Elise?" Aodhan's eyes went wide as he took in Elise, bedraggled dress and all. "H ... hi."

Elise gave him a winsome smile and a little curtsey. "Why, hello."

For a moment the two children just stood there, making

doe-eyes at each other. It was a bit odd, considering Elise looked like a miniature, non-yelling version of the queen and Aodhan looked like Kevighn's sister, except for the fact that he had hair the same color as Quinn's.

"We'll return soon." Ciarán jerked his head toward the doorway.

Elise looked to Kevighn for permission.

"It's all right, Elise." He should say something to the boy. His nephew. Who was still alive.

But there were no words.

Ciarán put an arm around his shoulders. "They'll be safe here. I think you need a drink."

"I … I think you're right." Shaking internally, Kevighn followed Ciarán back downstairs to the tavern, where the dark king pulled him onto a stool and shoved a mug of something in his hands.

"You found her quickly. I'm pleased." Ciarán sat down on the stool next to him.

"Is … why … what … " All the words jumbled in his head. Kevighn drained his glass without actually tasting the contents.

For a long moment Ciarán stayed silent, filling Kevighn's glass from a bottle on the counter. "I *told* you, over and over, that there was someone here I wanted you to meet. Quinn showed up with the child right about the time you were naught but a raging lunatic, hunting girls for the queen and bedding and drinking everything in sight. Every time I saw you, I wanted to tell you about him. But you were so angry, and ... " He closed his amber eyes and opened them again. "I had no words. I'd rather show you."

The words slowly penetrated Kevighn's brain, making the ideas stop spinning and settle down into something he might be able to make sense of. "You ... you're not insinuating that I'd hurt the boy? I'd never hurt Creideamh's child."

Ciarán shook his head. "No. I was afraid you'd take him from me."

"The leader of the dark court, raising babies and becoming attached to them?" Kevighn had no idea what to make of all this.

Ciarán took a pull directly from the bottle. For a moment hurt filled his face, a look out of place on a man so dangerous. "Aodhan knows I'm not his father, but he calls me such."

"Oh." Kevighn regretted his words. "*Aodhan.* Who named him?" He took another drink, this time noticing it was the honey wine Ciarán made himself.

"Quinn didn't say. Wasn't that your father's name?" Those unnerving eyes met his.

Slowly, Kevighn nodded. "It was. It's a good fire court name."

"Don't be angry with me. Please?" Ciarán took another drink from the bottle. "I've done my best to raise him the way you'd like. Every night I tell him stories about you."

Kevighn nearly dropped his mug in horror. "Please tell me they're stories appropriate for children."

Most of his adventures weren't.

A laugh escaped Ciarán's lips, lighting up his scarred face

under the hood. "We did have some good times that didn't involving drinking, stealing, killing, and whoring."

"We did?" Kevighn's face contorted as he attempted to recall such times. "I can't be angry with you … if anything, you should be angry with me. You're the king, and I'm just your humble servant. All these years, you've raised my nephew … is there anything you can't do, old friend?"

In some ways, Kevighn felt guilty, but in other ways, grateful. His past had been filled with dark times, and he hadn't been fit to care for himself, let alone a child. Part of him liked to think that raising Aodhan might have made him a better man, but deep down he knew it would just have ruined the boy.

He sighed, his head still spinning from this strange development. His sister's child had *lived*.

"But why? Why did Quinn do it?" he asked. Creideamh had been killed because of her abilities; it was common in such cases for children to face the same fate. Yet somehow Quinn had gotten the child spared, or hid him, and then smuggled him to the dark court. All very dangerous things, considering it broke the queen's law.

Despite this development, Kevighn still didn't feel remorse for killing Quinn. The man had been nearly dead anyway.

Ciarán shrugged. "Perhaps it was out of guilt."

"True. Though it doesn't make things better." Kevighn drained the glass and refilled it himself.

"Your nephew is a clever boy," Ciarán told him. "He's so much like you it makes my heart hurt. I know it doesn't bring Creideamh back. *Nothing* will bring her back. But Aodhan's alive, and he's a big boy now. He's been waiting for you to teach him, love him, be his uncle. As much as I need you and your many talents, especially with everything brewing, he needs you too. That's why I'm so glad you've decided to stop moping and come home."

Kevighn's heart broke a little, thinking of everything he'd missed because he was too angry to hear his friend tell him that there was some good left in the world.

"You have no patience for the small ones," Ciarán laughed, as if reading his thoughts. "He's at the perfect age for hunting, fishing, and all those things we loved."

Kevighn nodded; he was at a good age for a great deal of things. "I think I still have my bow from when I was a boy. If not, I'll make him one. But where will I keep him? I could take him back to the cabin, but I presume you still will have things for me to do..."

"Have you heard nothing I've said?" Ciarán made a noise of annoyance. "This is his home. We want this to be your home, too, like it was."

While he'd never abandon his cabin, there was a time when the tavern had very much been *home*. "It will be nice to have a home again. Someone to come home to. You mean for us to raise him together?"

That would not be unwelcome. Just being here brought back so many different feelings—some of which he wasn't ready to deal with just yet.

"*Them*," Ciarán corrected. "Him and the girl. I think it may work out." He signaled Deidre for another bottle.

Raising them both. Yes, that had possibilities, though he had a feeling someone would come for the girl eventually. She was too valuable to forget about.

For a moment Kevighn stared into his nearly empty cup, pondering this turn of events. "I have a nephew."

"You do." Ciarán put a tanned hand on top of his. "I've taken good care of him for you."

A stray thought made him suck in a breath. "What element can he command?"

Ciarán's lips twitched. "I'll let you figure it out yourself."

A nephew. The more he thought about it, the more the despair he'd felt for so long faded away. Something new began to take root in his heart. Something he hadn't felt in a long time.

Hope.

Taking the bottle from Deidre, he refilled his mug, and Ciarán's.

Kevighn raised his mug. "I think this deserves a toast."

"To new beginnings?" Ciarán raised his mug.

Their mugs clinked. "To new beginnings."

....

After many more rounds, the two of them staggered upstairs. They found the children in Aodhan's room—Elise curled on the bed, fast asleep. Aodhan, also asleep, sat on the floor, back against the bed, a small sword in his lap.

"You're teaching him to use a *sword*?" Kevighn hissed.

"You're just jealous because you don't know how to use

one," Ciarán replied. His hood was now down, fully revealing the scar across his olive skin and his short dark hair.

This was true. Kevighn was a little jealous. But he wasn't about to say it. "If she's to stay here, she'll need her own room. How exactly are we going to do this?"

They went back out into Ciarán's sitting room and sat down. "What did you tell her? How did you lure her away from her father?"

"The old king is dead. So is Quinn, for that matter." Kevighn recounted what had happened as they sat and drank even more.

"Ah, so you finally killed Quinn. How does it feel?" A bloodthirsty look gleamed in Ciarán's eyes as he leaned forward, resting an elbow on his knee. He never had liked Quinn much.

Kevighn shook his head and leaned back onto the chair. "Not like I thought. I don't regret it. Not for one moment, not even knowing that he'd given me Aodhan. But … I thought revenge should be sweet. It felt … anticlimactic."

"Yes, sometimes that happens." Ciarán nodded, elbows still on his knees. "I can't believe she turned up in Creideamh's tree house. I told you the Bright Lady hasn't forsaken you."

"The girl was trying to get to Magnolia. She has a tree house. She also loves Creideamh's tree house." Kevighn hoped his fair blossom was well, wherever she may be.

"Who's Magnolia?" Ciarán refilled their glasses from the bottle on the low table.

He sighed and took a long drink. "Where do I start?"

"Oh bother," Ciarán muttered, shaking his head in disapproval. "Who is she? Mortal? High court? Someone or something you shouldn't be falling for, as usual?"

"Probably all of the above." Kevighn held out his hand in an empty gesture. "And what do you mean, *as usual*?" He frowned.

Ciarán shook his head, ignoring his indignation. "Why don't you start at the beginning?"

"Fine." Over more wine, Kevighn told Ciarán all about Magnolia—about hunting her for Tiana, Magnolia not becoming the sacrifice, her choosing Stiofán, the queen making her one of them, and the breakup . . .

"Ah, so that's the girl," Ciarán whispered, tapping his chin with his finger.

"When I left her, she was still aboard her brother's airship." Kevighn's head rested on the back of the chair as he gazed at the wooden ceiling. His head popped up and he looked toward Ciarán. "She's the one who gave me the artifact pieces. I'd like to bring her here. I think she'd be an asset. Magnolia's smart, funny, good with plants and machines, and she's probably good with children; after all, she's a girl . . ."

"Stop." Ciarán raised his hand, expression darkening. "Kevighn, are you serious? You have *terrible* taste in women."

"I do *not*."

"Yes, you do. Must I give you examples? I hate to see you do this to yourself. Again. Also, if she's who I think she is, she's too young for you," he scolded.

Kevighn bristled. "I like them young."

"You're getting too old for that." Disapproval danced in Ciarán's eyes.

"Am not. And what do you mean *if she is who you think she is.*" If this wasn't Ciarán …

The look Ciarán gave him could make a lesser man spontaneously combust. "My spies keep track of many things, including the comings and goings of some young earth court princes, who are often in the company of a girl fitting Magnolia's description. In fact, she was just in the Otherworld. With them."

She was? His hands fisted. But that whelp had broken it off with her. Magnolia was safe with her brother in the mortal realm. "No, he can't have her."

"Obviously I need to keep you occupied." Ciarán looked unamused. "Let's not start any wars. Please. There will be time for rebellion later."

"Do you have something else for me to do?" Maybe he could find her, bring her here, where she'd be safe.

"Yes. Teach your nephew to hunt, spend some time with him. Help me keep the little princess happy and safe. The rebellion is starting sooner than intended." Ciarán shot him another look.

"It is?" That took him aback. "Elise is too young to rule, and we don't have all the pieces."

"I think that between Brogan and I, we may. Everything will come in time, but if we wait too long, there will be nothing of our beloved realm left," Ciarán said.

"What did Tiana do now?" That woman had no idea how to rule—not that anyone dared tell her. It would mean their death.

Ciarán looked at him with utter despair in his amber

eyes. "The queen recently changed the definition of *sword* to include long knives. She's been rounding up and executing people left and right, including..." His face contorted. "Several dark court boys. She's ordered her guards to execute them on sight; by the time I found out, it was too late."

"Long knives are *not* swords." Outrage rose inside him. Those not from the great houses couldn't carry swords; most peasants depended on long knives for protection and their everyday livelihood. "What's next, bows so no one can hunt for food?"

Slowly, Ciarán nodded. "That's what I've heard, but it's not official yet. It was one thing when her laws were just silly, but now they're harming people. *My people.* I won't stand for it."

Kevighn put a hand on his shoulder. "Neither will I."

"You're with me?" Ciarán asked.

He raised his glass. The queen couldn't be allowed to destroy their home, their people. "To death and beyond."

FIVE

The Faery Queen's Jewel

The sun fell on Noli's face and her eyes flickered open. V slept beside her in her bedroom. She must have fallen asleep in his arms. There were footsteps and a click.

"Get out of my sister's room, Darrow." Jeff stood in the doorway, pistol aimed at them.

V sat straight up, eyes widening as he caught sight of the pistol. "We're fully clothed. We must have fallen asleep while researching." He gestured to the still-burning candle lamp and the book on the floor, then hopped out of her bed with lightning quickness.

"Jeff, will you stop? I'm not going to be amused if you and Vix aim pistols at us every time we're together," Noli snapped, sitting up and scowling at her brother. She didn't need these sorts of shenanigans. There was enough to deal with.

"I … I'm going to my house to get some clean clothes," V stammered, then fled the room.

Noli's eyes narrowed at Jeff, displeased at his little game. "Happy?"

"He looks like a dandy in all that velvet. James can pull it off, but Steven can't." Jeff sat down, not even asking permission to enter, then helped himself to one of the cookies in the sack on her desk.

"It's the fashion in the Otherworld, and you know we came straight from there. It's a long story." She threw her legs over the side of the bed, smoothing her wrinkled Otherworld gown. "Can you teach me how to steal a jewel by tomorrow night? Please?"

Jeff blinked once, then twice. "Why?"

"Because tomorrow night at the museum ball, V and I will take a look at a gem purported to have been owned by a faery queen. If it's what I'm looking for, I'm going to steal it. It would be helpful if you'd give me some pointers." After all, that's what he and his crew did. They stole. She set the book on the desk. Going to the wardrobe, she pulled out the half-finished ball gown. Could she finish it by tomorrow?

"*Why?*"

V had asked her the same thing.

"I must keep the artifact out of the wrong hands and I think the gem is part of it. I've never stolen *anything*, and since it's a faery gem, the last thing I want is to be caught." Noli laid the gown on the bed and examined it.

"But *why?* I don't understand why this is so important to you—other than you're in love with Darrow, who doesn't deserve you," he grumped.

Noli spun on her stocking feet and faced her brother.

"I love V, and he loves me. Get used to it. As for the arti-fact... it's a staff, a magical one of great power. We discov-ered that much in our research. Nevertheless, I need to protect it because..." If V didn't believe the Bright Lady had spoken to her, Jeff certainly wouldn't. "It's difficult to explain. But if it makes you feel better, V doesn't understand either. He wants to research the thing to death first, but we should be stealing back the pieces Brogan already has, then locating the rest of them."

Jeff shook his head. "I don't understand all of this. But we can help if stealing this stone is really that important to you. Thad *is* a master thief."

The whole crew was in town? Brilliant.

"I can do it by myself if someone simply tells me what to do. I don't want to get you involved." The last thing she wanted was for them to get in trouble because of her. Noli examined the unsewn seams, the missing trim. "Besides, what would Vix say?"

"Vix wants you to figure out a way for us to elope with-out making Mother angry." Jeff smiled lopsidedly. "She said she'd rather be shot down by MoBatts over Deseret territory than sit through another wedding planning session disguised as brunch with Mother, Grandmamma, and the aunties."

Noli laughed, picturing such a fiasco in her head. "That does sound dreadful. See why I didn't want to go to Boston?" A sigh escaped her lips. "I'm not sure if I can finish this dress, even if I use the steam-powered sewing machine I built." She felt the slightest bit put out that her mother had left it behind. "I'm not as good a seamstress as Mama. What will happen to

Mama's dress shop? When I went out to do the shopping, I went by and noticed that it was still there, but closed up."

"Grandfather's trying to find a buyer. What do you need a dress for? You have plenty of dresses." Jeff made a face.

"It's for the ball, silly." She rolled her eyes, not expecting him to understand. "Now get out so I can dress and make everyone breakfast."

....

"No, no, no." Noli looked through the finished and half-finished dresses on the racks in her mother's little dress shop. No. None of these would be suitable for her to wear to the ball. What she ought to do was contact those with finished dresses and dresses in progress and deliver them to their rightful owners, since her mother only made dresses to order. There probably wasn't money to give back people's deposits. Some dresses were naught but a basket of fabric and trims.

Noli.

Noli stopped and turned. She was completely alone in the shop. "Who are you? Why are you talking to me?"

You're so silly. There's no one here but us, the sprite told her.

It's not the shinies talking? she replied.

The sprite paused. *There are no shinies here.*

No, there weren't. For a moment she buried her face in her hands. Yes, she'd gone around the bend. That was the only explanation. Even the sprite thought so.

You think too much. Let's go shopping, the sprite suggested.

She pushed the sprite away, along with thoughts of

61

strange voices and madness, and opened the parcels that had never been opened. Still, something wasn't right.

Also, the feeling that she needed to steal the gem drove her like someone might drive an auto. Jeff was now saying that she *couldn't* steal the gem, having made a quick stop earlier at the museum. It only made her more determined to be successful.

With a sigh, she opened another parcel. "Oooh." Lengths of imported silk brocade slipped through her fingertips. "Who did Mama order this for?"

We should make a dress from that, the sprite told her. *We'll be so pretty.*

I can't sew a dress in two days, especially out of that. But it was lovely. *Besides, burgundy isn't my color.*

We look pretty in any color, the sprite retorted. *Is silk a plant?*

Blinking, she opened another parcel, this filled with gold lace from France. *No, silk comes from worms.*

Oh. I'm not sure we're good with animals, but we could be. We could try making a dress with magic. Let's see what else there is. I have an idea.

Noli thought for a moment. *Make a dress with magic?*

Please? Can we try? If we fail, we'll just fix something else. We can use the burgundy brocade and see what other things we can find, perhaps some rosettes … and more lace. Lots of lace. And ruffles. We need a corset to go over the dress …

We can't wear a corset over our clothes here. Remember what Missy said yesterday? Noli replied.

And that is why we should. We're going to make her so mad. We'll be so pretty.

It had been a while since she'd seen the sprite this happy. The idea of making Missy jealous sounded…fun. *All right, we'll try for a little while.*

Noli went through all the various materials Mama had in the shop, assembling whatever the sprite wanted into a big pile, which included the brocade and lace.

May I have the body, please? the sprite pleaded. *I'll give it back. I…I don't know if I can do it with you in the body, I think it would be faster to just do it myself.*

Certainly, as long as you give it back. Noli relinquished control of the sprite and watched, so she could figure out what the sprite was doing and replicate it.

The sprite shaped fabric around one of the dress forms, molding it the way a sculptor might work with clay, literally merging the material together.

Is it pretty? The sprite preened at her handiwork.

It is. It wasn't actually something she'd *want* to wear, but not because it was ugly. The underskirt was cream silk and trimmed in gold lace, topped with the burgundy brocade, swathes of the gold lace from France, and brocade rosettes. It was…a lot. The giant skirt could easily hide several small children. The dress also had a train. Her eyes focused on the daring décolletage, trimmed in gold lace, which was most definitely…French.

Noli took back the body and examined the dress. There were no seams. Not even something allowing her to put the dress *on*. However, that was something she could handle. Perhaps she could find a way to get rid of the rosettes without the sprite getting upset.

Should we see if we can find accessories? the sprite suggested.

I have plenty of fascinators and gloves. But we can't make a corset and they're expensive. If it were going *over* a dress it would need to be "decorative corsetry"—something meant to be seen. The few she had wouldn't coordinate with the dress.

But... the sprite pouted.

It's pretty. I do appreciate your hard work. We'll get accessories later. Promise. Right now we need to find Thad and learn how to steal a gem.

If Jeff wouldn't help her, she'd find someone who would.

· · · · · · · ·

Steven sat in a chair in Quinn's office, reading up on the Staff of Eris. Noli was off doing... something, and he wasn't about to go anywhere near the Braddock residence without her. Jeff used to be so kind. Then again, he supposed if someone were courting Elise, he might be inclined to get a little sword-happy.

He flipped the page. Noli had been correct, right down to the Bright Lady herself ripping the staff apart. The only thing he couldn't find was anything about the stone.

Still, he wasn't sure he believed that the Bright Lady *spoke* to Noli.

"Darrow, we need to talk. Now." Jeff strode into the office, pistol very visible on his hip.

"I'm busy, Braddock." He didn't look up from his book. Two could play this game.

"Do you know where Noli is?" Jeff stood in front of him.

Steven marked the page with his finger. "At her mother's dress shop, finding something to wear to that dreadful ball she thinks we're going to."

"No. She's onboard the Vixen's Revenge, having Thad and Asa teach her how to steal a gem. I checked out the museum this morning, and I realized there's no way Noli can handle a job like this herself. *Especially* with her crazy scheme to steal it during a ball. I *told* her this." Jeff pounded his fist against the wall. "She won't listen. It doesn't help that the crew is completely enamored of her. Asa and Thad take orders from Vix, but for some reason Noli doesn't think she needs to listen to her. Or to me." He made a face.

V couldn't help but laugh. "Noli doesn't generally listen to anyone. This is *Noli*, remember? She hoverboards, fixes flying cars, and is a mechanic for air pirates."

"She listens to *you*," Jeff replied, not laughing.

"No, she doesn't." Otherwise things would have been different. "Your main objection isn't actually the stealing of the gem, but that she wishes to steal it herself." Steven rubbed his chin, trying to come up with a solution. Jeff nodded. "Perhaps *I* should take a look. I'd be able to tell if it were magic. If it isn't magic, then she'd have no reason to steal it."

Or go to the ball. He still couldn't believe Noli, of all people, *wanted* to attend a ball.

Jeff snapped his fingers. "That's brilliant, because I can't tell if it's magic or not. It just looks like a purple stone in a glass box to me."

He prayed to the Bright Lady that it wasn't magic. "Perfect.

Let me find James. I want to see the museum's exhibit on Dutch painters anyway."

....

"V, this is *so* boring." James shuffled past the wall of exquisite paintings. It was a traveling exhibition of Dutch Golden Age artists.

"Heathen." Steven studied a painting of flowers. Noli liked landscapes. He preferred paintings depicting every-day life. Unfortunately, they didn't have his favorite.

Just to irk his brother, he took his time, savoring the art-istry.

Finally, he allowed James to drag him into the room with the "fairy" exhibit. These mortals couldn't even spell it right.

As soon as he crossed the threshold, magic hit him squarely in the chest. "Flying figs."

"Language, V," James teased.

"You don't feel it?" Steven whispered, rubbing his mid-section.

"Other than shame at the really bad art?" James jerked his chin toward a painting of naked faeries cavorting in the moonlight. "No, I'm not you."

"That's probably a good thing," he replied. As Quinn had once put it, Steven was coming into some rather strange gifts. Ones he wasn't sure his father had ever noticed and ones he prayed his mother never knew about. His sensitivity to the changing tides of magic was one, his ability to sense those with the Spark, another.

Not wishing to draw attention by going straight to the magic, he slowly made his way around the room. Most of the items on display were paintings and sketches. There was a vase rumored to have been given to a family by faeries for luck that he swore his mother *literally* threw out of the big house once, before she was queen and they'd all lived there happily.

"That's one big stone." James practically pressed his nose to the glass case on a marble pedestal. Inside, a purple gem the size of a girl's fist sat on a white and gold pillow.

Steven sucked in a breath as he took in the sheer force of the magic the jewel possessed. "Bright Lady bless. What *is* that?"

"I'm not getting anything," James hissed back. "What do you feel?"

Steven put his hand on the glass, trying to read it the best he could. His hand yanked back as if it burned. "This may not be what Noli thinks it is, but this is most definitely ... you know."

The stone was quite magic. It was surprising no one had stolen it yet ... whatever it was.

They finished touring the gallery so that no one suspected anything. Finally, he and James left the museum and hoverboarded home in silence. They touched down in their backyard.

The door to Noli's backyard opened. A moment later, Jeff climbed through the loose board in the fence between their houses. His arms crossed over his chest. "So?"

Steven raked his hand through his hair. "I don't know what it is. But it's *not* something that should be in mortal hands. As much as I hate to admit it, Noli's right. We have to steal it."

"Fine. But there has to be a better way than Noli doing it alone. She needs to let us help her." Jeff's arms stayed wrapped firmly across his chest.

Noli climbed through the fence, a wrapped parcel in her hand. "Could you see Thad in a tuxedo and top hat? V, do you have anything suitable to wear tomorrow?"

"Probably." He'd just wear what he wore to the last affair he'd taken her to. It should still fit. Perhaps he should check on that.

Noli made a face at his reply.

Yes, he should check on that. Today.

"Noli, I've decided to help. Why do you insist on doing it by yourself?" Jeff huffed.

"Fine." Noli stood toe to toe with Jeff. "V and I will attend the ball. If I think I can take it without being caught, I will. If not, Thad and Asa can do it, but I can't pay you."

"Is this about *money*?" Jeff stepped back. "You're my sister. We'll steal something for you for free."

Her face fell. Steven put an arm around her waist to comfort her. Jeff glared. Steven glared right back and pulled her closer.

"I need to do it." Noli's jaw clenched in determination.

Ah, yes. Therein lay the crux of it. Noli believed she was the protector of this artifact, a duty bestowed upon her by a mysterious voice she heard while in a tree. She therefore felt that she personally needed to steal it.

"I believe you," Steven lied. "If she's telling you to do this, we'll do this together."

"We will?" Noli's entire face brightened, like the sun coming out from behind the clouds.

"Yes." It was one thing not to believe her; it was another thing to not believe her when Jeff didn't. Jeff made an annoyed noise. That made it all the better. "I'm not sure it's part of the staff, but it's not something we can leave in mortal hands. We'll figure it out." Steven toyed with her curls.

Jeff made another annoyed noise. "We're not finished discussing this."

Noli grit her teeth and took Steven's hand. "Yes, we are. V, let's see if your suit fits."

Steven allowed her to drag him inside his house and up the stairs. They recoiled when he opened his bedroom door. Whoops. He'd forgotten about the stench. What had caused it? Not that it mattered right now.

"Why don't you wait for me in Elise's room? I'll get it and change in James' room." He ran into his room, grabbed his suit out of the closet, and went into James' room. Steven kicked things out of his way. How did James function in such a mess?

He pulled on his suit. It didn't quite fit. Perhaps no one would notice.

Steven found Noli in Elise's room, which was still a mess from when Elise had fled in haste. She was sitting on Elise's bed reading a book, and looked up and frowned as he entered.

"That looks dreadful. Didn't you just wear it not long ago?"

He looked down at it, then back up at her. "I guess."

Setting the book on the bed, she came over to him and ran her fingers down his face. "I know you age differently. Did someone use magic to make you look, well, more like us?"

"Um, yes, when we came to live in this realm. I was disappointed that they made us so ... young. That's partially why everyone thought I was so smart. Father figured it would be better, that it would give us more allowances in adjusting. He used the magic in such a way so that James and I would be adults at about the same time here as we would in our realm. Why do you ask?" He stood inches from her. Steven liked being close to her without having to worry that Jeff or Vix would interrupt.

"You look ... different today. Different than you did yesterday. You're much taller, and you ... " A blush rose on her cheeks. "You look more ... like a man. I'm not sure how and why, but you do. I guess with your father being ... gone, the magic he used is wearing off."

"Oh, that makes sense. Magic generally undoes itself when the user passes on." He brought his face closer to hers, his dear, sweet Noli. "I really am almost an adult in my realm, so it won't be too much of a difference when it wears off completely. James, neither. Elise ... no, Quinn's with her. She'll be fine."

"Elise is older than you pretend she is, isn't she?" Noli's voice held no judgment.

"The matter of Elise is ... complicated." Actually, she was younger.

Noli rolled her eyes as she adjusted his suit. "Like she

thinks her mother is dead, and I'm not supposed to notice that she has the same sort of magic as you-know-who?"

Steven froze; he hadn't realized she'd figured out the similarities between Elise and their mother. "You can't tell a soul."

"I won't. She's naïve even for a little girl. It would be so easy…" Noli shook her head.

He knew exactly what she was thinking.

"Quinn will protect her with his dying breath, but finding her is very important. With Father gone, the family is my responsibility." He was failing at this right now, and it galled him.

She wrapped her arms around him. "Yes, it is. Now, does James own a suit? You simply *can't* wear this tomorrow."

"Noli, why are you stuck on this? Missy Sassafras is *nothing* compared to you." He ran his hand through her unbound hair. "She's not very smart. She probably has never read Aristotle or Shakespeare. She wouldn't know a Dutch Golden Age painting from a Baroque one. She can't fix an engine and probably grows lousy roses."

"But she makes superior scones." Noli glowered.

Steven leaned in until his lips brushed her ear. "I don't actually like scones. Now, what if I tell you what I've found regarding the staff?"

"It's bad?" She frowned.

"It can be terrible, depending on who wields it, but yes—according to what Quinn found, the circumstances leading up to the Bright Lady breaking it were quite dire."

"I see. So we absolutely need to protect the pieces." Noli looked solemn. "Even with all these things we need to do, I

71

think we should still apply to universities for next fall. I don't care where we go…I…I just want to go. Jeff says he'll help me pay for it if I don't get a scholarship. Which I probably won't."

That was a bit of a disconnect. She was behaving so strangely. How much of it was her being a girl, and how much of it was everything that had happened to her?

"Of course we can," he reassured her. She looked as if she might cry, and Noli wasn't as weepy as most girls. "Some of the applications I sent for have arrived."

Actually, applying to universities would give him something to look forward to. Steal a jewel. Duel his uncle. Find his sister. Attend university. Protect a world-altering artifact. Take back the kingdom. Marry the girl he loved. Just a day in the life of an exiled prince.

She gave him a smile as large as the sky. "Good. But we're still going to the ball."

SIX

The Museum Ball

Noli clipped a feather fascinator to her hair as she got ready for the ball.

Pretty, the sprite crowed as she caught sight of their reflection in the mirror.

"No. You can't go out like that, I'm sorry." Jeff blocked the door to her room with his body, a hand on each side of the door frame.

"You're not the boss of me, Jeff," she snapped, fluffing her carefully created curls to ensure they covered her pointed ears. "I'm tired of everyone treating me like I'm a little girl. Don't make me throw my knife at you."

His face fell as he entered her room. "I was making a joke. You . . . you look beautiful." A sigh escaped his lips. "The older brother in me doesn't want to acknowledge that you're not a little girl anymore. You're a woman grown, ready to make her own choices."

"Oh." She smoothed her voluminous skirts, then looked up at him in earnest. "I'm seventeen. I'm *not* a little girl anymore."

"No, you're not." Jeff shook his head, sadness in his eyes, as he sat on her desk chair. "Also, you're pretty good at throwing knifes. I saw you in the yard with James."

Earlier she and James had been having another sword lesson, which had ended with knife throwing, her favorite. "I like learning how to use a sword."

Noli pulled on net gloves, which she'd bleached then tinted with tea, trying to match the cream underskirt of the dress, and threaded gold ribbons through them.

"Are you really applying to all those universities?" Jeff rearranged the things on her desk. "I saw the applications on the kitchen table."

"Yes," she replied. V had brought over the applications and she'd started filling them out.

"Impressive." Jeff gave a nod of approval. "Your marks must be better than mine."

"Not really, but V seems to think I can do it." If he believed in her, then she had to try. She tucked a lace fan in her handbag. "Do I look all right?" Noli twirled in front of the looking glass, trying to glimpse the dress from different angles. She'd taken the rosettes off.

"You look amazing. Did Mother make the dress?"

"I did. Will you tie me up in the back? Please?" Not

knowing what else to do, she'd slit the back and laced it up like a corset.

Jeff stood and laced her up. "Well, that's different."

"That's the point." She took her new cream under-bust corset and put it over the dress. It was decorated with gold lace flowers. "Lace this up too, please?"

"What is *with* the corsets over the dresses? Aren't you supposed to wear them *under* your clothes?" Jeff's nose scrunched in confusion. "The corset tool belt you have makes sense, but this is just odd."

"It's a fae convention, but apparently it's making its way into this realm. I happen to like it." She'd discovered that at the corset maker's when she'd gotten the corset by trading fabric and things from her mother's shop.

He shook his head as he laced her up. "I'll never understand ladies' fashion."

Noli checked her appearance again in the mirror. "Perfect."

"Darrow better realize he's lucky to have someone like you," Jeff muttered.

"I do, Jeff. I do." V stood in the doorway. He twisted self-consciously. "Noli, do I look all right? James said I look like Father. I'm not sure if he meant it as a compliment."

Noli sucked in breath at the handsome sight in front of her. "You look like a gentleman."

She walked over and straightened the vest and cravat, which had been his father's party best. He did resemble Mr. Darrow a little, but not in a bad way.

"I never thought to use magic to make it fit." V tugged

at the cravat. "Will I pass? I feel odd wearing his suit. Like I'm wearing a costume."

She took him in from toes to top hat. He was a very cute man indeed. Noli adjusted his cravat, again. "You're perfect."

Jeff cleared his throat, still sitting at her desk.

V's eyes widened as he took her in. "You look *amazing*."

"I'm so glad you like it." Part of her preened, proud of the off-the-shoulder dress—and the entire effect the sprite had created. Even if the dress was *poufy*.

Poufy is pretty! The sprite told her. *And we look so very pretty.*

That we do, you did a good job, she assured the sprite.

V looks pretty too.

Noli gazed openly at V. *Yes, V looks really nice.*

If only Jeff and Vix weren't here …

"Will your skirt fit in my father's auto?" V frowned as his head flopped from side to side, top hat nearly falling off in the process.

Oops. She'd forgotten about that. "We'll figure it out."

Jeff sighed and shook his head slowly in resignation. "Have fun—and please don't forget to follow the plan." He eyed her handbag. "Do you have everything?"

Noli patted her handbag, which was a little large for the affair, but she needed the space in order to conceal everything. "I do. I even remember the plan."

They'd only been over it a hundred times. At least she'd gotten them to agree to doing things her way.

"Good." Jeff eyed V and patted the pistol at his hip. "Darrow, I'm watching you."

V straightened and gave a decisive nod. "Likewise."

"Ugh, you two. I'll be waiting downstairs." Grabbing her skirts, she left the room and marched down to the kitchen, frustrated by their silly boy games.

Vix sat at the kitchen table, cleaning her pistol. She looked up. "What a pretty dress. Not my style, but pretty."

"I appreciate the compliment." Noli untangled the train.

We will be prettiest, the sprite told her, as she fixed the skirts. *Missy will be angry. Perhaps she'll turn purple.*

She heard footsteps down the back stairs.

"I'm sorry, Noli." V joined her and offered his arm. "Shall we? The auto's out front. I've enlisted James as our chauffeur."

Noli took his offered arm. "Apology accepted. I just tire of you two sniping at each other. Now, let's steal ourselves a faery jewel."

....

"And here we are." James stopped the auto in front of the museum. The red and gold enameled steam-powered auto was a few years old but top of the line. He opened the car door for her.

Noli carefully extracted her skirts and train from the car and straightened them, as V got out and adjusted his top hat. A flying car, a giant purple Dragon model, soared overhead.

"I miss the Big Bad Pixymobile," she muttered. The unrepairable remains of her beloved flying car were in the shed behind the house, if Grandfather hadn't already carted them to the scrap heap.

"She was a good car." V put a gloved hand on her bare shoulder. "James, are you certain you don't wish to join us?"

James made a face as he climbed back into the car. "I'd rather eat ogre dung." He pulled out his pocket watch, which was on the chain she'd woven out of Charlotte's hair. James tucked it away and gave them a nod. "Enjoy."

After watching James race off, V straightened his top hat and offered Noli his arm. "Shall we, Miss Braddock?"

Grinning, she took his arm. "Why certainly, Mr. Darrow."

They walked up the museum steps slowly so she wouldn't trip on her skirts. V took the invitation out of his jacket pocket and handed it to the doorman.

The doorman looked at the invitation, then at them. Noli's belly knotted. He gave them a nod of approval. "Welcome."

They entered the museum lobby, checked in their wraps and his hat, and joined the line of couples to be announced into the ball. The strains of a waltz met her ears. Her belly didn't unknot as she remembered why she hated these sorts of affairs.

"Mr. Steven Darrow and Miss Magnolia Braddock," the man announced to the room.

Noli took a deep breath, well, as deep as she could with so much corsetry, and smiled as she and V entered the room. The main gallery had been cleared so there was room to dance, though fine paintings still lined the walls.

Couples, young and old, waltzed across the floor. Most women were festooned in ribbons and lace to the point where they resembled cakes in the bakery. A few older women sat along one wall. Chaperones. Several young women chatted in small groups, waiting to be asked to dance. All of Los Angeles society seemed to be in attendance. A few women craned their necks as she and V entered. Great. She could practically hear the whispers.

Perhaps this wasn't a good idea after all. No, that was what they wanted. Jeff, Vix, V … even Thad and Asa. No one thought she could steal the gem. But she could.

As for surviving the ball …

"Oh. You came." Missy sailed over, looking like a small steamboat in her navy and cream gown. All she needed was a hat with a whistle on it. Several girls trailed behind her, dance cards dangling from their wrists. Two whispered behind gloved hands and giggled.

No. She wasn't going to let them irritate her. Too much was at stake tonight.

"Missy, ladies." Noli had never bothered to learn all their names.

"Mr. Darrow, don't you look dashing? I'm glad you've returned from your travels. I can't wait to hear all about them." Missy took out her fan, fluttered it, and flashed him a look that was probably meant to be flirtatious, but instead made her look like a beaver.

"Miss Sassafras, ladies." V gave a little bow. "You all look well this evening." He sounded bored and uninterested, which Missy failed to notice, flapping her fan and leaning in as if he were telling exciting stories.

Missy looked down her pointed nose at Noli. "My, Noli, what an *interesting* dress."

Noli's cheeks burned with ire. *Interesting?* In society-speak, "interesting" was a code word for "ugly" and could be applied to everything from gowns to girls. The dress was different, but *not* interesting.

"I think she looks beautiful," V retorted. "Miss Braddock, may I have the honor of a dance?"

Before she could answer, V had her gliding across the floor to the *one-two-three, one-two-three* of the small orchestra. They twirled and whirled with the other couples to the rhythm of the music, not missing a step.

"Did I do that correctly?" V held her tightly to him. "You turned as red as your dress. I figured *interesting* is girl code for something."

"It is, and you did. I appreciate that." She had to move quickly and lightly to maneuver the skirt around the room; the train had a wrist-loop to help keep it from being stepped on. Several women gave her odd looks as they made their way around the floor. The bottom fell out of her stomach. "My dress really is ugly, isn't it? Everyone's staring."

V's cheek touched hers as they danced. "All eyes are on you because you outshine everyone else."

I told you we're pretty. The other girl is just jealous. She looks like someone tied a ribbon around a lump of fabric, the sprite assured her.

As amusing and accurate as that image was, Noli remained unconvinced.

The waltz became a polka. People changed partners. V held on to her tightly and she was grateful for it. She was in no mood to make nice while some old man danced with her out of pity so she wouldn't be drapery on the ballroom walls, sitting with the chaperones and undesirables.

"Polka, Miss Braddock?" He changed his hold on her.

"Why certainly, Mr. Darrow." Doing the polka in this dress was even more difficult than waltzing. She couldn't help laughing as she tried to keep her skirts from barreling into people.

V laughed. "That's a very large dress."

When the polka ended, he bowed and she curtseyed. They made their way off the floor. Noli prayed no one asked her to dance; if they did, the rules of society dictated that she had to accept.

"Would you like some refreshment?" he asked. V was always so good at playing the gentleman at affairs like these.

"Why, that sounds lovely." Finding the refreshment room would get them out of the ballroom so they could look for the jewel. Hopefully it wasn't in the same place as the food.

Missy shot her a nasty look as she took a place on the floor for the quadrille. Having danced with her partner on occasion, Noli almost felt sorry for Missy; well, Missy's toes.

Let's not dance with boys who are bad at dancing tonight, the sprite told her. The sprite loved dancing, but had little patience for inept partners.

Sounds good to me. Noli didn't like dancing with anyone but V.

In the refreshment room, no sooner had V brought her some cake when several women came up to her inquiring about her mother—and their dresses. Noli found herself promising to be at the shop the next day. V stood in a corner speaking with a group of young men, most of which she didn't fancy.

"Why are you standing in the corner eating cake and denying others the pleasure of your company?" Mrs. Sassafras gently chided. Now she looked like a lump of brown silk tied with a giant cream ribbon and trimmed in lace. The feathers of her fascinator were also cream, making her resemble an apple dumpling topped with ice cream.

"I like cake, Mrs. Sassafras." There wasn't much else to say.

I wish it were chocolate, the sprite told her.

Mrs. Sassafras looked around, frowning. "I'll escort you back to the ballroom. It's not proper for you to be hiding in here alone."

Noli took another bite of cake. Blasted societal rules.

"I dare say, I do like this decorative corsetry trend," she added. "Now, come along, dear. Your Steven will find you for the final waltz. I'm sure there are young men just waiting to dance with you."

Sure. Noli cast V a glance as she set her plate on a tray and Mrs. Sassafras herded her back into the ballroom and planted her in a chair. Not only was she apart from V, but she needed to find that jewel. Something she couldn't do from a chair in the ballroom.

The quadrille ended. Someone came over and asked Mrs. Sassafras to dance, leaving Noli all alone. No sooner had she left than Missy and her flock of courtiers accosted Noli. Considering it was improper for a lady to cross the ballroom alone, and that young women traveled in packs, Noli was stuck. She craned her head, hoping to see someone, perhaps a woman her mother owed a dress to, or any female she was halfway acquainted with. Everyone seemed to be going to the dance floor with their partners. Flying figs.

"I think I'm going to sit right here." Missy pretended to sit *on* Noli. "Oh, Noli, I didn't see you. Actually, I'm surprised they let you in. Truly, that dress is disgraceful."

The other girls tittered behind their fans.

Why was she putting up with this? She wasn't trolling for a husband. No longer did she need to be on her best behavior so her mother wouldn't be embarrassed. Why must she play by society's rules? After all, her mother wasn't here and she had no interest in *ever* being part of Los Angeles society again. She could *leave*. This chair. This room. Go find V and the jewel.

A weight lifted from her shoulders.

"I'm surprised they allowed *you* in dressed like that," Noli retorted. "You need to find a better dressmaker. It doesn't flatter you at all. In fact, you look like a boat."

Missy recoiled as if slapped. "How dare you speak like that to me? I'm you're better."

"No, you're not." Noli stood. "You're only invited because your merchant father is meddling in politics and it's the polite thing to do. Your parents make you go, because if you marry a truly wealthy man, with real social status and power, then it would cement their own precarious position. You're not accepted by true society girls, so you spend your time lording over anyone you can. Also, you're here annoying me and not on the floor, which means your dance card isn't full, and don't give me anything about being fatigued. You might be able to make a perfect scone, but you'll make no one a perfect society wife. Money can't buy class. You know it—and so do they. Now, if you'll excuse me." Noli marched away, desperately looking for a place to march to.

"Noli Braddock, is that you?" A blonde with a cascade of curls in a pink dress bounced over, accompanied by a brunette in blue and a brunette in lilac.

"Josephine? When did you return from France?" Noli took in the thin, pretty blonde with rosy cheeks and dimples. They'd been friends back when her family had social standing. Josephine had been in France for ages. Now, she was a *real* society girl.

"Who exactly is that girl in the awful dress? I keep seeing her at things. *Missy*. What sort of name is that?" Josephine took out her fan to hide her scornful look.

"I think it's short for Melissa. Her parents are new money." Noli tried to channel her mother when saying that. "She doesn't have very nice manners."

"My mother says that's the problem with new money," the girl in lilac retorted. "I'm Lillian, and this is my sister Vivian. We used to take dancing lessons together before my mother sent us to New York for polish." Lillian looked pained as she said that.

Noli nodded. "I remember all of you—especially you, Jo."

Lillian and Vivian had been among the friends who'd abandoned Noli years ago. But since everyone was pretending to be civil, she might as well do the same. It was infinitely better than speaking to Missy Sassafras.

"Do you still play the piano?" Vivian added. "I remember always being jealous that you were so much better than me."

"Were you now?" Noli hadn't had lessons in years.

"Why did you stop writing me?" Josephine frowned.

Noli looked down at where her shoes should be. The dress hid them completely. "Because I didn't have anything to say."

She'd stopped writing letters when the dark times started. No longer did she have gossip to share, because she'd moved to public school and been dropped by her old friends. She didn't attend parties or picnics or even the theatre. Her life became different. Unrelatable.

"But things are better now, aren't they?" Hope gleamed in Josephine's blue eyes. "My mother said you've returned to Boston."

"We did. My brother Jeffrey and his bride-to-be bought the house here in Los Angeles. I'm just helping wrap up our affairs."

"How very modern of you," Lillian replied without a hint of disdain.

Vivian eyed her dress. "What an unusual design."

"It's the latest in France." Noli bristled. Then her cheeks burned. Josephine had just returned from France.

"No, it's not." Josephine's grin grew wide, lighting up her doll-like face. "But I see what you did—and I like it. Ladies, we should do that. Also, you look so slender with your corset that way. I'm going to try it. So ... " She leaned in and lowered her voice. "We're going to sneak out and inspect the art. Care to be scandalous with us?"

Perfect. Noli grinned. "Why, Jo, I thought you'd never ask."

....

"You and Steven Darrow? I always thought James was more handsome." Josephine giggled as they ate cake in the refreshment room. Well, she and Noli ate cake, the other girls pretended to eat.

"James *is* attractive." Lillian's eyes held an appreciative gleam.

"I'm happy with V." Noli looked around. She'd found the gem; now, to find V so they could steal it and leave. As nice as it was to see Josephine, that wasn't the point of being here.

"Oh my," Vivian whispered behind her fan. "If that isn't the handsome devil now."

Noli turned and saw V enter the room and make his way slowly toward them is if he happened upon them and wasn't looking for her. Anything less would be improper.

"Hello." Noli smiled and introduced him to Josephine, Lillian, and Vivian.

He bowed. "If you would all excuse me, I believe Miss Braddock owes me a dance."

Josephine waggled her fingers at Noli as V escorted her out of the room. He didn't turn toward the ballroom. Instead, they found themselves alone in a dark gallery.

"I'm so sorry," V apologized. "I saw Mrs. Sassafras escort you out and it took me a few moments to find a way to politely leave the conversation. By the time I made it to the ballroom, you were nowhere to be seen. For a moment I thought that perhaps you'd taken Missy Sassafras outside." He gave her a lopsided grin.

"V." Noli gave him a little shove. "It's been ages since I've gotten in a fistfight. Besides, could you imagine? I did manage to take a peek at the room with the gem. It's not dark like this one. It's unguarded, but patrolled. I think I can do it. I have the decoy."

"Decoy?" His eyebrows rose.

She patted the heavy handbag dangling from her wrist. "It's in here. Thad gave it to me. We go, wait until the room is clear, you stand watch, I'll make the switch, and we leave."

V took out his pocket watch and checked the time. "James will be here soon. Are you certain? After all, Jeff and his men are standing by to help."

Like she would give them a chance to say *I told you so*.

"Let's try." Noli took V's arm and they entered the faery exhibit, analyzing the paintings until the room emptied.

Noli looked both ways; she touched the glass of the case holding the beautiful jewel, her belly nothing but nerves.

"What are you two doing in here?" a male voice asked from behind them.

Not knowing what else to do, she kissed V, long and deep, holding on to him with all her might. Then, she straightened and put a finger to her lips in what she hoped was a coy gesture. "Shhh. We're having a clandestine rendezvous." Noli winked, hoping to make it seem more believable—they were misbehaving, but not committing a crime.

"Oh, it's you. Aren't you supposed to be annoying

hardworking law enforcement officers in other locales?" Officer Davies didn't look—or sound—angry.

"Aren't you supposed to be off sending girls to reform school?" Anger welled inside her. He had to have known what Findlay House was like. For a moment she was back there as Miss Gregory poured cold water over her face ...

... she couldn't breathe ...

"We're just admiring the paintings, Officer." V put his forehead to hers. "Noli, it's all right. *Breathe.*"

Noli took one breath, then another, listening to his voice, as the memories of Miss Gregory and Findlay House faded away.

"That's it, darling, that's it," V soothed. Officer Davies left the room.

"I'm sorry I'm broken," she hiccuped, putting her head on his shoulder. Would she ever recover from everything that had happened to her?

"Let's go home. We'll let Thad take care of this," he whispered, his grip loosening.

No. She wasn't about to back down now. They were too close. Her hand found the fake jewel in her purse. Head popping up, she looked both ways. "Guard me."

Putting her hands on the glass, Noli used her magic to send out a pulse that would kill any monitoring device, even though she hadn't seen any indication that they used them. She lifted the glass dome and handed it to V. Carefully, just like Thad showed her, she edged the gem off with the new one, trying to keep the gem even.

Voices floated down the hallway and her heart quickened. *Steady*.

"Done." The real gem went into her bag.

V set the dome back on. "Perfect."

"What are you two doing?" Missy scoffed from the doorway. "You're not supposed to touch the exhibits."

Flying figs. Of course it would be Missy. What had she seen?

Blood roared in Noli's ears as she tried not to panic. "Have you ever seen anything so large?" she asked, trying to throw Missy off.

Missy squinted as if she didn't believe them.

"Miss Sassafras, would you honor me with a dance?" V bowed and offered her a hand.

What was he doing? Shouldn't they be trying to *leave?*

Missy put a hand to her lips and giggled, demeanor instantly shifting. "Why, of course, Mr. Darrow."

"Miss Braddock, I'll see you in the ballroom later." V took Missy's arm and led her out of the gallery.

Noli's jaw dropped. What had just happened? There went their speedy exit. As she headed toward the ballroom, her shoulders slumped. She wasn't sure whether she should feel rejected or angry, and didn't really notice when she bumped into two gentlemen she'd never seen before.

"Oh, pardon me," she muttered, not meaning it. She peeked into the refreshment room to see if Josephine was still in there so that she'd have someone to return to the ballroom with.

Why had V abandoned her?

What if he was actually *distracting* Missy? Yes, that must be it. After all, he knew what she thought of that dollymop.

"Done so soon?" Josephine's lips turned down in a slight frown as Noli joined them.

"We got waylaid by Missy and he's dancing with her out of politeness." Noli made a face, not bothering to pull out her fan to hide it.

"It wasn't very nice of him to abandon you," she replied.

"Have you met Missy?" Noli snorted.

Josephine smiled and looked at Lillian and Vivian. "Shall we return to the ballroom?"

The four of them walked down the hall. Shouts came from behind them.

Vivian made a face and fluttered her fan, though even that didn't hide her unladylike distaste. "Some people are *so* loud."

They returned to the ballroom. Immediately, Noli's eyes found V dancing the schottische with Missy. Actually, it looked as if V was herding Missy as she stumbled through the dance.

"She looks like an elephant," Lillian snickered from behind her fan.

"That's an insult to elephants," Vivian replied.

The music ended. Missy attempted an awkward curtsey, V bowed, and he returned her to the wall with the rest of the drapery. Then he approached Noli.

"Miss Braddock, may I have the honor of a final dance before we depart?" V asked.

"I suppose, Mr. Darrow." Noli took his hand and they

went onto the floor. A waltz started, which was infinitely better than a quadrille or any of those complicated dances that took forever. "Please tell me that you were distracting her." Noli tried not to make a face at Missy as they passed.

"Of course," V replied. "I *am* beginning to get an idea as to why she annoys you. She talks an awful lot about herself, when she's not gossiping."

Noli laughed. "That's Missy. After this, we should take our leave."

Realization crashed down on her. They'd done it. They'd gotten the jewel. Now to depart without incident. The music ended. She waved to Josephine, who was being led to the floor by Lillian's older brother.

"I'll call on you," Josephine mouthed as they left the floor after the dance.

Noli and V left the ballroom, collected their things, and walked down the front steps of the museum. James waited in the enameled auto, a bored look on his face.

"Steven, Noli, if I might have a word," Officer Davies called after them.

Panic rose inside her. Did he know? Had Missy told?

V gripped her wrist. "Relax. Allow me to handle this," he whispered.

Gulping to ease her fears, she nodded.

"Yes, Officer Davies?" V asked, holding her close. They weren't the only people leaving.

"Did you notice anything odd when you were in the gallery?" he asked.

"No, not at all," V replied. "Is there a problem?"

Noli's heart stuck in her throat and a million thoughts raced through her head—not one of them good.

"We caught two men trying to steal something; I wanted to know if you saw anything," Officer Davies said.

All the air whooshed out of her. He wasn't after them. Officer Davies shot her a look.

Two men. Noli remembered something. "After V left to dance with Missy, I saw two strange men in the hallway. By strange, I mean that they looked like gentlemen, but were unfamiliar to me. I don't remember what they looked like."

Maybe that would keep them off their path.

"Thank you, Noli." Someone called for Officer Davies. "Have a nice evening."

"You as well, Officer," V replied. They walked to the car and got in. James took off.

"So?" James gave them an expectant look as they sped away.

"We're good." Noli patted her handbag, the jewel inside. Elation still coursed through her—they'd done it. "Now, let's go home. I don't know about you, but I'm exhausted."

SEVEN

Complications

A click startled Steven awake. He rubbed his eyes and peered at the air pirate standing in the doorway of Noli's guest room, pistol drawn. "Vix, I'm nowhere near Noli."

Shrugging, she holstered her pistol and left muttering, "Breakfast is ready."

Steven dressed and padded down to the kitchen. His nose twitched at the smell of pancakes and his mouth watered. Everyone was there—Vix, James, and Jeff, and Noli cooking.

Jeff was sitting at the table reading the paper. The headline read *Jewel Stolen at Museum Ball.*

"You're lucky," he said, glancing up at Steven. "Apparently two men were caught trying to steal the gem. Then, while the police were busy with them, someone else *actually* stole the gem. The other men disappeared too. Noli was right—the ball was a great cover for a robbery."

Someone had stolen the fake. A load lifted off Steven's chest, then slammed down so hard he gasped. "What if they realize it's fake?"

"Wouldn't they have to be magic?" Jeff hid behind the newspaper.

Noli handed Steven a cup of tea, flashing him a large smile.

"Those would be the people I'd worry about." Steven took the offered cup.

"We'll handle them." Noli returned with plates of food.

"Are we doing more boring research today?" James stuffed food in his mouth.

Noli sat at the crowded table, on a fifth chair brought in from the dining room. "I need to be at the shop at ten. Jeff, if Jo comes to call will you please tell her where I am?"

"What you should be doing is getting that thing out of here." Jeff put away his paper so he could eat. "Go hide it in fairyland or something."

"We will; I'm just about finished. I'm going to see if Quinn sent us an aethergraph. I'm still worried about him and Elise." Steven took a bite. "Excellent breakfast, Noli."

Noli smiled, her eyes shining in the morning light. "I appreciate the compliment. I finished my applications this morning. Will you drop them off for me at Mr. Thompson's shop when you check for aethergraphs? Please?"

"That was fast." He took another bite of delicious pancake.

"I only completed three. I still have to ask some of my teachers for letters." Noli paused, fork halfway to her mouth. "Do you think the fact I'm not in school will affect my application?"

"Same as it will mine," Steven replied. "I'll send off yours and mine, though I only have one." It was odd that she could think about going to university at a time like this. But this was her dream, so naturally she'd be excited. "If you write some requests to your teachers, I can drop those off as well," he offered.

The look on her face said it all. He was actually looking forward to spending four years with her in the mortal realm, attending a university and learning new things. Being together without chaperones. After that, they could take his court back.

"I wish you all the best." Vix took a sip of tea. "Are you also going to university, James?"

James snorted. "Me, go to school voluntarily? Do you think Hittie and Hattie would let me work with them for a bit?"

Steven nearly spit out his tea. Hittie and Hattie were ornery female air pirate friends of Vix's. Hattie did seem fond of James.

Vix's eyebrows rose. "Doing what?"

"Gunning." James shrugged. "Noli, more sword lessons after you visit the shop?"

"Perfect." Noli grinned.

They finished breakfast. Noli gave Steven her applications and quickly wrote requests to her teachers. Back at his own house, the first thing Steven did was consult the book he and Quinn used for messages. He'd forgotten to check it yesterday.

The page was blank. His finger traced the spot where there should be a symbol. Two days ago, there'd been a triangle, which had replaced the circle and rectangle that had been there previously.

No symbol. That could only mean one thing.

Dropping the book to the ground, Steven ran all the way to Mr. Thompson's General Store. Chest heaving, he pushed open the door.

"Mr. Thompson, do you have any aethergraphs for James or Steven Darrow, or for Magnolia Braddock?"

Mr. Thompson returned with two papers. "I have one for Steven Darrow and one for Magnolia Braddock."

"I appreciate it." Steven handed the shopkeeper a coin. Noli's was from her mother. But the other...

Stiofán, something is wrong. Come as soon as possible.
—Mathias

Steven's entire being went cold. Mathias was a very good friend of Quinn's. As much as he hoped it wasn't true, this message wouldn't disappear or change.

Back at the houses, he found Noli and James gone. He moved all of Quinn's journals and research to Noli's room, where they'd be safe. After locating a schedule of airships to New York, he returned to town to visit the bank and buy some essentials. This time, he'd bring money before charging off on an adventure.

When Steven came home again, he found James giving Noli a sword lesson in her backyard. Jeff joined them too, his eyes shining with excitement.

"Noli, come quick," Jeff called.

Noli put down her sword, hiked up her skirts, and followed her brother into the house. Steven looked at James, who shrugged. They followed Noli and Jeff into what had been Mr. Braddock's office, which looked as if it had been set upon by bandits.

"You found it?" Noli's jaw dropped.

Steven cocked his head, wondering what Jeff had been looking for.

"You never thought to look in here, did you?" Grinning, Jeff bent under the desk.

She shook her head. "We're not allowed in here."

"Which makes it the perfect place to hide things." Jeff's hand shot out from under the desk, holding a glass jar stuffed with money. He emerged and waved the jar at Noli. "University fund. This should get you started."

Noli wrapped her arms around her brother, her eyes shimmering with joy. "You found it."

Ah, the infamous hidden jar of money. Steven had helped Noli look for it, and yes, this was one place they'd never dared look.

Jeff hugged Noli back, shooting Steven a pointed glance that clearly said *take that*.

"I dropped off the applications and your letters." Steven didn't know what else to say. He'd figured he'd pay for Noli's school. Somehow. He supposed all his father's money and the house were his now.

Perhaps they could sell the house here and buy one wherever they went to university. Then they could, for lack of a better term, "play house." Though he might have to marry Noli first. Mortal style, at least. Not that he minded.

He smiled. Yes, he'd marry her. Mortal *and* Otherworld style. Even with everything, he wanted to be with her forever. He was her other half. She made him a better man.

"What?" Noli laughed.

"I'd marry you in a moment." Steven's cheeks burned as he realized he'd said that out loud. Immediately, his hands flew up in surrender. "Please, no one shoot me."

"Please do it," Vix replied from the doorway, for once not aiming a pistol at him. "That way we could have a double wedding and Noli could plan *everything*."

Noli looked thoughtful. For a second her eyes took on that blank look that meant she was speaking with the sprite.

Jeff set the jar on the desk with a loud thunk. "We'll talk about weddings later."

Noli gave Jeff another hug. "Oh, Jeff, I don't need you to be a fussy old bodger too." She slid an arm around Steven's waist. "Is there any word of Elise and Quinn?"

His good mood faded as he remembered why he'd been looking for James and Noli in the first place. "Something's very wrong. Mathias needs us to come to New York."

"Why?" Noli's eyes widened.

Steven cleared the lump in his throat and shoved away the guilt he had for feeling more for the loss of Quinn than the death of his father. "I have reason to believe that Quinn is dead."

• • • • • • • •

"Uncle Kevighn, that was fun, can we do this again?" Aodhan's cherub face practically glowed with elation as they traipsed through the Blackwoods, bows and kill in hand.

Kevighn ruffled Aodhan's pale hair. "We'll go tomorrow if your father doesn't have anything for me to do; otherwise, we'll go again soon."

He had to admit, Ciarán was right. Aodhan needed him. Teaching him to hunt had brought back memories of his own misspent youth.

"May I come as well?" Elise trotted behind them.

"Of course." He gave the little girl a smile. Elise had refused to be left behind, so he'd taught the both of them. Elise was decent for a girl. Creideamh hadn't been a bad shot either.

When they reached the Thirsty Pooka, they entered through the kitchen. A staircase led directly to the hall with the secret passage to the living areas.

"Here, Grandma Luce, will you cook these for our supper please?" Aodhan handed the old woman their kill.

The small, elderly woman who ran the kitchen here took the animals from him. "Of course I will. Kevighn, I'm glad you're back."

"Me too," Kevighn replied. Old Luce had been grandmother and then some to him and Ciarán both. "Let's get cleaned up."

As they walked up the staircase and into the little hall, Kevighn could hear Ciarán yelling. He pushed the children through the passage. "I'll be there in a little bit."

He followed the voice toward its source—Ciarán's office, the one where he conducted official dark court business.

The office was very simple for a king. There was nothing but a few wooden chairs, a simple desk, a bookshelf crammed with books and scrolls, and a window covered with a heavy curtain. Ciarán, hood down, sat behind the desk, scowling at a large purple jewel in his palm.

"This is a fake! How could you get me a fake? It was real a few days ago."

"I . . . I don't know," one of men standing before Ciarán stammered, knees shaking. He was tall and not someone Kevighn recognized. "Perhaps someone else stole it. We weren't the only fae at the ball."

"What? Who else was there?" Ciarán's eyes burned with fearsome intensity.

Kevighn leaned against the doorway, watching.

The shorter man, named Lefty, rubbed his chin. "There were two. A blond boy and a girl . . . a pretty girl with dark hair and grey eyes."

The tall man shook his head. "She was a sprite, though."

"Sprites like shiny things." Lefty shrugged.

"Sprites aren't smart enough to steal a gem and leave a decoy," Ciarán snapped, his scarred face contorting in anger.

A dark-haired sprite and a blond boy at a ball. Could it be?

"Where were you?" Kevighn asked.

"Los Angeles. Why?" Ciarán shot him a look.

Kevighn came over to the desk. "I know a rather uncommon dark-haired sprite, one related to thieves, who unfortunately is sometimes in the company of a blond, sorry excuse for an earth court prince. Both of whom occasionally reside in Los Angeles."

"You mean the girl. *That* girl?" His eyebrows rose. "Why would she steal a gem?"

"Her brother's a thief." Kevighn eyed the gem. "May I?"

Ciarán nodded. "It's nothing but a hunk of glass."

"What should it be?" Kevighn examined it. It wasn't even some mortal semi-precious stone. It was literally purple glass.

"You two had best be off before I hurt you." Ciarán waved the men off.

"Yes, Your Majesty." They bowed and left.

Ciarán's attention turned to Kevighn. "Hunting lessons went well?"

"Aodhan shows promise. We had a good time." Kevighn set the glass gem down on the desk. "What *is* this?"

Ciarán sighed. "I think it's part of the staff. Well, if it was the *actual* gem, it would be."

"Is it?" So little was known about the staff, and the man who knew the most was dead.

"It's rather powerful in its own right. We can't let Brogan or Tiana have it." He frowned. "Who does she work for? Brogan? I need to know what pieces he has."

"Magnolia would never work for Brogan. But…" Kevighn sighed and shook his head. "Her brother does, upon occasion. She probably has no idea what it is. I never told her what the pieces became." While he trusted Noli with his life, there were some secrets he couldn't trust her with. Yet.

"Go get it from her." Ciarán said this with the easy air of authority.

Kevighn stared at him. "You want me to do *what*?"

"I need the gem. You like the girl. Go get the girl to give you the gem." Ciarán rolled his eyes. "It's simple. I don't care how you do it. Just don't come back without it."

Kevighn bowed. "Of course, my king."

Now *this* was a mission. After all, he was a huntsman, and he always got what he wanted.

EIGH+

Mathias' Place

"We're going *where* with *what*?" Noli's nose wrinkled with distaste as Steven ushered her and James through the bustling city street.

James made a noise of exasperation. "It's just a burlesque hall. It's a perfectly respectable establishment."

"One that requires code words and fluffy kittens," Steven muttered, not believing he was actually having this conversation. At least this time they were dressed like gentleman.

Noli straightened the skirts of her blue dress and scowled at James.

"You could have stayed behind," James replied, jacket squirming.

She hugged Steven's arm. "Never."

The doorman of the unassuming restaurant in a fashionable neighborhood stopped them with a scathing look.

"We have reservations under Gentry." Steven handed the doorman some coins.

The doorman handed one back and opened the door, his nose wrinkled in slight disdain as he sniffed, "It's ladies' night."

Steven pocketed the change. *Ladies' night?* Did he even want to know?

They entered and James walked over and gave the unfamiliar girl, clad in not much other than a red corset and bustle, a winsome smile. "Hello, we have a reservation under Gentry."

She appraised them, eyes lingering over him and James. "It's ladies' night."

"We're actually here to see Mathias. He's expecting us." James patted his squirming jacket. "We brought him a present."

"Follow me, then." She turned and waggled her bottom at James, leading them through the red velvet curtain down the hallway, past another doorman, and through more curtains.

Music greeted them, a thumping, wild music far from the waltzes and ballads of their earlier visits. The dim lights gave everything a rose-colored glow.

"V, is a burlesque hall the same as a joy house?" Noli's eyes went wide as she took in their surroundings.

"Not quite." He pulled her closer to him. If Jeff found out about this . . .

The hostess seated them. The tables had been draped in burgundy tablecloths, the chairs topped with velvet cushions.

Men wearing nothing but what might be bathing costumes brought drinks and supper to tables filled with women.

Women?

He took another look. Yes, nearly everyone at the tables were well-dressed women. Very scantily clad men wiggled onstage while women cheered and yelled things one normally didn't hear from ladies.

Oh. *Ladies' night.*

"You're such a prude," James teased, openly enjoying his discomfort.

"No, he's not." Noli turned her chair so her back was to the stage.

A man came over to take their order. Steven tried not to look at him, since his chest, and most of the rest of him, was bare.

"Whiskey for everyone," James said, as if nothing was out of the ordinary about this entire situation.

"I don't like whiskey." Noli's nose scrunched. "May I please have some honey wine... If you have any? I think that's what it's called. It's made of berries and honey?"

The man left.

"Have you ever *had* whiskey?" James asked.

"No. But I don't want any." Noli's arms crossed over her chest.

Steven put a hand on her arm. "Noli, what's wrong? Something's been bothering you since we boarded the airship."

Hopefully, it wasn't more voices.

"My mother expects me to return to Boston for Christmas." Noli sighed, shoulders rising and falling. "The good thing is that I think she might be marrying off Vix and Jeff under pretense—"

"Under pretense?" James made a face. "You mean she's going to throw them a surprise wedding."

"Unless I'm reading too much into the wording, I believe so. However, with Vix's hatred of wedding planning, it's better that way. Vix won't have to plan a wedding, and my mother can play mother to both the groom and the bride, planning everything just as *she'd* like."

Yes, she'd like it quite a bit. Steven could see it now.

"I wouldn't miss that for anything. But I have a feeling that..." Noli's face fell.

"That she'll want you to stay in Boston." Steven squeezed her hand. He knew she loved her mother, but Noli and Mrs. Braddock had very different ideas of how Noli should live her life. In many ways, he understood.

"Yes," Noli replied. "After all, why wouldn't I?" Her hands moved in an empty gesture and she gave a defeated sigh.

The waiter returned with their drinks. He winked at Noli as he set down her wine. Steven hit the table with his fist as the waiter left.

Noli's net-gloved hand covered his. "No half-naked waiter is going to sway me."

Then she blanked out for a moment. Steven wasn't sure he'd ever grow accustomed to this.

"What did the sprite say?" he asked, curious.

Noli's cheeks pinked. "She's admiring the men. Also, she thinks we need one of those unseemly red outfits the hostess was wearing, she wants *you* to wear one of the outfits the men are wearing, and she wants me to dance with you until you're not sad anymore." She squeezed his hand. "We don't like it when you're sad."

"Which is why we're going to drink away our sorrows." James raised his glass.

Steven suppressed a groan. Between his father's and Charlotte's deaths, James had been through a lot, but getting tipsy in a burlesque hall in New York City on ladies' night wasn't going to help. Not in a way that would actually be useful.

"Drinking won't bring anyone back." Noli patted James' arm. "I miss them too." The kitten poked his head through the top of James' coat. She laughed and scratched the kitten's ears.

"James, what do you think happened to Urco?" Seeing the kitten made Steven recall Mathias' hound, which made him think of his own. Urco had been his dog as a child, but he'd had to leave him behind in the Otherworld.

James shrugged and half-drained his glass. "I didn't see him at the big house, but then I didn't see any animals—no hounds, horses, or anything. Aunt Dinessa might know."

"That's a good idea." Perhaps Urco was in the palace kennels. Hopefully he was still alive. Steven missed him and should have thought to look for him sooner.

Noli cocked her head. "Who's Urco?"

"Urco's my dog. He's a fae hound. Technically they're not allowed in this realm, so I had to leave him behind when we were exiled," he explained.

"Oh. Do you miss him? I've never had a pet." Noli took a

sip of wine. It was a beautiful color, a sort of deep purple most unlike the wines he'd seen in this realm.

He thought of Urco; the pup would be full grown by now. "I . . . I do."

"Ah, you're here." Mathias appeared, well-dressed and elegant as usual. His hair was a blond so pale it was near white, his eyes a clear blue. He looked curiously at Noli.

"Mathias, this is Magnolia Braddock. Noli, this is Mathias. He's the friend of Quinn's I was telling you about," Steven said.

"It's nice to meet you." Noli inclined her head politely, but curiosity shone in her eyes.

"Come, join us." James patted an empty seat at the table.

Mathias looked at the kitten head poking out from James' jacket. "I summoned *you*; a gift is unnecessary, Séamus."

James shrugged and handed the kitten to him. "I like catching them."

Steven smacked himself in the forehead.

Noli's shoulders stayed hunched. She focused on her drink as the music changed and men came over to the tables and asked ladies to dance. "You have very good taste." Mathias indicated her glass. "It's imported from the Otherworld and there's a very limited supply."

"What happened to Quinn," Steven blurted, sick of pleasantries.

Mathias' lips formed a thin line as he passed the kitten to one of the half-naked waiters. "Quinn and Ailís were on their way here, taking refuge in various safe places. Then . . . something happened. All I know is that I was to meet him in Central

Park and take Ailís so that he could tend to something. When I arrived..."

"It was Brogan, wasn't it?" Noli's face contorted as she stared into the depths of her glass. "Another death that's all my fault."

"It's not your fault." Steven squeezed her hand, trying to ease her guilt.

"It was Brogan's men, but they had no reason to hurt Quinn." Mathias shook his head. "I fear they may have come for your sister and he died protecting her."

"Quinn's dead?" James' eyes went glassy. Quinn had been many things to them, including a father figure, since their own father was so absent, both figuratively and literally.

They would have to mourn later, especially if Brogan was after Elise.

"Where is she?" Worry swirled inside Steven like a maelstrom. It was his job to protect her; if anything happened he'd never be able to forgive himself.

Mathias shook his head. "I don't know. I'm so sorry."

"They didn't kill Elise, did they? She's a little girl." James paled.

Mathias raised his hand. "No. That's the problem. My attempts to locate her have been unsuccessful." He shook his head. "Quinn trusted me to protect her and I can't even find her." Pain crossed his face. "However, I think she escaped. I traced her to the portal in Central Park."

"Didn't you tell us that there wasn't a public portal here?" Steven's eyebrows rose.

"It's not actually public, even if it is in the middle of the park. From what I can tell, Ailís took it to the Otherworld. I don't know where she went. I can't speak wood faery—or tree. I'm hoping she took the portal to your family's home ... or perhaps to your mother."

Steven sucked in a breath. "Elise doesn't really understand the Otherworld; she was so young when we came here. She also thinks our mum is dead."

"Oh." Mathias' look turned grave. "Then you should go after her. Keeping her safe was of the utmost importance to Quinn."

"Indeed." His blood went cold. Elise, alone in the Otherworld? There was so much she didn't know.

James finished his drink. "Where in Central Park is it? We need to get her."

"Of course." Mathias punctuated this with a nod. "I'll take you there immediately."

"What about the body?" Steven asked. Quinn deserved a proper burial.

"What are your wishes?" Mathias folded his hands in front of him on the table. "If you have none, I'll be happy to take responsibility."

"I think he should be buried at the House of Oak, next to my father." His voice wavered slightly as he said that. He thought for a moment, wording his question carefully. "Do you think Quinn needing to tend to something has anything to do with the fact that someone may be ... interested in something he once researched?"

For a long moment Mathias stayed silent. "That's a probability. I've heard things that might involve objects best left undiscovered."

Steven nodded, not willing to offer more information at this time.

"Though Quinn was a man of many secrets," Mathias added.

Steven thought of the passage in his journal that mentioned Kevighn's sister. "Indeed."

Mathias led them out of the establishment and they caught a motorcab to Central Park. Dark was falling and Steven kept Noli close.

They came to a locked iron gate. Mathias gestured to them. "Anyone?"

Steven used his magic to open the lock. They entered the garden and walked through an arch of ivy. The moon's image reflected on a small pond.

He sucked in a breath. "This is beautiful."

Mathias led them to a large, old tree. Immediately, little wood faeries poked their heads out of knotholes and other hiding places. Nosey little things. James questioned the faeries. No longer afraid of using magic in this realm, Steven spoke to the tree itself.

Yes, there was no doubt that Elise had gone through here, though it had been used since. The tree said that she remembered where Elise had gone and could take them there.

"She passed through here," James told him. "The faeries remember her."

"The tree also remembers. Noli, let's go." Steven waved her over; she was speaking with Mathias.

James' face scrunched. "Should we really just barge into the Otherworld?"

"Swords out, I suppose?" Steven took his pen from his pocket, flicked his wrist, and it turned into his father's sword.

"Showoff," James muttered as he did the same to his boot knife.

"I want a sword." Noli's lip jut out in protest. "James says I'm doing better."

"V, I know you have more than one sword on you. Just let her use one of yours," James said with an easy shrug.

"I don't have a girl's sword." It was difficult to not make a face. No one touched his swords. Not even Noli.

"We'll find one for you," James assured her.

"Mathias, we appreciate your help." Steven gave him a wave.

Mathias waved back. "Good luck with your search. I hope you find her. Please don't be afraid to come to me if you ever need assistance."

"That's a kind offer." Steven put his hand on the trunk of the tree. Noli and James did the same. He reached out to the tree with his mind. *Please, take us to where you took her.*

• • • • • • • •

Kevighn walked the streets of New York, pulling his coat tighter, favorite cane in hand, top hat poised jauntily on his head. Once, it had been here, not San Francisco, where he sought amusement. This time he tracked Magnolia. Why was she here?

At the door of the club, he frowned. This was a fae establishment. Not what he expected.

Whose place was this? Kevighn sent out tendrils of magic. Oh, *this* was where Mathias was hiding? Figured. But what business would his fair blossom have with the likes of Mathias? He paid the doorman and walked inside.

A very scantily clad girl in red sashayed up to him. "May I help you?"

He smiled at her and tipped his top hat. "I need to speak with Mathias."

"Oh, do you, now?" Her look grew coy. "Do you have an appointment?"

"I'm here on behalf of Kyran Dempsey." He passed her a coin. She flounced off. He looked around at the lobby filled with well-dressed men. Some were led to a dining room and others past a velvet curtain behind the podium.

The girl returned, pale. She gave him a little bow. "This way, sir."

She led him down a hallway, and into a small office. "He'll see you shortly."

This was much more opulent and cluttered than Ciarán's office. The back wall was entirely filled with books, with a fireplace on one side. Kevighn took a seat across from the desk.

No, Noli wasn't in this building. But she had been. Again, why?

"Kevighn Silver-Tongue, you're no longer working for the queen?" Mathias entered the office, looking like the same pompous bastard as always.

"You have no right to judge me," Kevighn snapped. "I'm working for Kyran again. He'll be *very* interested to know your whereabouts."

Mathias spread his hands. "I am but a humble businessman."

"Bullshit." Especially the *humble* part. Spoiled high court trash.

Mathias' blue eyes narrowed. "This is *my* establishment. You have no authority here. If Kyran has anything to say to me, then he should do it himself."

He remained standing, towering over Kevighn, trying to be imposing. But Kevighn's years in the high court had made him immune to such posturing.

"I'm tracking a girl for him. Her name is Magnolia Braddock. She's probably traveling with two young earth court princes. How long ago was she here, why was she here, and where did she go?" Kevighn eyed him, daring him to not be forthcoming with the information.

Mathias crossed his arms over his chest, expression chilly. "Why?"

Ugh, he was still an ass. "That's none of your business. Now, tell me or I will—"

"Shut up, Silver." Mathias pounded his fist in the middle of the desk. "You can't command me to do anything. Leave or I'll have you thrown out."

Kevighn stood; anger raged through him. "You'll pay for this."

"You wish," Mathias smirked.

"A war is brewing. If you know what's good for you, you'll get your loyalties straight. Oh wait, you don't have any." Kevighn shoved his way past Mathias and stalked out of the building. That was fruitless.

Where did she go from here? Kevighn followed the tracking spell back to the garden in Central Park, the one he'd followed Elise through.

What? Unless the princes know about their father's death and were tracking their sister.

Kevighn rubbed his hands together, hoping they wound up at the Thirsty Pooka and that he could get there first. Yes, this would be quite interesting.

NINE

The Thirsty Pooka

Noli looked around the eerie, forgotten wood, a half-dead tree behind them. Why had Elise come *here*? Something about this place felt familiar. She looked around, studying the area. It seemed like she'd been here before, yet it was different. Oh, the rundown house was gone. This was where she'd run once, fleeing Kevighn's advances.

Without really thinking about where she was headed, she began to walk.

"We're in wild lands," V said, close behind her. "It's not quite the same as the pure magic I showed you, but close. We should be careful."

He pulled out his sigil, a sunburst of gold wire with a green stone at its center. It was the mark of his house, the House of Oak. If you looked closely, you could see the image of a tree, the branches and roots intertwined.

"What are you doing?" Noli squinted at the medallion in his hand. Once, she'd had one; she still missed it. Right now, V was forbidden from giving her another.

"Tracking her, just like I tracked you. It doesn't work as well in the mortal realm, which is why we used the other spells," V explained. He muttered something, holding it in his palm. In his other hand he kept hold of his unsheathed sword. James did the same.

They walked through the chaos. Suddenly everything changed, like they'd crossed an invisible line. They stood in a grove of trees. Creideamh's grove. Without waiting for the boys, Noli made her way to the base of the big tree in the center. The sweet smell of the star blooms she'd planted made her nose twitch in delight.

Little wood faeries accosted her, pulling her hair and sitting on her nose, trying to tell her something.

"Now *that's* a tree house," James breathed from behind her.

"It's all right," she soothed, wishing she could understand faery speech. "They're with me. We're looking for a girl. Did she come through here?"

They replied in a flurry of incomprehensible sounds.

"Slow down," V told them. "One at a time." He frowned. "It seems as if Elise was trying to get to your tree house, but the portal brought her here instead."

"To my tree house? But it's not a portal." Noli's nose scrunched.

"I don't think Elise understands how portals work." V

cocked his head in thought. "Since your tree house isn't a portal, the portal must have taken her here."

James turned around and around, taking the place in. "But where *are* we?"

It did make sense. But why did they have to come *here*, of all places? Hopefully Kevighn wasn't present. That could be very, very bad.

"What?" V's eyes bulged as one of the faeries spoke to him. "Noli, the faeries said that they told her to wait here for you. Why would they do that?" His face fell and with it, so did her heart.

Noli exhaled, stomach churning. "I've been here before," she admitted quietly. There was no sense in hiding it. "This is Creideamh's tree house."

"Oh. She was Kevighn's sister, was she not?" V frowned, and James just blinked.

"Indeed." Noli sighed again as a little pink faery perched on her shoulder to comfort her, sensing her distress. "We're behind Kevighn's cabin, the one where he kept me when he brought me to the Otherworld. I...I spent a lot of time in this tree house when I was here." As much as she wouldn't admit it to V, those hadn't been unhappy times. She'd enjoyed being in the tree house, taking care of the gardens.

"Oh. This is Kevighn's place?" The light went out of V's face.

Tears pricked Noli's eyes. She hadn't done anything wrong, but V's distress made her feel guilty.

"Where's Elise?" she asked the faeries. "Is she still here? In the tree house? V, why can't I understand them?" It came out as a partial wail. How come V and James understood the faeries but she couldn't?

You're not listening right, the sprite interjected. *Listen with your heart, not your ears.*

What? How exactly did one listen without using ears?

Just… here.

Noli felt herself shoved out of the body and the sprite took over. *Give me the body back,* she snapped at the sprite.

I can't explain. I have to show you, the sprite replied.

"Tell me again?" Noli asked the faeries.

All of the sudden, she heard a sweet but high-pitched voice, something like a bird chirp. As the chirp continued, words emerged.

Did you get that? the sprite asked her. *Kevighn took her. She went with him because he said he'd keep her safe until he found you. He sent a faery to tell you he was taking her to the Thirsty Pooka in the Blackwoods. Can we go there? That sounds fun. Also, Kevighn is nice to look at.*

May I have our body back? She still wasn't quite sure what the sprite had done.

Did I help? The sprite liked to be helpful.

Yes, so much. Noli assumed control of her body once more.

"Noli, are you all right?" V steadied her. "That was—"

"Really strange," James finished.

"Kevighn has her." The words stuck in her throat.

Outrage flashed in V's eyes. "Why would he do that?" Then he listened to the faeries. "And where's this place he took her? The Thirsty Pooka?"

"It's in the Blackwoods," Noli whispered. That was also where Kevighn had told her she could find him.

"The Blackwoods is dark court territory." James went pale. "Why would he go there?"

The pieces were starting to fall together, but only just. "Kevighn once belonged to the dark court, you know," Noli said. "He rejoined it after Tiana exiled him. Also…" Her hands twisted. "When you were talking to the tree and the faeries in the park, I was speaking to Mathias." She met V's eyes. "He told me that 'Kyran' was an alias of the dark king."

The air hissed out of V. "So when Kevighn paid your brother for the artifact pieces, he'd gotten the money from Kyran. That means that the dark king knows about the artifact."

"If he does, why would he allow Kevighn to dispose of the pieces in the mortal realm? Wouldn't he keep them and use them for himself?" James rubbed his chin in thought.

"Perhaps Kevighn lied." V's voice went sharp and his eyes narrowed.

"Kevighn doesn't lie," Noli snapped. Not about that. He'd promised.

"Yes, he does," V retorted.

James held out his hands. "Knock it off. We need to figure out *why* Kevighn would take Elise to the dark king."

"For the same reason Brogan wants her. Elise is the high queen's only daughter. She'd make a good hostage or pawn." V's shoulders fell in defeat. "*I'm* supposed to protect her. Now the dark king has her—that's even worse than her being in the hands of Brogan or Tiana." The hand not holding the sword fisted around his sigil, knuckles white.

"I … I'm pretty sure she's safe. Kevighn sent a wood faery with a message for me to find him at the Thirsty Pooka." Noli's voice shook. She liked Elise and didn't want anything bad to happen to her. "Perhaps he truly just happened upon her and wishes to return her to us."

V's face contorted in anger. "Not likely." He marched off, sword in hand. "Coming?"

"Um, V. We can't just march into dark court territory." James ran after him.

"V, wait," Noli called. Usually, he was the one calling for her to wait while she charged off to do something without a plan.

"Why?" V halted, giving them a scathing look.

"We're *earth court*. Also, our mum is the high queen. They'll probably kill us as soon as we enter their borders." James shrugged. "Also, do you know where the place is? Because I don't."

V held out his palm. "We have the sigil."

"And what good will that do us when we're attacked for being in the wrong place at the wrong time? Is it really that smart to blindly traipse across dark court territory?" James rolled his eyes. "Think, V. I'm tired of having to be the brains of this outfit."

"Yes. We need to think," Noli echoed. "We have to get her back. What should we do?" But she knew what *she* had to do.

"Maybe we should return to the big house and figure out

where we're going?" James suggested. "Also, we may want to get Tiana involved. If Ciarán has Elise that might be best."

"I'm not getting *her* involved. Not yet." V's face and voice went tight. "Elise thinks our mother is dead. Also, I'm a little afraid of what Tiana might do when she realizes Elise's potential. She's just a little girl now, but she *will* be a threat soon. Very soon. We all know what Tiana does to her competition."

James' expression went grave. "Oh."

If anyone were capable of harming their own child, it would be Tiana.

V put his sigil back around his neck, then raked his hand through his unkempt hair. "I don't like the idea of Kevighn having her."

"I don't either, but we can't just barge into the dark court. We're of no use to her if we're dead," James pointed out, putting a hand on his shoulder.

V shook his head. "As much as I hate to admit it, you're right. Let's return to the big house and see if we can come up with a plan. Preferably one that doesn't involve Tiana."

"I like that idea very much," Noli replied, grateful V was thinking rationally again. Tonight she'd get Elise back herself.

....

Noli waited until the light in V's room went out. Boots in hand, she crept down the hallway, wishing she had a better weapon than her little knife. From what the boys had told her, and the little she knew about the dark court, the Thirsty

Pooka was probably dangerous and filled with creatures who wouldn't hesitate to kill an earth court prince on sight.

She, on the other hand, wasn't exactly any court. Therefore she had no enemies. At least she hoped not.

Well, except for Brogan.

Still, they had to get Elise back, and she didn't know what else to do.

"Where are you going?" James blocked her escape.

Startled, Noli nearly dropped her boots. "I . . . "

"Where *are* you going, Noli?" James grinned.

Noli hid her boots behind her back. "Um, nowhere."

While she didn't think James would wake V, she didn't want to push her luck. V *would* stop her from going alone, and James had a point; the boys couldn't walk in with her.

"Sure." James turned and went the opposite way. He stopped and gave her a look. "Coming?"

Her insides quivered. "Where?"

"Don't go all V on me. Come on." James walked down the hall.

Noli trotted after him and found herself in his messy room, which teemed with memories of Charlotte. The dressing screen, cosmetics on the bureau, a ribbon lying on the floor. James opened the wardrobe and brought something out. He set a long, gold object covered in jewels in her hands.

"I found this earlier today and thought you'd like it," he said. "If you're heading into dark court territory, you'll need it."

"What is it?" It was heavy—and beautiful. Even V's sword, the one that had belonged to his father, wasn't this ornate.

"It's a girl's sword. Don't start any wars. Remember, you stab people with the pointy end." James slung it over her back and grinned. "Don't worry about V. I'll take care of him. Be safe—and bring her back. I believe in you."

Noli smiled. Someone believed in her. These days, she'd felt like such a liability, but James' statement made her feel lighter, braver. "I appreciate this."

Oooh, it's pretty. Can we go now? I want to see the tavern. They're fun, right? the sprite said perkily.

Shush, we're going for work, not play, Noli admonished. *We need to get Elise. You like Elise, remember?*

Yes, she's good at tea party.

The sprite did enjoy a good game of tea party.

Now, Noli told her, *let's go get Elise.*

....

All the confidence drained from her as she eyed the tavern on the other side of the trees. She had felt like invisible eyes had born into her back the entire time she'd trekked through the Blackwoods, setting her on edge.

A little purple light landed on her nose.

"Oh, hello there." Noli recognized her as one of the wood faeries from Creideamh's tree house—although not one who'd been there earlier today.

The faery chirped.

"What?" Noli concentrated, and the chirps faded into words. "Oh, Kevighn sent you? Yes, I know he has Elise. I appreciate you finding me."

The faery nodded. This must be the one he'd sent with the message.

"This place is frightening." Noli watched as two creatures—she wasn't sure what they were called—ambled inside. They were large, hairy, and ugly, with axes slung across their backs. They made air pirates look like members of a ladies sewing society.

"Who are you and what are you doing here?" A large man in black with a crooked nose stood behind her. A dagger hung from his belt.

"I…" Her belly sank as she turned and took a step back.

The ugly man with him elbowed him. "I think she's here for us. Why else would a sweet little sprite come to a place like this?"

The first man leered in a way that made her squirm. "Kiss me, you pretty thing."

Grabbing her, he mashed his face to hers, trying to shove his tongue into her mouth. She struggled against him. When she opened her mouth to scream, his large, wet tongue entered her mouth and she recoiled. Her fingers found the knife in her boot. She stabbed him with it, then wriggled out of his grasp.

"Hey, what was that for?" the man yelped.

"I'll give you something shiny." The other man grabbed her and shoved her to the ground, ripping her sword from her and flinging it aside. A shriek tore from her mouth as he ripped her dress. She kicked and screamed. He smacked her across the face. "Shut up."

"Let go of her or I'll tell my father," a small male voice ordered.

The man sneered. "And who's he?"

"Me." A deep, commanding voice reverberated through the forest. "Aodhan, you're not supposed to be out here at night."

Noli couldn't see who'd spoken, but that voice demanded respect.

"The little faery said she needed help," the boy replied, coming into her line of sight.

"Leave," the voice told the man on top of her.

"Of course, I...I'm sorry." The man climbed off her and ran as fast as he could away from them, as did the other, both clearly afraid of whoever was with the boy.

A boy with pale blond hair and a bow across his back bent down and picked up her knife and sword. He handed them to her as she sat up. "I think these are yours."

"I appreciate your assistance." She put the sword back around her and tucked the knife into her boot. "You...you saved me." That man could have done horrible things to her. Noli shook. Perhaps this wasn't such a good idea after all.

"It's all right. You're safe." The boy crouched down and smiled, all the way to his yellow eyes.

Something about that boy's smile reminded her of Kevighn. It was probably the bow and quiver on his back.

A tall man in a cloak, the hood shadowing his face obscuring who he was, offered her a hand. "Are you all right?"

Gulping, Noli nodded, allowing him to help her stand.

"Why are you here?" His voice dripped with authority.

There was something familiar about him, but she couldn't quite place it.

"I … I'm Noli Braddock." The little purple faery landed on her outstretched hand. "I … I'm looking for Kevighn Silver. He sent me a message and told me to come here."

"She's Elise's friend," the little boy added. "I'm Aodhan."

"Do you know Elise?" Noli's heart skipped a beat. Maybe this would work out after all. She didn't relish the thought of returning to the big house without Elise.

The boy nodded. "She's my friend, too."

The man held up a hand. "Aodhan, go inside, please."

Her belly churned; she wasn't sure she wanted to be left alone with him. "I need to take Elise home."

"No one will hurt you. Just come with me." His voice was far from soothing, yet not actually ominous. Several men in dark clothing came up beside him.

Aodhan put a hand on her arm. "It's all right, Noli. My father will protect you." With a smile, he scampered into the darkness.

"How do I know that you won't harm me?" She tried to keep her voice from trembling.

"Because I know who you are, and I have no wish to start a war. However, we need to talk … " The man gestured toward the tavern.

Noli didn't move. He knew who she was? That didn't calm her nerves one little bit. She peered into the dark hood, trying to see who he was. "I don't even know your name."

"You may call me Kyran."

The air hissed from her teeth, and then Noli curtsied. "Of course, Your Majesty."

She was in the company of the dark king himself. *He* had Elise.

Unseen eyes bore into her back as Ciarán ushered her into the tavern and sat her at the bar. She'd never been in a place like this. Her nose wrinkled at the stench of beer and unwashed bodies. Creatures she'd never seen before watched her in ways that made her skin crawl. The two creatures she'd glimpsed earlier, the ones with the axes, threw knives at a dartboard.

A very short woman stood on a box behind the bar. She looked at Ciarán and her eyebrows rose. "She's a little young."

Ciarán, hood still up, shrugged. "This is business."

"'Bout time you hired a nursemaid for the brat." She grinned. "Though Luce might not like it. Also, keep her away from *you-know-who*."

He gave the woman a sharp look then turned to Noli. "What would you like to drink?"

"Um, do you have any honey wine?" She had a feeling no one drank tea here.

He signaled the bartender and she handed him a bottle and two glasses. "I made this myself." Ciarán poured two glasses.

She looked at the bottle. "You gave this to Kevighn Silver."

He raised his glass. "I did. So you are Magnolia?"

"I am. I'd like Elise back, please. I appreciate you caring for her, but I need to take her home." Noli took a small sip, allowing the sensation to roll over her tongue and explode down the back of her throat. Ah, summer in a bottle. She could think of no better description.

"I'm surprised a sprite would come here alone." His eyebrows rose.

"I wasn't always a sprite," she retorted. She had little patience for verbal games.

"Indeed." He took a sip of wine.

It was unnerving how he kept his hood up, which was probably the point.

"How did you know? Spies?" she asked. According to James, both the high court and the dark court had spies everywhere. Tiana and Brogan had even had spies in the big house.

He shrugged. That would probably be *yes*.

"Kevighn sent me a message telling me to come here." Shivering, Noli pulled her cloak tighter around her. "Is he here?" If he'd lied … so help him. She'd smacked him before and wasn't afraid to do so again.

"No, he isn't. However…" He gave her a pointed look. His eyes were a peculiar color, golden brown like a piece of amber her father had shown her once. They were quite different from Kevighn's yellow eyes.

The following silence weighed heavily in the air of the pub; words that weren't there whirled through her head, making her nervous.

Noli broke the silence before she screamed in frustration. If Ciarán wouldn't speak plainly, then she would. "May I please have Elise?"

"The girl is safe. She shouldn't be roaming the Otherworld unattended." Slight disapproval tinged his voice.

"It's not as if I'm the one who lost her." Noli tried to keep her temper in check. This wasn't how she expected the dark king to be.

"True." He took another sip.

The silence was the worst part—which was probably his intention.

Noli's belly dropped. "Are you *keeping* her here? There are people who won't appreciate that." Like V. Like the queen.

"I'm keeping her safe. The last thing you need is for her to fall into the wrong hands." Again, the slightest hints of disapproval set her on edge.

"I *know*." She'd classify him and Kevighn as being the *wrong hands*.

For a moment Ciarán studied his glass and the liquid within. "It's such a pretty color, don't you think?"

"May I *please* have Elise back, *Your Majesty*." She mimicked her mother in a way she hoped was "forcefully ladylike."

His lips twitched. "What will you do with her once you have her back?"

Noli blinked. What would she do indeed? It wasn't as if they could leave Elise at the big house—or take her with them. The last thing she wanted was to put going to university on hold to raise a little girl. They weren't about to ask the high queen to babysit, either. Quinn was gone. What else could they do?

"Either keep her with us or send her to school in the mortal realm where she'll be safe," Noli finally said. Yes, V's family probably had enough money, and her mother would help find a suitable place. Elise could go to school near wherever she and V went. Her mother also liked Elise. Perhaps she could be the daughter Noli could never be . . . at least for a little while.

He nodded. "Not, say, take her to her mum or uncle?"

"No."

The dark king folded his hands in front of him. "I propose a trade."

"She's not yours to trade." Anger bubbled inside her. She *had* to get Elise back. Now.

"Now, what is that mortal saying? About possession and the law?" He gestured to the pub. "This is my territory. You're just one girl, and a sprite at that."

Noli crossed her arms over her chest. "What if I just tell her mother? She won't like this."

"Do you think she'll be pleased that she's here to begin with? Who do you think she's going to blame, hmm?" He toyed with his glass. "Perhaps not you, but your friends. Do you really want to do that to them? You're in love with the elder one, aren't you?"

Her heart skipped a beat. That's exactly what Tiana would do, too.

"What do you want?" she demanded.

"You stole a gem from the museum in Los Angeles. Bring it to me and we'll talk." Ciarán polished off his drink. "Now, I think you should leave before you get into more trouble. You'll pass to the portal unharmed, as long as you go directly there."

No, a voice said. It was the same voice she'd heard before. *Don't give it to him.*

How did he know about it to begin with—or that she had it?

"What gem?" Noli asked. "I don't have a gem. You must be mistaken."

"I suppose you don't want her back, then. I assure you, she'll be safe and well cared for. My son is quite attached to her."

Son? That must be the boy with the pale hair and the bow. The dark king as a doting father was also something she hadn't expected.

No. She couldn't give him the jewel. But at the same time, they had to get Elise back. Perhaps V had an idea, not that she wanted to leave Elise here.

The dark king gave her an expectant look.

"Why should I trust you?" She eyed him, trying to see him through the shadows of the hooded cloak.

"Can you really afford not to? Besides, I might be able to help you." His look remained bland, yet expectant, as he leaned his elbow on the bar like they were exchanging pleasantries.

"You know where my father is?" The words just leaked out. As soon as she said them, she realized he was probably referring to her *other* issue.

Ciarán just looked at her, that silence pressing down, whispering unsaid things in her ears. It would be so easy to give him the jewel in exchange for Elise. In fact, V and

James would want to. They didn't understand. Well, *she* didn't understand. Still…

"Never mind. I don't need your help." She pushed the whispers away. As much as she wanted herself back, she wasn't ready to deal with monarchs again—beyond getting Elise.

"Don't you?" His eyebrows rose, but that was all he said.

The silence crushed her, the screaming voices making her flinch.

Finally, he stood. "It's time for you to go."

"I want to see her." She didn't stand.

"It's late, she's asleep." He nodded toward the door, indicating she needed to leave. Now.

"Why do you want the gem?" There had to be a way to get Elise back without giving it to him. It just didn't feel right. Even in exchange for Elise.

He took her hand and pulled her up from the stool. "Why do *you* want it?"

"I'm just keeping it safe." Her mouth clamped shut. Flying figs. She hadn't meant to admit she had it.

"For whom?" he pried, taking a step toward her.

"Does it matter?" Two could play this game. Wait. If he wanted the gem, did he in fact have other pieces? Could she get those too?

He marched her to the door. "You *can* trust me. Steer clear of Kevighn. You don't want him, believe me. Stay with your prince."

The doors closed behind her and suddenly she was alone in the darkness without even the little purple wood faery.

Trust him? Perhaps she could. Unlike the queen, or

even Kevighn, nothing about him screamed *disingenuous*. Perhaps he also wanted to protect the jewel. Despite the obvious, everything inside her told her to trust him.

The greater question was, did she *want* to?

TEN

Tempers

Steven sat straight up in bed, a cold sweat blanketing his body. A sense of wrongness crept through him. A glance at the window revealed that it was still night.

He tiptoed down the hall and cracked opened the door. Noli usually kept her things in Elise's old room when they visited, which was filled with girlish things and paintings of butterflies and flowers. Since she'd been in a bit of a snit tonight, she'd gone to sleep in here instead of in his room.

"Noli, are you all right?" Silence. "Noli?" Steven crept in, not wishing to wake her if she was asleep, but needing to make sure she was all right.

The bed was empty. Where could she be? He checked the library and the adjoining garden. Nothing. Steven trudged out to the faery tree in the middle of the hedge maze since sometimes she liked to visit them when she couldn't sleep.

No Noli. Where could she be?

Panic rose inside him as he raced to James' room and threw open the door. "James, Noli's gone."

"I'm sleeping, Stio." James buried his face in his pillow.

He ripped the blankets off James. How could he sleep at a time like this? "We need to find her. Now."

"She'll be back soon." The pillow muffled James' voice as he grabbed the blanket and yanked it over his head.

Steven's heart stopped as his brother's words sank in. "You know where she is?"

"Yeah."

"Where?" He yanked James out of bed and onto the floor with a thud.

"Ow." A wounded look crossed his face as he rubbed his arm, looking up from the floor of his messy room.

Remorse filled Steven. "I'm sorry. I … I'm just worried. Where is she?"

James leaned against the bed, still on the floor. "She might be a little different now, but you can't keep her wrapped in cotton wool."

"What are you talking about?" He shifted his weight from foot to foot. At the moment he had little patience for his brother's nonsense. They needed to get Noli. The weapons, clothes, and other things strewn across the room distracted him. The only orderly part of the room was the top of the bureau, which held girlish items. Charlotte's things.

"She's not Elise and she'd not dumb. Treat Noli like Noli." James shook his head. "Also, why were you so mean to her?"

"What? I wasn't mean. She was the one who was cross." His nose wrinkled at the thought.

James tilted his head back so it rested on the bed. "Yes, you were. After you found out the tree house belonged to Kevighn you were cold to her all night. Which made her grumpy."

"No, I was—" Raking a hand through his hair, Steven sighed. Maybe he *had* been a little short with her. "I don't like to think about the time she spent with … him." The mere thought made his blood boil.

"Relax." James rolled his eyes. "Noli loves you, you love her. Trust her. She trusts you."

Steven plunked down onto the rumpled bed. "You're right. Kevighn just makes me so … angry. Where did she go?"

"She went to get Elise back." James stood and yawned, looking a bit like a cat as he stretched. "I'm hungry. Since we're awake, we should have some food and wait up for her."

Steven's jaw dropped. "She *what*? Of all the dumb things."

"Don't be a fussy old bodger," James huffed. "It makes sense. We can't just walk into dark court, but *she* can. She'll be back with Elise in no time."

Steven's mind reeled. "You actually expect Kevighn, Ciarán, or whoever to simply permit her to *take* Elise?"

He couldn't be that naïve.

"Why not?" James yawned again, then shuffled out of the room.

Ire rose within Steven and he yelled, "Where do you think you're going?"

"If you're going to yell at me, yell at me over food," James called from down the hall.

Steven punched the door frame. How could James have *let* her go? And Noli, how could she just leave? What if...

His knees buckled. What if she went because she *wanted* to see Kevighn?

"Whatever you're thinking about that's making you turn that particular color, just stop. Come on, breakfast will be served in the library shortly. I'm sure the girls will be hungry." James stood in front of him with an amused look on his face. "She'll be *fine*."

Without replying, Steven shoved passed him. As he dressed all he could think of was Noli going to see Kevighn alone. Of course she'd sneak off. Guys like Kevighn *always* got the girl. He tugged on his boots, seething inside. What an idiot he was.

He stormed down the hall, plopped down on the settee, and glared at the door. The library was usually his favorite room in the big house, filled with books and memories. Darkness obscured the view outside the big window and the glass door, leading into a small garden. Since their return to the Otherworld, this library in the wing they'd grown up in had become the hub of the house. Right now it held no comfort. He punched the back of the settee.

"Why are you so angry?" James, now dressed, occupied his favorite chair. A breakfast tray sat on the table and he poured himself some tea.

"It's obvious. Noli wants to be with *him*, not me." Steven glared.

Tea spurted out of James' mouth and he laughed, choking on tea. His cheeks flushed as he thumped his chest. "Don't be an idiot. If Noli didn't want to be with you, she *wouldn't*. Certainly, I'd never put up with you treating me the way you do her. Just let it go and grow up."

"What?" He shot to his feet in a fit of rage. How dare he?

James grabbed his shoulders and *shook* him. "V, snap out of it."

Steven blinked. What was happening to him? Why *was* he so angry? "What if some dark court fiend hurts her?"

"For someone who wants to be king you sure don't understand much about Otherworld politics. No one wants to start a war." James helped himself to a bowl of hot cereal, steam rising off the top in inviting tendrils.

Unconvinced, Steven sat, anger still sucking at him like leeches. "What if someone *wants* to start a war?"

James glared at him. "She'll be *fine*."

With a heavy sigh, Steven picked up a piece of fruit, not wanting to think too much about what James had said. He glowered at his brother. "She better be."

．．．．．．．．．．．．．．

The cereal, rolls, and tea had grown cold. James snored softly in his chair, one arm covering his face, the other dangling over the side. Steven stared at the doorway, a million feelings swirling and festering inside him as he waited for her to return.

Why did the Bright Lady torture him so?

His father was dead. Quinn was dead. His sister was

missing. When he went to seek revenge, his uncle wasn't there. The love of his life had run off to meet another man.

The weight of his responsibilities threatened to suffocate him. If Tiana hadn't sent him on that fool's errand, he would've been there when the men came to kill his father. His father—and Quinn—would still be alive.

All Tiana did was ruin his life. His family. She'd even ruined Noli.

Standing, he knocked back over the settee. "I hate you," he bellowed. "I hate you, I hate you, I hate you."

Something moved near the door. "I'm sorry. Whatever I did, I'm sorry."

He turned and saw Noli in the doorway, face crestfallen.

"Noli, where have you been?" Steven rushed to her, his anger fading.

James sat up. "You're back." He looked around. "Where is she?"

Her shoulders slumped. Dirt streaked her face and her dress was torn. "I don't have her."

"What, Kevighn wouldn't give her to you for a kiss?" Steven snapped. She'd run off and didn't even have the decency to bring Elise back?

Noli flinched as if struck.

"Relax, V." James turned to her. "What happened?"

"Kevighn wasn't there. Ciarán was. He has her. He said…" She hiccupped. "He said he'd trade her for the jewel."

"Oh, all right then. Let's get the jewel and take it to him." That seemed simple enough. The last thing Steven wanted was for Elise to get corrupted by the dark court.

She looked up at him, eyes wide. "We can't give it to him."

"We can't leave Elise there. She's my *sister*." Anger ignited within him. His sister was worth more than some...*thing*.

"But who knows what he'll do with it. It's dangerous." Her lower lip jutted out and her eyes met his.

"The dark court hates Tiana. Who knows what they'll tell Elise," Steven retorted. "Whose side are you on?" Sure, the gem was powerful, and probably shouldn't be in his hands...but the exact same thing could be said about Elise.

"Stop." James put his hands out as if trying to create a barrier between them. "Why is everyone so angry?"

"Why did you let her run off to meet Kevighn?" Steven snapped, getting in James' face. "You're my *brother*."

"I didn't *run off* to meet with Kevighn. I went to get Elise. We were out of options," Noli retorted, voice rising. "What is going on here?"

Steven wanted to tear his hair out. "I can't believe you. Noli, I thought you loved me."

"I...I do love you." Her voice choked. "How could you doubt that?"

Still, he couldn't staunch the torrents of anger flowing through him. "So, that's how you show it, by running off? Admit it, you love him."

"Kevighn? No. I don't love him. I love *you*, you fussy old bodger." She frowned, biting her lower lip. "What has gotten into you? I'm sorry I didn't get Elise, and I know it was stupid to go alone, but it was all I could think of. You know I don't always think my plans through..."

He stood in front of her, rage propelling him. "But you

didn't get her back, and now you won't even give him what he wants—"

"Prince Stiofán, what is going on here?" a female voice snapped. A dainty, green-clad figure rushed past him right toward Noli.

Steven realized his hand was raised as if to strike. Aunt Dinessa's small body curled protectively around Noli as she glared at him. Her blond hair hung nearly to the hem of her deep green dress.

"I ... I'm sorry, Aunt Dinessa." His cheeks burned as his arm dropped to his side. Where *was* all this anger coming from? It wasn't like him.

"Good." Aunt Dinessa gave him a scolding look, her body still blocking Noli from him. "There's so much yelling in this room, I thought I'd happened upon a den of fire court ruffians by mistake. Earth court princes mind their tempers. Certainly they don't strike someone they love." Her eyes narrowed, voice filled with rebuke.

His shoulders slumped as he watched Noli sob into Aunt Dinessa's dress. She was right, even though he never actually hit Noli, his behavior was unacceptable, especially given his age and station. What *had* gotten into him?

"I ... I'm sorry, Noli. I'm so sorry," he apologized.

"Now what is going on here?" Aunt Dinessa's green eyes bore into him in a way that reminded him so much of his father.

Steven sighed, fearful she'd tell Brogan. "It's complicated."

"I might be Brogan's twin, but I'm not him," Aunt

Dinessa retorted. "My politics haven't changed much since you left; if anything, my beliefs have gotten stronger."

"Why are you here, Aunt Dinessa? Not that we don't love to see you," James said, turning on the charm. "Should I call for tea? This is cold."

Her eyes went alight with mischief. "I snuck out to tell you that Brogan returned late last night. I ... " Her expression went bashful, cheeks pinking. "I wished to see if I could still do it—sneak out, that is. Brogan forgets that just because I'm a grown woman, it doesn't mean I don't remember all those ways out of the palace we discovered as children."

"You always know the best things," James replied.

"Why don't I help Noli get dressed and we can all go together," Aunt Dinessa offered.

Steven's eyes fell on Noli, who looked up at him with betrayal etched on her pretty face. Still, he couldn't quite get past the curtain of anger.

"You don't have to go, Noli." He felt the need to say it. However, since Dinessa didn't know the true purpose of their visit, having Noli join them would be useful.

Noli's eyes narrowed in defiance. "Why?"

"Don't mind V, he's being an idiot." James waved his hand in Steven's direction. "We'll go see Uncle Brogan and figure everything out later."

Sniffing, she nodded, still looking so ... wounded.

Aunt Dinessa gave him a pointed look, one that reminded him of his father, and turned her attentions to Noli. "Noli, will you show me your room? I lived in this wing when I was a girl."

After the women left the library, James strode over and punched him in the arm.

For a moment, Steven just stared at him. "Whose side are you on?"

"There are no sides, moron. Don't lose Noli. She's the best thing to ever happen to you. Now get your sword," James snapped.

He rubbed his arm, trying to understand James' mood. "What about Elise? We can't just leave her there."

"We'll go take care of Uncle Brogan, then get Elise." James shook his head. "I don't understand the thing with the gem. We should bring it with us and make the trade. Yes, it's dangerous, but is it more dangerous than Elise in dark court hands?"

Steve nodded in agreement. "You as the voice of reason disturbs me. But yes, I'll get the jewel and my sword."

• • • • • • • •

Elise opened her eyes. Aodhan hovered above her, yellow eyes wide.

"What's wrong?" Elise sat up, trying not to bump heads. She had her own room right next to his. She'd made them a connecting door by talking to the boards. He'd promised not to tell anyone. It was nice having a secret with someone her own age.

"Uncle Kevighn and Father are fighting." His face crumpled as he sat on her bed. "Also…"

"What?" She put a hand on his arm. Aodhan was odd, but sweet and kind. If only her brothers were more like him.

"She came last night." His eyes shone with several emotions.

"Who?" Elise cocked her head.

"Noli." He looked away. "Father told me not to tell you, that it would make you upset."

"Noli came and left?" It felt like being stabbed. Noli. James. Steven. Father. No one ever had time for her.

"She did. I saw her. You were asleep." Aodhan nodded. "Uncle Kevighn and Father are fighting about her. I know where she is. Perhaps we can go to her."

Elise wrapped her arms around herself. "Why? They don't want me."

No one wanted her but Quinn … and he wasn't here.

Aodhan put a tentative arm around her. "I want you."

She buried her face in his arm. Sometimes she got so lonely. "It's nice to have a friend."

"I'll always be your friend." He snuggled close to her. "I … I can't hear all the fighting, but it sounds like Father sent Noli away without letting her see you."

Elise blinked, betrayal slicing through her. "Why would he do that?"

"Because she's bad for Uncle Kevighn?" His face scrunched as if he were repeating words he didn't understand.

"What does that mean?" she asked. Why would Noli leave her here? Weren't she and Uncle Kevighn friends? Though her father didn't approve of Noli, either.

He shrugged. "I have no idea. Who is she, anyway?"

"She's going to marry my older brother. Noli's quite nice, and has a tree house, and lives on the other side of the fence." Elise thought for a moment. Noli was like an older sister. She wouldn't leave her here without good reason. "Do you know where she is? Do you know how to get to Los Angeles?" That would be faster than waiting for her to return.

"Noli went to the House of Oak. Is that in Los Angeles?" His forehead furrowed.

Elise thought for a moment. *House of Oak. House of Oak.* She closed her eyes, picturing a grand house with large trees. A memory emerged.

"We lived there, a long time ago, before we moved to Los Angeles," she whispered. "It's... it's so different there. Did you know that in Los Angles not everyone has magic? In fact, we have to hide it from the mortals."

Aodhan's jaw dropped. "You lived in the *mortal realm*? I want to go there so badly."

"Mortal realm?" That sounded so... odd.

"There's our realm, the Otherworld. Then there's the mortal realm. Think of them as books on a shelf with no bookends. Parallel and independent, but if something happens to one, they all fall down. We have magic, mortals don't," he explained.

"Oh. So, there's more than an ocean between the Otherworld and the mortal realm?" She really didn't understand everything that had happened when she was young, and no one ever explained it to her. Actually, she thought where they lived was overseas, like Europe.

"You have to take a portal. Did you come through the portal with Uncle Kevighn?"

Portal? "I took a tree."

"A tree is a portal," he said. "Not all trees are portals, but all portals are trees. Is there a portal near the House of Oak? We can find Noli. She's not alone—"

"My brothers!" Her excitement faded. Once again, Noli and her brothers were on some adventure without her. "I never get to go on adventures. I never get to do *anything*." She pouted.

"Why don't we sneak out, have an adventure, and find them?" Aodhan asked. "If they're not there, we'll just come back."

As much as she liked the idea, a frown tugged at her lips. "Won't we get in trouble?"

Aodhan grinned. "Probably."

"All right then. After all, my brother James always says if you don't get in trouble, it's probably not worth doing." She grinned back. Finally, an adventure of her own.

"He sounds fun. Let's sneak out while they're still fighting." He stood and offered her a hand up.

They got a few things and crept down the stairs. Elise couldn't help but giggle.

"Shhh." Aodhan put a finger to his lips.

They snuck out through the big kitchen where Grandma Luce worked. She often gave them treats. They looked both ways to see if anyone saw them.

When they went outside, she gazed up at the pink sky. "Why is the sky not blue?"

"The high queen makes the sky, and this queen likes pink." He gestured to it.

"Oh." That seemed . . . arbitrary. "Can we use magic here? I'm not supposed to use magic back home unless I'm having a magic lesson."

"Of course you can." He looked back and forth, checking to see if anyone watched. "All right, let's make a run for it. On three?"

She took his offered hand. "On three. Let's go have an adventure."

ELEVEN

Actions and Reactions

Kevighn just stared in disbelief at his best friend. Had he misheard? "Ciarán—"

"I'm saying this because I care about you, *stay away from the girl*. You don't actually have feelings for her. You're just in it for the hunt. You're not a failure if you don't catch her." Ciarán gave him a stern look from the other side of his desk.

"I'm not in it for the hunt." He made a face right back. "You're the one who told me to get the gem from her." Kevighn's arms crossed over his chest, tired of arguing. He'd just missed Magnolia's departure from the pub. And she'd been *alone*. Blasted odd time conversion between the realms. Sometimes it was moments, other times hours or days.

"A mistake. But ... " Ciarán held out his hand in an empty gesture. "Now the girl will bring the gem to me."

"Are you actually going to allow Elise to go with Magnolia? It could work. She's on our side, and she'd be a good ally. She hates Tiana. We could entrust her with protecting Elise, making sure the girl is brought up properly so that when it's time for her to take her place as high queen, she's not twisted and broken but pure and good. Not to mention, Magnolia can probably get us the pieces of the staff that Brogan has." Kevighn's mind spun as he considered the possibilities. Yes, this could work.

Ciarán rubbed his chin, one elbow on the desk. "How do you know we can trust her?"

He rolled his eyes. "Use your magic." That's what got him to where he was—his ability to see into people's souls.

"We'll see." Someone called for Ciarán and he stood. "Why don't you find Aodhan and take him hunting or fishing? I haven't been able to give him much attention lately."

"You keep him very ... sheltered." Kevighn stood, too. Aodhan didn't even realize that the man he called "father" was leader of the dark court.

Hurt flashed in Ciarán's eyes. "I was waiting for you. I didn't want to take too many liberties."

Kevighn rubbed his temples and sighed. "I'll take the children out for a while ... if you'll find something interesting for me to do. I'm so bored *I'm* willing to sneak into the earth court palace and steal the pieces Brogan has."

Not that he minded spending time with Aodhan; however, with everything brewing, he wanted to be useful. He went down the hall and through the secret passage to the private living areas.

"Aodhan? Elise? Who wants to go hunting?" he called. Nothing. He listened for giggles and running feet as he checked their rooms and the playroom. No one. Perhaps they'd gone to the kitchen for a snack.

In the kitchen, Luce hunched over the stew pot, reigning over her little dominion.

"Have you seen the children?" His nose twitched in appreciation. Whatever she was cooking smelled delicious, but that was where her magic lay.

Luce shook her head. "They're probably off playing. Aodhan is happy for a playmate."

"True." His belly growled. "May I have some, please?"

"Of course." She handed him a bowl of stew and a hunk of hot bread.

Taking a stool, he sat down. He'd have something to eat while waiting for them to return.

· · · · · · · ·

Noli stared up at the incredible tree-palace as she followed V, James, and Aunt Dinessa. It never ceased to amaze her. Giant wooden spires and turrets shot high into the air. They and the entire palace were *formed of trees*, oak trees taller than even the rowans guarding it. The palace reminded her of a giant, grandiose version of Creideamh's tree house. Guards patrolled along the top. A moat encircled it, the tree-palace's giant, gnarled roots gripping the ground to form the moat's bridge.

Aunt Dinessa had been very protective, staying close to her and shooting V dark glances. What had gotten into V?

151

When his hand had risen to strike, it was as if some other man had gazed out from his eyes.

Dinessa led them to a secret entrance.

Noli…

Noli looked around. It was that voice again. What did it want from her?

We should take the shinies while we're here, the sprite told her.

What? *That would be stealing.*

It's protecting. We can do it while the boys are busy.

Hmm. Considering she was angry with V, it could be just the thing. She could protect the pieces *and* get revenge on Brogan for everything he'd done—to her, V, and James.

Aunt Dinessa rubbed Noli's hand. "Don't worry; we'll have cake for breakfast while the boys speak with Brogan."

"Of course." She needed to keep up the charade that this was a social call, not the prelude to a duel. However, Brogan would probably expect it.

Cake for breakfast? I like her, the sprite replied. *Maybe she'll have green cakes.*

Noli's favorite cakes were the green ones sometimes served in the Otherworld; they tasted of marzipan and were filled with cream.

I like her too, Noli replied. Dinessa was caring, kind, considerate, compassionate. Everything Brogan and Tiana weren't. She was also quite dainty and graceful, reminding Noli of a person-sized wood faery. It was difficult to believe Dinessa and Brogan were twins.

Noli's sword bumped under her cloak. Dinessa frowned, but she didn't say anything. After all, the boys had theirs.

Noli shot V a look as they walked. He'd ignored her for the entire journey. How could he believe she loved Kevighn? Idiot.

Dinessa opened a door. "Noli and I will be in the tea garden. You go find your uncle."

"Of course," V replied. Without so much as a glance at Noli, he led James through the door. She and Dinessa climbed one more flight of stairs.

"Boys are dumb," Noli muttered, feeling the tiniest bit guilty at not staying by V's side.

Dinessa nodded and opened another door. "Yes, they are."

The moment they entered the suite of rooms swathed in green, a door flew open.

"Dinessa, where have you been?" Brogan demanded.

Unlike the last time Noli had seen him, when he'd been in gentleman's dress, Brogan wore Otherworld clothing, complete with a green velvet waistcoat. He wasn't wearing a sword that she could see. He didn't seem to notice Noli, so she stood very still, hoping it would stay that way.

"Your nephews have come to visit," Dinessa replied, non-plussed. "They're in the green sitting room. You should greet them."

"I hardly think so." He glowered, his green eyes narrowing. His hair was a curly dark blond like James', and he had the same build and features as Mr. Darrow.

"Always so grumpy in the morning. Let's find them."

Dinessa put an arm around his waist, in a gesture so soft and tender it seemed wasted on the likes of Brogan. She shot a look at Noli that clearly said *I'll be right back.*

They left, and Noli felt a sigh of relief shudder through her. She was grateful that Brogan hadn't noticed her.

Let's find the shinies. They're close. I can hear them, the sprite urged.

She could? If sprites were smarter they could take over the Otherworld.

That would be no fun, rulers think too much, she retorted.

Um hmm. *All right, lead on, but you can only have the body until we find them.*

Will my body be pretty? I want to be pretty. I want my own name, too.

Why don't you think of one then? Noli replied as they crept out the door they'd come through and into another room, the sprite in charge of the body.

Can't you hear them singing? the sprite asked.

Noli didn't hear anything. The sprite led her through a series of connecting rooms, then stopped.

We're here, the sprite whispered.

Noli felt herself take possession of the body. The room she stood in was masculine, yet opulent. The wooden walls were hung with tapestries and swaths of silk. Thick rugs carpeted the floor. A desk sat in the corner. There was a case of books and papers.

Brogan had an office? But being a king wasn't all duels and parties.

Now, where would he keep the pieces?

Behind the curtain, of course. Tricky.

What? Noli walked to the nearest tapestry. On it was a giant golden lady surrounded with flames. The Bright Lady? *Behind here?* Carefully, she peeked behind the tapestry. Nothing but a smooth wall. She put her hand on the smoothness. Something pulsed under her palm. *Reveal your secrets, please?*

A knothole appeared. She reached inside and pulled out a silken bag. Still hidden partially by the tapestry, like she was hiding behind the parlor curtains, she peeked in the bag. Golden pieces winked at her. A breath hissed from between her teeth. Yes. She reached in the hole again and pulled out a small, battered book. Quinn's missing research. Excellent. The book went in her handbag and the bag she attached to one of the loops of her under-bust corset. The golden sword bumped against her hip. Her hand hovered over the knothole. *Hide yourself.* The wall grew flat.

Noli ducked out from behind the tapestry. Now, to find Dinessa and have some cake.

"Where do you think you're going?" Brogan stared at her. "I wondered who those little feet belonged to. They're far too dainty to belong to my nephews—and they're too smart to steal from me."

Caught. Fear rooted her to the ground.

"I got lost," she stammered, grasping for words, trying to figure out how to get away.

He held out his hand, an expectant look on his face. "Give me what you took, little thief, and I'll have your hands instead of your head."

"These are not for the likes of you." Noli bolted out the nearest open door.

"Stop, I command you," he bellowed.

Noli found herself in what must be Brogan's bedroom. The only way out she could spy was a balcony and the doorway she'd just come through. She went onto the balcony and hid, back pressed against the wall, hoping he'd leave.

"I know you're there." He stepped onto the balcony. "Who do you work for, little sprite? Ciarán?"

Not knowing what else to do, she unsheathed the sword James had given her. She took a deep breath. *Pointy end first.*

Noli jumped out and slashed at Brogan, cutting his sleeve. Droplets of blood decorated the thin gash on his arm.

"Treachery," he yelped, stepping toward the edge of the balcony. "Guards!"

"I don't think so." Noli hopped so she stood between him and the doorway, drops of his blood glistening on her metal blade. "No one hurts my family—and that includes V." She slashed at him again, this time catching him in the chest. "You made me ill. You killed V's father and Quinn, and you tried to hurt Elise."

He held out his hand and threw her across the room without touching her, like he had aboard the Vixen's Revenge. She flew through the doorway of the bedroom and hit the floor with a thud. The sword skittered across the floor toward the giant bed, inches from her grasp.

"What if I did?" He gave a chuckle more suited to a mad scientist in a penny dreadful than a king. "Also, remember,

I'm hardly defenseless, little sprite," he growled, entering the bedroom. "You're a dreadful swordswoman."

Brogan towered over her, putting a boot in the center of her chest when she tried to roll over and get the sword.

"I still know what you did—not just to myself and them, but with the artifact and what you're going to do with it," Noli spat, trying to creep over to the sword so she could cut the muscles in his legs and escape.

"Do you now? That will go with you to your grave. Stealing from me was a mistake. The last one you'll ever make." He took a long knife from his belt, one she hadn't noticed before.

Noli stretched out, fingers brushing the hilt of her sword. *Almost there.* She taunted him, buying herself time as she scooted across the rug: "How could you do that to your own family?"

Green eyes danced with madness. "You have no idea. If you only knew … "

"She's lying." Noli's hand gripped the sword's hilt. *Victory.* "Whatever Tiana promised you, it's a lie."

"What's going on here?" Dinessa called from outside the room.

"You know not of what you speak. I can hardly expect the likes of you to understand." Brogan dove at her with his knife.

"Brogan, no." Dinessa ran in with a flurry of skirts.

At the same time, Noli thrust her sword up, trying to protect herself from his blade with her own. A squelch and two cries pierced the air. Looking up, she saw Brogan's eyes bulge, her sword through his heart; blood was spurting everywhere like a demented fountain. Dinessa gazed at her, eyes wide, blood spreading across her pretty green dress.

"Dinessa!" Noli scrambled up. What was going on?

"Take the land," Dinessa whispered, hand over her heart, blood flowing over her pale fingers. "You have to deal a death blow and take the land or there could be a war."

"But you…" Horror spread through Noli—she hadn't meant to hurt Dinessa. She liked her. Why was Dinessa bleeding when she'd stabbed *Brogan*?

Dinessa nodded slowly. "We're twins. That's why he keeps me here, a near-prisoner."

Noli still didn't understand. She knew they were twins, but what was the connection? Her attention turned to Brogan, who was trying unsuccessfully to plug the holes in his body, his face contorted in dismay as he propped himself up on the corner of the bed.

Voices yelled in the distance.

"Listen to me, Noli. You need to spill your blood on the ground, plunge the sword into the drops, invoke the Bright Lady's name, and take the land." Dinessa sank to the ground, fading. "Hurry. I believe in you."

"I'm sorry." Tears blurred Noli's vision. "I didn't mean to hurt you." She still didn't understand.

"I forgive you. Be good to Stiofán. He loves you." Dinessa's eyes closed and she slumped over.

Noli sniffed. Brogan lurched toward her, knife in hand. More people entered the room, but she didn't pay them any heed.

"This is for you, V. This is for you, and your family, and your father." Taking the sword in both hands, Noli brought it down across Brogan's neck with all her might, sawing through the meaty flesh and severing his head.

Here goes nothing. She sliced open her left palm. *Ow.* As she shook her hand, drops hit the lush carpets on the wooden floor. With her right hand, Noli plunged the sword right through the carpet, into the floor, her left palm smarting as she wrapped it in her skirts. Her right hand still rested on the hilt of the sword. What did she do now?

I'll tell you what to say. After all, you were stealing the pieces for me. It wasn't the sprite, but the voice. *Say, "By the land, the Bright Lady, and all that is good, I, Magnolia Montgomery Braddock, claim this as mine for my eternity or until the magic itself no longer makes it so. And this I swear."*

Should she? But it sounded right. Noli took a deep breath. Here went nothing.

"By the land, the Bright Lady, and all that is good, I, Magnolia Montgomery Braddock, claim this as mine for my eternity or until the magic itself no longer makes it so. And this I swear." She put her left hand on the hilt, still bleeding, and fisted her right hand over her heart, because it felt correct.

"What is going on?" a voice demanded.

"Interfere at your own peril." Someone else's voice escaped from her own lips.

Tingles enveloped Noli's body, turning into a million pin pricks.

Hold on. You're strong. I know you are, the voice told her. *This isn't what I had planned for you. But it will be better this* way. *You can assemble the staff and raise the girl who will wield it with grace, not anger. You can be my body and fight those who rebel… like Her… She will fight, but I will be still no longer.*

Noli's body felt as if it were burning on a pyre. *Who are you? Are you the Bright Lady?*

No, silly, the voice laughed, but it was gentle, not taunting. *I am everything… and nothing. I am greater than Her, yet weaker. I am tired of being kept hungry because you fae can't keep your leaders in check.*

If she wasn't the Bright Lady… *Are you the magic? The land?*

Magic. Land. Aether. I am whatever you wish to call me. And I have chosen you.

What? Why her? *I can't do that. I'm no chosen anything.*

In time you will be.

Why me? Her mind spun like an out-of-control carousel.

From the moment the queen made you, I felt you. You were interesting to watch. Then when you were in the tree and so kind. Hmmm…

Insecurity crept through the pain. *What?*

No, no. This won't do. But I'll grant you a favor to demonstrate my good will.

Her body felt like a living Tesla coil. *What's happening?*

Be kind to her. You have a good heart, Magnolia Montgomery Braddock who tells stories. Take care not to lose it, lest I be forced to turn my wrath upon you. Your love will help you. He has a good heart, too.

The voice faded as did the sizzle. Her eyes flickered open and she sank to her knees, spent, hand still on the sword as she looked around her at Brogan and Dinessa's headless bodies. Blood seeped from her hand and covered her skirt.

Guards stared at her, unmoving, swords drawn. V and James stood there, jaws open.

"Noli, what did you do?" V took a step forward, but didn't touch her. He looked pale, like he'd been punched in the stomach.

"Um, V." James came up beside him, taking in the situation with big green eyes. "I think Noli just took the earth court."

TWELVE

Long Live the Queen

"What?" Steven hissed, trying to wrap his mind around the gruesome sight. Something *had* happened with the magic, and his chest ached from the backlash.

Before him was chaos. Blood. Bodies—two headless, one naked. Who was the unclothed girl with hair like honey? Noli remained on her knees, a golden sword in the ground, blood everywhere, a stunned expression on her face.

There were more shouts as people poured into the room. Everyone just stood there, gazing at the young woman covered in blood in the king's bedchamber. The air was so thick with magic even the guards dared not move any closer.

James stepped forward and bowed to Noli. "I, Séamus of the House of Oak, second son of first son Domhnall, acknowledge that Magnolia, first daughter of the House of…Tree, has rightfully and legally taken the earth court."

He got down on one knee and put his fist over his heart. "Long live the queen."

Steven's knees buckled as the gravity of the situation hit him with the force of a speeding train. James gave him a wild look.

"I...I, Stiofán of the House of Oak, first son of first son Domhnall, acknowledge that Magnolia has rightfully and legally taken the earth court." He got down on one knee, mimicking James' gestures, too shocked to do anything else. "Long live the queen." The words came out shaky as he tried to process what had happened. Noli had *what*?

Yet something had happened with the magic, something *big*.

"What?" Noli's face was a mask of terror.

James put a finger to his lips. "Accept," he hissed.

"I...I accept." Her whispered words rang through the room with the clarity of bells.

The magic shifted again, swirling and changing so fast and forcefully that if Steven hadn't eaten so long ago it would have come back up.

James stood and gazed at him expectantly. "Aren't you going to do anything?"

Steven stood there, his gut still reeling from the violent shifts in the magic as he replayed what had happened in his head.

"Fine," James huffed. He held out his hand to Noli. "Your Grace?" James helped her stand, then turned to address those gathered in the room. "Her Grace would like someone to take care of this. Aunt Dinessa will be buried at the

House of Oak. Uncle Brogan..." The look James shot Steven pleaded for him to interject.

All Steven could do was gaze at Noli, the pooled blood soaking into the carpets and the wooden floor.

"We'll deal with that later," James finally said, with a disappointed shake of his head. "I'm sure there's much to take care of. We'll attend to Her Grace and she'll see visitors later." No one moved and he shot them a pointed look. "That *was* an order."

People began to move. *Her Grace*. Noli had killed Brogan and taken the kingdom. Steven's belly lurched as he stumbled to his feet.

"V?" Noli shook as her gaze shifted to him. The naked girl stood beside her, taking everything in with giant honey-colored eyes.

"I..." His heart pounded. Noli had taken the earth court by force from Brogan, a kingdom that was supposed to be *his*. Spinning on his boots, he ran out of the room. He ran until his chest heaved. Leaning over a railing, he tried to gather his wits.

He stuffed a knuckle in his mouth. How could she have done this to him? She knew that taking back the earth court was his dream...and she'd yanked it out from under him.

Here he thought she loved him. Steven punched the rail.

"All right, idiot, what's your problem now?" James stalked over to him.

"I can't believe she'd betray me like that." He felt like he'd been stabbed.

"Do I need to hit you? The last thing she'd ever do is

betray you. Now, I have *no idea* what happened back there, but knowing Noli, it was probably an accident," James replied. "However, we do need to discover what happened and create an official story *before* everyone comes—and you know they're going to come."

Steven recoiled at his brother's words. "Why should we help *her*? She just took our kingdom from us."

James' expression soured. "You're a moron. Noli has no idea what just happened. She's in shock and needs us. Tiana will be here shortly and Noli *has* to have it together before she arrives."

He crossed his arms over his chest. "The kingdom was supposed to be mine."

"Um, it *is* yours. Noli just took it for you." James shook his head. "You two do everything together. Certainly that's not going to stop now."

"Noli has *no idea* how to run a kingdom," Steven ranted, fingers raking through his hair. "I've spent my *entire life* planning for this—either being trained by father, or plotting what I'd do once I got the kingdom back." He had notebooks *full* of carefully detailed plans.

James rolled his eyes. "I *know*. She can't do this alone. Your dreams have just come true. The kingdom is now yours. She'll probably even let you use all your plans."

"What are you talking about? It's not mine," he snapped, anger and confusion whirling inside him. "My best friend, the girl who I thought loved me, just *stole* my dream. She didn't even *ask*." His hands fisted. "She *knew* what this meant to me, she knew I wanted this."

James stared at him with sheer and utter disbelief. "Fine." He shoved his sword in Steven's hands. "Go kill her and take the kingdom. Not only can she not defend herself, but she has no idea what happened. She's waiting for you to come and explain all this to her and make it right, like you always do."

Steven stared at the sword in his hands. James' sword. "What?"

"You can be king in one of two ways. Either kill Noli and take it from her, or stop being stupid, tell her you love her, and go be her king." James' face flushed with passion and rage.

"I ... " He shook his head. "I can't be her king."

James' voice hushed as pain flashed in his eyes. "I thought you loved her."

"I ... I do. But *she* took the kingdom, a girl. One that knows nothing. She can't even use a sword and magic. How will that make me look?"

James smacked him upside the head. "Will you swallow your pride? They're going to eat her alive without your help. You're right, she knows nothing. But with you, she can do it. You know why? Because you can do damn near anything together. If you don't help her, someone's going to kill her and take the kingdom in days, and they're not going to be nearly as easy to defeat. Not to mention the first thing they'll do is exile us ... if they don't kill us outright."

"Ow." Steven rubbed his head. "Will you stop hitting me and calling me names?"

"Start acting like a prince ... or a king," James snapped.

"Do you remember those lectures father gave us? The ones about how our actions define us?"

"I remember." It was difficult not to roll his eyes. Their father used to give them *a lot* of lectures.

"This is a defining moment. It's time to take our kingdom back. Are you going to kill her or marry her?" James got very close to him, eyes daring. "She's our *friend*. I never pegged you for a prideful coward. I'm beginning to think Jeff is right and Noli *is* too good for you." He marched off, leaving Steven with the sword in his hands.

Unfortunately, James was right. Pride was getting in the way of thinking logically.

When Noli lopped off Brogan's head, it was for him. She'd said so. Yes, he'd dreamed of that moment for years...so many years...but at the same time, he'd always hoped there'd be another way. He was a man of words, not swords. Darling Noli had given him a gift.

Now he should give one to her.

"Prince V?" A sprite with a mass of honey-colored hair he could only call a mane looked up at him with big, honey eyes. Her...décolletage...threatened to spill out of her green dress. Ah, the naked girl. Someone must have dressed her. He still didn't know who she was—or why she'd been naked. Something about her seemed familiar.

He eyed her. "Yes?"

She twirled. "Am I pretty?"

He blinked, not knowing what to say. "Yes, you are."

The girl's lips broke into a wide smile. "I'm so glad. I

wanted a pretty body. I'm going to call myself Miri. Isn't that a good name?"

"Yes, it is." What was going on here? Who was she? Obviously, she knew him.

"Noli is very sad and scared. Will you come give her a kiss and make her feel better?" Miri batted her eyes at him. "I suppose the sad thing about having my own body is that I'll never get to kiss you again. It would hurt her if I kissed you." She perked up. "But there are *lots* of other boys to kiss and dance with. I'm going to have so much fun." She tugged on his wrist. "Come."

Her words penetrated his head, bouncing around until they made sense.

"Are you the sprite?" he asked. There was no other explanation.

Miri's head bobbed. "Now I have a body of my very own so I can be fun and Noli can think a lot and be boring. That's why I need a name."

"How did *that* happen?" If the sprite had her own body, what had happened to Noli?

And how?

She shrugged. "Noli hurt the bad king, then *whoosh*, the lady, the one that talks to us, came and talked to Noli and said things and said she'd give Noli a present. And I hurt." Her eyes widened. "So, so much, then..." Miri clapped her hands. "I woke on the floor looking at Noli, who was her, but different, and I was now me." She jumped up and down, then tugged on his wrist again. "Now, come."

"Noli's herself again?" Steven's heart leapt. "Take me to her."

Half-running, the sprite pulled him into Dinessa's room. The scene before him made his heart break.

"I don't understand," Noli sobbed into James' shoulder. "Brogan was about to stab me and it just…happened. Dinessa's the one who told me to put the sword in the ground. I didn't mean to hurt her," she hiccupped. "Why did she die, too? I don't understand. I didn't even mean to kill Brogan. I just wanted to get the pieces."

"I know." James patted her back. "I know. Accidents happen. Dinessa and Brogan are twins, if you hurt one, you hurt the other as well."

"Oh." Noli looked crushed. "I had no idea."

Miri looked at Steven expectantly. "She's sad."

"Do you want to be helpful?" he asked Miri, keeping one eye on Noli.

She nodded so hard he thought her head might fall off.

"First, you're now one of Noli's, I mean, Her Grace's, handmaidens. Your job is to help her," he told her. "Can you do that?" Sprites liked to be helpful. They also liked to gossip.

"Oh yes. Noli's boring, but I love her. We're sisters." She clasped her hands to her overly large bosom and bounced.

"Good. First, go down to the kitchens, find the chatelaine. Tell her you're one of Her Grace's handmaidens and someone needs to get the old king and queen's suite ready for her. Then, tell her that Her Grace wants you to prepare for her to hold an audience with her subjects. Finally, I know you love Noli, so part of your job, not just today, but for always, is to help others love her. Can do you that?" He'd probably given her too many tasks.

She looked at Noli, who still cried into James' arms. "I can. It will make her happy?"

"It will be helpful."

"I like to help." She smiled, then left.

"Here." Steven walked over to James and Noli and shoved James' sword into his hands. "I don't need this." His fingers stroked Noli's unbound hair. "Don't cry, Noli. Please?"

Noli peered up at him with teary eyes. "V? I'm so sorry."

"Oh, darling." All his anger, all his pride, faded away. "I … I'm not angry." He looked at James. "May Noli and I talk? We have a lot to do in a short amount of time."

James nodded. "Plan C?"

"You remember?" He actually had several detailed plans on what would happen once he took the kingdom. Plan C would be best for this particular situation.

James grinned, attaching his sword to his belt. "Of course. As much as I made fun of those, they actually make sense."

"I don't have my notebooks," Steven added. They were at the big house with other things he'd taken from Los Angeles.

"Let's get this started before Tiana comes; then we'll get the notebooks." James left, closing the door behind them.

"Come here." He bundled Noli into his arms and held her to him as her body shuddered under his fingers. Someone had given her a clean dress and wiped the blood off her. "Now, what happened?"

She told him about stealing the pieces and the resulting

encounter with Brogan. "I didn't mean to, it was an accident," she whispered over and over.

He held her at arm's length and gazed into her beautiful eyes. "It wasn't an accident. We can't have an accidental queen. We can't mention the artifact. No. You avenged Brogan for me … as an act of love and devotion." Steven's cheeks burned. "I mean … if you still want me."

"Of course I do, you fussy old bodger. I *love* you. Even when you're being idiotic. But … " Her face fell. "I didn't mean to take killing your uncle away from you. It all happened so fast."

"I know." They sat on the edge of Dinessa's bed and he pulled her into him. "You know I'd rather fight with words." He ran his finger down her tear-streaked cheek. "I'm going to be a man and take this as the gift it is."

"What do you mean, *queen?* And why is everyone calling me *Your Grace?*" She made one of her adorable confused faces.

"You *took* the kingdom. There's a difference between just killing the current monarch and actually taking over a kingdom … which is why most of the time no one simply tries to kill a monarch, because then the court would be leaderless and there would be too much bloodshed as families warred for the throne," he explained. "You must meet very specific qualifications in order to actually take a kingdom, one of which is that you have to be an adult." His face screwed up. "But we're not adults—and you're not from a great house, nor do you wear my sigil, though you are technically mine, so I suppose that somehow met the magic's requirements."

"Oh. I suppose so." She gulped. "Technically, I *am* an

adult. It occurred when Queen Tiana did...whatever, she did to me."

That made sense.

"I'll spare you the details, but you're an earth court adult who can use a sword. Not everyone has the right to bear a sword. Where *did* you get it?"

"From James." She rested her head on his shoulder.

Of course she did.

Back to the matter at hand. "Then, after you kill the current monarch with a sword, you have to follow certain steps to transfer the kingdom to you, which you did. The Bright Lady found you worthy. James and I acted as witnesses. You accepted. And now you, my love..." He stroked her hair. "You're the new queen of the earth court."

"I...I'm queen? But how can I be queen? We're not married yet." Her eyes went wide.

Oh, Noli, still so innocent in so many ways.

"You're queen in your own right. Like Tiana. Only..." Steven's cheeks burned. "Unlike her, you have the right to have a king. If you want one, that is." After everything, he didn't want to presume. James was right; he'd been a moron. "Also, I'm sorry for being an idiot. I know you always act in my best interest."

She sat up and smiled. "Apology accepted. My first act as queen will be to make you king. My second act will be to clear your family's good name...if it still needs clearing." Noli looked around. "Who do I tell to make it so?"

James was right. She knew nothing. But she had him.

"Noli, do you mean it? Do you really wish to make me

your king? Marriage is different here in the Otherworld." He took her hands, heart leaping while his stomach lurched. Noli made him a better man.

"Of course I do. This is your dream. You're getting your kingdom back." She beamed.

Any remaining doubt and anger faded away. "We're getting *our* kingdom back. It's going to be a lot of work, but we can do this together."

"We always get through everything together. Besides." Her smile turned bashful. "I don't know how to rule a kingdom."

Their foreheads touched. "Fortunately, I've spent my entire life preparing for this."

Her face fell. "I can't be a queen. I can't even be a lady."

"Noli, this is our kingdom. We can rule it however we'd like—within reason. We'll be more... relaxed. We'll become a haven for inventors and creators. We can have royal gardening competitions, and"—he grinned—"a royal tree house. We get to make the rules." None of his plans called for shaking things up, but then again, he'd never planned for an uncommon queen like Noli.

Still, this could work. No, it *would* work.

"A royal tree house?" Her eyes gleamed. "I want one of those hover chariots like the queen has... only I want it to go fast. Perhaps we'll have races."

Now that could be fun. "We'll help each other, too."

"Of course. That's what we do—make each other better." She planted a kiss on his nose.

His finger brushed her ear. The point was gone. For a long moment he studied her. She was just as pretty as before, though her looks had become a little more refined and digni-fied ... as a queen's should be. The curls had returned to her hair, only they weren't quiet as unwieldy as they'd once been. Gently, he put his hands on her temples and read her magic, something he should have done before and never had.

"That tickles," she laughed, twisting slightly under his touch.

"Noli ... " He sucked in a breath, she had *a lot* of magic. "You're not a sprite anymore."

"I know. She took the sprite out of my head and made me myself again." Noli flung out her arms. "I feel fabulous."

"I'm so glad." He kissed her. Noli was back. A sprite could never be queen. However, he had a feeling Noli didn't quite realize that she wasn't mortal. There couldn't be a mortal queen, either. "Noli ... "

The door opened and James marched in. "I hope you've forgiven each other and kissed and all that because we have work to do."

Steven would talk to her about that later. "Yes. Impres-sions are very important. What happens today will define how people see you as leader."

"You mean *us*, don't you?" Noli made a face.

"Technically, since *you* took the kingdom, you have to actually marry V in order for him to be king." James grinned, clearly taking pleasure in this.

Noli nodded. "That makes sense."

"So ... " James' smile stretched so wide it threatened to expand past his face. He gestured to Steven and Noli.

It took a moment for Steven to understand. "You want me to propose right now?"

"Not this second, if you'd rather not," Noli whispered, a tentative hand caressing his face. "I know it's sooner than we expected. But I want you to be my king, and that means we'll have to marry at some point, won't we? We always knew it would happen someday."

Someday. It had seemed so far off. After university, when he became an adult and faced Brogan. Now that far-off day was here, so much sooner than expected.

Steven gulped as his gaze fixed on Noli. "I was hoping not to have to do this twice, but I will. If you truly want to be an *us*, then we should be an *us* from the start. Like always, we'll make it up as we go along."

Her entire face lit up. "Really?"

"Really." Actually, they usually made things up as they went along because she deviated from the plan. But that was also one of the things he loved about her.

"What do you mean, do this *twice*?" She cocked her head.

"I should ask Jeff for your hand, to be proper. Well, mortal realm proper." The idea of asking Jeff made Steven nervous. Vix and her pistol made him even *more* nervous. What if they said *no*?

Noli laughed. "Jeff will be angry if you deny him that."

"Yes, he will. Engagements in our realm are different. We don't use rings. But when we go back to the mortal realm, I'll buy you one and ask your brother, and then we'll be proper in both realms." He had a feeling that would be important to her.

"Do I get two weddings?" she teased.

"Unless you want to tell your mother about being a faery queen, then you do, actually," James said.

"Oh. Yes, that." Noli went ashen, probably realizing what she'd done. She'd changed their lives *so much*.

But James was right, Steven realized. He'd achieved what he'd wanted for so long. They had their kingdom back. It might not be the way he'd planned, but the important thing was *they had it back*.

Also, he'd soon marry a woman who was strong enough to *take* a kingdom. The inner strength needed to take it and face the Bright Lady was something he'd glossed over. Anyone would be proud to be with such a woman.

Still, the tiniest bit of doubt niggled at the back of his mind.

No. He pushed it away, focusing on the moment. On her.

"Anytime now. We have things to do." James shifted from foot to foot.

"We can just tell them we're engaged, if you'd like to wait to propose until there's a more romantic moment," Noli offered.

This probably wasn't her idea of the perfect proposal, either. Even though she wasn't as silly as many wellborn girls, who believed marriage to be their defining moment, she'd probably had something worked out in her head as to how it should be.

He stood, standing her up. "Are...are you sure you want to do this?"

Steven's belly clenched as he waited for her answer. He partially expected her to say no.

She nodded. "If I have to rule a court, you have to do it with me."

"Once we do this there's no going back, it's not like an engagement in the mortal realm." He held her hands tightly.

"Like ending an engagement—or a marriage—is easy to begin with?" she laughed.

"All right." His heart pounded as he pulled out his belt knife and cut his palm. He took her palm, still weeping from the gash she'd given herself before and pressed them together. "May our love be as vast and strong as the very magic that binds us together. May our love be blessed and bound so that we shall never part, even when our bodies fade away. By the Bright Lady and the land herself, make it so." He nodded at Noli as he intertwined their fingers.

"By the Bright Lady and the land herself, make it so," she whispered, her eyes never leaving his.

The tingling started in his toes. Magic surged through him, probing and testing, making him want to let go of Noli, but he refused. He knew magic was invoked in the ritual, but he never realized it felt like this.

Do you regret it? a voice whispered in his ear. *After all, she killed your quarry, she took your prize.*

The anger he'd felt before rose up inside him, stoking the flames of fury. She took the court. She killed Brogan. She snuck off to see Kevighn. Maybe he should just…

He shook his head, shaking away those feelings of doubt, of wounded pride.

No, he answered back. *I don't regret it. She didn't steal my prize. She gave me a gift. I . . . I don't think I could have actually brought myself to kill Uncle Brogan.* The admission hurt, but it was the truth. *I love her and we're going to do this together . . . just like everything else.*

You do love her. The voice sighed. *It's so beautiful. Because she loves you so much, I've been testing you to see if you were worthy. You have passed.*

Noli had been *right?* He sucked in a breath. The Bright Lady *was* speaking to her. And testing him? Was that where the anger and doubt had come from? It must have been. *Why me?*

I have a special job for the both of you.

You do? I am but your servant. What do you need me to do? He felt . . . humbled, and honored.

It will be revealed in time. For now, I approve of, and bless your union.

I . . . I appreciate that. Magic continued to sear through him. But he wouldn't let go. He'd never let go.

My path is not an easy one. May your love always be strong.

The burning sensation subsided and he opened his eyes, looking at Noli, who blinked.

"I . . . I guess that's a *yes,*" she whispered.

"She . . . " It had been real.

Noli nodded. "Yes. I didn't realize engagement was like that here."

Actually, they didn't have engagements, not like what Noli knew in her realm. They had betrothals, but that was different. He wasn't about to give his mother the power to forbid him from marrying her. They'd speak of it later. Surely, Noli wouldn't mind the fact that he'd just married them magically. She'd still get her wedding, both here and in the mortal realm. He'd see to it.

"Are you done now?" James twisted uncomfortably.

Steven looked at Noli. He grabbed her and kissed her. Her eyes went wide. Looking at James, he released her and grinned. "I'm done now."

"Good. Here." James put a ring on Noli's hand. "Since we're all the House of Oak here, you should wear it."

Steven eyed the tiny ring. "Where did you get that?"

"Same place I got this." James looked smug. "A queen needs a crown, especially if you're going to face Tiana." He placed a crown of metal oak leaves on her head. "Perfect."

"Really, James?" Steven's voice hushed. "What exactly are we doing here?"

"Plan C, sending a message." James' chest puffed up. "What else tells Tiana that we're here to stay more than Noli wearing her crown and ring? After all, she has no claim to them anymore. They're Noli's. Also, don't you owe her a gift?"

Noli touched the crown, running her fingers along the metal leaves. "They were hers?"

"They've belonged to many, many queens, not just her, and I'll get you a proper gift," Steven assured her, his belly twisting a little at the ire this might invoke. However, his brother had a point about messages. Also, subtleties were wasted on Tiana.

"And finally." James put the little golden sword around

Noli. "You should never be far from your weapon or your guards. We'll continue your lessons."

Noli paled. "People will try to kill me?"

"They might." Steven wrapped an arm around her. "James, where did you get that sword?" It wasn't their mother's sword.

James shrugged. "I found it at the big house. It's a girl's sword, so I thought it would be perfect for Noli. Now, come on. I found some allies and they need to meet with us before Tiana arrives. Also, I need to put the artifact pieces, Quinn's research, and the jewel someplace secure. Is father's safe in his private library too obvious?"

"The jewel is here?" Noli shot him a hard look.

"I didn't want to leave it at the big house where it might be stolen. Kevighn's broken in before—he might do so again," he lied. Also, they still needed to get Elise back. "How do you know the combination?" But then that was probably where Tiana's crown and ring had been.

James grinned. "Secret. Now … allies, they're waiting … "

Allies? Then again, most swore allegiance to his uncle not because they supported him but to avoid exile—or death.

Steven had a thought. "Do we have a moment?"

"A quick one." James made a face of boyish disgust. "No, we don't have time for *that*."

He swatted James. "Not *that*. If I'm really going to take a stand against Tiana, it would make sense to greet her while wearing Father's crown."

Noli grinned. "I like that idea. I don't care if we didn't have a wedding yet. You're already my king."

His heart leapt. Noli was his. Forever. But first things first. "James?"

James took something out of a bag and placed a crown in his hands, a larger, more masculine version of Noli's. His grin went wide. "I thought you'd never ask."

THIRTEEN

Adventures

Kevighn doubled over the table in the tavern kitchen like a drunken ogre as the magic punched him in the gut. He hadn't felt a shift like that for some time. Lunch finished, he'd been nursing a glass of ale while waiting for the children to return. If they didn't come back soon, he'd go find them.

"Kevighn, Kevighn." A panic-stricken Ciarán jogged into the kitchen.

"Did you feel that?" Kevighn rubbed his stomach. "What happened with the magic?"

Ciarán shook his head. "I don't know, but we have no time for that."

The terror on Ciarán's face made his belly churn. "What happened? What did Tiana do now?" he asked.

"I think the children are missing."

"Missing? I thought they'd gone out to play?" Kevighn froze. Missing?

"Aodhan left me a note." Ciarán clutched something in his hand so tight his knuckles went white. "It says *gone adventuring, back later.*"

That sounded like something he and Ciarán would have done as children, not that they ever bothered to leave notes. "Does he often do that?"

"Never. He's not even supposed to go beyond the glade without me." Ciarán crumpled the note in his hand.

It was interesting how protective Ciarán was of the boy, considering how wild the two of them had been at that age. Adventuring in the Blackwoods would have been a given. Still, with how important those children were, Kevighn could also see why he was panicking.

"It doesn't seem like something Elise would do, either. She's such an obedient girl," Kevighn replied. Especially when compared to Noli.

"I have no idea why they'd do such a thing." His eyes glimmered in a way that made Kevighn instinctively lean back. Ciarán could be unfathomably rational at times, but he hadn't gotten his position through reason.

"How are we going to get them back?" Kevighn asked.

"*We?*" Ciarán's dark eyebrows rose. "You're the one who wanted to do something interesting. Find them."

"Let me get something to use for a tracking spell." He stood at the order, giving his glass of ale a forlorn look. Later. Orders were orders.

Ciarán shook his head. "Aodhan's hard to track. I wonder where he got that?"

Quinn always had been difficult to find. "Elise then? I'm sure they haven't gotten far."

"Here." He took the sigil off from around his neck and handed it to Kevighn. "Use this."

Kevighn pulled his hand back, gazing at the near black stone that went red when held to the fire, wrapped in a spider web of silver wire. It was the sign of a once great house, a house made great again when Ciarán took the dark court. It had been stupid, but when you were that age stupid things often sounded like good ideas. At least they'd been successful.

"Go on." Ciarán sighed. "You can touch it."

Usually a peasant such as him *couldn't*. Though he trusted Ciarán with his life, old habits were hard to break.

"I noticed you gave him a sigil." Kevighn gingerly took it from him, not completely relaxing when nothing happened.

"I was protecting him." A hint of defensiveness tinged his voice. By giving the boy a sigil, Ciarán had made Aodhan part of his family.

Kevighn held up his free hand in surrender; he took no issue with that. It was more than he could do for the boy.

"For that I'm grateful. You took care of him when I couldn't." Kevighn felt the tiniest stab of guilt for that, even if it had been for the best.

"I have one for you, too. When you're ready. I'd give it to you now, but I don't want you to run again." Ciarán's look softened.

"What?" Kevighn nearly dropped the sigil.

Ciarán put a hand on Kevighn's arm, steadying him. "Kevighn, you've been my family for a long time. You've finally come home and we want you to join our family for good."

All he could do was stare at his old friend. Him, gifted with a sigil? They were closer than brothers, but this was a gift beyond gifts—even greater than Ciarán making sure his cabin and Creideamh's grove remained intact after his exile. Still, the implications...

"You know the word of power associated with it. Go find them and bring them home." Ciarán closed Kevighn's fingers over the sigil, the touch suddenly so much...more.

Things he hadn't felt in a long time overwhelmed him. Kevighn held the sigil to his chest, in a fist over his heart. This was much more than a mere order. "I...I will. I promise."

•••••••••

Elise clutched Aodhan's hand as they walked through the tall rowan trees, which cast ominous shadows around them. They'd been walking for *ages*.

"Does any of this look familiar?" Aodhan asked. "I'm hungry."

"Me too." Her stomach growled. They'd already eaten the cookies they'd brought. "I was so small, I barely remember." Elise gazed up at trees so tall she couldn't see their tops, obscuring the pink sky. A pink and purple sky! If she were queen she'd pick a more sensible color, like blue.

Aodhan consulted the map he'd taken from his father.

"I think we're close. Why don't we ask the wood faeries? In a place like this there's bound to be wood faeries."

"That's a great idea. Do you wish to call them, or should I?" Elise stayed close to him. Maybe this wasn't such a good idea. There was so much...space.

"I can call them, if you'd like." Aodhan gave her a bashful smile.

"Please?"

Aodhan closed his eyes and sent out a silent call to the wood faeries.

Something hit her. "Ow." Elise looked around as she rubbed her midsection. "Did you feel that?"

Aodhan nodded, frowning. "I...I think something happened to the magic?"

"The magic?" Her nose scrunched at the odd idea. "How can anyone feel magic?"

"I do...and apparently so you do. Not everyone does. But the magic is alive, so why wouldn't we be able to feel it?" He shrugged as if it were a perfectly ordinary explanation.

"How can magic be *alive?*" That sounded so...strange.

His expression crumpled. "How can you say that?"

"I...I don't understand." That face he made hurt more than being hit by a rock.

Slowly, he nodded. "Maybe it's because you lived in the mortal realm. Don't worry," Aodhan squeezed her hand. "I'll tell you all about our world."

"I'd like that." Perhaps he could explain all the things no one would ever tell her about.

Little balls of light flitted around them—pink, blue, purple, yellow, green.

"We're lost," she told the fluttering faeries. "We're looking for my home, the House of Oak. Are we nearby?"

The faeries said that they were.

"Good, could you take us there? Please? I'm hungry," Aodhan replied.

"Are Noli and my brothers there?" she added. "Oh, they just left? We can wait for them." She looked at Aodhan. "Is that all right?"

He nodded. "As long as there's food."

The faeries guided them to a little garden. Elise saw a beautiful tree, ideal for climbing. On the other side of the garden was a big picture window with a seat perfect for curling up with a book. There was also a glass door.

Elise walked up to the door and peered inside. It was a library, filled with books. On the low table sat a tray with tea, fruit, rolls, and empty bowls.

Aodhan opened the door. "Let's go inside."

"Should we?" No one was in the library and it felt... wrong.

"It's your home." He walked right in.

"True." She followed, ignoring the feeling that she was doing something naughty.

Making himself at home, he plopped down on the settee and eyed the food on the table. "The tea is cold. It looks like the remains of someone's breakfast. Should we go find the cook and have her make us something?"

Elise had no idea where to find... anything. "I'll warm

the tea for you." Taking the porcelain teapot in both hands, she focused on warming the tea inside until tiny puffs of steam escaped from the spout. She poured him a cup and handed it to him. "How's that?"

Aodhan took a sip and made a face. "It needs sugar, but it's hot enough. I appreciate you doing that. It's a handy trick."

"It is, isn't it?" She handed him the sugar bowl then poured herself a cup.

They stuffed themselves with leftover food.

"Should we explore a little?" Aodhan patted his stomach contentedly. "Will you show me your room? Do you have one?"

Elise nodded slowly. If only she could remember. "I must. We should look for it."

They walked down the hall, opening doors and peeking inside.

"That room's messy." Aodhan made a face as they looked in a room with weapons on the walls and clothes on the bed and floor. A dressing screen stood in the corner.

"I think this is James' room." Elise's eyes fell on the girlish trinkets on the dresser and she frowned. James didn't like girls much. "Perhaps it's Steven's room . . . though he's rather tidy."

They went to the next room, which was impeccable. A stack of books and some pens sat on the desk.

"This room is *very* clean," Aodhan replied.

"This *must* be Steven's room." Then who did the girl's things in James' room belong to? Perhaps Noli was using his room and he slept elsewhere.

Aodhan opened another door and peered inside. "This room is quite girly. Do you think it was yours?"

Elise took in the butterflies painted on the walls, the ruffled curtains and bedclothes. She ran her fingers down the length of the dresser and opened the wardrobe, which held two sizes of dresses—too small and too large.

"This ... this is my room." She touched the butterflies. "James painted these for me. Noli must be staying here." They looked like Noli's dresses—and that was her valise.

"Why does your room have an extra bedroom?" Aodhan peeked through a door.

"For my nursemaid, of course." If she scrunched her eyes tight she could almost see her, hear her voice.

"What should we do now? I'm bored." Aodhan shoved his hands in his pockets.

"Should we explore?" Elise took his hand and they walked down the hallway and right into a large man.

"And who might you two be? What are you doing here?" He eyed them in a way that made her skin crawl.

"I'm Elise Darrow; it's nice to meet you." She bobbed a curtsey. "I'm looking for my brothers Steven and James. Have you seen them?"

He grabbed them roughly. "You two shouldn't be here. Come with me."

"Let go." Aodhan yelled, thrashing against his grasp. "Elise lives here."

"No little girls live here. Just big ones." He tried to drag them down the hall.

Aodhan squirmed out of his grip, then grabbed Elise's

hand and pulled her out of the man's clutches. The children tore down the hall, trying to get away from him.

"Get back here, you little intruders," the man bellowed, chasing them.

They raced into the library, out the garden door, and across the grounds until their chests heaved and hearts raced.

Outside, Aodhan looked around, panting, no one in sight. "I think we lost him."

Elise nodded as she tried to catch her breath. She could use a drink of water. "I agree. I'd still like to wait for my brothers, but I don't think we should stay inside."

"I agree. Let's explore outside," Aodhan said.

Hand in hand, they wandered through gardens filled with fragrant flowers and giant trees. They found themselves on a path lined by giant hedges as tall as they could see. Everywhere they turned were more hedges.

A dead end faced them. Aodhan frowned. "How do we get out of this place?"

Elise grinned. "I suppose we could walk *through* the hedge instead of doubling back."

"How?" Aodhan eyed the thick wall of green shrubbery.

"We ask them nicely, of course, silly," Elise teased. She put her hand on the wall of green. *Will you let us through?* She frowned at the hedge's reply. *What do you mean it would be cheating? What's a hedge maze? Please let us through.*

The hedge parted, making a hole large enough for her and Aodhan to climb through.

"How did you do that?" Aodhan asked.

"Magic. I can talk to trees. It's how I made the passage

between our rooms, remember?" she told him. Once again, they were on another hedge-lined path, though there were no dead ends in sight.

"You can also heat tea," he added.

Her cheeks warmed. "Shhh, that's a secret. No one's supposed to know I can do things not earth magic."

"Oh, I won't tell. My father has fire magic, so does Uncle Kevighn."

"Do you?" She wasn't exactly sure how it worked, though everyone in her family had earth magic.

He scuffed the dirt path with his boots. "I'm not supposed to talk about it either."

"Oh. I won't tell." She crossed her heart.

Aodhan looked around, voice hushed. "I can do lots of things, including earth magic. I don't think you're supposed to be able to use more than one element."

He was like her? Excitement bubbled inside her. "I know. My tutor never wants me to use my other types of magic, beyond earth magic, except when I'm learning to control them. We're the same, then—we both can use lots of elements?"

What a great secret to share!

"I . . . I guess so." Aodhan beamed and squeezed her hand.

"You don't look like your father, with his dark hair and tanned skin. You have your uncle's eyes. Was your mother pale?" It was so blond it was near-white, like Quinn's. She missed her tutor. Perhaps he was here someplace, too.

He shook his head. "I think she looked like Uncle Kevighn. Another secret? My father's not my real father. I don't remember my parents. My mother was Uncle Kevighn's sister."

"Oh." Elise squeezed his hand. "I don't remember my mother much, either."

They continued to wind their way through the maze until they came to a giant oak tree. Gnarled and crooked, filled with knotholes, the branches stretched far and wide, its roots a visible tangle at its base.

"What a grand tree," Elise breathed. A faery tree if she ever saw one.

"Let's play a game," Aodhan suggested.

"What would you like to play?" Little balls of light climbed out of the knothole and watched them. She waved. One of them waved back.

Aodhan tapped her shoulder and took off running. "Tag."

"I'm going to catch you, Aodhan," she yelled as she chased him around the tree. Every time her fingers brushed his shirt, he escaped from her grasp. "You're so fast."

"Catch me if you can." Aodhan's foot caught on something and he tumbled. "OW!"

"Aodhan." Elise took off running. She peered into the strange, long hole. Aodhan huddled at the bottom, cradling his right leg. "Are you all right?"

He looked up at her with wide, yellow eyes. "My leg hurts."

Elise looked around; there were two strange, long holes in the ground. There was also a mound, about the same size and shape, next to them, covered in rocks. A wilted pink flower sat on the top of it.

"What *are* these?" She also noticed a tiny one near the tree.

"I don't know. Can you get me out of this hole? My leg hurts so much." Aodhan sniffed.

The hole in the ground was deep, and if his leg was hurt he probably couldn't climb out. If she got him out, they still couldn't walk back to the big house.

"I ... I don't know." A little ball of green light sat on her shoulder. "Aodhan's hurt," she told him. "Can you please find Steven, James, or Noli and bring them here? We need help." The little faery agreed and flew off.

Elise walked over to the hole and frowned. "Perhaps I can pull you out?" She lay on the ground, not caring if she dirtied her dress. Her arms stretched until their fingers brushed.

As hard as she tried, she just couldn't do it.

"Can you stand at all?" she asked.

He shook his head, lower lip quivering, but he didn't cry.

"All right then." Elise carefully climbed into the hole and sat down next to him.

"What are you doing? Perhaps you should return to the house and find help." He didn't sound too keen on her leaving.

She shook her head, remembering the large man. "No, I'm *not* leaving you alone. Besides, one of my brothers will be here soon."

Aodhan nodded, resting his head on her shoulder. "I hope so."

Elise stroked his hair. That's what Steven did when Noli was upset. "Don't worry. They'll find us."

FOURTEEN

Aftermath

Noli felt sick to her stomach as she took in the imposing room. "I thought we were meeting Tiana in your father's study," she whispered, afraid to speak loudly in such a place.

"This *is* Father's study." V squeezed her hand, his father's crown resting on his tousled locks. "It's not actually meant for studying. That's what his private library is for. This room is meant for one thing."

"Intimidation?" She gazed at the vaulted ceilings, the rich furnishings, the fact that there were only two chairs—one very nice chair on one side of the table and one not-so-comfortable one on the other.

"Exactly. You sit here." Steven took her to the large, green chair and pulled it out for her.

"Me? Where will you sit? Should we call for another chair?" Noli took the offered seat.

He shook his head. "You're the queen. You took the kingdom. I'll stand right here next to you. I won't leave your side unless you ask. I promise."

"Good. I...I'm nervous." Having him by her side would be a small comfort. She was so unsure about everything. About meeting Tiana, about meeting her subjects.

Subjects. She had subjects. Just the thought boggled her mind.

"Take that, Missy," she muttered. Missy Sassafras would *never* have subjects. "Tiana will sit there?" She eyed the small chair on the other side of the ornate wooden table, not looking forward to facing the high queen. At least V was with her. She always felt, with him, as if she could accomplish nearly everything—though this was much more daunting than mastering Latin or fixing a flying car.

"Yes. We won't offer refreshments. This isn't a social call. This is where we draw the lines. Remember what we discussed." He squeezed her hand.

With her free hand she rubbed her temples. "All this intrigue makes my head hurt. I didn't understand half that meeting. I'm just glad we have allies. We can trust them?"

"I trust Elric. I've known him all my life." V's smile put her at ease.

"I got that idea when he saw you, hugged you, and told you it was about time you took back the kingdom," Noli replied.

"Him, Bran, Padraig—we're going to need them. I'm so glad they remained loyal to my father. They were some of his most trusted advisors. They'll help us weed out those who might cause us trouble." He rubbed his chin. "We should give James a job. Something important, but not so important he won't want it because he thinks it will be too difficult."

"I'll think about that. V?" She looked up at him. "There's something that's been bothering me. How did Brogan take the kingdom without killing your father? Was it because of his exile?"

"Brogan had succession right, because of my age. When you have succession right, it is possible to take the kingdom without killing someone. For example, my father could have voluntarily passed the crown to Brogan, had he wished to follow Tiana. However, I knew I'd have to take it from Uncle Brogan because he'd never give it to me willingly. Father was exiled by Tiana *first*, so Uncle Brogan could take it by succession right without killing him."

She blinked, trying to process everything. "Otherworld politics are complicated."

He grimaced. "You have no idea."

"I'm glad I have you." Otherwise she'd be completely and totally lost. She still felt bad about Dinessa. Perhaps that was one reason why V hadn't been too eager to kill Brogan.

V leaned over and gave her a kiss. "I'm glad I have you."

Footsteps echoed down the hall. They straightened, letting go of each other's hands.

The herald came to the door, dressed in green and gold livery. He cleared his throat. "Your Grace? Her Royal Majesty, High Queen Tiana, is here to see you."

Noli took a deep breath in an attempt to quell her nerves. "Please, show her in."

Tiana strode in, wearing a pink and purple gown as diaphanous as the one Noli had worn to the museum ball. More. Only the entire dress was covered in beads, the under-bust corset pink. Pink and purple roses opened and closed as they festooned her blond hair. As usual, the centerpiece of her coif was her crown of clock hands with the five-circled crest of the high court in the center.

"Your Majesty." Noli stood. "Please have a seat." She gestured to the uncomfortable chair, trying to channel her mother, who excelled at being gracious to people she didn't like.

Tiana looked around the room and sniffed in distaste. "I never did like this room. Let's meet in the green parlor instead." She glanced at the empty table. "There's not even tea. Why are you playing dress up? I thought I said that you could no longer be together."

Steven nodded as if indicating for Noli to reply.

"This is a business meeting, not a social call, Your Majesty." Noli tried not to grit her teeth as she gestured to the empty chair. "Please, have a seat."

"Fine, I'll indulge your little charade." She sat. "Stiofán, you're in *so* much trouble. Taking the kingdom without permission." Tiana clucked her tongue. "What *will* your father say?"

Noli took her seat, anger at Tiana's words rippling through her. "He's dead. Brogan killed him. That's why I killed Brogan. That's right, *I* killed him, not V. Me. I killed Brogan and took the kingdom as an act of my love and devotion to V."

All the blood drained out of Tiana's face. That wasn't how

they were supposed to do things. Oh well. By her expression it was clear that the queen hadn't known of Mr. Darrow's demise, which offered some relief. But only some.

"Lies." The queen's face contorted. "All lies."

"No. They're not." V stood beside Noli, shoulders squared. "Uncle Brogan sent earth court guards to kill my father. Believe what you will—it doesn't actually matter to me."

Her eyes narrowed. "Is that any way to speak to your mother?"

V's eyes narrowed back. "This isn't why you're here."

"I'm here to see who overthrew Brogan, of course. Because the new king is *still* my loyal subject." She focused on V, ignoring Noli completely. "How exactly did you do it, Stiofán? Who were your witnesses? I hope it wasn't Ailís; she's too young for such things."

"I took it, not him," Noli interjected, trying to deflect the queen. "*I* killed him with *my* sword. V and James were my witnesses. This is *my* kingdom."

Tiana's eyes bulged, then she threw her head back, her laugh a tinny cackle. "How could a *sprite* take a kingdom? The Bright Lady would never allow it. You're so funny."

"I'm not a sprite anymore." Noli couldn't help but grin as she said that. "Also, my first act as queen is to make V my king." She looked up at V, smile widening.

"No, you don't have my permission." Tiana bristled, looking very out-of-sorts.

"I wasn't actually asking your permission, Your Majesty." Noli gentled her tone slightly. No good would come from angering the queen, but they couldn't afford to put themselves in any position where she might be able to tell them *no*. An order from the high queen must be obeyed.

Even by her.

"Don't you want me to be king...Mum?" V gave the queen a pleading look, the fake kind Noli often gave her own mother when trying to get her way.

The queen brightened like the afternoon sun. "You...you called me *Mum*."

"You *are* my mum. I love Noli. Believe or not, she took the kingdom—for *me*. I think you, of all people, could appreciate that." V squeezed Noli's hand and smiled at her. "We would very much like your blessing."

Noli could do without her blessing. The point was for the queen to *not* make their lives miserable.

The queen studied them, the corners of her blue eyes crinkling slightly. "I told you to break it off with her. This is disobedience."

"You told him to break the stone in my sigil, but you'd already given me to him," Noli reminded her. "We will be married and have the coronation simultaneously. We'll let you know when it is."

When in doubt, assume permission.

"My, you two are crafty." Tiana's hands folded into her lap, expression smug. "I didn't expect this from either of you. Certainly"—she looked down her nose at Noli—"I didn't expect *you* to be able to *take* a kingdom. You still must obey me. I *am* the high queen."

"Yes, Your Majesty. Though I am hoping we can come

to…agreements…peacefully." Noli repeated the words she'd been told to say. They were much more diplomatic than the ones she'd prefer to use.

"Is that a dare?" Tiana's eyes gleamed.

"Of course not, Your Majesty." But it was.

Tiana threw up her hands in motherly frustration. "Fine, you impulsive children. Take a kingdom. Get married. Go run your own lives. But don't come crying to me when things get hard."

It was difficult not to grin at the queen's outburst.

"We appreciate your blessing." V's voice remained tempered but his eyes danced in delight.

"Yes, indeed," Noli lied. Why was Tiana being so agreeable? Worry crept through her, but she'd ponder the queen's ulterior motives later.

For a moment Tiana looked young, innocent. "Is your father truly dead?"

V nodded. "He is. I'm sorry."

"I did love him, you know." She dropped her hands to her lap and stared at them.

Silence coated the room, the air fraught with emotion so heavy Noli feared suffocation.

The queen stood, shattering the moment as she fluffed her skirts. "You must come for tea soon so we can discuss everything. Bring Ailís. Is she staying with you or would you like me to care for her?"

"We'll let you know what we decide, your offer is kind," Noli replied. No. The queen wasn't getting Elise. At least she didn't know Ciarán had her—or order them to hand her over.

"Congratulations on achieving your dream, Stiofán." The way the queen said it made it sound of little consequence. "Magnolia, since you have no handmaidens, I'll lend you Breena and Nissa, they miss you. I know good help is hard to find."

Noli stood and shook her head. "Really, it's not necessary—"

"Tut, tut. You *must* have handmaidens. There's so much you have to learn, you poor dear backward girl. Don't worry, I'll *personally* help you." Her smile didn't reach her eyes.

"Really, Your Majesty, it's not—"

"No, no." She waved them off with her hand. "After all, you're part of the family now. It's the least I can do. Don't have your wedding tomorrow. Have it the day after. In the evening. Oh, and don't make me look bad." Without even a backward glance, the queen flounced out.

Noli counted to ten before blurting out, "What just happened?"

"She accepted us taking the kingdom, and our marriage, though now she thinks she'll actually be able to rule through us—which isn't allowed, and she won't like it when we remind her." V offered her a hand up. "You're getting two handmaidens, and we need to find the seneschal and let him know that Tiana requests that our wedding and coronation be moved up to the day after tomorrow."

She sighed, putting her head in her hand, elbow on the table. "That's what I thought happened."

"That went far better than it could have. Nicely done, Your Grace." V kissed her.

"I don't need a handmaiden." Not that she actually minded Nissa and Breena. "Or lessons on how to be queen from her. I'd rather eat gears."

"We're going to have to allow the loan of the handmaidens. After all, it's better to have the spies you know than the spies you don't. We'll work on the royal lessons."

"I really don't understand all this." She shook her head.

"You'll get used to it." He put an arm around her. "Now, for the difficult part. It's time for you to meet the great houses of the earth court."

• • • • • • • •

The air grew chilly and Elise wished she'd thought to bring her cape. Instead, she huddled closer to Aodhan. Thirst burned her throat. The wood faeries had been kind, bringing them berries and acorn caps filled with water. But there was just a sip in an acorn cap and she hated to burden them, since it was probably quite the trip for such little beings. She could leave Aodhan and find water, but she feared someone taking him away—like that man.

Instead, they waited. He told her all sorts of things about the Otherworld that she didn't know. In exchange, she told him about the mortal realm. It was proving difficult because he'd never seen flying cars or airships. Perhaps she could show him the way she showed things to wood faeries.

"Here's a flying auto. This one was the one Noli had before she and V broke it." She sent him the image, mentally, of Noli's blue-winged auto. "Can you see?"

He sucked in a breath. "And you *ride* in it? That's wondrous!"

"It takes you places, like a carriage without horses. There are also non-flying autos—and hoverboards. My brothers love to hoverboard." Elise showed him a mental picture of hoverboarding.

"I *want* one." He grinned. "Do you have one?"

She shook her head. "Girls don't hoverboard, silly. Though Noli does sometimes. But she's different."

"How?" His face screwed up.

"My father says she's not a proper girl. That's why he doesn't like her spending time with us. I suppose it's because she likes to do things boys do and her family is poor." Elise shrugged, not really understanding what that had to do with anything. "But she's always nice to me. I hope she becomes my sister. I've always wanted one."

"I miss my father," Aodhan sighed.

"I miss my father too, and Quinn. He takes care of me and teaches me things." She looked up at the darkening sky, going from pink to a dusky purple. "I hope they come soon."

He put his head on her shoulder. "Perhaps you should return to the house and get help."

"I don't want to leave you—they'll come." They had to.

They sat in silence for a long time with only the little faeries for company. The green faery, the one she'd sent for help, came barreling toward them, chattering so fast she couldn't understand.

"Elise," James called in the distance. "Elise, where are you?"

"James, James, over here," she yelled. Hope swelled inside her.

Her brother stood over them, a rucksack over his shoulders. His eyebrows rose. "You can get out of *that*."

"But Aodhan can't. I . . . I didn't want to leave him." She pulled him closer. "He's hurt."

"Oh, hello there." James peered at them through the darkness and waved. "All right, let's get you out." He set down the rucksack.

Elise scrambled out and helped James hoist Aodhan out of the hole.

"Can you walk?" James asked as he helped him stand, arm around his waist.

Gritting his teeth, Aodhan took a tentative step, winced, and shook his head.

"Hold this." James handed Elise his rucksack.

Its weight made her sink as she slung it over her shoulder. "What's in it? Rocks?"

"Steven's books." He rolled his eyes. "Up you go." James put Aodhan on his back and took Elise's hand.

Elise looked up at her brother. He looked . . . different, but she couldn't quite place it. "I appreciate you coming for us."

"I'm glad Steven sent me back to get his dumb books. Otherwise we might not return for days." He squeezed her hand.

She looked at the holes in the ground. "What are those for?"

His shoulders sank a little. "Do you remember Aunt Dinessa?"

Elise shook her head. "No."

"Well...she..." He inhaled and exhaled. "She died this morning."

Elise put a hand to her mouth. "That's horrible. What happened?"

Even though she couldn't remember, it was still a dreadful thing.

"It...it was an accident." James' face crumpled a little as he gave it a long glance. "I always liked Aunt Dinessa. She was fun."

"It's a *grave*?" Even though her mother had died, she didn't remember any of it.

He nodded and gulped as they walked.

"What about the other empty one?" She looked back at it.

"That one...I...I'm sorry Elise." He squeezed her hand. "That one's for Quinn."

"Quinn?" She put a hand to her chest as if it could keep her heart from breaking. "But...but I was just with him. He...he told me to run. Oh." Her shoulders slumped. "The men who were chasing after us...they got him, didn't they?" Tears streamed down her face.

James pulled her close as they made their way through the maze. "Quinn died protecting you."

All she could do was cry. Quinn was gone. Who would love her and take care of her now?

"Don't cry." Aodhan's hand stroked her golden curls. "It'll be all right."

"What will I do without him?" she hiccupped. He taught

her, cared for her, played with her. While everyone else went about their lives, she knew that he'd always be there.

James shook his head. "We'll manage."

"The filled-in one … is that Mother's?" She gave it a wary glance.

"Nooo." James made one of those faces that meant he was hiding something. "We … we'll talk about it later."

Later usually meant *never*. "But I want to know," she pouted.

"Later. Right now we have to help your friend here. Who is he?"

"I'm Aodhan," Aodhan replied. "My father runs a tavern— the Thirsty Pooka in the Blackwoods."

"His uncle is Noli's friend, the one with the tree house. Kevighn," Elise added.

"Is he now? It's nice to meet you," James replied.

They emerged from the maze and walked in a direction different from where Elise and Aodhan had come from.

"Where are we going?" Elise asked.

"To V and Noli. We'll fix Aodhan there. I'm not much of a healer," James replied. "Aodhan are you in a lot of pain? Should I do something about it?"

Aodhan shook his head. "I'm fine."

Elise knew he wasn't. She also knew, growing up with Steven and James, that this was a boy game, pretending it didn't hurt when it actually did.

They walked and walked, then took a portal. Then they walked some more. They came to an area filled with giant trees. Men in green and gold watched them. James pulled out his sigil so it showed and they didn't bother them.

"James, we're supposed to keep them hidden," Elise whispered.

"In Los Angeles, but not here. I…" He looked at her. "Someone will explain everything."

Her jaw jutted out. "You *always* say that and no one ever does."

"This time someone will, promise." James smiled and squeezed her hand. "I'll need you to tell me everything, too, but not now…later."

"An exchange?" Something was going on and for once she wanted to know what it was.

"Yes."

"Look at this, Elise," Aodhan breathed.

Before them was an enormous tree, as big…no bigger… than a mansion. In it was a house…no…a castle—made *entirely* of trees. A grand tree castle, with turrets and a moat.

"Where are we, James?" It looked a little…familiar.

James patted her shoulder. "This is the earth court palace."

FIFTEEN

A Step Behind

Kevighn frowned as he followed Ciarán's sigil dangerously close to the earth court palace. This wasn't good. The only thing worse would be if Aodhan and Elise were at the high palace itself. He'd spent the day on a wild goose chase, one step behind the children. He'd finally tracked them to the House of Oak, only to be redirected *here*.

Ever since he'd left Magnolia in San Francisco, he was always a shade too late. Too late to properly kill Quinn. Too late for the gem. Too late to find her. Too late to get the children.

A heavy sigh slipped from his lips. How much closer dare he creep? The palace came into view through the tall trees. There seemed to be something happening, people coming and going from the giant tree-palace. Their demeanor seemed too somber for it to be a party.

"Halt. State your business." The point of a sword pricked Kevighn's back.

Earth court guards always were sneaky buggers, not to mention he *was* creeping through a forest.

Kevighn held up his hands and turned around. "I'm Kevighn, emissary for the dark king."

"And you're here because?" The sword didn't waver.

"Same as everyone else." He gestured to the palace, trying to bluff his way in.

"Nice try. Come back in two days." The guard poked him with his sword. Bushes rustled and Kevighn had a feeling more guards had joined him.

"Ah, but you see, the dark king insists." What *was* going on? Perhaps someone there knew what had happened with the magic earlier.

One of the others emerged from the growth and grabbed his wrists. "Earth court only. Come back in two days."

The guards frog-marched him to the palace borders.

The one with the sword gave him a shove. "If I see you again we won't be so nice."

Defeat echoed in every step as he slunk toward the nearest public portal. There was nothing left to do besides tell Ciarán. *Two days*. He'd return and steal the children back then.

What if they hurt Aodhan? The urge to tear into the palace and take his nephew by force surged through him.

It all depended on who had the children and that required information. Hopefully if Ciarán didn't already have it, he could obtain it—quickly.

Also, what *was* happening in two days and what had

occurred with the magic? Was it connected? It felt a bit like when Tiana had become queen. It would be nice if Tiana was dead, though that probably hadn't happened.

The Thirsty Pooka teemed with young women. Ciarán sat at the bar speaking with them one at a time. Kevighn watched as some were sent away and others were told to wait at a table. Curious.

"Is it ladies' night, old friend?" Kevighn braced for the backlash that would happen when he told the dark king that his son was being held by the earth court.

"As qualified as you are, I specified earth court or someone who can pass." Ciarán waved on a girl with blue-white hair. "A moment if you please," he told the waiting ladies. He and Kevighn walked to a corner of the bustling tavern. "I'm interviewing handmaidens."

"Why?" Kevighn eyed the girls, some of them very comely.

"A gift for the queen. Now … please tell me you found them." His eyes gleamed, not with anger … but worry. Aodhan brought out the dark king's softer side.

"I found them, but I didn't bring them back." Kevighn braced himself. "I … I'm afraid they're in the earth court palace."

Ciarán's eyes flashed. "Of course they are."

"There's something happening in two days, something you're invited to. I would say that would be the time to retrieve them, but I can't help but worry about how they're being treated. Especially Aodhan." The boy was all he had left of his sister, his family.

Ciarán shook his head. "You told me that she was

uncommon, but I thought you were being a romantic fool. When I met with her I didn't appreciate her craftiness even though she has the stone. Somehow she's managed to acquire both children and probably whatever pieces of the artifact Brogan already possessed. I truly hope you mean it when you say she'll be our ally, because I'd hate to be foes with someone so cunning and canny. And with her connections to the high queen—"

"Who and what are you talking about? None of this makes sense." What did it have to do with all these young girls? Kevighn's neck practically snapped as a redhead walked by.

"Stop looking at them. They're not for you." Ciarán moved in front of him, blocking his view. "I was speaking of Magnolia. I had no idea she was that clever."

"What about Magnolia?" He craned his neck. So many lovelies.

"Remember when you felt something amiss with the magic?"

Kevighn rubbed his gut in remembrance. "What of it?"

"Today Magnolia *took* the earth court. I knew she kept company with earth court princes who sought the throne, but never would I have seen this coming." His hooded face filled with awe. "I know taking one of the elemental courts is different from when you helped me take the dark court, but still. She's a girl. A young girl. I know enough about elemental court politics to know she at least had to kill Brogan with a sword. Brogan's an excellent swordsman."

"Well, that prat was in charge of the king's guard before

he took the throne," Kevighn replied. Stupid earth court princes and their stupid swords. "Wait. Did you just say *Magnolia* took the throne? Not that whelp of an earth court prince, but *Magnolia*?" His little blossom had *taken* the court? "But that means..."

"It means she's officially out of your league." The dark king's look dared.

"What if I act as intelligence? I could spy on the court for you..." Could he bring himself to spy on her?

Ciarán gestured to the waiting girls. "I have people in court, but I want to get someone close to her. Hence, trying to find someone who could pass as a lady's maid."

"Don't bother; she has no patience for silly girls." Kevighn shook his head, mind reeling. "She's *queen*? In her own right?"

She was smart, clever, strong, oh, she was strong. But to *take* a kingdom?

"Yes. She's holding court with her subjects right now. The coronation's in two days."

Kevighn blinked. "I never did understand the custom of throwing a party after you take a kingdom. It seems like part taunting, part allowing your enemies to observe you closely." He couldn't stop his mind from racing. Magnolia was queen. It would be difficult but maybe...

"Kevighn, it's *over*." Ciarán put his hands on Kevighn's shoulders. "She's marrying that prince. She never was for the likes of you anyway. You *know* this. You've *always* known this."

He took a step backward, something in him crumbling.

There was truth to his old friend's words. Part of it was the hunt, infatuation. Still, he didn't like to lose.

"He's going to end up killing her just like Quinn killed Creideamh," Kevighn protested.

"She's *not* Creideamh." Ciarán shook him so hard his head rattled. "What do I have to do to convince you? Stop living in the past. Embrace what you have." He sighed. "I don't have time for this. Do you think Magnolia will hurt Aodhan?"

That question caused him to pause. "No. I don't think she'll hurt anyone."

Ciarán shrugged. "She killed Brogan."

"He deserved it." He raked his fingers through his hair. "If she's queen, hurting Aodhan will start a war. That's probably not how she wishes to begin her reign. Couldn't you send a missive monarch to monarch and work something out?"

"She's not going to *give* me Aodhan. Even if she will, I'm sure the prince or someone else won't allow it. Aodhan's too valuable." Ciarán shook his head. "She has the jewel, she's the queen, she has Elise, what could I give her? I'm not ready or willing to give her the pieces of the staff I've acquired."

Kevighn thought about what he knew of Noli. "The queen did turn her into a sprite..."

He waved his hand. "My reports show she's a sprite no longer. Something happened—something big, though what I'm not sure. Also, would the Bright Lady truly permit a sprite to be queen?"

"True." How *had* she managed that? "Ah! Magnolia's

father got lost in the Otherworld. If you could find him or anything regarding him…"

"He's probably dead. We should just steal Aodhan back in two days. But we'll send someone on it anyway, who knows when the information might prove useful."

"It would make her happy." Kevighn knew she wanted him back…

Ciarán smacked him. "Snap out of it."

"Ow." He stepped closer to Ciarán. "Why do you care so much?"

"Why do you think?"

Kevighn's heart caught in his throat; this was all too much. He turned, every part of his body screaming for him to flee.

A hand grabbed his wrist, but it wasn't rough. "Don't run. By the Bright Lady, don't run again." Ciarán's voice went raw, and so many things Kevighn wasn't ready to see lurked in his amber eyes.

Ciarán sighed, still holding onto his wrist. "Look, why don't you help me choose a girl to send to her, then we'll have a few drinks and figure out how to get Aodhan back."

Kevighn closed his eyes and opened them again. That look remained on Ciarán's face. He still wasn't quite ready to deal with these old feelings. They weren't unwelcome, but acknowledging them meant putting this life aside. For good.

Instead, he nodded. "Yes. Let's go look at pretty girls and then get very, very drunk."

SIX+EEN

Elise's Return

Steven put his arm around Noli as they walked up the stairs in the private wing of the earth court palace, their audience with the nobles finished.

Noli rubbed her temples. "That didn't go too badly. Did it?"

"It was fine. We have to expect a little chaos, all things considered." Like Noli not being from a great house. Like only his presence keeping some of the lords from taking her down right there. Like not looking as if he were taking over while simultaneously not revealing Noli's ignorance of their ways, which proved to be beyond difficult. He had a newfound appreciation for statesmanship.

If only his father were there to talk to. As Machiavelli would say, "*The more sand has escaped from the hourglass of our life, the clearer we should see through it.*"

His father would have been *livid* that Noli had managed to take the kingdom, but perhaps the act would have shown him that she was worthy of his respect.

Two guards stood in front of a double set of doors. One opened the door when they approached.

Steven led her inside, giving her a kiss. "Welcome home, Your Grace."

"Where are we?" Noli looked around the large front parlor.

"The royal suite. This will be our home when we're at the palace. For now we're going to be spending a lot of time here. There's a lot to do." The doors closed silently behind them.

Noli sunk down into a settee. "What did I do, V?" Her voice choked a little as she put her head in her hands, elbows on her knees. "The nobles hate me. I think that big guy is going to murder me in my sleep."

"Lord Adair always secretly wanted the throne. It's going to be difficult. But we can do this together." Steven sat, putting an arm around her shoulders, trying to comfort her. He didn't like to see her upset, but at the same time, this was something they'd have to deal with—and succeed at. No matter what.

"You can have it. I … I don't know if I can do this." She closed her eyes.

He bundled her into his arms. "Noli, I want nothing more than to do all this for you. These are my people; I know them. I understand statecraft. I can do a lot, but I can't do everything for you."

"Why?" Her face was buried in his chest.

"Because this is your kingdom now. If you relinquish it to me, it makes you look weak, which makes you a target. However, at the same time, using my knowledge and expertise makes you look wise. We'll have to balance everything carefully."

Already, he'd been approached by three houses besides his own who'd sought assurance that he was the real power behind the throne. Part of him wanted to say *yes*. He wanted to be the true king, and he knew that Noli would allow it.

But he also knew that wouldn't be right.

In the end, he'd assured the nobles that everything would be fine. This was going to be difficult. However, failing wasn't an option.

She sat up. "Can we eat supper now? I've barely eaten all day."

"I can get you something. What do you want, cake?" Miri, the sprite, emerged from another part of the suite.

Noli jumped, surprise crossing her face. "What are you doing here?"

"I'm your handmaiden; I was getting everything set up for you." She smiled. "I'll get you some food."

"Miri, find a maid and *they'll* get the food," he said gently. Two of them to teach. "Why don't you have someone send up supper and see if James has returned?"

She nodded and left.

"Handmaiden? I now have *three sprites* as handmaidens?" Noli's eyebrows rose.

"We'll give them plenty to do," he assured her, sensing

her panic. "After supper we need to meet with Bran, Elric, and Padraig."

"I don't want to meet with anyone. I'm hungry, tired, and I want a bath. Oh, all my things are still at the big house. I don't suppose you sent James to get them? And the piece of the artifact, that should be here with the others. Are you certain the things are safe?" She pulled her knees to her chest and rested her head on them, her back leaning against him.

"Yes, James retrieved it, and yes, they're safe. I don't think he got any of our personal things. Not yet. We're still in survival mode." His arm wrapped around her. "We've met with the houses, but we have the audience tomorrow for the general subjects, not to mention you need to be prepared to meet with the different court leaders, we have to go over the coronation procedures, and you must be briefed on what's happening in the earth court and the Otherworld. Tomorrow, in addition to the public audience with your general subjects, you're meeting with the seneschal to go over protocol—"

"So many meetings." Unhappiness dripped from her voice.

"Yes. There are a lot of meetings. We'll meet regularly with Bran, Elric, and Padraig—daily in the beginning, perhaps even more. We'll often meet with the houses, as a group and individually. There will be regular audiences to hear grievances from your subjects. Sometimes you'll meet with other leaders, other groups, we'll also throw parties. There's a bit of a season here, too. Though we have a little time before that starts."

"There is?" Her head popped up and she made a face. "I suppose people have to get married somehow."

"At least we don't have to go through it." He planted a kiss on her temple. "It will be *fine*." How would they manage? It had been less than a day and already she was falling apart. There was no time for weakness.

"Yes, we will, and soon we'll go to university. I suppose we'll return every other weekend to take care of things?" She brightened.

"Noli … "

Her face fell at his words. "What?"

"Never mind." He didn't have the heart to tell her that she'd dashed their dreams of going to a mortal university. She'd bound herself to the land. Never again would she return to the mortal realm for more than a visit. Noli belonged to the Otherworld now.

The door flew open and James walked in—and he wasn't alone.

Happiness overwhelmed him.

"Steven." Dirt smudged Elise's face and dress as she flung herself at him.

Standing, he picked her up and swung her around. "Elise, you're safe."

"Why did you leave me?" Elise looked at Noli with hurt-filled eyes.

Noli stood and hugged her. "They wouldn't let me take you, but never mind, you're here now."

Steven looked at James. This was beyond unexpected, but welcome. "How?"

"They were at the big house. But this one's hurt." James set the blond boy on his back in one of the chairs. "This is Aodhan."

"He's my friend," Elise explained.

"I'm fine." Aodhan gazed at them with wide yellow eyes.

"Except for the fact you can't walk." James shook his head. "Steven, will you help me? Oh, I guess you're just Stio, now?"

Noli shook her head. "I'm not calling you Stiofán."

"Why?" Not that Steven minded, but James had a point. It was time to put their mortal names aside, at least while in this realm.

"Someone has to keep you honest." She grinned.

"Stiofán." Elise frowned at him. "You only get called that when you're bad."

Ah, yes, this would be difficult.

"It's my real name. Just like James is Séamus and you are Ailís."

Her eyebrows rose as if she didn't quite believe him. "What's Noli's real name?"

"Magnolia." Another thing against her in the eyes of the royals. It was such an obviously mortal name.

Elise rolled her eyes in a way that reminded him of James. "I *know*. Her other real name."

"That's all the name she has." Maybe they should give her one so she'd fit in better.

Steven turned to Aodhan. "Let's take a look, shall we?"

Who was he and where did she find him?

He watched as James scanned the boy's leg. As much as

James said he wasn't, he truly was better at this. His time with Charlotte had made him very good at things like scans, minor healing, and taking away pain.

"I think it's just a bad sprain," James told him. "Second opinion?"

"Show me how." Noli crouched down next to him.

Noli's lack of magical knowledge was something else he'd have to work on.

"Not now." Steven brushed it off. The less people knew about her ignorance, the better. How quickly could he turn her into the ideal queen? If she were perfect then people would realize that they should be as honored to have her as a queen as he was to have her for his wife.

"Oh." Her face fell.

"What are you doing?" Elise peered at them, forehead furrowing.

"Why don't the two of you go do something," Steven replied, anxious for Elise to be off. "But don't go far, Noli, we still have to meet with everyone."

"Fine." Noli took Elise's hand and marched out of the room without a backward glance.

• • • • • • • •

"Are you hungry?" Noli led Elise into the next room. It reminded her a little of the queen's tearoom at the high palace. Oh yes—this would have been Tiana's sitting room, back when high queen was merely the queen of the earth court.

Did she get to redecorate?

Elise nodded. "Yes, and thirsty. So is Aodhan." She looked around the room. "I don't remember this place."

"Ask your brothers about it." Noli didn't know what else to say. She plopped down at the small, round table. "When Miri returns we'll have her bring supper for everyone. Maybe we can find you a new dress."

Elise also sat down at the table. "All my things are at the restaurant. The one Aodhan's father runs."

"Aodhan's father?" Noli recalled their encounter at the Thirsty Pooka.

She nodded. "Your friend Kevighn is his uncle."

"Kevighn is his uncle, but his father runs a restaurant..." Noli was trying to make sense off all this. Yes, that was why he looked familiar. This was Ciarán's son, the one who'd saved her with his bow that night at the Thirsty Pooka.

"That's not his real father. Aodhan's parents are gone," she added.

Noli sucked in a breath. Aodhan had Quinn's coloring and Kevighn's eyes ... was he perhaps Creideamh's child, who for some reason had been hidden away in the dark court?

The idea boggled the mind. But most importantly, she had possession of a boy who Ciarán called "son" and Kevighn called "nephew." How many pieces of the staff did the dark king have? Surely the boy would be worth all of them. This had possibilities.

Elise looked around the sitting room. "Where do I sleep here?"

Noli's head, heavy with fatigue, rested in her hand, elbow

on the table. "I'm not even sure where *I* sleep. We'll ask Miri. Are you all right? Did anyone hurt you?"

"Of course not. Aodhan's father is quite nice, and Uncle Kevighn is teaching me to use a bow and arrow." Elise's chest puffed with pride.

Uncle Kevighn? Oh, V would love that.

"I think I'd like to learn to shoot a bow," Noli told her.

The door opened and part of her deflated when Miri walked in, not V.

"Supper's on the way." Miri looked at Elise. "Hello, I'm Miri."

"I'm Elise. It's nice to meet you." Elise yawned. "Supper sounds splendid."

"Miri, can you please tell the kitchens or whomever you asked about supper to send it for five, not two? We found James and Elise." Noli suppressed a yawn of her own.

Miri's honey-colored head bobbed. "Good, perhaps we can play tea party later."

"Oh, I'd like that." Elise stifled a yawn. "Perhaps tomorrow. I'm quite tired."

"She'll need a place to sleep. Also, her friend Aodhan is staying with us a few days. He'll need a place to sleep as well." Her belly rumbled. Couldn't Miri have brought her a snack? Also, she wanted to be far, far away when they played tea party, but the two of them occupying each other would be a good thing, indeed.

"Her room is the girl's room, isn't it?" Miri's head cocked to one side. "And James' room is one of the boy rooms? Aodhan can stay in the other boy room since you and V will be staying together in the big room." She gave a satisfied nod. "Yes, I'll make sure all the rooms are clean since I think they only fixed up one boy room for James."

It took a moment for Miri's rapid-fire chatter to permeate her brain, which currently had the consistency of cold treacle. Right—this was their family apartment, and James, V, and Elise all had rooms here, just like at the big house.

"There's a bathing tub." Miri's eyes went wide. "It's sooo big." Her hands stretched out to indicate it, nearly smacking Noli in the head in the process. "After supper, would you like a bath?"

"That sounds heavenly. Oh." Noli drooped. "I have a meeting after supper."

"After that, but before you sleep. I'm finding you clothes and things." Miri stayed chipper and upbeat, and it was a little difficult to not smile.

"I think I'll need that bath after the meeting." Possibly cake.

"What about my things?" Elise asked. "Also, may I have a bath before bed? And a story?"

Miri looked her up and down, then tapped her finger to her chin. "I think I can do that. All of that. Noli, I...I mean, Your Grace, would you like me to help Miss Elise get ready for bed while you're in the meeting?"

Elise's head bobbed as if she *wanted* Miri to help her.

Gah. Hunger was making her grumpy. Miri was a kind, gentle, helpful person. Actually, this would be a good task for her.

"Please? It would be helpful to me if you would see to Elise as part of your duties."

Miri beamed. "I like to be helpful. Oh, should I have our friends help? I'm so happy you brought them to visit. Perhaps tomorrow we can all play Mintonette. Elise can play with us." She clapped as she said that, eyes dancing with joy.

Friends? Oh. "Breena and Nissa? Yes, they can help you as long as everything I need gets done. But you're in charge, so you can decide who does what."

"I can do that?" Miri's giant honey eyes blinked once, then twice.

Noli put a hand on Miri's shoulder. It was so strange to see her instead of just hearing her. "Of course you can, you're capable of more than you think."

She'd always come through when she needed her to. Miri beamed at the praise.

"What's Mintonette?" Elise cocked her head. "Is it a game? I do love games."

"Oh, it's a wonderful game." Miri clapped her hands under her chin and did a little dance. "We'll teach you tomorrow."

Personally, Noli hated Mintonette—especially the way they played it in the Otherworld.

"Miri, will you make sure they bring supper for everyone now?" Noli prodded before she and Elise chattered on about nonsense all evening. Yes, the two of them should get on quite well.

"Of course." Miri gave an awkward curtsey and left.

"Who's she? I like her," Elise asked.

"She's my handmaiden. They're like nursemaids for grown-up girls," Noli replied at Elise's confused look.

"What?" Elise giggled, putting a hand to her lips.

Noli shrugged. There was really no better way to explain it to a child. "They are. They make sure you eat, fix your hair, help you dress, keep you from getting into trouble, and amuse you when you're bored. Miri is a very good hair-braider, and tells silly stories."

"I like stories." She yawned again.

"Elise? Only use earth magic around Nissa and Breena, all right? Actually, on second thought, only use earth magic at all unless you're with James, V, or me, and if no one else is around. It's very important." The last thing she wanted was for Elise to be in danger—or someone telling the queen of her abilities.

"I understand. It's like when we are in the mortal realm then?" Her voice went glum.

"For now. But you can use earth magic all you like."

"Who will teach me magic now that Quinn's…" Elise's lower lip quivered and her eyelashes fluttered as she tried not to cry.

Noli pulled Elise into her arms. Was it her, or had Elise gotten smaller? "I need a magic tutor, too, so perhaps we can learn together?"

It was sad that a little girl knew more magic than she did.

Elise titled her head up and blinked, a look of hurt on her face, lower lip still quivering. "I didn't know you had magic."

With a heavy sigh, Noli toyed with the little girl's hair.

"I didn't always. Now I do, and I have to learn how to use it. But we'll find you a tutor and whatever else you need."

She frowned. "We're staying here?"

"For now." Sending her back to the mortal realm still seemed like the best option, but there was too much going on to think about that right now.

A maid walked in with a tray; she set it on the table and bobbed a curtsy. "Your supper, Your Grace. The rest will be up shortly."

Noli's stomach gurgled in happiness as she appraised the awaiting feast, complete with dessert. "I appreciate all this. You may go."

The maid left.

Elise looked at the food. "This is for us?"

Noli poured a cup of tea, took a sip, and let out a happy sigh. "Yes, the boys can eat later."

....

"Noli, are you even paying attention?" V half-snapped.

Noli wriggled in the uncomfortable chair in what V called the "war room"—a small room with a round table and maps on the walls and shelves filled to overflowing with books and scrolls. There were no windows, and the dim light only enhanced the sleepy feeling brought on by a full stomach and a long day.

"My apologies," she muttered, trying not to yawn. "It's been a long day and I didn't sleep last night."

"The queen doesn't need to apologize." Padraig gave her

a fond smile, green eyes gleaming, as he patted her arm with a gnarled hand. "I think we all feel that way right now."

Out of her new advisors, she liked the elderly Padraig best. She'd never seen one of the fae that old before, if his hunched form and long, white hair were any indication of age.

"But there's so much to do before the audience tomorrow. If the coronation is the day after tomorrow, they'll need to be briefed on the other courts." Elric, the chancellor, held up a list.

Bran waved his hand; he was a nondescript, quiet man who seemed very good at fading into the background. "It can wait until morning."

Elric harumphed. From the moment Noli met him she understood why V trusted him. He and V were a lot alike in personality. While she'd put her faith in V, Elric's appearance reminded her far too much of Mr. Darrow for her own comfort. Apparently they were related.

"I say we forget to invite the other courts." Padraig's blue eyes twinkled.

"If only we could," Noli muttered. The high queen would find fault with everything, she was sure. Over the years she'd heard newly married girls speak of their horrific mother-in-laws. She was about to get the worst of the lot.

"I think Elric's right," V agreed. "We should probably—"

"I'm *old*," Padraig mock-grumped. "Old and tired and these bones need rest. We can reconvene at breakfast, if that's satisfactory." He shot her a look.

"That sounds perfect to me. We'll adjourn tonight and meet here tomorrow for breakfast," Noli replied before V or

Elric could get a word in edgewise. Hot tea would make these meetings more bearable.

"Noli, I don't think—" V's lips puckered. "You're right, Your Grace. We'll adjourn until the morning." Unhappiness tinged his voice. But he'd gotten more sleep than she had.

Padraig leaned in and whispered, "Don't let them push you around." He stood and announced, "I'm going to sleep. This has been quite the adventure today."

Noli stood too, anxious to find that hot bath Miri had promised. A snack wouldn't go amiss either. She looked at V, who had his head bowed over Elric's infernal list while deep in conference with the chancellor. "V, are you coming?"

Still examining the list, V waved his hand. "I'll be there soon."

"All right then." She exited the room and looked around. How did she get back?

"If I may, Your Grace?" Bran arrived at her side, standing not much taller than she. "You shouldn't be wandering about by yourself. Tomorrow you'll have proper bodyguards."

Bodyguards? *Inside* the palace? But some of those great houses did seem to want her dead. "Yes, of course."

They walked in silence through the quiet palace halls.

"Your Grace, exactly what are your plans for the dark king's son?" His voice was soft but matter-of-fact.

Her eyes bulged and it took her a moment to pull herself together. "Who?"

"It's my job to know what happens in the palace—and your kingdom. Now, what are your plans for the boy?" Bran asked. There was something in his brown eyes that made her think twice about underestimating him.

"Ciarán has something I want. But I won't harm the boy." She kept her voice quiet.

"A trade, I see. Is the dark king aware of what you desire?" he prodded.

"Yes." Noli wasn't ready to tell anyone about the artifact, but Ciarán would figure out what she wanted. How close were they to having all the pieces?

He nodded, stroking his chin. "Have there been any... negotiations?"

"No. But since he's coming in two days, that's as good time as ever for the trade, isn't it?" A bit of uncertainty crept into her voice.

Bran inclined his head. "Perhaps. We can discuss this more tomorrow. I just wanted to be aware of your... intentions."

She saw they were nearly at the guarded double doors marking her private chambers.

"Of course. He's safe and taken care of. We can send him a missive if you think it would help," she offered.

Bran gave her another nod, but didn't reply to her question. "Be careful as to what you allow those handmaidens of the high queen's to see. Also, don't be surprised if other households and courts gift you with servants. You must accept Tiana's without question, but you might be *particular* about where other servants are placed."

More spies.

"That's good advice. Now, what exactly is your position here in the palace?" she asked.

A smile crept across his thin lips. "Why, I should think it would be obvious."

The uniformed guard opened the door to her chambers. Bran bowed. "Until tomorrow, Your Grace."

"Until tomorrow." She entered and the double doors closed behind her. Later she'd ask V what Bran did. Right now, she'd find Miri and that hot bath.

....

Ahh. Just what she needed. Noli allowed the scented bubbles to envelop her as she slid into the steaming water. Miri hadn't exaggerated about the size of the bathing tub, which resembled a woodland pond, complete with living greenery around it.

Closing her eyes, she allowed the heat to soothe everything away. How was she going to do this? Why did she have to be so impulsive?

Like the day she'd taken the Pixy out for a joyride, today was a day she regretted.

The door flew open.

"Noli, you should be in bed. You *said* you were too tired to continue." Annoyance dripped from V's voice. "If you weren't tired, you shouldn't have ended the meeting."

She was tempted to flash him one of Jeff's favorite rude gestures, but instead she kept her eyes closed. "In case you've forgotten, I didn't get any sleep last night."

"If you hadn't run off to meet with Silver, you would have," he scolded.

Her eyes snapped open. "Last night I didn't sleep because I was trying to get your sister back. Now, will you allow me to bathe in peace? Please?" Noli's voice cracked a little, not liking how he was still holding that against her.

V's entire being fell. "You're ... you're right. Enjoy your bath, you deserve some quiet."

The door closed and she closed her eyes again. She stayed there warm and happy until the water cooled and the door opened again.

"Would you like me to help you out now?" Miri bubbled.

Noli opened her eyes and saw Miri standing there with a giant towel and a silken robe. She yawned. "Please. If I stay in here any longer I'm going to fall asleep."

Miri dressed her in a nightdress and braided her hair. Yes, handmaidens were nursemaids for grown-up girls. But they were also quite helpful when you were too tired to do things yourself.

"Do you need anything else?" Miri inquired.

"No, and you should go to bed, too. You've had a long day yourself." Noli yawned.

"I like Elise." Miri smiled. "She's sleeping now."

"Oh, I should check on her ... and Aodhan." It seemed like the right thing to do. She followed Miri to the opposite end of the cavernous suite.

"She's right here." Miri pressed a finger to her lips as she pushed open a door.

The room was reminiscent of Elise's room at the big house, only the four-poster bed had a canopy and curtains. There were no paintings of butterflies or flowers covering the walls. In the middle of the enormous bed lay a small, blond girl in a ruffled nightdress, a doll clutched tightly in her arms as she slept.

"I used my magic to make clothes fit her." Miri glowed with pride. "Nissa and Breena had *no idea* we can do that."

"You're so good at it, too." Quietly, Noli tiptoed over and pulled the blanket over Elise, taking a moment to trace her fingers over the little girl's downy cheek. Then, closing the door behind her, she returned to the hallway where Miri still stood.

"Where's Aodhan?" Noli looked up and down the hallway. Even here the walls, floors, and ceiling were made of polished wood. It was like she'd imagine it would be inside a knothole—a very posh knothole, where even Grandfather Montgomery would come to tea.

Miri grabbed her hand and led her to another room. As soon as she opened the door, Noli knew this room was once V's. Books lined the walls, with several missing, their empty spaces reminding her of a gap-toothed grin. Everything was in greens and browns, simple, clean, and utilitarian, yet elegant. Well, if men's things could be called *elegant*.

Aodhan lay in the grand but canopy-less bed. He looked so vulnerable. Innocent.

No, she'd never hurt him. None of this was his fault. She'd return him to his family as soon as possible.

His eyes fluttered open. "Oh, hello again, Noli."

"Hello, Aodhan." She leaned against the doorway, a little embarrassed since she was in a nightdress and dressing gown. "Are you feeling better?"

Aodhan got up on his elbow. "Much. Will I go home tomorrow? I think my father will be worried about me."

"It will probably be the day after, but I'll make sure he knows you're here." If he didn't already. Also, she wouldn't be surprised if Kevighn tried to steal the boy back at some point. She should tell V. It wouldn't do to have Aodhan taken before she'd gotten the other pieces of the artifact from his father.

"Will..." Aodhan frowned. "Will Elise stay here?"

The sadness in his voice made her heart wrench. "She should be with her family, just as you should be with yours."

Lips pressing together, the boy nodded slowly. "Perhaps we can play sometime?"

Noli bit back the words *but of course.* Could they, with Aodhan being who he was? But then again, if his father had been Quinn, wouldn't that make it all right? However, were people supposed to know that? If they did, would it endanger the boy in some way? Obviously, there were reasons Aodhan had been hidden in the dark court and didn't simply join Quinn in exile in the mortal realm.

Instead, she plastered on the same half-smile her mother did when trying to not exactly lie while not telling the entire truth. "We shall see. In the meantime, you should go back to sleep."

Noli closed the door, surprised to see Miri waiting for her.

"Do you want to tuck James in, as well?" Miri gave her an innocent look.

She stifled a laugh at the idea. "No, James can tuck himself in."

"Oh." Miri just stood there.

"Go to bed." Noli yawned. "I can find my own room." Hopefully.

"Let me show you." Miri took her hand and led her to her bedchamber. "Good night."

"Good night." Opening the door she slipped inside the dark room. Bed at last. She kicked off her slippers and climbed into bed.

Arms wrapped around her. "There you are."

Noli rolled over and gazed at V, stifling a gasp of surprise. She hadn't expected him to be done with his meetings.

V pulled her to him, so that her head lay on his chest. "Let's go to sleep, Noli. We have a busy day ahead of us tomorrow."

Sleep. Yes, sleeping in his arms sounded splendid.

"Do you regret all this?" she whispered.

V gave her a long and smoldering kiss. "Not for a moment. Good night, Noli. I love you."

Noli got cozy under the blankets, using V as a pillow. She could hear his heart thumping in his chest. The sound was comforting. "Good night, V. I love you too."

A Hunting We Will Go

Kevighn's head pounded. He opened his eyes and stared at an unfamiliar ceiling. What had happened? He rolled over, half-expecting to see some strange female sleeping beside him.

The bed was empty, and he remembered that he was at Ciarán's.

Last night's events came back to him as he sat up and rubbed his head. Yes, last night, after learning his fair blossom was lost to him forever, he'd gotten *very* drunk. Stretching, he padded out of bed. Ciarán always knew the best remedies for hangovers.

Ciarán's room was empty, as was his office. At this time of the morning the tavern was closed. The smell of baking bread wafted from the kitchens. He found Ciarán sitting on a stool in the kitchen at the small table in the corner, like an ordinary man. Mug in hand, he hunched over something, frowning.

"So serious so early?" Kevighn plopped down on the stool next to him, head pounding.

Ciarán set the paper in his hands in front of Kevighn. "She wants to trade Aodhan for our pieces of the artifact."

He read the missive, written in Magnolia's own neat but girlish hand. It was succinct and polite.

"Did you expect any less?" he replied.

Ciarán turned the mug around in his hands and sighed. "No."

"Do you have any intention of making the trade?" Kevighn eyed Ciarán's mug, since Luce was nowhere to be seen in the cozy kitchen. She was probably out in the garden.

Standing, Ciarán walked over to the stove. "No."

"Should I steal him back tomorrow?" Something twanged inside him; while he understood that the game was over, he still wasn't sure he wanted to see Magnolia wed that earth court whelp.

"I have a feeling she'll be expecting that. But we should try." Ciarán busied himself by taking down containers and mixing them into a mug, to which he added hot water from the kettle atop the stove.

"She won't harm him." This he said more to himself than anyone else as he laid his head on his folded arms.

"No, and Aire will make sure of that—good choice, by the way." Ciarán carried the steaming mug over and set it before Kevighn. "I'd thought a lady's maid would be the best choice, but your idea was much better. It also puts me at ease to know someone I trust will take on this role."

Kevighn took a sip of Ciarán's brew, allowing the taste

to roll over his tongue and wake up his senses ... and hopefully the rest of him. Ciarán had a knack for making potions that actually tasted *pleasant.*

"Aire has grown up." When Kevighn had left the dark court to be the old high queen's huntsman, she'd been but a girl, her older brother their friend. Now she was one of Ciarán's best female soldiers, and off to the earth palace to pretend to be a guard and spy for the dark court.

"Children grow up." Ciarán took his seat.

"Yes, they do." His sister had and one day his nephew would as well.

For several moments silence coated the kitchen. Luce returned, giving each of them slices of hot bread thick with jam. The jam was made with those berries Noli liked so much, the same kind that Ciarán used in his wine.

Finally, Kevighn felt nearly ... normal, though a warm bath and a change of clothes wouldn't go amiss. He only wore one shoe.

"What are we going to do about ... " Kevighn indicated Noli's missive with a sweep of his hand.

"I want you to find her father. You're the best tracker I have. Not that I expect you to discover much. But I don't want to give her what she's requested." Ciarán polished off his bread and jam.

"I understand completely." Relief flooded him as he drained his mug. If he was out searching for Noli's father he wouldn't have to attend the coronation—or the wedding. "It could take a long time, if I find anything at all," Kevighn added. "After all, something probably ate him as soon as he arrived."

"True." Ciarán rubbed his chin. "However, you *will* attend tomorrow's events with me."

Kevighn's mood soured. "Why?"

"Because I'm your king and I command you to." Ciarán straightened himself, looking every inch the dark king, even without his hood. Perhaps it was the scar, or his regal bone structure, or the imposing look in his eyes.

He drooped. "Yes, Your Majesty."

Ciarán's look softened. "Who will help me steal Aodhan back if not you? Perhaps we can steal Elise back as well— even if they are expecting us."

"True." However, if he reunited Magnolia with her father she'd be grateful ... and he knew precisely where to start his hunt.

....

The protective magic of the House of Oak was much stronger than the last time he'd muscled his way in. Also, this time, he needed to go all the way *into* the house.

Kevighn crossed through a small garden, the one where he'd found his fair blossom crying in a tree. No. She wasn't his fair blossom anymore. As much as he wished it wasn't so, she belonged to someone else—and there was nothing he could do about it.

With a heavy sigh, he opened a door, which led into a library. Using the stealth that had earned him his position as huntsman, he crept from room to room until he found what he sought. Magnolia's room.

The feminine room hummed with her essence. Now, was it here? If it wasn't, he'd need to go into the mortal realm, to her home in Los Angeles.

He didn't see her toolbox. Her valise caught his eye, her enchanted bag that held much more than one would expect.

It felt almost...indecent...to open it. Kevighn pulled out item after item until finally his hand clapped around the handle of the battered brass toolbox. *Victory.* Setting it on the bed, he put everything else back inside the bag so it didn't look as if he'd been there.

Once the box served its purpose he'd return it, after all, he knew how much it meant to her. Looking both ways, he darted out of her room and went back the way he came. Hopefully, he could use the toolbox to track her father.

As soon as he left their lands, he began to whistle.

EIGH†EEN

Secrets

"Noli, will you take a walk with me?" V asked as they left the war room.

"A walk would be nice." She'd been cooped up all morning—and this afternoon she had an audience with her subjects. Just the thought made her shiver. Yes, being outside among the trees would keep her from screaming in frustration.

"Good." He took her hand and squeezed it. "We have amazing gardens, though would you mind if we stopped by the kennels first?"

Kennels? Dogs lived in kennels. Oh. "You found Urco?"

V's eyes gleamed. "I think so... I hope he remembers me."

"Of course he does." She squeezed his hand back.

As they walked down the hallway, Noli sensed movement behind them. Guards. James had selected them himself. One of them, named Aire, was a girl. With her cap of brown hair and her uniform, she looked like a boy at first glance, much like Vix did—which was probably the point. V had made noises about it until James explained that girl guards could go places boy guards couldn't.

They wove through the palace. All the hallways confused her—it would take ages for her to learn to navigate this place.

Her entire body relaxed the moment fresh air kissed her face.

V led her past the stables to the kennels. "Urco," he called. "Urco." He gave a strange little whistle.

There was a rumble and a black dog the size of a small pony leapt at V, knocking him to the ground and licking his face.

"Urco, I missed you so much, boy." V wrestled with the hound right on the floor of the kennel. A few people stopped and stared, probably not expecting a near-grown prince to behave in such a fashion.

Noli had to admit it was cute. Endearing, even.

Urco's head popped up and he eyed Noli. Unused to dogs, especially ones so very large, she took a step back.

"Easy, Noli. If you run, he'll make chase, he'll catch you, and it won't be good for anyone." He popped up from the ground and put an arm around her waist. "Urco, this is Noli."

Urco sniffed her and she tried not to show fear.

"He's so big," she breathed.

"Here." V took her hand in his and showed her where to scratch Urco behind the ears. His fur was silky soft beneath her fingers and his tail thumped the ground so hard the floor vibrated.

V leaned over and whispered something to the dog. "Come, Urco." He gave another whistle, took her hand, and they walked out of the kennel, Urco bounding behind them. "Urco's a good hound. I wouldn't mind keeping him in the wing with us—it would make me feel better."

"They're fierce, aren't they?" She'd heard stories of fae hounds tearing people to shreds, not to mention she'd seen them, once, when Tiana had sent the Wild Hunt after her.

"Yes, and smart." He nodded in agreement. "Much smarter than mortal dogs."

They walked hand in hand through the magnificent grounds. Unlike the high queen's gardens, which were showy and perfect, these were more natural—vegetable plots, herb gardens, flower beds, forests.

"Where will the royal tree house be?" Noli swung V's hand as they walked. He'd promised her a tree house and she intended to hold him to it.

His eyes gleamed. "Let me show you."

They came to a flower garden; the sweet smells making her nose twitch in delight. In the garden sat a faery tree—it wasn't overly large or grand, but ...

"It's perfect." Letting go of his hand, she ran to the tree. Little faces peeked out of the knotholes. High-pitched squeals filled the air as they perched on the gnarled roots of the tree. The boy wood faeries bowed and the girls curtsied.

"What's this?" she whispered. Never before had they greeted her like this.

V linked his arm through hers. "They're greeting their queen."

"What do I do?" Noli asked. They kept bowing. It was so odd.

"Nod and say, *you may rise*," V whispered to her.

She bobbed her head. "You...you may rise." The words felt so odd on her lips.

Two faeries brought her a flower.

"I appreciate that," she told them, accepting it. "This would be the perfect place for a tree house. Don't you think?" She could see it now...

V put a hand on her shoulder, body close to hers. "This was always Aunt Dinessa's favorite place."

Her heart wrenched. Dinessa. Who was dead. Because of her. Tears pricked her eyes. Once again, it was all her fault. "I...I'm sorry, V."

"It's not your fault. I understand." He tilted up her face with his fingers. "She understood, too. She always knew that someone would eventually kill Brogan, and that she would also die. Aunt Dinessa made her peace with it long ago."

Noli couldn't even imagine that.

They took a seat at the base of the tree, leaning against the trunk. Noli spread the skirts of her green gown out around her. Urco romped through the garden, but politely—neither chasing the faeries nor disturbing the flowers.

Noli put her head on his shoulder. "I'm afraid for this afternoon. Why would the people listen to a mortal girl like me?"

V scooted closer to her, his arm around her waist. "Noli . . . you're . . ." He took a deep breath. "You're still not mortal."

"What?" She jumped backward out of his arms, as if burned. "But I'm me again."

"You are . . . but you aren't." He raked his hair with his hands. "You got your personality back, but you're not mortal. A mortal could no more be queen than a sprite."

The impact of his words hit her in the chest like a cannonball. "What do you mean I'm not mortal? I have to be mortal." Her voice rose in pitch and she chewed on her lower lip. If she wasn't mortal, what was she?

Sensing her unease, several wood faeries flew over and settled on her shoulders. One played with her hair.

"I'm sorry, Noli." He took her hand and she snatched it away. "But you're you again, isn't that more important than being mortal? I'm not mortal, James isn't mortal. You can still go into the mortal realm to visit—"

"You mean go to university." Her heart tightened. V was hiding something, she knew it. "We'll get things settled here and then we'll attend university and come back on weekends . . . won't we?" She tried to keep the wail out of her voice. Her dream was everything.

"Noli." V's face went tight. "I . . . I don't think we can do that. We can visit the mortal realm. We really should spend Christmas with your mother. But even if we could get things to a point where we could leave for an extended amount of time, you can't be a recreational queen—going to school during the week and being a faery queen on weekends. I . . . I'm sorry Noli." He pulled her to him, her body heavy and limp. "But the mortal world isn't your home anymore. You belong to the Otherworld now."

"But we're going to university." It was difficult to force the words out. "I... I sent off applications. I'm going to be a botanist." She looked up at him, eyes blurry with tears. "How can I be a botanist if I don't go to school?"

Silence. All she could hear were the sounds of dreams shattering.

He stroked her hair. "We'll go to the Academe, if you'd like, though at first we'll probably have to settle for private tutors while we get things situated."

The Academe was the Otherworld version of a university.

"But can you even study botany here?" Her dreams, her secret, dear dreams, crushed like a bug under the heel of a shoe.

"You're queen of the earth court—soon you'll be able to control any and all plants, both here and in the mortal realm. It's botany, just with magic." He gestured to the garden. "And this place, this garden, is always cared for by one of the royal family. You can have a garden, a tree house, a workshop... "

"It's not the same," she hiccupped.

"I know." He wrapped his arms around her. "But you have me. We'll... we'll start a new life. Me, you, James, Elise."

She guessed sending Elise to school in the mortal realm was out of the question.

"But I don't want this," she wailed. "I never meant to kill Brogan. I was just trying to defend myself. Your dream has always been to come here and be the king, but me... I just wanted to be a botanist."

Everything was ruined all because of a rash action that had seemed good at the time. That seemed to be the story of her life.

"I know." His voice was soft and tinged with regret. "We can do this together. The Bright Lady chose *you* to be our queen. She wouldn't have done that without a good reason."

What did the Bright Lady have to do with this? It was the magic that chose her. Then again, he believed everything was the will of the Bright Lady.

A thought struck her like lightning. "When did you know I wasn't mortal?"

It crawled under her skin, making her squirm away from him. The wood faeries continued to try to soothe her.

"Um … when I read your magic yesterday." The blush rose on his cheeks, high and red. "Considering you'd just taken the kingdom it didn't seem the right time to tell you."

"It didn't?" Anger swirled inside her like a dervish. "And not going to university—you knew that yesterday, too, and didn't think to tell me?"

"You have a lot going on. It wasn't as if I was intentionally lying to you," V fired back.

She flew to her feet. "My dreams are crushed. I will *never* be able to accomplish them—meanwhile, you have yours even quicker than expected. How could you not tell me? I thought you loved me."

"I do love you. I know this is difficult, but you have to think about the entire scheme of things now. You're not only responsible for yourself, but a court. There's so much to learn, people to impress, a kingdom to manage." He tugged on her hand. "It's going to be another long day. Why don't you sit next to me and have a little rest before someone finds us with urgent matters to take care of."

She couldn't quell the stream of anger and betrayal flowing from her. He knew how important her dreams were.

"What else didn't you tell me?" Her arms crossed over her chest. "Um ... " His face went scarlet.

"Steven Darrow you tell me this instant." Noli's voice went up the octave.

Betrayal flashed in his eyes. "Why, so you can yell at me some more?"

"Fine." She ran out of the garden. V didn't follow her, which made her heart drop.

A couple of guards followed her, but she ignored them, bumbling around the grounds until she heard familiar shrieks. Wiping her face with her sleeve, she squared her shoulders and sailed into a small garden. A Mintonette net had been set up. Nissa and Breena played Miri and Elise as they lobbed the golden ball back and forth over the net using nothing but magic.

James lounged nearby on a blanket with Aodhan, watching the girls play.

"It looks as if they're having fun." Noli plopped down ungracefully next to James.

He shook his head. "Stupidest game ever."

"I agree." She shook her head.

"Where's Stio?" James' head whipped around.

"Who?" Noli brought her knees to her chest as she watched. Miri and Elise's team seemed to be winning.

"V." James fell backward onto the blanket, conjuring images of lazy summer picnics in the hills and hoverboard rides.

Things according to V she'd never experience again. She opened her mouth to ask James, but closed it again. Not only was Aodhan right there, but V didn't lie. Delay or omit the truth, yes. Lie, no.

While she understood that he was trying to protect her, she didn't appreciate it and it didn't lessen the sting. That dream had gotten her through so much—her father disappearing, Jeff leaving, her friends abandoning her. It was all she had that was hers alone.

Now it was gone.

"Are you well, Noli?" Aodhan peered at her with a gaze older than his years. "You look like you need a strong cup of tea."

"I . . . I'm fine," she sighed. "And I don't know—or care where V is."

The game ended and Elise, in a pretty, pale green dress, ran over to them, the others following.

"Your Grace." Miri bobbed. "Can I help you with anything?"

"Yes, please, can we help you with something?" Nissa chirped.

Elise tugged on Noli's sleeve. "Why does everyone keep calling you that?"

"Later." James brushed her off.

A deep frown creased Elise's face as she looked around. "Where's Dadaí?"

James shuddered a little as he exhaled. "Later."

Her face screwed up in a petulant pout. "I want to know *now*."

The pain in her voice wrenched Noli's heart.

"Elise … later," James sighed.

Elise made a huff of frustration—something Noli understood completely.

Noli looked up at the sprites, who gazed at her expectantly waiting for orders, a half-baked plan forming in her mind.

"Breena, Nissa, I'll need a dress for my audience this afternoon. Could you please make sure I have everything I need? Also, check on my dress for tomorrow. I will need other dresses of course—and my dresses from the big house. Also, Elise will need a wardrobe as well." There. That should keep them busy.

"Of course, Your Grace." Nissa and Breena curtsied and flounced off.

Miri's lower lip quivered as her gaze followed her friends.

"I have a special job for you. Could you please have someone bring a lunch up to the tea garden for Elise and me? With little sandwiches and cakes and tea?" Noli looked at Elise. "I thought we'd have a lunch, just us girls …" She looked at James. "And no boys."

Elise gave Aodhan a long look. "That sounds nice."

"Yes, Your Grace." Miri bobbed. "Perhaps the cook has some of those green cakes you like." She bounded off.

Noli stood. "Elise, let's have tea."

And if she happened to tell Elise everything her brothers wouldn't tell her … well … they shouldn't be keeping secrets from her anyway.

. . . .

Steven entered their suite of rooms. It felt so odd to be back. They should redecorate; it would make him—and Noli—feel more at ease. Urco trotted at his heels. Hounds were extremely loyal and protective. Having Urco around would be as good as any charm or spell. Better.

James and Aodhan sat in the parlor playing a game.

"Where's Noli?" Steven looked around. Hopefully, she'd had enough time to cool off. There was work to be done and she needed to be in top form for this afternoon.

James made a face. "She and Elise are in the tea garden. No boys allowed. Did you and Noli have a fight?"

Steven looked at Aodhan; he didn't want to say too much with the boy present. "Noli's under quite a bit of pressure. However, I couldn't hide certain . . . realities from her."

"Oh." James' look went sly. "So you explained your *engagement?*"

"I didn't get that far." He still didn't understand why she was so angry. Certainly, she'd wanted to be a botanist. But now she was a queen. Didn't all girls secretly wish to be queens and princesses? Plans changed. It was time for her to grow up and stop being selfish. Because of her impulsiveness, they were now running a court.

James studied the game board and moved his piece. "It's Noli. She'll come around. Just make sure you say you're sorry. Girls like that."

Steven's nose wrinkled in distaste. "But I didn't do anything wrong."

"All the more reason to apologize." James looked at Aodhan. "Girls are a lot of work."

"Are they? I don't know many girls." Aodhan's head cocked to one side. His hair was nearly as pale as Quinn's. He moved his piece across the board.

Who *was* the boy? He'd ask Noli, since apparently she'd already sent word to his family.

But the boy's eyes … where had he seen eyes like that before? They didn't seem like earth court eyes.

James eyed the board. Couldn't James see that he was wide open? Steven moved his piece for him. "There."

"That's cheating." Aodhan pouted.

"Is it?" Steven's eyebrows rose. "Aodhan, what house do you belong to?"

The boy frowned. "House? My father runs the Thirsty Pooka."

Steven took a step back. Dark court. Where had Elise found a dark court boy? Oh, Kevighn and Ciarán had held Elise at the Thirsty Pooka.

"I see. What were you and Elise doing so far from home?" he asked, curiosity piqued.

Aodhan moved his piece, trying to regain his ground. "Elise and I went on an adventure. Will I return home tomorrow? I miss my father—and my uncle."

"I'll have to speak to Noli, since she's arranging it." What did Noli know?

"I have this. Is that what you mean by house?" Aodhan withdrew a sigil unlike any Steven had ever seen. The near-black stone contrasted with the web of silver around it.

Not earth court. Yet did the dark court have actual houses? He'd always thought it was naught but misfits and outcasts. Interesting.

Right now he didn't have time for this. He needed to check on Noli, then they had a meeting to prepare for her audience. His stomach rumbled. Yes, lunch was in order as well.

"I'm going to check on the girls." Maybe they had some food left. "Urco, stay here." Steven made his way to the tea garden and knocked on the door.

"Who is it?" Noli called from the other side.

"It's me." He went inside the garden. The fragrance of flowers greeted him. Elise and Noli sat in chairs that looked like trees, under a canopy of moss and ivy. The wooden table held a full-on tea party, complete with more food than two girls needed to eat. He was so famished that he'd even eat dainty girl food.

"Go away. I'm angry with you." Noli glared at him over her teacup, which looked like a leaf.

Elise's lips puckered. "I'm mad at you too."

His heart sank as he stepped all the way into the gardens, the moss floor squishing under his boots. "Why are you angry with me, Elise? I thought I was your favorite."

Her little arms crossed over her chest and she gave him a look that was *very* Noli-like. "Why didn't you tell me?"

"Tell you what?" His heart raced. "Noli...what did you do?" There wasn't time for this.

"She told me everything. How could you keep that from me?" Tears glistened in Elise's blue eyes.

Steven's jaw dropped as the bottom fell out of his stomach. She didn't...

"Noli, how could you... you have no right—"

"Yes, I do. No one likes to have the truth kept from them," Noli spat. "She's here, in the palace—which she remembers. People refer to me as *Your Grace*. Breena keeps calling her *princess*. I had to tell her something." Noli switched to Latin. "I didn't tell her that her mother is still alive, or is the high queen, but considering Tiana will be at the coronation tomorrow, you need to tell her something."

"She's my sister, not yours," he huffed. Noli's presumptuousness galled him.

"You can't keep her in the dark forever. I know you keep the truth from people to protect them, but it still hurts us." She switched languages.

Miri entered and bowed. "Your Grace? You're needed; the seneschal has more questions."

"Now, if you'll excuse me, I have things to attend to." Noli shot out of her seat.

"Noli, wait." He grabbed her arm and she glared, wresting herself from his grasp.

Elise pushed past him, hurt in her eyes. "I'm going to play with Miri."

Didn't they understand? He was doing his job—protecting those in his care. If they'd stop being selfish and think of the overarching scheme of things, then they'd understand.

With a sigh, he sat down in one of the chairs and helped himself to a tiny sandwich. How could Noli do that? She knew very well why they'd kept Elise in the dark.

James and Aodhan appeared in the doorway.

"What a nice garden." Aodhan's eyes fell on the table. "Oh, lunch." He hobbled over to the table, stuffed one of the tiny sandwiches in his mouth, and sat down.

"Are you all right?" James grabbed a cake of his own, remaining standing.

Steven raked his hands through his hair. "I don't think I'll ever understand girls."

James patted his shoulder as he took a seat next to him. "No man ever will."

NINETEEN

Misunderstandings

Fatigue pressed down on Steven as he went over the coronation checklist with Bran and Elric. Noli had been chilly toward him all day. She'd been a bit awkward during the audience; he'd have to give her some pointers for the coronation. He glanced over at her as she went over her parts for tomorrow with Padraig.

Tomorrow, she had to be perfect.

Finally, Padraig left. Noli stood and yawned. "If you will all excuse me, I still have lines to memorize for tomorrow."

Without so much as a glance, she left the room, guards trailing her. Bran left to take care of other things.

Steven sighed and looked at Elric when they'd finished the list. "Anything else?"

"Go to sleep," Elric told him. "Tomorrow's a big day."

"You're right." Steven left.

Familiar voices drew him as he walked down the hall. He saw Bran and Noli together, a bit away from the guards as if not to be overheard. Bran handed Noli something. She opened it and frowned.

What exactly would Noli and the court spymaster have to talk about? And the letter ...

He crept closer so that he could hear.

"Tomorrow we'll need extra security—especially around Elise and Aodhan," Noli told him softly. "I wouldn't be surprised if Ciarán tries to use the festivities to steal the children."

"Both? Or just his son?" Bran replied.

Son?

"Both. Under no circumstances can we allow either child to fall into dark court hands." Noli tucked the letter in her pocket.

Bran's eyebrows rose. "You don't plan on returning the dark king's son? That could have ... repercussions."

"No, I'll return him—a child should be with their family, but Ciarán won't get him back for free." Determination crossed her face.

What was going on here?

Steven strode over and joined them. "Aodhan's the dark king's son?"

"Shhh ... not so loud," Noli hissed.

"And you only thought to tell me now?" Anger coursed through him.

Her expression turned bland. "You have so much else going on, and I just haven't had the time. Besides, I can take care of this myself."

"Are you negotiating with Ciarán—alone?" The outrage increased. She had no experience in this sort of thing. One misstep…

"I wouldn't call it negotiations, and I know what I'm doing." Her attention returned to Bran. "We're going to need very tight security." Noli frowned. "I hate to keep the children away from the festivities, but it might be best, especially given everyone in attendance."

Everyone meant Tiana. If he didn't tell Elise about their mother before tomorrow, things could get…sticky.

Steven nodded. "Yes, Elise won't like it, but you have a point. We can't have the dark court, or anyone else, taking the children."

"I'll make sure the appropriate people are in place," Bran replied. "Good night, Your Grace, Your Highness." Bran left.

"What is going on?" Steven hissed, trying to sort everything out. Aodhan was the son of the dark king? Was that what the sigil meant?

Noli shook her head. "Not here."

In awkward silence they walked to the suite. Once inside, he looked around the front parlor. No one. Good. But this late, the children should be asleep. It would be all right if James heard. For safety, he drew the soundproofing glyph anyway.

"The little boy sleeping in my old room is the *son* of the dark king?" Steven's mind raced as he took a seat on the settee. That meant Ciarán ran the Thirsty Pooka, presumably under his alias. Odd that the dark king would run a seedy pub, yet at the same time, he was the high queen's foil. It made sense.

"Well…" Noli twisted her hands, one toe tracing the ground in front of her. "Ciarán calls Aodhan his son and has raised him, though he's not actually his father. However, Kevighn is his uncle." Again, she gave him that look.

"Wait—" He blinked, trying to process all this.

She looked away. "Considering that Creideamh and Quinn were…together, I think Aodhan might be Quinn's son. After all, the boy has Kevighn's eyes and Quinn's hair."

Steven sucked in a breath. "But how did Aodhan end up in the dark court? If he really is Quinn's, he should be here with us."

Noli held up a hand. "My knowledge is spotty, but Kevighn and Creideamh were fire court, and they took refuge with the dark court, which was, I think, where Creideamh met Quinn. Also…" Her voice quieted. "Creideamh had earth talent. That's not good, is it, if someone from the fire court has earth talent?"

"Flying figs." The epithet just slipped out. "No, it's…it's punishable by death—or exile. Which makes Quinn's journal entry make sense…and if there was a child…" He tried to piece together Otherworld law in his head. "The child would die as well."

"So the child was hidden in the dark court, possibly as an apology to Kevighn…" Noli looked away. "It seems like something Quinn would do. Also, Mathias said that Quinn was a man of many secrets."

Secrets indeed. A wife and child Steven never knew about. Could that be why Quinn had followed his father into exile? However, wouldn't he have heard of something such as this?

"Obviously, we don't know the entire story," he said slowly. "It's probably best to not let anyone know of our suspicions—otherwise, we might have to uphold the law."

"What?" Noli blanched.

"Sometimes we might have to enforce the law—which only can be changed by the high queen. For example, current law prohibits anyone not from the high queen's line from having the talent of more than one element. The monarch of the court where the person is found is the one responsible for ensuring they are exiled—or killed." Steven held her gaze. She needed to understand being a ruler was far more than parties and pretty dresses. Sometimes they were in charge of unpleasant things. Not that he wished to condemn an innocent child to death.

She gulped. "Oh."

"What are you seeking from Ciarán?" He eyed her. "Do you miss Kevighn and want to trade the boy for him?"

"Don't be an idiot," she spat. "What do you think I'm asking for?"

It took him a moment. "Oh, because you need to protect the pieces."

He'd forgotten about the staff and the jewel, with everything going on. He should check to make sure they were secure in his father's safe—and think of another place for them.

"Yes." Noli nodded, pacing back and forth. "He won't yield, but I didn't expect him to immediately. Which is why we can't allow him to steal Aodhan back tomorrow—or Elise."

"You're right. We'll keep them here with Urco and some guards. Then I won't have to explain Tiana." Steven raked his hand through his hair. There were so many things to think about—too many.

"You'll have to eventually," she snapped.

"I'll deal with her in my own time." Anger about what she'd done earlier sloshed over him like ice water. "I can't believe you told her."

"And I can't believe you hid things from me. Losing my dreams and mortality might not be of consequence to you, but they are to me." Her eyes danced with irritation.

"Tomorrow is important," Steven said grimly. "You need to appear like a queen ... an Otherworld queen who *took* a kingdom, not a mortal girl who got the throne by accident. Be very careful not to do or say anything that lets anyone know that." Scolding leaked into his tone. She wasn't taking this as seriously as she should.

Noli grimaced as if she'd eaten something bad. "Are you done lecturing me? I'm going to bed—and you, Steven Darrow, are *not* welcome."

Spinning on her heels she marched down the hall. A moment later he heard a door slam.

Urco whimpered and slunk into the living room.

"Come here, boy." Steven scratched Urco's head. He didn't really understand Noli's fury. However, he still hadn't told her that they were married. Maybe he should tell her before tomorrow? Perhaps not.

Elise still wasn't speaking to him and he needed to do some damage control on that, though he had no idea when. Didn't Noli understand *anything?*

He sighed again and patted Urco. "I suppose you and I will be sleeping on the couch."

Was he making a mistake? Had his parents been right about Noli the entire time?

Steven rubbed his temples. Perhaps everything would look brighter in the morning.

••••••••

Noli stood in the throne room, heart in her throat. Later today this vast and opulent room would be filled with Otherworld elite, the likes of which made Boston society seem like a dancing class.

"Now, after that, Stiofán will join you on the dais. You'll hold hands, declare your love in front of the Bright Lady, then Stiofán will be crowned and you'll proceed through the hall and out the doors," the seneschal instructed.

"That's it?" She frowned. While she expected Other-world customs to be different, she'd thought there would be ... more ... to marriage here.

Not that she and V were on speaking terms right now. After all, he'd slept on the couch last night.

"Did you hear me, Your Grace?" the seneschal asked. "What precisely did you have in mind?"

Her gaze shifted to V. "It's fine." She shook her head. "I just ... never mind."

The last thing she wanted was to betray her mortalness—well, former mortalness—or endure V's scolding for doing so. Again.

"Are you certain?" The seneschal frowned.

No, she wasn't.

V gave her a glare that meant she wasn't being regal enough.

Inwardly, she sighed. On the outside, she squared her shoulders and shook her head. "No, no. You've done a terrific job."

She glanced over at V, and his look said she'd still done something wrong. Her frustration built. What else did he want from her?

"If there's nothing else, then I have things to attend to." The seneschal gave her an expectant look.

"That...that will be all." Noli waved her hand like she'd see her grandmother do when dismissing servants.

The seneschal left, leaving her and V alone with Padraig, who'd be overseeing the actual ceremony.

"Noli, you *have* to be more regal," V hissed. "Also, what was that?"

"I...I just thought my wedding would be different." Noli looked away. A dress made by her mother and a veil attached to a coronet of flowers. Her father walking her down the aisle. Music. A lavish reception. A fancy cake.

Her family.

All those thoughts she shoved away. No, like V promised, she'd get a proper wedding eventually.

He always kept his promises.

She loved V with every fiber of her being. Yet this was all so much, so fast... and so different. Why did she keep making bad choices?

Her gaze fell on V, who was still looking at her expectantly.

Was he one of those bad choices?

No. He wasn't.

She swallowed hard. This wasn't how she thought it would be. Yet at the same time, there was nothing she could do that wouldn't make it worse.

Eyes misty, Noli looked away. "I... I need to look over everything one last time."

"Yes. It must be perfect." V nodded in agreement. "*Excellence is not an act, but a habit.*"

"Aristotle said that." If he was quoting Aristotle, he was serious. Excellence she could understand. But perfection? She gulped. *Noli* and *perfect* were never used in the same sentence. Try as she may, she'd never be the perfect faery queen.

Would V end up hating her for it?

Worse, would she hate herself?

"Excuse me." Taking a deep breath, Noli fled the room as gracefully as she could.

TWENTY

Following Orders

Kevighn frowned, Magnolia's toolbox in hand. In front of him sat a stretch of wild lands, an expanse just a few shades shy of the chaos of the pure magic itself. Strange creatures and dangerous beasties lurked in the wild lands, usually feeding off lost travelers. This particular area was quite dangerous because it was riddled with pockets of wild magic.

Could Magnolia's father—or what was left of him—be in there?

Unfortunately, Kevighn didn't have time to search further. If he wasn't back in time to attend the coronation . . . Ciarán wasn't one to disobey.

Especially if you valued your life.

He'd return tomorrow.

....

Kevighn walked up the back stairs of the Thirsty Pooka. Footsteps echoed behind him and he turned.

"Where have you been?" Ciarán scolded, hood up, his clothes the kind he usually wore when acting as dark king, not tavern owner.

"Doing as you ordered. Also, I figured I should dress suitably." Kevighn held up a bundle he'd retrieved from his cabin.

Ciarán nodded. "Good. I think our best opportunity to find the children will be during the party after the ceremony. If we're lucky, they'll be running around with the other children and it will be easy to make contact. I'll leave slipping away with them to you."

"Of course, Your Majesty. If we're unlucky, it will offer cover for me to find them." If he was occupied, it would mean less time he needed to spend looking at Magnolia and that whelp of a prince playing happy couple.

Ciarán clapped Kevighn on the shoulder. "This is for the better." His eyes bore into Kevighn's own.

Suddenly, Kevighn understood. His head bowed.

Ciarán lifted up his chin so that their eyes met again. "Your family is waiting for you."

"I know." Kevighn couldn't look away, yet he had no other response than those two words. Two little woefully inadequate words. He turned, releasing himself from Ciarán's touch. "I'm going to get dressed."

"Did you find anything?" Ciarán asked.

"Perhaps . . . but I'll hunt more tomorrow." He walked up the stairs without looking back. Putting aside Magnolia meant setting aside an era; that he was ready to close this chapter of his life. That he was done mourning Creideamh.

He should. Ciarán had been waiting for him far too long—longer than he'd ever wait for anyone. It wouldn't be disloyalty. Creideamh would want him to continue on with his life, especially caring for her son.

Still, it didn't make it any easier.

· · · · · · · ·

Elise twirled in her new party dress, so fluffy and soft. "It's suitable, Miri?"

"You're perfect." Miri bounced as she clapped her hands.

"I can't believe that Noli and Steven are getting married—and that she's a queen and he's a king. It's like something from a story." Though she was still vexed with Steven. Why had no one ever told her that she was a princess? A princess! All her friends would be jealous.

Miri let out a happy sigh, hands clasped under her chin. "It is, isn't it?"

There was a knock on the open door and Aodhan hobbled in, dressed very nicely.

His eyes grew big as he stopped right in front of her. "Elise...you...you look nice."

Elise put her hand to her lips and giggled. "You do as well."

"Do you think my father or uncle will be at the party?" Aodhan frowned. "Noli said that I might go home today."

"I don't know." Though she didn't want him to go.

Steven entered, wearing an elaborate green and brown outfit with embroidery on it, his sigil visibly around his neck, their father's ring on his hand, a sword at his side.

"Are you here to take us to the party?" Elise asked. "Do I get to be the flower girl? I've always wanted to be one."

Her brother shook his head. "There are no flower girls in Otherworld weddings."

"Why wouldn't Noli want a flower girl? She's queen—she could insist." Elise pouted. "How is my dress?"

"Elise...you and Aodhan aren't going to the party. You're to stay here with Miri," Steven told her.

"What?" she and Miri said at the same time.

"Miri," Steven's voice gentled. "It will be most helpful for you to stay here and play with Elise and Aodhan. At some point James will come up and play with them so that you can have a turn at the party."

"Oh, all right." Miri nodded, looking a little disappointed. "I know all sorts of games we can play."

Elise tugged on Steven's shirt, not understanding why, once again, she was left behind. "But I want to go."

"No." Steven crossed his arms over his chest in a way that reminded her of their father.

"You're not my dadaí." Elise's eyes squinted and her lower lip jutted out. She was tired of being told what to do.

"No, I'm not. But I'm in charge and you're not going. Now, I need to go." He left.

"He's quite frowny for someone getting married," Miri murmured. "Oh well. I'll go get some games." She left.

Elise turned to Aodhan. "I wanted to go."

Aodhan's eyes went alight with mischief. "Why don't we sneak out?"

"Oh, that's brilliant. After all, Steven never said we couldn't leave—just that we couldn't attend the party. We'll play with Miri for a little while, then distract her and sneak out."

As much as she hated to trick Miri, they couldn't have adventures with her around.

"How will we do that?" Aodhan's eyebrows rose.

She grinned. "We'll play hide and go seek. Miri is a very good hider."

He laughed. "This will be fun."

Elise went giddy inside. Who thought not listening would be so enjoyable? "Yes, indeed."

TWENTY-ONE

The Coronation

Noli wrapped her arms around herself as she stood all alone in the small but richly appointed antechamber of the throne room. So many feelings bombarded her that she couldn't sort them out.

Not that it would help.

Queen. She was about to become queen. A faery queen. Something bedtime stories were made of. Not that before this year she'd even believed in fairy tales.

Her life would never be the same. As much as she loved adventure, it seemed her adventures and decisions simply got her into trouble. Each one of those poor choices—which had seemed good at the time—had thrown her life into a tailspin. Even she knew impulsiveness wasn't a good trait in a leader.

A heavy sigh escaped her lips and she smoothed the skirts of her elaborate green gown, the brown corset covered in gold embroidery, filling the fabric with a scene of trees and leaves, which matched that of the dress and long train. Certainly, it was exquisite—her mother couldn't have done better.

The door opened and V entered, looking dashing in his own finery. Padraig followed in an elaborate robe, carrying a wooden staff.

"Do you remember your parts?" V grilled, without even a *hello* or *you look nice.*

"Yes," she snapped. "You just heard me go through them *three times.*"

"The pronunciations have to be perfect. You have to be perfect." He stood very close to her and she instinctively took a step back at his vehemence.

"Children." Padraig's voice cut through the silence. "And you are children, especially to someone as old as I. You need to cease this."

"Cease what?" V's brow furled in puzzlement.

Padraig took their hands in his gnarled ones. "Fighting. A house cannot be divided. You are about to take on a huge responsibility—and must work *together*, not against each other. Marriage is work; it's about compromise and respect. It's possible, believe me. I've been happily married for a very long time. It's not without its lumps and bumps, but that's life."

He turned to Noli and continued. "Stiofán is correct, Your Grace. You need to make a good impression, and the both of you being united will go far in sending a strong message. But Stiofán, no one is perfect, and Magnolia, you're capable of far more than you give yourself credit for. Believe in yourselves—and each other." He squeezed their hands and released them. "Now, I'm going to check on the seneschal. I'll leave you to patch things up before we begin."

With a little bow, he exited the room, leaving her and V completely alone—the guards positioned outside the antechamber.

"I'm not perfect," Noli whispered, Padraig's words giving her strength. "I'll never be the perfect queen, though I hope to learn to be one who does a good job, but…" She turned away. "I don't want you to hate me because I'm not perfect and I don't want to hate myself."

"Noli." V's arms wrapped around her from behind. "How could you think that?"

She spun around to face him, still in his arms, their faces very close. "Because for the past few days every word that comes out of your mouth is negative. According to you, I'm not doing a single thing right—and that hurts on so many levels." Her face contorted in pain but this time she didn't look away. "Everything's different now. All my plans… they're gone. I'm scared and confused. I…"

Before she could finish, his lips covered hers, swallowing the rest of her words.

Noli pulled back, eyes narrowing. "Don't you dare think that you can just kiss me and make it all better, Steven Darrow."

"Why not?" For a moment V looked innocent… boyish.

Her shoulders rose and fell as she sighed. "I… I'm sorry I told Elise. I was just so angry."

"I'm sorry, too. I should have told you everything that

first night." His arms brought her to his chest and she could feel his heart thumping, even through all his layers.

"Yes, you should." She rested her head on his shirt, which was both soft and scratchy. "But I forgive you. Can you still love me even if I'm not a perfect queen? It doesn't mean I'm not taking things seriously, it's just…"

"Of course I love you." His lips brushed the top of her head. "And I'm sorry. You're right—I should be more supportive. I'm used to this life, but you're not. I thought that if I didn't turn you into the perfect queen then it might ruin everything. But…"

He held her at arm's length, catching her in the snare that was his gaze. "I also don't want to ruin *us*. What we have. I had this image of everything in my head. You'd think I'd know by now that even the best-made plans go astray. It's going to take some time, but I think we can be excellent rulers without being perfect. I'm not perfect, so I shouldn't hold you to perfection either. This is going to be a big job and it'll be much easier if we work together. Padraig is right about that."

"I agree, and I'm going to hold you to all that you just said." The words went far in easing her heart. She leaned forward and captured his lips with hers in a long and lingering kiss, continuing it even when the door opened.

"Ugh, you, two," James muttered. "At least you're not fighting."

Steven broke off the kiss and ran his hand down her face. "I'm sorry this isn't your dream wedding. Things are different here. And, being a guy, I didn't truly understand how much weddings mean to mortal girls. I promise I'll give you your wedding with all the trappings. Your mother can make your dress; Jeff can walk you down the aisle—"

"And Vix can follow you with her pistol." James laughed.

"Do you forgive me?" V ran his hand through her unbound hair.

"Only if you forgive me." She kissed him again, this one fleeting. "We can do anything together—including run a kingdom. The best things are a bit unconventional, don't you think? Different isn't always wrong."

V's face broke into a grin as he slowly shook his head. "No, it's not. I have a feeling that before too long things in the Otherworld are going to change—and different is going to be exactly what we need."

"No more secrets?" she asked.

"Um …." V's cheeks flushed. "Wemightbealreadymarried."

"What?" She tried to make sense of his words.

James chuckled in the background.

"Remember when I asked you to marry me? Right after you took the court, when *she* spoke to us?" His entire face went red.

She nodded, recalling how powerful the magic had been.

"We don't actually have engagements. That was how you marry someone here. What we're doing now is just a public ceremony—though sometimes you do both together." His eyes went wide. "Please don't hate me. I tried to tell you and you ran from the garden. I was afraid that if I didn't do it right then, Tiana would forbid it."

Noli drew a finger down the scar on her palm, remembering

the moment. "It seemed like an awful lot of magic for an engagement, and it makes sense why what we're doing feels so ... ceremonial. And no"—she took his hand—"I'm not mad. I'm glad you told me."

V caressed her face. "I love you so much."

"I love you too." They were married by magic? Well, it wasn't actually the strangest thing to happen to her. In a way she was glad, and she understood V's reasoning.

The door opened again and Padraig walked back in. He gave them a long look. "Is everything better now?"

"Yes," they replied in unison.

Padraig gave a satisfied nod. "Good. Now, if you'll come with me, we have a coronation to attend."

....

The music started and Noli gulped, trying not to shake as she stood by the throne room doors. She looked toward Padraig, who stood at the very back of the room by the throne. He nodded, indicating it was time.

The long train of her gown was carried by a group of little girls in pale green—one from each of the great earth court houses. Two men flanked her, one carrying her crown, one a sword; each item on a green pillow. Lord Adair, the one who wanted her throne, was carrying the sword. Having him walking next to her with a weapon did nothing to quiet her nerves.

As practiced, Noli walked slowly down the aisle, trying to smile but not look around. This was it. She wished V was by her side, but he wasn't. Not yet. That came later.

The walls of the cavernous throne room were swathed with tapestries depicting the history of the court. The room was packed with people, some of whom she'd never seen the likes of before. Many wore earth court colors, but it was easy to pick out the delegations from the other courts. Queen Tiana and her entourage had the best seats.

Noli resisted the temptation to look for the dark court. However, she found V and James sitting with the House of Oak. It was too bad Elise wasn't permitted to attend. She'd probably love it, not to mention she should be helping to carry the train.

At the very back of the room was a high dais. On it sat a single chair—the old, wooden, intricately carved throne where the ruler of the earth court had sat for as long as there'd been one.

When she reached the dais, Noli stood in front of the throne but didn't sit, as instructed. The men with the crown and sword took their positions on each side of it.

An elaborate cloak was wrapped around her shoulders, and then she sat down. The little girls arranged her train and stepped back. The music stopped, the room falling into an eerie, reverent silence. Padraig stepped forward to address both her and the crowd. A crowd which focused their full attention on her. The high queen smirked and Noli's heart pounded in her ears.

Padraig spoke in what V termed "the high language"—a language so old it was practically lost, used only in ceremonies such as coronations. According to V, even the scholars at the Academe had problems translating texts in the language.

Part of why she'd been having trouble with the parts she had to say was because pronouncing the language proved difficult. Also, though Padraig had given her an overview, the idea of saying something without knowing exactly what it meant made her uneasy.

Padraig nodded and she answered. He continued to ask her questions and she responded. Essentially, he asked if she was prepared to take on the honor and duty of the earth court. He also asked if there were any objections.

Noli held her breath, expecting someone—anyone—to speak out, to challenge her right then and there for the court.

No one did.

Still, she remained as tightly wound as a pocket watch.

Lord Adair came over and offered her the sword, which she took, stating that she accepted the responsibility of defending her court and people with her life. At least that's what Padraig told her she said. As her hand curled around the hilt, she felt a little shock course up her arm. It wasn't enough to make her cry out, but it was enough to remind her that this was very, very real.

As Padraig continued with the last bit, her eyes found V, who gave her a smile and nod of approval. James outright grinned. It was difficult to not grin back. It took all her concentration to stand and swear upon the Bright Lady and the magic itself that she would be the new queen, serving and protecting the court until she died or was deemed unworthy.

Taking the sword, she cut her hand, offering her blood as sacrifice to both the Otherworld and her people.

The air around her sizzled, like it had when she'd taken

the court—and when V had proposed, no, married her. She closed her eyes, steeling herself for the pain ... but it never came. Neither did the voice. A gentle breeze fluttered through the room, even though they weren't outside. A murmur lit through the crowd as the breeze swirled around her, rustling her skirts and her unbound hair.

"She has spoken," Padraig said softly in the high language.

Someone helped her put the sword around her. The man with the crown walked over to Padraig. The old man took the crown and held it up, showing it to all assembled as he spoke the traditional words in the high language as to what it represented. Then, he set it on her head, giving her a smile, eyes gleaming. Tingles shot through her, though they were minty, not painful. Fanfare blared in the background. He took her hand in his, which was bony and leathery but strong, and led her around the dais, presenting her to the room as the new queen.

"Long live the queen, long live the queen," the crowd chanted as the earth court subjects bowed, acknowledging her new position. However, the grimaces of some of the lords of the great houses didn't escape her. V and James no longer sat with their house. It was nearly time for their part.

Padraig led her to the throne and she sat once again. The music resumed. V progressed up the aisle, alone, looking handsome in his court best, his father's sword at his side.

This should be reversed. Something stabbed her, not regret or jealousy, but it was still a feeling that *she* should be walking down the aisle to meet her groom.

Perhaps, given everything, she should send James into

the mortal realm to aethergraph Vix about making the surprise wedding a double.

Noli caught movement out of the corner of her eye, and she saw James holding V's crown on a pillow. Her eyes fell on Queen Tiana, who sat primly in a ridiculously diaphanous purple and gold dress that took up two chairs.

Would the high queen object? Would someone else object? Her chest tightened. No. Everything would be fine. Taking a deep breath, she focused on V.

Padraig nodded, and she stood. V joined her on the dais and they faced each other.

Never had she expected to marry this young—though plenty of girls did. But deep in her heart she'd wanted to marry V for a long time.

It wasn't as if her dreams would have to go completely by the wayside. She could study plants here, invent, and continue to learn new and exciting things.

V's left hand clasped her right wrist, her right hand clasping his left wrist. One of the little girls handed Padraig a basket. The old man began a very long, traditional speech in the high language about duty and marriage. Taking a piece of ivy out of the basket, he wound it around their wrists as he spoke, binding them together—a symbol of their joining not only as husband and wife, but as king and queen.

The entire time, V gazed at her, a smile on his lips, and it was all she could do to not melt into a puddle like some insipid maiden in a penny dreadful. Even if they'd already been married by magic, this was still a special moment.

V was hers. Forever. No one could separate them now.

Padraig turned to them and switched languages. "Queen Magnolia, do you accept Prince Stiofán, first son of the House of Oak, as your partner and king, to rule alongside you through good times and bad, for the good of the court and all who dwell in it?"

She gazed at V. "Yes, I accept."

"Stiofán, first son of the House of Oak, do you solemnly swear upon the land and the Bright Lady to serve and protect your queen, the earth court, and all who dwell within, with your dying breath?"

V nodded. "Yes, I, Stiofán, first son of the House of Oak, solemnly swear upon the land and the Bright Lady, to serve and protect my queen, the earth court, and all who dwell within, with my dying breath."

He might be speaking the words to the crowd, the magic, and the Bright Lady, but his eyes stayed on her. Her heart caught in her throat and her belly fluttered.

James came forward and handed the crown to Padraig.

Padraig raised the crown in the air, said a string of things in the old language, then set it upon V's head.

Noli watched as his entire being glowed, not with magic but with pride. He'd done it. His dream of becoming king had finally come true.

And she'd helped.

Standing to one side, Padraig made a sweeping gesture with his gnarled hand. "May I now present Queen Magnolia of the earth court, and her King, Stiofán."

Her heart roared in her ears and she leaned forward, capturing V's lips with hers, kissing him as deep as she dared with such an audience. When she broke off the kiss she realized that everyone in the room, including Padraig and V, were staring at her.

Noli's cheeks burned. "He didn't say, *and now you may kiss the bride?*"

V laughed. "No. That's not a usual part of the ceremony. But you may kiss me whenever you wish, Your Grace."

Pulling him close to her with her unbound hand, she kissed him so deeply she could hear Padraig clear his throat.

Her heart continued to roar in her ears when she released him. She could hear giggles and whispers in the audience. Noli glanced at James, who rolled his eyes and mouthed *mushy*. Queen Tiana sighed and shook her head, not in disapproval but in resignation at the folly of youth.

No one seemed especially scandalized. Good.

The fanfare played again, and, with their wrists still bound together with ivy, they progressed out. People bowed in respect as they walked down the aisle. It was difficult to simply look at everyone and smile, when all she really wanted to do was jump up and down and giggle like an over-sugared debutante.

As soon as they cleared the throne room doors she squeezed his hand and grinned. "We did it, V."

With his free hand, he reached up and ran his hand through her hair. "Yes, we did. You … you look beautiful, by the way. I forgot to tell you earlier."

She leaned in and gave him another kiss.

"None of that." He grinned. "We have a party to attend."

Noli pretended to pout as they walked down the hall. She could see guards fall in behind them. After the guards would be the guests: first the other monarchs, followed by the earth court houses; and then everyone else. They would all head to the ballroom for a very large party followed by a long and official banquet with the courts, houses, and other important people.

"V," she whispered, leaning toward him. "You're king." Suddenly, everything hit her all at once.

"Are you all right?" His eyes gleamed with concern as they entered an out-of-the-way sitting room so they could have a few moments alone before they went to the reception.

Noli took a long look at the man who would be by her side forever, for better or worse. Despite everything that had happened her entire being burst with the love she felt for him.

She smoothed his hair, which didn't lie flat even with the crown. "I couldn't be better."

TWENTY-TWO

A Change in Plans

"Ready or not, here I come," Elise called, trying not to giggle. She opened her eyes and Aodhan silently joined her. As quietly as they could, they snuck out of the chamber.

Whew. They entered the front parlor. Urco looked at them and stood. She put a finger to her lips, hoping the giant dog understood. He followed them, but didn't bark.

Elise put her hand on the door and held her breath as she opened it. She and Aodhan exchange glances as they slipped out, Urco on their heels.

A guard stepped out in front of them. "Where do you think you're going?"

Elise froze. What did they do now?

"We're hungry," Aodhan lied, giving the guard an innocent look.

"I'll send for a maid." The guard herded them toward the door with his body.

"What are you doing out here?" James appeared, still in his fancy clothes, a covered plate in his hand.

"They're hungry, Prince Séamus," the guard told them.

"Thought so." James held up a plate. "I stole us some treats. Why don't we go back in the room and eat, then play a game?"

Elise eyed him. James was much more fun than Steven. She turned and looked at Aodhan; after all, the point was to find his father.

"In." James herded them back inside before they could speak, Urco following. "Aodhan, you'll see your father soon. Noli promises. Elise, I know you're upset about missing the party, but believe me, they're not that much fun." He set the plate down on the low table in the sitting room and uncovered it, revealing all sorts of sweet and savory treats, making her mouth water.

Aodhan frowned. "Aren't parties supposed to be fun?"

"They all remind me of Charlotte." James closed his eyes and bowed his head, his face contorted with a pain Elise had never quite seen before.

"Who's Charlotte?" She helped herself to a pastry.

James' shoulders rose and fell. "I'm surprised Noli didn't tell you about her. She was an amazingly wonderful girl whom I loved very much."

"Where is she? May I meet her?" Her brother was sweet on a girl? She'd never known James to be interested in girls. Were the pretty things in his room hers?

He shook his head, eyes opening, though barely. "She would have loved you. But she died. We used to go to parties together."

"I'm sorry." Elise put a hand on his arm. So many people they loved had died—their parents, Quinn, their aunt and uncle she couldn't quite remember, James' girl.

"Me too," Aodhan replied, mouth half full of food.

They ate and ate until all the food was gone.

"What should we play now?" James looked around.

"We should find Miri—we were playing hide and go seek," Elise admitted, feeling bad for tricking her.

James rolled his eyes. "Yes, let's go find Miri. After all, I promised her I'd come up so that she could attend the party."

· · · · · · · ·

Kevighn sat in his seat, still as stone, knuckles turning white as he watched Magnolia join herself to another man. It was merely a simple public ceremony, which meant the two of them had already bound themselves to each other.

"Will you stop?" Ciarán hissed.

"I . . . I'm sorry, Your Majesty." A little sigh escaped his lips. "She looks lovely, doesn't she?" As radiant as only a woman in love could be.

"He looks like his father."

Kevighn studied Stiofán. Yes, he did look like the old earth king.

When Magnolia kissed Stiofán with such passion, Kevighn's heart broke. It was done.

Ciarán gave him a stern look, then it softened. "Why are they kissing?"

"A mortal custom." Kevighn tried not to watch.

The couple left, and then the monarchs followed. Tiana went first, followed by the water court, the air court, and the fire court. Finally, Ciarán and the dark court.

Everyone proceeded to the grand ballroom, which had been stuffed with so much greenery that Kevighn could almost imagine himself outside. The ceilings were excessively high. Music played and tables were piled with delicacies—and a giant cake. Noli's doing for certain. He recalled how much she adored cake.

He glanced at Ciarán. "I'm going to find some refreshments." They exchanged a knowing look, and Kevighn left the table. Of course he wasn't really getting food, but it wasn't as if he could say out loud that he was going to look for Aodhan. The fact he hadn't seen Elise at the coronation worried him.

Kevighn wandered around, trying not to let it bother him that most people openly shunned him. Then again, he was an exile and shouldn't even be at such an event. Only the fact that he wore dark court colors, and came with Ciarán kept him from being thrown out. Not that he would mind.

A waiter walked past, holding a tray filled with glasses of wine. He plucked one off, drained it, and set it on the tray of a waiter collecting empty ones. When another tray passed he helped himself to one and sipped it, walking around the perimeter of the room, searching for any sign of Elise or Aodhan, praying Magnolia didn't have them hidden away some place.

The high queen and her entourage brushed past, and he flattened himself against the wall hoping she didn't see him.

When Tiana passed without comment, he exhaled. Like she had eyes on the back of her head, she spun on her heels, glared at him in a way that would incinerate a lesser man, harumphed, then sailed on as if nothing had happened.

What did she think of the girl she disliked *taking* her old court and marrying her son?

As he prowled the edges of the ballroom, an odd feeling washed over him. It started in his spine and trickled up into his shoulder blades. Every time he tried to discreetly look around to see who—or what—watched him, he saw nothing.

Neither did he see the children.

Hmmm. Perhaps it was time to leave the ballroom, especially before he saw Magnolia. He wasn't happy for her, not one bit. Stiofán would hurt her, not to mention that the great houses would eat her alive because she was common—and formerly mortal. Those who liked to think themselves elite wouldn't welcome her into their ranks with open arms, especially given how unique she was.

No. It was better he allow Ciarán to keep him busy so he didn't have to watch them ruin her. Just like they'd destroyed his sister. One would think the earth court would nourish, but it only seemed to kill.

Slinking along with the stealth of a hunter, he exited the main doors. Several large, uniformed, earth court guards blocked his path as soon as he crossed the threshold. Ciarán's girl wasn't among them.

"Where are you going?" the guard demanded, hand on the hilt of his sword.

"I just wanted to get some air." Kevighn tried to slide between them.

One grabbed his wrist in a vise grip. "This way."

The guard marched him back into the ballroom and into a small—and well-guarded—private garden. Kevighn wandered around the garden, which seemed to lead *nowhere*, probably on purpose so party guests wouldn't meander into the more private parts of the palace—exactly what he needed to do.

Re-entering the ballroom, he ducked out the other exit, pretending he needed to use the washroom. Again, he was met by guards, escorted there *and back*. As soon as he returned to the ballroom, he saw guards openly watching him. His stomach sank.

He tried to sneak out a third time.

Another guard withdrew his sword and blocked Kevighn's path. "You need to stay in there, Silver, or I'll personally escort you to dark court territory."

Silver. The guard knew him. Or at least of him. The realization caused him to stumble back into the ballroom and grab the first glass of wine he found. Not far from the dessert tables, Kevighn leaned against the wall, sipping the red liquid. It wasn't nearly as good as what Ciarán made, but would suffice.

Someone was having him watched, which would make retrieving Aodhan impossible.

"Hiding, Kevighn?" Magnolia stood before him, radiant

in her gown. She no longer wore a train on her dress or the elaborate cape, but the crown of leaves decorated her wavy hair, the sword at her side.

"Magnolia." Startled, Kevighn sloshed wine over the rim of his cup, leaving red splotches on the wooden floor. "I'm not congratulating you." It came out more like a pout than anything else.

"I don't expect you to." She looked around, as if looking to see if anyone was watching... probably that whelp of a prince. However, he wasn't a prince anymore—or a whelp for that matter. At least they weren't still tied together with ivy.

"Are you having me watched?" He took a sip of wine.

She shrugged. "Is Aodhan who I think he is?"

"Perhaps." It would be dangerous to speak of such things here.

Her head tilted as if she was considering this. "He looks like her, doesn't he... except for his hair."

"You figured it out?" Kevighn's heart skipped a beat. This was dangerous knowledge.

Magnolia's smile went coy. "If I did, I'd keep such a thing to myself. After all, knowledge can be dangerous. I won't harm him."

"I know." That was the only reason why this hadn't been elevated into something more.

"You should go home." Without a look back, she left him alone.

A few moments later, Ciarán found him. "You're still here."

"I'm being blocked." He sighed. "Every time I make a move, a guard is right there."

"She's shrewd." Ciarán shook his head. "We're not getting him today. However, she gave me her word that she wouldn't harm him."

His eyebrows rose. "You spoke to her?"

"It is good manners to offer my congratulations." His eyes narrowed. "I might be dark court, but I'm not an ill-mannered brute. Since our business is done, I think we should depart."

"But..." He was unused to failing. The idea of *leaving* without his quarry made his hackles rise.

Screams rang through the crowd and people started to run. Kevighn stood rooted to his spot as the cries intensified, though he wasn't sure what had caused the screaming. Maybe this would be a good time to look for Aodhan.

His skin hummed in a way that meant fire magic was at work.

Fire magic?

His stomach sank. If this was an attack, his place was at Ciarán's side. With a few quick steps, he closed the gap between them and reached for a bow that wasn't there. Dammit, all he had was a long knife.

Hand on his knife, he turned, catching a glimpse of the airy shape of a transparent lizard—something that could almost be mistaken for a shadow.

The magnificent wedding cake burst into flames.

TWENTY-THREE

Salamanders

Shrieks filled the ballroom. Steven's hand found the hilt of his sword as he looked around the room for Noli, who'd been flitting around speaking to everyone in a way that would make her mother proud. Out of the corner of his eye he saw a shadow; then the wedding cake burst into flames. He jumped back. Noli. Where was Noli?

"Salamanders," someone whispered behind him. "We should go, Your Majesty."

Someone else replied, "No, if we leave now, they might think we're behind it."

Steven spun around to see Ciarán and Kevighn.

"*Are* you behind it?" he demanded of them.

Ciarán didn't have his hood up, and Steven had never seen him up close up like this. It was difficult not to stare at the scar marring an otherwise handsome face.

Kevighn scowled at him, his eyes narrowing, and Ciarán shook his head. "Why would we do that?" Ciarán asked.

Oh, let him list the ways. Instead, Steven just glared.

Noli ran over to them, an exasperated look on her face. "Stop bickering and help me. We need to work together." Without waiting for an answer, she hiked up her skirts and ran off.

"She's right, you know." Ciarán pushed up his sleeves. "Kevighn."

Kevighn sighed. "Of course, Your Majesty."

"Noli, wait." Steven ran after her, dodging the people running and screaming. Salamanders were fire elementals—dangerous, tricky beasties who had the ability to become partially intangible and slink in the shadows.

Everywhere he turned, little fires were set as the buggers slid from place to place wreaking havoc as they went. A delegation from the water court worked to quench the tiny fires popping up all over the room, but it seemed that for every one quelled, two more started. Guards tried to evacuate people in an orderly fashion, but it didn't stop him from nearly being trampled.

Where was she? Steven craned his neck.

A shriek pierced the air and he turned just in time to see a little girl standing there, frozen, as a flaming tree fell toward her.

"Hold on." Noli swooped in, as if to push the girl out of the way.

"Noli!" Steven rushed toward her. What was she doing?

Her hand went out, and the flaming tree *stopped* mid-air

as Noli and the girl escaped harm's way. Where had she learned to do *that*?

"V, help me," she called.

What could he do? Earth *could* quell fire, though that wasn't really in his area of expertise. They worked together to quench the flames, glad the smoke wasn't thick.

"Everyone, do what you can," Noli commanded. "If you can't, get out and help anyone hurt or afraid. Also, can anyone in fire court catch those blasted things?"

People stood there, watching. "You heard her," Steven told them. "Fire court, try to catch them. Water court, take the largest fires. Earth court—and anyone else—take what's left. Go."

They worked together to both put out the fires and keep everything flowing—delegating tasks, ordering a room set up for the injured, and such.

When the fires seemed to be extinguished, and no new ones popped up, Steven surveyed the area. Giant charred patches pocked the room. Most of the greenery had burned. Food was strewn across the floor. The party was officially over.

He just hoped there weren't any casualties. This wasn't how he wanted to start their reign. How *had* salamanders snuck into the palace . . . or had they been *let* in? *By whom* and *why* were the next questions that sprang to mind.

Uliam, king of the fire court, trudged over to him, fine red and black clothes singed, soot on his face. "Your Grace, the salamanders have all been caught. I would like to assure you that we had nothing to do with this."

"We appreciate your court's assistance," Steven replied.

Of course they'd say that they didn't do it. That's what the fire court did. *Deny, deny, deny.*

"It was the dark court that proved most useful." Uliam frowned and rubbed his red beard.

"They did?" Surprise flowed through Steven's voice.

Uliam shrugged. "Considering everything, it makes sense; I just never expected them to actually *help*. I'd think they'd slip out the back door at the first sign of trouble."

"Indeed." Considering what? Oh, Noli mentioned that Kevighn had once been fire court. Had the dark king been fire court as well? Out of the corner of his eye, Steven caught Noli trying to move something heavy by herself.

Uliam's eyes followed Steven's own. "I will follow your reign with great interest."

Sure, so he could find their weaknesses and exploit them.

"I beg your pardon, but I believe my assistance is needed." Steven scurried over to the entrance to the garden; two trees had fallen, blocking the door. "Noli, what are you doing?"

"Someone's trapped. I can't lift it." Noli's dress was torn, her hair a mess. "Hold on," she told someone.

Little cries came from ... somewhere.

"Let me help." Steven wished James was here, but he was with the children, which was the better scenario. He took a deep breath, then put his hands on the tree. "On three ... one, two, three ... " Grunting, they lifted it, but only a few inches.

"Can you wiggle out at all?" Noli asked whoever was stuck.

The only answer was more cries.

"We need to lift it higher," Steven told her. "On three ...

294

one, two, three..." Putting his back into it, he tried to lift it even higher. Suddenly, it got lighter, rising several more inches. He looked over to see Ciarán assisting them. "What are you doing?"

"Helping. I agree with Her Grace—we should work together," Ciarán said as he helped lift the tree.

"Exactly." Noli gave a satisfied nod. "Now, can you wriggle out of there?"

A little nose peeked out, followed by a furry, pointed face, little ears, and several tails, though he couldn't see how many. It limped over to Noli and made a little cry of thanks. They let go of the tree and Steven exhaled in relief.

Noli crouched down and peered at it. "Oh, you're hurt. Please don't be offended, but I'm going to pick you up and carry you to where they're tending the wounded. It will be faster that way." She gathered the little red fox-creature in her arms and swept toward the door.

"Is she *carrying* a kitsune?" Amusement tinged Ciarán's voice.

Steven glared at the dark king. Generally, one didn't carry a fox-elemental like a pet, but it was a child, injured, and she did ask. Sort of.

"We're not enemies." Ciarán wiped his hands on his dark cloak.

"We're not friends, either," Steven hissed.

The dark king shrugged. "Suit yourself."

A boom rumbled through the room with the force of an earthquake and a ball of exploding fire engulfed the part of the room where Noli had headed.

"Noli!" Steven called.

Ciarán swore. "You need to get everyone out of here. Uliam said his men killed no salamanders; apparently they lied. As a defense mechanism, salamanders leave behind an orb that explodes shortly after death."

Elric hustled over to him. "Your Grace, thank the Bright Lady I found you—"

"Not now, evacuate the room, there may be more explosions," Steven ordered. "Noli, Noli…" He ran *toward* the explosion right as another orb exploded, sending bits of burning wood careening toward him. Holding out his hand, he deflected the fragments, carving a pathway.

But it did nothing to quell the flames and smoke.

"Noli, where are you?" he yelled. The thick black smoke choked him and the heat burned his face. This was different from the small fires. This grew rapidly, creating noxious fumes.

"V, help me. I can't hold it back…" Noli called from beyond his vision.

Steven ripped off part of his shirt and wrapped it around his face to keep out the smoke. "Noli, where are you, talk to me?"

"I'm over here." Her voice held a frantic edge.

Flames surrounded her. The kitsune was cradled in one arm, and her other arm was out in front of her, glowing green. Separating her and the kitsune from the flames was a shield of green light. What was she doing?

Miri appeared beside him, her face smudged with soot.

"Tell her to put it out. She's already tapping into the magic; she can use it to put all the fires out."

"What?" He eyed the very odd sprite. "Miri, you need to get out of here. Go help those who are injured."

"She can do it. I believe in her." Miri turned and disappeared.

Tapping into the magic? Steven's hand went to his forehead. Of course. Noli was a ruler in distress. Theoretically, the magic that composed the court itself could answer her— though, to his knowledge, it hadn't come to the aid of an earth court monarch in generations.

"Noli, tap into the magic," he called. Was that how she'd been doing everything? Unconsciously tapping into the magic?

"What?" She shot him a desperate look as the green shield flickered.

"Ask the magic of the earth court to come to your aid and use it to put out the fires." He wasn't sure what else to do. Taking a step backward to avoid the flames, he used his arm to shield his face from the heat. But he wasn't going to leave her. He'd sooner cross the rapidly building wall of flames himself.

Her face contorted and she gulped, nodding slowly.

"I believe in you," he added.

The green light imploded, becoming a glowing orb in front of her. She *threw it* like a golden ball in a courtier game. The moment she hurled it, the light spread, tendrils creeping out like fog, smothering the flames.

Steven took a step toward Noli, but saw the look of total

and utter concentration on her face as she shone with shimmering green light. The fog coated the room like a blanket, filling every corner and crevice, pooling around their legs and limbs. It was cool but not cold, dense but intangible, smelling of oak trees and moss as it covered him, obscuring his vision. He peered through the fog and could see the flames dying out. For a moment the room held nothing but silence. Finally, the fog lowered and the smoke evaporated, leaving breathable air.

Elric stood at his side, eyes focused on Noli, who still glowed. "Is she..."

"I believe so." Pride rang through Steven's voice. "That's my Noli. She's going to be unconventional. At times she'll make the both of us want to tear out our hair. But no one tries harder."

Noli's eyes closed. As her hand moved, the fog shrunk toward her as if she were a magnet.

"Look, Your Grace." Elric gestured to a wall that had been charred earlier and was now flawless.

"Flying figs." As the fog receded, the wood *healed* itself, as if she were calling on the magic to cure the living trees that formed the palace.

Elric's face screwed up in confusion. "While I have heard Your Graces and Prince Séamus say that, I don't quite understand what the phrase means."

"It's a swear—a silly, mild, made-up swear." His eyes stayed focused on Noli as she gathered the fog to her. The room was still a mess with things strewn everywhere, but no longer were there any holes or charred bits in the walls.

The fog shrank until it was nothing but a small orb hovering over her hand. She closed her hand around the ball and it disappeared.

Her eyes snapped open and focused on him. "V."

Immediately, she sank toward the ground.

"Noli." In a few quick steps he reached her, his hand gripping hers as he pulled her to her feet. The kitsune was still resting in her arm, looking up at him with curious green eyes.

She gave him a small smile. "I think I overextended myself." Her words were shaky; actually, *she* seemed to be shaking. "Let's get this little one to the healer—and its parents. Sorry, I don't know if you're a boy or a girl."

"Come on." Steven put an arm around her waist and led her to the room that had been designated the infirmary. Her face was quite red, but he wasn't sure if it was from the fire or exertion. Noli leaned on him heavily, and he prayed to the Bright Lady that she'd be all right.

"Your Grace, you're injured." Elric came up to them, a worried look on his face. "Please, come with me to the healer."

Noli scowled. She didn't like doctors. "I need to find its family. Also, there are people far more injured than I. I should be helping, not using valuable resources unnecessarily."

Elric's lips pursed. His eyes fell on the tiny kitsune in her arms. "Ah, I believe I know where his parents are—and they're quite worried. I suppose you wish to bring him to them yourself."

"I do." She smiled at the little kitsune. "He's also hurt."

A sigh of resignation shuddered through Elric. "Come with me."

Not knowing what else to do, Steven stayed by Noli's side.

Elric led them to a worried-looking couple. They were in hybrid form—fox ears and tails, slightly pointed noses, creamy skin, green eyes, and dark hair—hers almost black and intricately braided, his a dark brown.

Steven tried to discreetly count their tails, since that was a mark of rank. Nine, the highest rank—which would be why they were in attendance. Kitsune were generally affiliated with either the high court or the dark court, and he was unsure which they hailed from.

"He's hurt." Noli held the kit out to his parents.

The father bowed. "Your Grace, we are most grateful to you for saving our son."

"Yes, we are in your debt." The mother bowed as well, then took the kit from Noli's arms.

Noli smiled at the parents. "It was nothing, but he's hurt. Elric, please make sure they see a healer."

With that, she turned and went off in another direction.

Steven caught up with her and put a hand on her shoulder. "Noli, where are we going?"

"We're going to tend to the injured and help where we can." The resolution in her voice—and her poise—made him nearly stop in his tracks.

"Why?" When had Noli become such a lady, not a simpering lady, but a true *household general,* the commander-in-chief of hearth and home. In some ways a court was an enormous household.

"Because that's what Queen Victoria would do." A blush

rose on her cheeks. "It's the only queen I know of—and I don't know *that* much about her."

He wasn't sure if Queen Victoria would personally tend to the sick, but he couldn't see any harm in indulging Noli. No one would give her a task that put her in danger.

"Oh, where's Miri? I need her to check on the children." Noli craned her neck.

She found Miri and sent her upstairs to check on the children and James. Steven followed Noli around while she comforted those who were afraid, fetched cups of tea, and reunited separated families.

Noli was in the middle of telling a group of children a story when Lord Adair strode over to them and Steven's stomach sank. The urge to scold Noli for not being regal enough bubbled to the surface and he swallowed hard, gulping it down.

"Lord Adair." Steven plastered on a fake smile.

"Your Graces." The Lord seemed stiff, as usual, his ridiculous handlebar moustache bobbing as he spoke. "Lanie, it's time to go."

"Must we, Dadaí?" A little girl in a torn, pale green dress pouted. Steven recognized her, both as one of Noli's train bearers and the girl Noli had saved from the burning tree.

"Yes." His noble face remained stoic, but his blue eyes softened as he gazed her. Lord Adair turned to Noli. "Your Grace, I … " It looked as if it pained him to say the words.

Noli grinned. "It's fine, Lord Adair. Am I not supposed to protect everyone in my care?"

"Indeed." The word was carefully neutral. "Lanie?"

"Yes, Dadaí." With a heavy sigh, Lanie stood, then gave a very proper little curtsey. "Your Graces." She smiled at Noli. "I like the story; I'd love to hear the end another time."

"Of course." Noli smiled all the way to her eyes, her cheek still smudged with soot.

Lord Adair led his daughter away. Bran caught his eye, then left the room.

Steven put his hand on Noli's shoulder. "I'll be right back."

"Of course." She returned to the story.

He went out to the hallway and looked both ways. No one. Steven continued down the hallway, then saw movement again. Turning down the hallway, he saw Bran waiting for him.

"Is everything all right?" Why did he say that? Of course things weren't all right. Someone had deliberately attacked his palace, his court, his kingdom.

His wife.

Bran gave a little bow. "Her Grace seems to respond well in stressful situations."

"That she does…I…" He shook his head. Steven should keep his worry that the people might not appreciate such an involved queen to himself.

"We will need to debrief. Do you think you can tear her away?" Bran asked.

"Indeed. Do you have any information about who caused this?" Steven asked. Bran always made him a little nervous.

"My men are working on it, Your Grace. This could…get complicated."

"Yes, it could." Steven remembered something. "Does the dark court have houses, like we do? I know little of the dark court."

"A few." Bran nodded. "Mostly they were disgraced or exiled houses that sought refuge within the dark court, then flourished."

"I see." Steven rubbed his chin. "The dark king belongs to such a house?" He recalled Aodhan's sigil. Sometimes entire houses were cast out of their courts. The only choices were the dark court or going into the mortal realm.

"Yes. Though that was more recent. Ciarán sought to bring honor to his dishonored house by taking the dark court from the previous ruler during the ogre rebellion. You were but a boy, so I don't know if you recall that."

He didn't. Tomorrow he'd read everything he could on recent dark court history.

"It was a fire court house, wasn't it?" he asked.

"Yes," Bran replied. "Silver is fire court as well, though naught but a peasant. However, he was the dark king's right hand man during all of that. It looks as if he's decided to reclaim that position."

Kevighn, the right hand of a monarch? That surprised him.

"Should we be worried?" Steven wondered.

"Perhaps. After all, Silver was chosen to be the old high queen's huntsman *because* of the prowess he demonstrated in the dark court. Not only did he and Ciarán take the court, but they quelled the ogre rebellion in one swoop. However, they aren't our current problem." Bran gave another nod. "I'll gather your council and we'll meet soon, if that pleases Your Graces."

Actually, Steven preferred to retire upstairs with Noli. But duty called.

"Certainly," he replied, "though Her Grace will want supper and hot tea. We'll be there as soon as I convince Her Grace to have her injuries tended to."

A smile played at the corners of Bran's lips. "Good luck with that."

Steven turned and walked back toward the room. Good luck indeed. He'd need it.

....

"I promise a healer is nothing like a doctor." Steven had Noli's arm in a firm grip. He needed someone to look at her injuries before all the healers left.

It was getting quite late and arrangements had been made for the injured and their families. Everyone else should be leaving if they hadn't already. The grand banquet had been postponed. They also had a meeting to attend to. But first...

"Must I?" Noli's nose wrinkled.

"Yes," he assured her. "The patients have been seen to, the children are fine, and now it's time for you to get looked after."

He was relieved that James and the children were safe upstairs and the dark court hadn't used the distraction to kidnap them. A shadow fell over him and he put a protective arm around Noli.

"If it isn't the happy children," Queen Tiana simpered. "Magnolia dear, I'm so sorry that everything ended like... this..." She made an empty gesture with her dainty hands, crown gleaming in the lamplight.

"It's fine," Noli replied. "I wish all balls were this exciting, though I could do without the injured, destruction, running, and screaming."

It was difficult not to laugh at such a Noli-like answer. The queen sniffed. "Yes... but to have your reign marred with such a thing..."

Noli paled.

Steven squeezed her hand. "If you'll excuse us... Mum."

The moment he said *mum*, Tiana softened. "Of course, of course." She gave them a coy smile.

Steven led Noli off. "Don't listen to her. Coronations *often* end in disaster."

"They do?" Noli perked up.

He wasn't actually sure about that, but he didn't want Tiana's words to upset her. In fact, he hadn't realized the high queen was still here. He hadn't seen her since before the salamanders attacked and he'd assumed that she'd left like so many others. Then again, she had probably found her handmaidens and pumped them for information.

"Now, let's get your injuries tended to." He gave Noli a soft smile.

"Will you get looked over, too?" She eyed him.

"Yes—and I'll even hold your hand." Anything for her.

A slight smile played on her lips. "Why didn't you say so in the first place?"

....

Supper eaten, he, Noli, and their advisors sat in the war room, though Padraig looked half asleep. Elric read over a list, frowning to himself.

The door opened and the seneschal walked in. "Your Grace?"

Noli looked up. "Yes?"

The seneschal bowed deeply, eyes red. "My most humble apologies for your party being ruined. I—"

Noli waved her hand. "Please stand. It's not your fault. It happens, besides, it was a lovely party and we'll just have to throw another soon."

Relief flooded his face. "Of course, Your Grace, after all, we really should still hold the banquet with the other monarchs at a later time."

"Go ahead and plan that for whenever everyone can attend. I'll leave it all in your capable hands." She smiled. "Again, the party was lovely. Good work."

"I appreciate your kind words, Your Grace." He bowed and left the room.

"That was charming," Steven whispered to her. "More *What Would Queen Victoria Do?*"

"More like my mother." Noli shook her head in amazement. "I actually learned things from her. But don't tell her I said that." She grinned.

Elric looked up from his list. "Are we ready?"

Noli glanced at Steven. "I believe we are."

"There were no fatalities. There were a number of injuries, but only a few are serious and the healers assure me everyone will be fine," Elric reported. "We should make sure the queen of the water court understands how appreciative we are that she not only allowed her hand-maidens to assist with healing the injured, but after seeing Her Grace tend to everyone, she herself assisted. I hadn't realized that she was such a skilled healer."

Padraig snorted. "The best healers *are* water court."

It was one of those handmaidens who'd seen to Steven and Noli.

"Of course," Noli told Elric. "We should express our appreciation appropriately; will you please make sure the proper person sees to that?"

He inclined his head. "Of course, Your Grace."

Steven looked at Bran. "The fire court did it, didn't they?"

"Them or the dark court," Elric mumbled. "Nothing but hoodlums and ruffians."

Noli peered at them over her teacup. "We shouldn't make assumptions without all the facts."

"Her Grace has a point," Padraig said. "Bran, any ideas?"

"It's the fire court, of course," Elric interjected.

Bran shook his head. "One would think...but I'm not certain."

"You're not?" Steven and Elric replied in unison. If not them, then who?

"No," Bran continued. "I've spoken to the guards and

had the wards checked. The salamanders didn't force their way in, which means they were let or brought in by someone."

"They weren't let in by our own people, were they?" Noli frowned. "Not that I'd like to think one of our guests would do such a thing."

"If it wasn't the fire court, then it was Ciarán and his ruffians," Elric huffed.

"Why?" Noli cocked her head. "Yes, yes, I understand that the fire court is our opposite, but *opposite* doesn't necessarily mean *enemy*. Also, I think we're greatly misunderstanding the dark court."

"Her Grace needs more time to understand the histories of the courts and our relations with them," Elric scolded.

"At this time we can't prove anything." Bran frowned. "Despite the obvious, both the dark court and fire court appear innocent, but I will continue to investigate this most thoroughly."

"If it's not them, *who* could it be?" Steven asked. There weren't any other options that he could think of.

Bran tapped his chin. "There are rumors of a new rebellion forming, against whom I'm unsure. They could be behind it. Also, perhaps it was someone within a court acting unofficially. We need to look beyond the obvious—since it would be a natural assumption for it to be the fault of the fire court if salamanders were used."

"You mean someone from another court might use salamanders and think they'd get away with it because the fire court would be blamed?" Noli's face scrunched.

"But don't you need to control fire in order to control salamanders?" Elric replied.

"I suppose you could catch them and release them without bothering to control them." Padraig shrugged. "Obviously, we're not going to discover who was behind this tonight."

"No, we're not." Noli looked thoughtful.

"I still vote for the dark court or fire court," Steven muttered. It was the logical explanation, no matter what Noli thought.

"I as well," Elric added.

Padraig stood. "If it is all right with Their Graces, I believe we should adjourn?"

Elric held up a hand. "I have a question for Her Grace. How did you know how to tap into the magic in order to stop the fire? Your performance today was quite impressive. I was under the impression that your training in magic has been … minimal."

Noli took a deep breath. "I acted on instinct—and, well, V told me I could do it."

A scowl crossed Elric's face as if her answer was unsatisfactory.

"I believe that's enough, chancellor. Yes, I know there's much to do—people need to be reassured, we need to take stock of any remaining damage, create a plan, keep investigating, and such. However …" Padraig, who was still standing, looked stern. "I think, given what today represents, we should allow Their Graces to retire?"

Elric's face went red. "Yes, of course. We'll convene in . . . say, the afternoon? No sense meeting early."

Noli perked up. "Of course. I'll see you then."

Steven held out his hand to Noli. "If I may?"

She stood. "But of course."

He put an arm around her waist. Hopefully the children would be asleep and everyone else would make themselves scarce. Yes, this night represented quite a bit—and hopefully she'd see it the same way.

TWENTY-FOUR

Tonight

"That was the worst day ever," Kevighn mumbled, hunched over the bar at the Thirsty Pooka. Magnolia had gotten married, salamanders attacked, and they hadn't retrieved Aodhan. "I need another drink, Deidre," he told the bartender.

He'd had several already, since Ciarán had gone right upstairs to take care of some business. Kevighn was still drinking when the dark king came back down to the bar.

"You drink too much." Hood up, Ciarán went behind the bar, grabbed a few bottles of wine, and headed for the kitchen.

Kevighn followed Ciarán up the back stairs into his private quarters. This place was quiet without Aodhan. Mere days and already it felt like home again.

But Ciarán was right. While he loved his cabin, this place had very much been home to him once. After his parents had been murdered. As he and Ciarán made their plans. As they fought to keep hold of the dark court after taking it and starting a new order.

And then he'd left…

When Ciarán had needed him most, he'd left—abandoned his old and dear friend and joined the high court, of all things. Not that one could really ignore an order from the high queen.

Sure, he'd been hurt, but none of that—the women, the drugs and drinking—none of that had brought Creideamh back.

Killing Quinn hadn't brought her back either.

Kevighn slammed his fist into the nearest wall. "Stupid, stupid, stupid."

"You're an idiot. Fortunately, you're a lovable idiot." Ciarán's hand clapped his wrist. "Come on." He shoved him up another set of stairs, sat him down someplace, and put a bottle in his hand.

"I thought you said I drink too much." Kevighn took a pull right from the bottle, not even tasting it.

"You do. Let everything go." His voice went quiet. "It's time."

Kevighn shook his head. "But my sister trusted me."

"She did—and it wasn't your fault. She knew that; otherwise, do you really think Aodhan would be here with us?" Ciarán threw back his hood and gazed into the quiet night. The only light and noise came from the tavern itself.

"I haven't failed on a hunt in a long time," Kevighn admitted. "Perhaps I'm losing my touch." First Magnolia, now Aodhan. Looking up, he realized that he sat next to Ciarán on the roof of the tavern. He'd been so lost in thought he hadn't noticed. It had been a long time since they'd sat up here.

Ciarán shook his head, taking the bottle from his hand. "You're not losing your touch. No one's perfect. Not me, not you. We'll get him back. Please tell me you have a lead on Magnolia's father."

He recalled that odd place of wild magic. "Yes. I'll go tomorrow."

"Good." Ciarán drank directly from the bottle then handed it back to Kevighn.

"What if we don't find him? It's been a long time." Kevighn looked out into the dark and endless sky.

Ciarán sighed. "Then we'll make the trade."

"We will?" Kevighn did a double take.

A derisive laugh escaped Ciarán's lips. "Yes, I might actually make a deal. My son—and you—mean that much to me. But it's not as if she knows how many pieces we have. Also, we're going to have to work together eventually to assemble it. Probably sooner rather than later, given everything. Even if the girl's not ready."

"True." Kevighn stole a glance at Ciarán's face. The hood had slipped down and something . . . something in those amber eyes made Kevighn's stomach tighten, and not in a bad way. "What were you meeting about just now?"

"While we were all at the earth court for the party, Tiana had one of the villages under *my* protection raided and dragged off an inventor and several boys carrying long knives." Ciarán pounded the roof with his fist, snatched the bottle of wine, and took a long pull. When he finished, his eyes glowed with anger. "Aire's brother is leading a team to get them back. I've sent extra soldiers to protect the other villages, but we must put a stop to this. You do know the high queen is one of the few people who could have set the salamanders loose on the wedding."

"And the last person anyone would blame," Kevighn replied, coming to that conclusion himself but having the sense not to say it. It would be treason. But she could control *all* the elements. Even fire. "Will the little girl be enough?" Elise was just a child.

"Children grow up. Also, *anyone* is better than Tiana." Ciarán sighed. "We need to start gathering our usual allies, to see who in the other courts feels the same way. We can't do this alone."

That was treason also.

Ciarán took another long drink, then handed it to him. "You can finish it. I brought another bottle."

Kevighn took the bottle and downed it. He had a feeling he'd need it. "Why do you trust me?"

"Grief can make us idiots. You've always been there for me when it counted." Ciarán's voice went raw. He leaned forward, elbows on his knees. "You were there when we'd go adventuring as boys, when I took over the tavern, when I had this crazy idea that perhaps I, some disgraced fire court brat with no parents, could become king of the fiercest court. That means something to me."

"You were there for me, too." Kevighn set the empty bottle

down on a flat space before he dropped it and it rolled off the roof.

"That's what family does." Ciarán scooted closer and reached into his cloak pocket. "It's time to take your place in this family." He held out a sigil, one identical to his and Aodhan's.

Kevighn's heart sped at all it implied, and he knew that Ciarán meant this gesture in many ways. Sometimes he wondered whether he'd brought all those girls into his life in part to convince himself that they were what he wanted. Not Ciarán. Not someone from a great house. Not someone who was now *king*.

Not someone far too good for a peasant such as himself.

"Take it, you fool." Ciarán's eyes glowed in the darkness.

There was no one outside of Creideamh that Kevighn trusted more…and Creideamh was gone. If a rebellion was brewing, his place was here. Also, there was Aodhan. His sister would never forgive him for neglecting her child.

He gazed up at Ciarán. "It doesn't matter that I'm common?"

"Has it ever?" Ciarán asked.

Kevighn sucked in a sharp breath. No, it never had. "I accept."

"Good." Ciarán placed the sigil around his neck.

Kevighn picked up the medallion and examined it. "I never thought I'd have one of these."

"You're a fool." Ciarán's look grew fond as he opened a new bottle of wine. "Now, let's drink. To freedom and family." He raised the bottle, took a drink, and handed it to Kevighn.

"To freedom and family." The two things that mattered most to a man. The two things Kevighn intended to keep, no matter what the cost.

••••••••

"A penny for your thoughts, Noli?" V's voice pulled Noli out of her rumination as they approached their suite. The guards opened the doors and they went inside.

As the doors closed behind them, she looked around the front parlor. It was empty except for Urco, who lay on the settee gazing at them with wide eyes.

"Good evening, boy." V went over and scratched Urco behind his ears.

"I've been thinking." She'd been mulling things over in her head that she didn't dare speak aloud in the war room. V might trust their advisors, but she wasn't ready to speak treason in their presence.

"About what?" V continued to lavish attention on Urco, who thumped his tail against the settee. It was nice that he had found his dog.

"Um…" Noli looked around. "First, I need to check on the children." She went down the hall to glance in on Elise and Aodhan, who slept soundly. Good. When she came back into the parlor, V was still playing with Urco.

He looked up at her expectantly from his place on the floor.

"Can you do… what did you call it? A glyph?" She took a seat on the settee, her belly tight.

"The soundproofing spell?" He frowned. "It is a glyph, but I'm not sure I called it that."

"Oh. But can you? And teach me? Please?" So much had been running around in her head since she'd taken the kingdom, it seemed like every day more information appeared in it and she wasn't sure how—or why. Perhaps she was tapping into something like when she'd accessed the court's magic.

That had also been very strange . . . and all too comfortable.

But Noli wasn't ready to share any of this with V. It was too odd sounding, and she didn't want him to worry.

"Of course I can." He took a seat beside her. "I expect that we should send for magic tutors for everyone—you, Elise, James, me . . . "

"Probably. I . . . I suppose we're raising Elise?" Not that she minded, but she could barely care for herself, and now she had a kingdom, a husband, Elise . . . it was overwhelming.

"What else would we do with her? I thought for certain Tiana would demand to see her tonight." He frowned slightly.

She'd wondered the same. "We could always send her to school in the mortal realm; she can be my mother's perfect ladylike daughter."

V opened his mouth in protest, closed it, cocked his head, and then nodded. "That might be an option, depending on how things go. It could be safer for her. But we should keep her here for now."

"Of course. Now . . . how do you do the spell?" Noli watched as V showed her several times how to work the spell, which was a lot more complex than simply drawing a symbol in the air.

Finally, she got it to work.

"Very good," V said. "Now, what's on your mind?"

"The salamanders." Even though they had the spell, she spoke softly. "I'm not convinced it was the dark court, fire court, or rebels."

"Who else could it be?" V's face screwed up in thought. "It would have to be someone who could control fire."

Noli nodded, forming her words carefully. "Who else can control fire? Who would no one expect—or even mention, because the very words are dangerous?"

V paled. "Flying figs—but do you actually . . . no . . . why would she?"

Noli shook her head. "I don't know. But she's cold, calculating, and crazy. I overhead some people talking about how she's terrorizing dark court villagers, stealing their inventors, killing people who possess certain types of weapons. I'm not as good at history as you, but even I understand that those actions can cause a rebellion. Also, she accepted us marrying and taking the kingdom *far* too easily. I should have expected her to do something. The worst thing that you can do to a bride is to destroy her wedding."

His lips made a hard white line and he gulped. "This is dangerous. Believable, but dangerous. You can't tell *anyone* other than me."

"Why do you think I didn't mention it in the war room?" she replied. At least he believed her.

"We can't even put Bran on this. But we can ask him about the rebellions." V continued to pet Urco absently.

"What does Bran do?" Noli asked, cheeks warming. "I know I should know, but I don't."

"Oh, he's our spymaster." V shrugged.

"Ah, I see." A spymaster. Since the high court and the dark court had spies, she was grateful they had some as well.

"Anything else?" V asked.

She shook her head. He taught her how to undo the spell.

A sleepy Miri, in a nightgown, padded out. "I thought that was you. Would you like a bath?"

"I can do it myself," Noli replied. A bath sounded perfect, but she felt strange having people do everything for her. It had been so long since she'd had servants.

"Nonsense. I'm awake. Do you need anything else?" Miri bounced up and down on the balls of her bare feet.

"No, just run the bath and go to sleep please. It's late." Noli yawned. It had been a long day—at least there were no early meetings tomorrow.

"Of course." With a little bow, Miri scampered out.

V gave her a long look. "If you're going to take a bath, I'll go wash up elsewhere."

He leaned in and gave her a kiss, long and lingering. Her belly tightened as his arms curled around her. She tangled her fingers in his hair as she met his hungry mouth with hers.

When he pulled back, he brought her to him. "I'm sorry your wedding was ruined."

Noli shook her head. "It's odd, but it didn't seem like a real wedding." Her cheeks warmed. "I mean, yes, I understand we're married, but I suppose I'd be a lot more hurt if it was the kind I've always expected. Does that make any sense?"

"It does." He gave her a bashful smile. "I promise we'll go to Boston for Christmas. I'll propose properly. But we don't have to have a double wedding if you don't wish to. We can wait."

V looked so adorably awkward talking about such things. She smoothed his hair with her fingers and gave him a little kiss.

"I love you, V." She patted Urco on the head, then stood. "Now, I'm going to take that bath."

His eyes gleamed. "Yes, you do that. I'll be waiting."

....

Noli lay back in the scented bath, eyes closed. One of the things that would take getting used to was that she seemed to always be surrounded by people. At least she had this lovely, giant bathtub. Though she had to order Miri to go to sleep and not wait up to help her get ready for bed. She was capable of doing that herself.

Closing her eyes, Noli half-dozed in the water until it cooled and her fingers had gone pruny. She climbed out and dried herself off. Miri had said she'd left nightclothes for her.

Noli picked up a bundle of white, which slid under her fingers like the finest of silk. What was this? She unfolded it to find, well, she supposed it was a night dress, it was long, but had no sleeves, and was elaborately embroidered with white thread and pearls, as if it were meant to be seen.

Her entire body flushed. This was essentially her wedding

night. Even though a proper girl shouldn't know these things, she knew exactly what happened … and wanted it.

She slid on the silky garments. They made her feel beautiful and grown up. Noli brushed and braided her hair so it wouldn't get tangled and put on the matching robe. Taking a deep breath, she entered the bedroom.

V lounged on the bed in naught but a nightshirt, reading something, hair damp from his own bath. He looked up at her and a blush rose to his cheeks. Setting his reading on the nightstand, he gazed at her in a way that made her heart leap.

The room glowed with candles. There were flowers everywhere, their perfume delicate, yet sensual. Rose petals sprinkled the top of the bed.

"Miri left these for me. It's so soft. Feel?" She walked over to the bed, trying to be beautiful and confident. So many emotions fluttered in her belly.

V pulled her onto the petal-covered surface and ran his hands over her shoulders and down her arms, pulling the robe with it, her skin sizzling where his fingers caressed her.

"You're beautiful," he whispered, voice warm on her ear.

"So are you," she breathed back, running her hand through his still-damp hair. Fresh out of the bath, he looked quite … ravishing, and it made the fire in her belly grow. Leaning forward, she kissed him as he peeled the robe off her. "You're mine, V."

He put his arms around her and leaned forward, gently lowering her to the bed, his eyes never leaving hers. "Yes, I am. I love you so much, Noli. I'm yours, forever, to do whatever you wish with. What do you command of me?"

Those soft words awakened everything. Her back arched slightly in anticipation.

"Love me forever." She tilted her face up, asking for a kiss.

"Only if you love me forever in return." His lips brushed hers as his hands slid under her back, bringing her to him, deepening the kiss.

"I love you, so much." Noli lost herself in his green eyes. "I feel like I can do anything with you by my side."

His kisses trickled down her neck. "I feel the same. Now, what do you wish of me? Do you wish for me to kiss you here?" He kissed her collarbone. "What about here?" The kiss went a bit lower.

"Oh, that tickles." She laughed and wiggled as he kissed her again and again.

"What about this?" He took a flower and ran it down her face, her body curving as he trailed it down to her navel, then kissed her through the fabric of her nightclothes. "So…"

A coy smile spread across her face. "You know exactly what I want."

She was a faery queen. All those old-fashioned things her mother had drilled into her no longer applied—if they ever really had.

V kissed her on the lips. His kisses got lower and lower, which made her body shiver with anticipation.

His eyes danced. "As you wish, My Queen."

She pulled him to her and kissed him with all her might. The past few days had been difficult, but she no longer regretted any of it. Regret wouldn't change things. It was time to accept this new fate and give it her best—and she could, with V by her side.

V's hands caressed her body. A happy sigh escaped her lips and she surrendered herself to the one she loved most.

TWENTY-FIVE

Discoveries

Steven gazed at Noli, who slept peacefully, her head on his bare chest, curls tickling his nose. He tried not to sneeze, afraid it would wake her. The sneeze came out anyway, and even though he tried to stifle it, her eyes fluttered open.

"Good morning, V." She gave him a sleepy smile.

"Good morning." He kissed her on the forehead. "I...I love you." Last night...

Words couldn't begin to describe it.

Her hand caressed his face and she smiled. This wasn't sleepy; no, it was coy, and it assured him that last night had been everything she'd wanted.

"We can do this," he told her, filled with a new sense that perhaps this *would* turn out all right in the end. "We'll work together and do what we need to in order to recover from the attack, we'll create and implement a plan for the kingdom, we'll go to the Academe and study. I'm sure you can study plant magic—that's a bit like magical botany, don't you think?"

"Magical botany, I like that. Though perhaps I'll start with that tutor first." She yawned. "I'm so tired. I don't know if it was all that magic, or the stress of yesterday, or..." A blush rose to her cheeks in a way that made him want to kiss her and start last night all over again.

So he did.

"V..." She laughed and pushed him away, gently.

"I'll see about those tutors today. Elise's nursemaid, too. And..." He pulled her close. "Since we don't have meetings this morning, perhaps after breakfast we can hunt for a good place to set up the royal workshop? Then we can send for your things from the big house, and when we go back to the mortal realm we can get whatever you like from your house."

Noli glowed with happiness. "I'd like that so much. Last night all I could think of was how much easier it would have been to fight the fires if we'd had our hoverboards."

That was his Noli, always thinking about better ways to do things.

"V...I hate to change the subject, but...when will they expect us to have children?" She gazed up at him. "I know we used magic to prevent them, but I have no idea what people will expect here. In the mortal realm it would be my duty to have them as soon as possible, and...I'm not ready," she blurted. "We have so much work to do and I don't want to disappoint anyone, but—"

He stroked her hair, soothing her. "No one will expect

us to have children right away—especially given that everyone here pretty much considers *us* children."

"Oh good." She sighed with relief. "I'd like to make our dreams come true and spend time with you before little feet pitter-patter about this place. Also, we have Elise."

"I'm not ready to be a father," he admitted, glad she shared his feelings. "You'll probably be ready to be a mother before I'm ready to be a father, because girls always seem to be more ready for these things."

She shoved him as she laughed. "That's not very modern of you."

"But it's true," he mock-pouted. "We'll need to come up with a cover story for your mother, something that explains us being out of touch and not visiting much."

Noli nodded in agreement. "But we should tell Jeff and Vix the truth."

"Yes." As much as he didn't want to, it would be helpful. "I...I was thinking we could tell your mother that we're studying abroad, since she doesn't like airships—and that we'll be terribly busy with our studies and such. We can work out a system for messages with Jeff, and James can retrieve them for us. I..." He took a deep breath. "I think we need to examine the rest of Quinn's research on the staff, especially what Uncle Brogan had, and send James to track down any remaining pieces. Maybe he can even work with Jeff."

"Or Hittie and Hattie." Noli laughed. "I never got to meet them, but they sound like fun."

He shook his head, remembering the sisters. "I think

you'd get on well with them. Are we protecting the pieces…or have things changed?"

Steven wasn't sure if the Bright Lady still spoke to her.

Noli drew the glyph in the air. He should set strong protections around their bedroom as well. After all, there were spies among them.

"I think we're going to need to assemble it once we have all the pieces. We need to find out what pieces the dark king has," she admitted.

The last thing he wanted to do was to work with Ciarán. However, she had a point.

"How exactly do we do that?" he asked. Stealing them wasn't going to work.

"We could ask him," Noli replied. "Also, I think we'll need to start preparing Elise to take the throne." She put up her hand when he opened his mouth to protest. "We can do it covertly. But we've been charged with ensuring that she's the right type of queen to wield the staff. Which unfortunately isn't…"

It wasn't Tiana. He gulped. "I know."

Would it really come to this? He was unhappy with his mother, but he didn't want to kill her. Perhaps they could discover a peaceful solution and solve things with words instead of swords.

"We should think about regents as well, someone to rule on her behalf and advise her until she's of age. We can't be regents, and James isn't of age. Though he'd refuse anyway." Steven sighed, this was even more complicated than he'd expected it to be. "Quinn would have been perfect."

"One thing at a time." She squeezed his hand. "I think breakfast might be in order before we decide to change the Otherworld as we know it."

He kissed her neck. "I suppose."

"That's not what I meant by breakfast," she laughed as she tried to get up.

Steven pinned her to the bed and grinned. "No?"

She wiggled out, then pinned *him*. "This is better."

"Is it?" He liked this playful, feisty Noli, her nose touching his, her grin wide as the Cheshire Cat's. "Why don't you show me?"

• • • • • • • •

Kevighn sat up with a start, blankets around his waist, light streaming in through the window. Where was he? What had happened? He rubbed his throbbing head and looked around.

This was Ciarán's room. Last night . . .

His fingers went to the sigil around his neck. No. Last night wasn't a dream.

Nor did he regret it.

A hand clasped his wrist, eyes meeting his. "Don't run— and that's an order. I'm through being patient with you."

"I won't. Not ever." He meant every word. Why had he waited so long?

Yawning, Kevighn turned to look at Ciarán, who sat up as well. "I want to get an early start," Kevighn told him. "The sooner I find Magnolia's father, the sooner we can bring Aodhan home."

"I was thinking … perhaps Aodhan could become care-taker of your sister's grove and tree house—if it's all right with you," Ciarán said quietly.

Kevighn took a deep breath. "Yes, the grove has been neglected for too long. I think he's of a good age for that."

His sister's grove deserved a real caretaker. Who better to do that than her son?

"Excellent." Ciarán stood and got dressed. "Take what-ever provisions you need."

"I will. I hope I won't be gone too long." Kevighn dressed as well. "Do you want to come with me? It's been a long time since we had a reckless adventure."

Ciarán put a hand on his shoulder. "I'm always up for a good adventure—and I never shirk from a fight—but when you have people under your care, you can't be reckless for recklessness's sake."

Kevighn threw a shirt at him. "You sound like your father."

"He was a wise man." Ciarán balled up the shirt and threw it back.

Kevighn pulled on his shirt and they went downstairs, where old Luce was baking the day's bread. She took one look at them and put the kettle on, then went down into the cellar. When she came back she made them tea and fried sausages.

Fried sausage sandwiches went well with Ciarán's hang-over remedies. Which they both needed. Maybe he *did* drink too much.

"Where exactly are you headed? Do I need to ask for

safe passage on your behalf?" Ciarán asked as they ate at the table in the kitchen.

Safe passage? Ah, yes. When adventuring on another court's lands, it was customary to ask for permission. A new life meant playing by a new set of rules.

"I . . . I don't know, precisely," Kevighn replied slowly. "I was just following the tracking spell. The place itself is in the wild lands, riddled with patches of wild magic. Can people survive wild magic? I don't know much about it."

Luce toddled over and slapped a coil of rope in front of him. "You'll need this. Be quick, time runs different in them patches."

That was good to know. "What's the rope for?"

"It can be very easy to become distracted and lost. Before you enter, tie one end to something, then the other around your waist so you can find your way back and not wander around forever. It's enchanted, so there will always be enough," she added. "Also, mind your thoughts. Wild magic is meant to be formed."

"I appreciate that, Luce." He smiled. Luce, being ancient, knew all sorts of useful things.

Ciarán put a hand on his shoulder. "Don't do anything stupid. We want you back."

Kevighn wasn't quite ready to say it out loud, but he wanted to come back, too.

....

Toolbox in hand, Kevighn entered the wild lands. Everything around him was dark and dismal, as if something had sucked the color and the joy out of it.

Yet it wasn't lacking in life. No, the gnarled branches seemed to claw at him as he passed. Strange birds called from twisted trees. Rocks popped up from out of nowhere to trip him. Wild lands often took on a life of their own, which was why many didn't like to travel through them. Also, the threat of being eaten by the odd creatures that lurked in these parts was high if you didn't know how to be stealthy and smart.

He followed the tracking spell until he came to a place where everything just ... ceased. While the wild lands were ordered chaos, the patches of wild magic were akin to dense fog.

Frowning, he gazed into the wild magic, then redid the spell several times—just in case the sheer amount of magic had wreaked havoc with it.

No. Mr. Braddock, or what was left of him, was in ... *that*.

He took the coil of rope out of the basket and tied one end to his waist and the other to a nearby tree like Luce had instructed. Taking a deep breath, he entered the magic.

TWEN+Y-SIX

New Beginnings

"If it's not the dark court or the fire court, then who could the culprit be?" Elric grumped as they wrapped up their daily meeting in the war room.

"Everything is … inconclusive." Bran frowned.

Noli and V exchanged glances. With every passing day, they grew more certain that Tiana was behind it. Not that they could say so, even to Bran.

"Is there anything else we need to address today?" Noli asked. The injured had returned to their homes, the remaining damage to the palace had been repaired, the banquet had been rescheduled, and things were slowly settling into something that might be considered normal.

Padraig shook his head. "Not that I can think of."

Elric looked over his list, frowning as he checked things off. "No, Your Grace."

Bran shot her a glance that meant he needed to speak to her alone.

"Then I think we're done." She smiled and stood.

As usual, V and Elric put their heads together, consulting lists and books, researching and planning everything to death. She left the room and, as expected, Bran followed.

"Your Grace?" His voice went low. "When *do* you expect to make the trade with His Majesty for the boy?"

"I'm not sure, I haven't heard back from him." Strange. What was he waiting for? "I'll send another missive." Of sorts. She knew exactly what would garner a response.

"I see. Your Grace." Bran left without another word.

What an odd man.

Noli returned to their chambers. Their things had been retrieved from the big house; tutors and governesses were being found; Quinn's journals and research had been brought back from Los Angeles and ensconced in V's father's private library, which V had taken over as his own. There hadn't been much free time, but gathering all the pieces of the staff was a priority. She had a feeling she wasn't just supposed to protect the pieces, but that she was going to have to *assemble* them—and ensure that Elise could wield the staff in a way that wouldn't anger the magic.

"Hello, Noli," Aodhan said as she entered the sitting room. He and Elise were sitting on the floor around the low table, playing a board game that was a bit like chess.

"Aodhan, would you like to write your father a letter? I won't look, I promise." Yes, a letter from Aodhan would be much more effective than anything she could say.

"I'd like that very much. Would you like me to do that now?" Aodhan captured one of Elise's pieces with his own, causing her to pout.

"Please?" Noli eyed the board. "I'm sorry, I have no idea how to play this game. But once he's done, let's go out to the garden. I want to try something. Perhaps you both could help me."

She needed to be outside. Gah, there were so many meetings. Indoors. How did anyone stand it? Shouldn't all of earth court be *outside*?

Elise brightened. "Oh, good. I'm tired of this game anyhow."

Aodhan stood and grinned. "You're just mad because I always beat you."

"Am not." Her cheeks flushed.

"Are too." Eyes dancing, he left the room.

Noli helped Elise put the game away.

"Why do I need a governess? Isn't Miri enough? Am I not going back to my old school in Los Angeles?" Elise made a face as they sat down on the settee.

"We're staying here for now, and apparently you need a governess, not a nursemaid. Also, for some reason, sprites can't be governesses," she replied. Urco came over and begged for affection. Noli scratched behind his ears in the way he liked. "Don't you like Caít?"

Evidently, lesser royals often took on positions like governesses and such for royal children. Caít was a cousin, and she reminded Noli far too much of Charlotte with her impish ways. She'd be moving into the palace soon to start her duties. V had wanted to find a governess for Elise before Tiana gifted them with one.

Elise reached out to pet Urco. "I like Miri."

"Me too, and she'll still play with you." Noli smiled. "Why don't you find Miri and ask her to get us a picnic, and I'll check on Aodhan?"

"Perfect." Beaming, Elise set off to find Miri.

....

"This is hard," Noli told V. He was helping her form a tree house out of the faery tree in the earth court palace's flower garden. V had the faery tree at the big house—and now she had this one, at the palace. However, she missed her tree back in Los Angeles.

"It is hard, isn't it?" V replied as they worked. "They say it took hundreds of people to craft the palace. I'd always thought it was an exaggeration, but now I believe it."

"This is fun," Elise chirped as she helped.

Noli looked over and saw her and Aodhan both hard at work on their part of the tree house construction. He had such an intense contemplative expression on his face.

"V—" She nodded toward them. Aodhan had earth talent. Like his mother.

What else could the boy do?

He sucked in a sharp breath. "I see."

James stood below and gazed up at them. "What are you doing?"

"Making a tree house, silly," Elise laughed.

They'd made quite a bit of progress, and it actually looked like a two-room house without a roof, and missing a wall.

"Sounds boring." James plopped down on the ground below and helped himself to the remains of their picnic, feeding crumbs to some wood faeries who thought eating was more interesting than helping. "V, are we still going to the big house tomorrow?"

"Yes, we are. Also, did you see to those things I asked?" A look of concentration covered V's face as he made a window in one of the walls under the direction of a cadre of wood faeries.

"What things?" Noli directed the branches to weave together, creating a roof.

"Surprise. Here, let me help." V helped her finish the roof as Elise and Aodhan brought the last wall up to meet it.

They climbed down from the tree and observed it. Several little wood faeries sat on Noli's shoulder. One was the purple faery from Kevighn's who'd decided she liked it here better. A green one sat on Elise's head.

"What do you think?" Noli asked everyone. It was simple, with two rooms and several windows, but they could add on to it later.

"It needs furniture, like Uncle Kevighn's," Elise told her.

"My Uncle Kevighn has a tree house?" Aodhan asked. His limp was gone and he seemed in good health.

"You should ask him to take you there," Elise replied.

"Ours is better." V's arms wrapped around Noli protectively. His tone was jealous, but he didn't comment about "Uncle Kevighn."

"It is," Noli replied. It actually was, in many ways, though that hadn't been her sole intention. "I give you, the Royal Tree House." Her gaze traveled around the garden. "We need more roses—oh, and star blooms. I'd like to plant them around the base of the tree." She'd grown partial to the fragrant night-blooming flowers.

James lounged on the grass with Urco. "Oh, we got a message from Queen Tiana asking if we needed anything."

"Star flowers from her greenhouse, of course, in every color. Also, I want a hover-chariot like she has," Noli replied. "What?" she added at V's expression. "If we don't tell her something, she'll give us the Otherworld equivalent of a white elephant."

Her gaze fell on Elise, who was frolicking happily with Aodhan. They needed to do something about the fact that Elise thought her mother was dead. Soon. Before the queen made good on her invitation to come to tea and give royal lessons.

V chuckled. "You're right."

"I suppose I can make the tables and chairs." James stood. "V, do we have any royal engagements tonight? We could have supper here."

Noli and V exchanged looks.

"No, no royal engagements tonight," Noli replied. "I like that idea, don't you?" She looked at the children, who grinned with excitement.

"Supper, here?" A scandalized look crossed V's face.

"Oh, don't be a fussy old bodger," Noli laughed.

V shook his head, a grin playing on his lips. "All right, a tree house supper it is."

········

At the big house, Steven stood by the faery tree and the three tumuli, which were now filled in and covered in white rocks. He supposed his father and Dinessa should have been entombed in the family plot, where he'd had Brogan buried. But it had seemed more fitting for them to be here. They'd always loved it here, and now Quinn, in death as in life, was at his father's side.

But the more he read of Quinn's journals and research, the more he realized how little he truly knew about the man.

Noli squeezed his hand and gave him a small smile. She'd come with Elise and James to pay their respects. Aodhan had stayed behind with Miri. It wasn't his place to tell the boy who his real father was.

"I miss you, Dadaí." Elise put a bouquet of flowers on his tumulus. She placed another on Quinn's. "Quinn." Tears streamed down her face as she flung herself on the grave. "Quinn." Over and over she sobbed his name.

Noli took a step forward to comfort her.

"Let her cry." Steven pulled Noli closer to him and he buried his face in her shoulder as he finally allowed himself to mourn the man who'd been more of a father to him than his own.

Eventually, he let go of Noli and picked up Elise, holding his little sister to him. She rested her head on his shoulder.

He took Noli's hand as well, which was slightly awkward with Elise in his arms.

"Let's return to the big house. We'll have a snack, see if there's anything else we need, then go back to the palace," Steven told them.

"I like that idea. My toolbox wasn't in my valise when my things were brought over." Noli glanced over at his brother. "James?"

James held a bouquet of flowers in his hand. "I … I'll be there in a bit."

Without another word, he disappeared.

"Where's he going?" Elise asked as they walked to the big house.

"He's going to visit Charlotte. She's buried not far away," Steven said softly. With everything that had happened, it was so easy to forget that he'd lost her not long ago. But if the Staff of Eris was all he suspected it would be when they assembled it, no one would have to endure the sacrifice ever again.

....

"No peeking." Steven covered Noli's eyes with his hands as they stood right off her flower garden before a little cottage that looked straight out of a fairy tale.

"Why?" Noli laughed.

"I owe you a wedding present, remember?" He couldn't keep the grin out of his voice. He was quite proud of what he'd been able to do for her—in secret, too.

"Oh, but I don't have anything for you." Disappointment rang through Noli's voice.

"I have everything I want. Also, you created the tree house." Steven pressed his lips to the top of her head, then removed his hands. "Open."

She opened her eyes and gasped at the small building in front of them. "Is this a secret hideaway just for us?"

Why hadn't he thought of *that*?

"Look." He opened the door. The place looked like a cross between a cottage and a barn. "Behold the royal workshop."

None of the spots they'd found in the palace had been right for her workshop, so he made her one of her own. He led her inside.

"This is … this is amazing." She examined the work bench, the cupboards, and everything else. "I want to get the rest of my tools from Los Angeles." Her face fell. "I can't believe I lost my father's toolbox."

"Maybe you left it on the Vixen's Revenge?" Steven wrapped his arms around her. "We'll ask Jeff. Do you like it?" His belly twitched in apprehension. It had been difficult to find the time to create this for her in secret with everything else they had going on.

Noli turned around and gave him a deep and passionate kiss. "It's the best gift ever."

"What are you going to do first?" he asked.

She thought for a moment. "I think I'm going to make a hoverboard."

"That's my Noli." He wouldn't have her any other way.

TWENTY-SEVEN

Reunions

Kevighn opened his eyes, which he hadn't realized he'd closed. The disordered chaos of the wild lands had disappeared. All around him was something that reminded him of walking in a dense fog—only this haze was pale purple and had an appearance more akin to champagne bubbles.

His hand went to his waist, the enchanted rope still tied tightly around it. The other hand clutched the toolbox, following its pull through the blind nothingness. He couldn't see anything *but* the magic, not that he'd expected to.

Mind your thoughts. Luce's words returned to him. Yes, he should focus on the task at hand—but not so much that it took on a corporeal form. He'd heard tales of men going mad or their fears coming to life and chasing them to death.

"Mr. Braddock?" Kevighn called, trying to keep his mind blank. "Mr. Braddock, are you here?"

Being surrounded by nothing unnerved him. A light. Yes. That's what he needed. He held out his empty hand and it began to glow. Perhaps he didn't have much magical training—or natural talent—but he could make a light. A trick mastered long ago through his many misadventures with Ciarán.

While there was naught for the light to illuminate, it went far in settling the uneasy feeling coating him.

"Kevighn, is that you?" someone called through the mist. "Kevighn, come here. I have something for you."

His heart skipped a beat. He knew that voice.

"Magnolia—" Kevighn shook his head. It was either the magic taking on the voices of his subconscious or a fae who preyed on lost travelers.

Focus. He needed to keep his wits about him. Magnolia wasn't for him. He understood that now. But that didn't mean he still didn't have a certain fondness for her.

"Mr. Braddock?" he called as he followed the pull of the spell deeper into the mist.

"Kevighn, where are you? Why haven't you come, why won't you help me?" another female voice sobbed. In the distance a crumpled form appeared.

Creideamh.

On instinct, his feet moved toward it, even though it wasn't in the direction indicated by the spell. He stopped short. No. It wasn't her.

"You swore you'd always protect me," she sobbed. "Help me, brother." The figure reached out, taking on her appearance more surely with every passing moment.

"NO." Kevighn's yelp echoed through the void as he clapped his hands over his ears the best he could while holding the toolbox. "You're not her. You're not her." He took off running.

Keep it together. Taking a deep breath, he pushed everything out of his mind and continued running as he called for Mr. Braddock.

No one answered.

He passed through a veil and found himself in a tiny grove—whether it was natural, part of the wild lands, or a figment of the chaos, or even from his own imagination, he was uncertain.

Grass lay under his feet, and at the center of the grove stood a shady tree. Under it, sat two men and a woman, all in sensible but well-made mortal clothing, having a picnic.

"Henry, try these sandwiches." The woman offered a man a plate. Her mousy hair was up in a dowdy style, her glasses doing nothing to accentuate her face.

"Of course, Etta." The man smiled as he took a sandwich.

Kevighn froze. That was Magnolia's smile. Not to mention the man looked like an older version of Jeff, right down to the cleft in his chin.

"Excuse me, are you Mr. Braddock?" Kevighn prayed this wasn't his imagination. But the spell ... the spell pulled him right toward the man in the suit, sitting on the blanket, briefcase and top hat next to him as if he was on a lunch break.

The man looked up. "Why, yes, I am. Am I supposed to be meeting with you? I'm afraid my pocket watch has stopped working."

"It's still lunchtime," the other man—blond, assured—said with a wave of his hand.

"I'm not your meeting, but I'm Kevighn Silver and I've been looking for you." Lunchtime? A picnic? But time ran differently, and the magic here was so wild that perhaps even a mortal could control it.

Oh. There was *so much* Spark in this little group. But then, Magnolia had gotten it from someplace. Perhaps their collective thoughts had formed this place and they thought they were back in San Francisco, eating lunch, not lost in a void of wild magic in another realm.

"You're looking for me? Are we acquainted?" Surprise danced in Henry's eyes.

"No, but I'm acquainted with your daughter—she's sent me to get you. I need you to come with me. Though you're all welcome. This is your team, Mr. Braddock?" Kevighn could hardly leave people here. Magnolia had told him that her father's entire team of engineers had disappeared along with him.

"Noli? But she's just a girl, and you're a man grown…" Mr. Braddock's expression contorted. "What treachery is this?"

How did he explain this? Frowning, Kevighn tried to figure out a way to get Mr. Braddock to come with him. He felt an odd tugging sensation—not from the tracking spell, but from someplace else. Oh well, he had other things to think about.

"Is that my toolbox?" Mr. Braddock frowned.

Kevighn held it up. "Yes, it is. I used it to find you. Do

you … do you believe in aether? You and your team were in San Francisco to help rebuild the city. While there, you fell into a pocket of aether released by the earthquake. Your family misses you, Mr. Braddock—and I'm sure your families miss you as well," he told the other man and woman. "Please come with me, and I'll make sure you're reunited with your loved ones."

It was close to the truth, since to the mortals, magic was aether. However, they'd actually fallen through a tiny tear between the two worlds, which opened up when an earthquake devastated San Francisco. An earthquake that had originated in the Otherworld—when Annabelle took her own life to prevent being sacrificed.

Something that was partially his fault.

A look of horror crossed Etta's plain face as she studied him. "You came from out there, didn't you?" She pointed at the nothingness behind him. "If we leave this place, we'll get lost and never return, like Daniel." Her voice went quiet and she gave a little sniff.

Ah, so they *were* aware something was amiss. Who was Daniel?

"How do we know you're not some creature who will lure us away and eat us … " Etta took out a handkerchief and blew her nose.

The tugging grew stronger. What was that?

Kevighn turned to Mr. Braddock. "Aether is odd. Time passes differently. Magnolia isn't a girl any more. She's a lovely young woman who fixes flying cars and isn't afraid of anything. Jeff flies an airship. He even has a girlfriend. Please, we don't have much time. Come with me. I'll return you to your family. They miss you."

Henry Braddock gazed at him with wide, soulful eyes, a look that reminded him very much of Magnolia. "You're not a figment of my imagination?"

"No. And your wife… she's still waiting for you to come home." What was that tugging? There was a jerk and he found himself taking a step backward from the force. What? He looked down and saw the rope around his waist…

Was someone *tugging* on the rope?

"Eady?" Henry's face brightened.

"We won't get lost in the void." Kevighn pointed to the rope around his waist. "That's what this is for. I'll explain everything, but we don't have time. Let's go. Please." Kevighn held out his hand as the tugging increased. "I promise not to harm you."

Henry Braddock stood.

Etta's eyes pleaded. "Henry, don't go…"

Henry shook his head. "Noli. Jeff. Eady… I… I miss them so much." Henry offered her his hand. "It'll be fine." His attention turned to the other man. "Ned, are you coming?"

Ned took a deep breath then turned to Kevighn, eyes narrowing. "You will take us home?"

"We have a stop or two on the way, but I will, I promise. No tricks," Kevighn assured him, nearly stumbling backward as the rope pulled. "Please, I… I think our time is up."

The three mortals gazed at him.

"Stay very close to me. In fact, we should hold hands."

Not that he wanted to, but a sense of urgency filled. "I won't chase after anyone who wanders off."

"But what about Daniel?" Etta's lower lip quivered.

Henry patted her shoulder. "It's time to go, Etta."

A burning sensation filled Kevighn's chest. He looked down and saw his sigil glowing. "By the Bright Lady, Ciarán," he muttered. Yes, time to go indeed. "Let's go!" he said to the group. "And we should run."

They held hands, and Kevighn gave a few tugs on the rope, hoping it would send a signal to Ciarán—or whoever was on the other side.

The rope responded in turn, half dragging him as they ran, trying to keep up.

"Can we slow down?" Etta huffed and puffed.

"My briefcase." Henry stopped. "I should get it. My wife gave it to me."

The tugging didn't stop.

"I'm sure your wife will get you another." Kevighn herded them through the chaos, hoping that their quickness would keep any apparitions from appearing. The last thing he wanted was to hear his sister's pitiful cries.

Etta stopped. "Daniel, Daniel…" She turned and looked at them. "Don't you hear him calling?"

Kevighn stopped short, the rope nearly cutting him off in the middle. "No, I hear nothing. Do you?"

The gentlemen shook their heads.

"Let's get him." Etta let go.

"No." Kevighn grabbed her wrist. "It's not him. We're in a pocket of pure aether. It will deceive you. We need to get going, we're almost out." He hoped. The rope tugged again, winding him. Kevighn tugged back.

Etta struggled against his grip. "Let me go. Let me go."

Henry put a hand on her shoulder. "Daniel's gone, Etta. Please…."

"No," she shrieked like a banshee, fighting him. "No."

"Etta. Stop." Ned wrapped his arms around her. "Come on."

"Daniel." Tears flooded her eyes as she sobbed.

Kevighn couldn't help but feel sorry for her. He hated to see a woman cry. "Here." He shoved a handkerchief at her. "I'm sorry, but we need to go." The rope pulled him forward. "The faster we go, the easier it will be."

"It'll be all right." Ned put arm around her waist.

They took off at a run, the rope continuing to pull him in. Finally the mist gave way to the wild lands.

Ciarán stood there, hood down, a rope in his hands. Relief flooded his face. "Bright Lady bless, I thought you'd never come out."

Kevighn's heart skipped a beat. "How long have I been gone?"

For Ciarán to look like that … it made his heart hurt.

"I've been tugging on this damn rope all day. I waited four days before coming." Pain flashed in his eyes.

He'd been gone five days? It felt like moments.

Henry looked around at the wild forest surrounding them. "Where are we? This isn't San Francisco."

"No, it's not. I'm Kyran. Have you ever wondered where aether comes from?" Ciarán gestured around him. "It's here."

348

"Aether is naught but children's stories," Ned scoffed, still holding the sobbing Etta.

Kevighn shook his head. "Believe what you will." They'd probably have to alter everyone's memories before returning them to the mortal realm anyhow. "We'll return you to your homes soon, I promise. Mr. Braddock, Magnolia will be so happy to see you. So will your son and wife."

"So this is him." Ciarán appraised him thoughtfully. "And who are these people?"

"Ah, please forgive my manners." Henry smiled. "I'm Henry Braddock. I'm an engineer. And this is my team ... well, what's left of it." His voice went soft. "I trust you'll help me figure this out? I know I shouldn't just go with you, but ... I ... I know something's not right, and I miss my family."

"I'm going to take you all to my tavern. You'll be my guests, and you'll be quite safe. Now, please, let's go. I don't know about you, but I'm hungry." Ciarán nodded and began to walk, his guards following.

Ned spoke softly to Etta, who still sobbed.

"Daniel ... was he part of your team?" Kevighn asked Henry.

"No." He shook his head, a mournful look on his face. "It was so strange. One moment we were examining a bridge, the next moment we were ... well, in a place like this." Henry gestured to the wild lands. "The first to go was Adam. There was a beautiful woman who called to him, and then ... " He cringed. "It was like something from a nightmare."

A baobhan sith probably. "She killed him?"

"Yes." Henry exhaled sharply.

"You're lucky all of you didn't die," Kevighn told him. These mortals, dripping with the Spark, would make someone a very tasty snack.

"Yes. Mark was next. We wandered into that….that strange purple mass. He saw a monster, one we didn't. He ran and we…we never saw him again." Henry bowed his head. "We all saw Daniel, though, standing there, talking to us. Daniel was Etta's husband. We knew him very well. Only he died of cholera last winter. That was when I truly realized that we were someplace strange. I heard people calling to me— my wife and Noli. It was enough to make a lesser man mad. When we happened upon that…that place…it was far easier to pretend we were back in San Francisco, on a lunch break, than face…well…everything."

"I understand." Kevighn gave him a little nod. Yes, forget-spells for everyone. It would be better that way. He went over to Ciarán and put a hand on his shoulder. "Where's Aodhan? Is he all right?"

"He misses us." Ciarán's look went far away. "Her Grace even had a letter delivered from him. I've never met a monarch quite like her."

"She's different…trusting, innocent." Kevighn kept his voice soft.

"Her intentions are pure. I believe she'll make a good ally." Ciarán looked at the mortals. "What a bounty."

"What do we tell them?" His gaze fell on the weeping Etta.

"What we need to. Then, I suppose, we'll make them forget. Except for her father. We should ask her what she wants."

That was unexpected.

"Do you really think we can be allies with the *earth court*?" Kevighn asked. Considering that he and Ciarán were originally fire court, it was a lot to swallow.

"I think we can be allies with Her Grace. Do you know that she wants to arrange visits between Elise and Aodhan?" An incredulous look spread over Ciarán's face. "Next thing you know, she'll ask us to teach Elise fire magic."

"Someone needs to teach the girl. It's not as if they can simply bring in tutors without advertising Elise has those gifts. I have a feeling they'll want to keep her abilities a secret from Tiana," Kevighn replied. "We have people who can use all elements among the dark court…"

Ciarán's eyebrows rose. "Someone will notice her going back and forth. Perhaps…" He shook his head. "If it were another time, I'd entrust her to Mathias."

"Mathias is a traitor," Kevighn snapped. After all, he, too, had assured him that his sister would be safe with Quinn. Then the bastard ran off and hid like a coward.

"Like Quinn, Mathias was never part of our court." Ciarán shrugged. "We knew they were trouble the moment they entered the tavern."

Quinn had come into the Thirsty Pooka for research, looking for odd bits of knowledge. His half-brother had tagged along for amusement. Ciarán had never liked Quinn, though he'd liked Mathias well enough. Kevighn couldn't stand that pompous ass.

"I'm sure Magnolia has ideas," Kevighn muttered. Even sending the little girl to live with air pirates would be better than her living with Mathias. "This could be our chance to get the jewel."

Ciarán shook his head. "It's safe with Her Grace. We need her help. I ... I used my gift on her without her knowledge at the coronation—let's just say you were correct."

Kevighn blinked. "What?"

He laughed. "Things are about to get *very* interesting. Especially when we reassemble the staff. It's a good thing that you detest being bored."

"I do." Kevighn glanced over at the three mortals, who huddled together, speaking softly. "Now, let's get Aodhan back."

· · · · · · · ·

Noli put her sword around herself, then smoothed her hair. It was time to take Aodhan home. Having the boy write a letter had done the trick.

"Ready?" She turned to V, who was sitting on their bed.

"I don't like this." V frowned, pulling on his boots. "We should meet someplace neutral. What *is* he exchanging Aodhan for? I can't help but feel as if we're walking into a trap."

"I don't think it's a trap." Noli shook her head. "Aodhan should be back with his family." All the missive had said was that they'd make an exchange. She *hoped* it was for the pieces of the staff.

"But if he's really Quinn's son ..." V shook his head.

"Quinn and my father were cousins. I looked it up. They were so close because Quinn was raised here at the palace. Sort of the poor relation foisted off with people who didn't want him. Apparently my father was the only one who really accepted him, which was also why Quinn worked so hard at his studies, so that he could be accepted in his own right as a scholar."

All the pieces fit together. "That makes sense, but I thought he was a prince."

"Technically, he is—though not from the direct line, like my father." V's forehead furrowed. "Their grandfathers were brothers? Or was it great-grandfathers? Anyway, there are a lot of lesser princes and princesses, though few hardly ever use the title. It was different for Quinn because he grew up here and my father brought him in as a brother. At least that's what I found. Also, he was..." V's cheeks pinked. "An indiscretion, apparently."

"Oh." So even with magic to prevent children, there were still *accidents*.

The bedroom door burst open. "I don't want Aodhan to leave." Elise stood there with an enormous pout on her face, hands on her hips. "Why can't I go with you?"

"Because you need to stay here," V retorted.

"That's not *fair*," she wailed, face turning pink.

"I know." Noli walked over and comforted her, feeling bad for the little girl. "I know it's not fair. But I'll bring back your valise. Why don't you and Caít go and decorate the tree house for me? Could you do that?"

"Me?" Elise's face lit up. "Could we have a tea party there when you return?"

"What a grand idea. Miri can have the kitchen make those green cakes I like." Noli needed a break so badly that she'd even play tea party, as long as there was tea and cake. The work had been nonstop. Meetings and meetings and meetings and so much work. Her head threatened to explode from too much information. She hadn't even had time to try out her workshop—and she still couldn't find her father's toolbox.

Even V was grumpier from lack of sleep.

"I don't want him to leave," Elise sniffed.

"I know you'll miss Aodhan, but he needs to go home." Not that Noli wanted him to leave either. She, too, had grown used to having him around. However, he wasn't theirs to keep, even if he made Elise happy.

"I know." Elise's voice went glum as she looked at her shoes. "But I'm lonely."

"You have Caít, a magic tutor, and Miri, not to mention Breena and Nissa will gladly play with you *whenever* you wish." Though Noli didn't really like Tiana's hand-maidens spending much time with Elise.

Just yesterday Tiana had asked them all to come to tea very soon—and bring Elise. She'd also sent Elise a mechanical pony. They hadn't given it to Elise yet. Noli and V needed to discuss how to handle everything, including whether or not to tell Elise the truth about Tiana, before Tiana told it to her. In some ways it was surprising the queen had waited so long, but then this was Tiana, and rationality never seemed to factor into the situation.

"Let's say goodbye to Aodhan." Noli took Elise's hand

and they found Aodhan in the sitting room playing with Urco. He was fully healed and quite ready to go home.

Elise threw herself into Aodhan's arms. "I'm going to miss you."

"I'm going to miss you too." Aodhan hugged Elise tightly, exuding a tenderness only seen in the pure-hearted love of children. "But we'll still play and visit."

They both looked at Noli expectantly.

"Of course you will." She'd have to figure it all out, but she couldn't stomach the thought of keeping them from one another.

"No." V stood there ready to go, a scowl on his face. "Noli, this won't … we can't … "

"Don't be a fussy old bodger." She scowled right back. "Yes, it will be tricky, but we'll find a way. It will be good diplomacy."

V raked his hand through his hair. "Diplomacy that will get us killed."

"Isn't that the best kind?" James appeared, sword at his side, a grin on his face.

"Ugh, you two." V shook his head.

"Isn't that my line?" James' grin grew.

Noli looked around. "Elise, go play with Caít and Miri. We'll be back in a little while."

Elise clutched Aodhan's hand. "Don't forget me."

He gazed into her eyes. "I couldn't if I tried."

With a grin, Noli ribbed V. "How can you deny that?"

"It's the company he keeps that I take issue with." V let out a heavy sigh.

Noli shook her head. "You sigh too much. Let's go."

....

"*This* is where the dark king resides?" V scowled at the tavern as they approached.

"If you keep scowling, your face is going to freeze that way," Noli retorted. At the same time, she could understand his uneasiness. Bran, Elric, and even Padraig didn't like the idea of *them* going to the dark king to make the trade. They all thought Ciarán should come to the palace. Which made sense. But she knew deep down that Ciarán wouldn't betray them.

Unlike the last time she'd been to the Thirsty Pooka, it was daytime and quiet. The door opened as they approached.

Noli looked at Aodhan and squeezed his hand. She steeled herself and stepped through the doors, trying to remind herself to be regal. This time she was here officially, as queen.

The place was empty, except for a few people sitting or standing near the bar. They were nearly all in black, and every one of them was a large man. Probably the dark king's most trusted guards. A few men lurked on the staircase and balcony overlooking the main room. Were there no women in the dark court?

"Father." Aodhan let go of her hand and darted in, running straight into Ciarán's arms.

Hood up, Ciarán was standing in front of the bar, in plain sight of the door. He bent down and scooped the boy up. "Ooof. I won't be able to do that much longer."

Aodhan laughed, face alight with joy. "I didn't grow that much, Father."

"Perhaps not, but I still missed you." Ciarán set him down.

"I missed you, too." Kevighn embraced Aodhan.

There was something different about Kevighn, aside from the fact he wore all black, though his bow was still slung over his shoulder.

"Of course *he's* here," V muttered, still hovering in the entrance.

"Shut it," James hissed, giving him a push so that they were all inside. They only had a handful of uniformed guards with them, including the girl Aire. Noli liked her.

Noli gave the dark king a small curtsey and joined him by the bar. There was no bartender. No, the tavern wasn't open for business—not the refreshment business, at least.

"We've returned your son to you unharmed, Your Majesty," she said. "Do you have what I requested?" She wasn't sure she liked so many people present, but she couldn't let that show.

"Here are Elise's things." Ciarán handed her Elise's valise.

"She'll be happy to have this back." Noli handed it to James, then returned her attention to Ciarán. "The items?"

"I have something better." Ciarán looked like a cat who'd found the cream pitcher.

Her belly lurched. What treachery was this?

V put his hand on the hilt of his sword and took a step forward.

"Stand down, young king." Ciarán gave him a sharp look.

"You, as well, Prince Séamus. I'm not betraying you. Rather, I have gone to great lengths to secure a very generous symbol of our goodwill."

"Did you now?" She eyed him. What could be better than pieces of the staff?

"We'll need to work together soon, for the good of the Otherworld." His eyes were really the only thing visible under that hood. "You have shown me that you're trustworthy. I wish to do to the same." Ciarán nodded to Kevighn, who disappeared into a room behind the bar.

Aodhan tugged on Ciarán's cape. "Father, what's going on? I don't understand."

"I know, and I'm sorry." His voice was firm, and he didn't tell Aodhan any more.

"Noli's my friend. You're not going to trick her, are you?" Aodhan's eyes went wide.

Someone made a comment in the background about earth court being no one's friend.

"You *are* my friend, aren't you, Noli?" The boy took a step toward her, eyes beseeching.

"I'm friends with kind people. As long as there's kindness in your heart, you try to do what's right, and treat others the way you wish to be treated, you will always have a friend in me, Aodhan. Elise as well." She smiled at him. He was such a kind-hearted boy.

A few people snorted at her words—from both delegations. Ciarán gazed at her, a dark eyebrow rising, but didn't say anything.

Kevighn returned, a few people following, and addressed

her. "Your Grace, do you remember what you asked me to do, so long ago…"

V shot her a dark look as she thought for a moment.

"I…I found him." Kevighn didn't meet her eyes. Something was in his hand.

"He found more than him. But I'll be generous and give you all three." Ciarán sounded so regal as he said that.

"What?" Noli squinted at what was in Kevighn's hand. "Is that my toolbox? How did you get that? I have been looking all over the place for it."

"I…I used it to find someone. Here." Kevighn shoved the box into her hands. "There's someone who wants to see you."

In front of her stood two men and a woman. One of the men…no…it…it couldn't be. Could it? Noli looked closer. Her knees went weak.

"Papa?" She gazed at the dark-haired man. "Is it really you?" She turned to Ciarán. "If this is a trick…"

"It's no trick, Your Grace." Kevighn took his place by Ciarán's side.

"Eady?" Her father walked over, eyes large. "No, you're not Eady. Noli? Is that you?" He took a step back. "But you can't be my daughter. My Noli's a little girl, and you…you're a woman. A beautiful woman."

"Papa." Noli handed V the toolbox and threw herself into his arms as if she were still small. "Papa, I missed you. I never gave up hope that you were still alive. Never ever." Almost. But not completely. Tears pricked her eyes as she buried her head in his broad shoulder.

Her father's arms wrapped around her. "This place is very strange, but thank you for sending your friend to find me."

She tipped her face up. "Be careful with your thanks here."

He was here. Alive. In the Otherworld. Flying figs, how would she explain everything?

"Where's your mama?" He looked around.

"I'll take you to her soon. Jeff, too." Oh, how happy they'd be!

"Do you remember Etta and Ned?" Papa asked, arms still around her.

"Of course." Noli smiled at them, a little afraid to ask where the rest of his team was. Etta was the first married career woman she'd ever met, and was brilliant at sums and figures. Noli glanced over at Ciarán and Kevighn. "There are no words to express my gratitude."

"I suppose we get no pieces of the staff then?" V muttered.

"Will you stop being a fussy old bodger? Getting my father back is worth it. It . . . " Emotions threatened to overwhelm her brain and shut off her thinking, her words. "You've been gone for seven years, Papa."

"I'm sorry." His eyes misted.

He looked as if he hadn't aged a day. Was it possible that he hadn't?

"It's not your fault. Mama will be so excited." Just the thought made her giddy. "Oh, and if Jeff and Vix are truly getting married you'll get to see." What would her father make of Vix?

"Jeff? Married?" Mirth flowed through her father's voice. "But if it's been that long…" His eyes fell on V. "Steven? Is that you? Where are your glasses?"

"I … I'm glad you're back, Mr. Braddock." V put an arm around Noli's waist, then dropped it, cheeks pinking. "Um…"

"Oh dear, this should be fun," James laughed.

"Papa, you remember Steven and James Darrow, don't you?" she said. The look on V's face made her want to laugh; he flushed all the way to his hairline.

V took a deep breath. "Iwanttomarryyourdaughter. IwasgoingtoaskJeffbutnowthatyou'reback…"

Her father took a step back, bewilderment crossing his face. "Are you that old, Noli?"

"I … I'm seventeen." Noli's cheeks warmed. She hadn't expected V to blurt it out so. "Steven's taken care of me all those years you were away."

Her father's eyebrows rose. "Why are you all carrying swords … and why are you *here*? No one will tell me much, but I'm pretty certain we're … elsewhere."

"We are." She gulped. "We're in the place aether comes from. Some people can cross back and forth. V and I are among them. It's … it's a bit of a story."

"I see." A haunted look took up residence in his eyes. "I suppose much has happened since we've been gone?"

"It has." More than she ever hoped he'd know. It would just hurt him. "But you're fine. And soon … soon I'll take you to Mama."

"Do you find the exchange satisfactory?" Ciarán looked smug—and amused.

"I do, Your Majesty." She couldn't stop grinning.

"Your father was missing?" Aodhan came over to her. "I'm glad you have him back."

"I'm glad your uncle is good at finding people." Noli patted Aodhan on the head. "You be a good boy for your father and uncle."

Aodhan nodded.

"If I may." Ciarán jerked his head to a corner.

Noli glanced over at her father, who was in deep conversation with V and James, then joined Ciarán.

"I think it would be best to wipe their memories of all of this," Ciarán murmured. "They've had traumatic experiences while here in the Otherworld. Also, I'm not certain how much you want your mortal parents to know…about everything…"

She sighed. He had a point, though she wasn't sure she liked the idea of mucking with their minds.

"All right, but what *will* they remember? There's no way to hide that they were gone for so many years," she said.

"They'll recall being caught in the aether, Kevighn finding them, and then returning to Los Angeles—well, the other two will. Your father will remember being reunited with you. But this…" Ciarán gestured to the pub. "Not to mention everything else they've heard and seen."

"Caught in the aether?" Noli cocked her head, pondering that. It could work.

"That's close to the truth. They were found in a pocket

of wild magic, so to them it felt as if days had passed, not years, which is why they haven't aged. I think it would be best, especially for the woman. She's not very … strong … " Ciarán glanced over at Etta, who looked a bit bewildered.

"She's more one for facts and figures than stories. People like that don't enjoy having their realities challenged," Noli agreed. "So, you'll return Ned and Etta to Los Angeles, and my father—"

"Excuse me, Your Majesty." V put his hand on her shoulder, his eyes dancing. "Noli, he said *yes*."

"He did? Oh, V." She threw her arms around him. "I … I have my father back."

"I'm so glad." V held her tight. "That will also make things easier for your mother … she'll have him … since … "

"Oh, right." Reality hit her. "Yes." She'd just gotten her father back, after all these years, and now she'd barely see him.

V cupped her face in his hands. "Cheer up. He's back. We'll visit. I promise."

She gulped, her throat growing tight from so many feelings all at once. "I know. So … what do we do … if we erase his memory we can't head back to the palace … "

"I suppose we'll just head to your mother's a little early." V smiled bashfully. "That's why we've been working so hard, so that I can take you to Boston. We can't stay long, but you can have Christmas with your parents and see your brother get married."

Tears leaked out of her eyes as she held V tight. "Can James get Elise and meet us there? I don't want them to feel left out."

V planted a kiss on top of her head. "James can also put your toolbox in your workshop where it belongs and bring Elise her valise."

"Oh, Elise will be excited about that. I can't wait to see my mother dote on Elise." Noli's fingers traced his jaw. She really ought to give the toolbox back to her father . . .

Ciarán cleared his throat, reminding them of the task at hand. "Excuse me, but have you decided how you'd like to proceed, Your Grace?"

Christmas. She was about to spend Christmas with her mother and father, with Jeff and Vix, James and Elise . . . and V. When surrounded by those you loved most, who needed presents?

She exchanged a look with V. "Yes, yes we have."

It was time to give her mother the best Christmas gift ever.

TWEN+Y-EIGH+

The Best Presents

"It's your move, Uncle Kevighn." Aodhan grinned. They sat on the floor of the sitting room, the game board on a low table between them.

Kevighn studied the pieces on the board, then looked to Ciarán for help, since he never was good at this game. Ciarán shook his head, hiding his smile.

With a huff, Kevighn moved a piece, hoping the move was a good one. "They were kind to you?"

"Did you know the earth court palace is made from living trees?" Aodhan moved his piece, cheerfully capturing Kevighn's. "They were very nice. I spent most of my time with Elise and Miri. The room I slept in belonged to Elise's older brother. I . . . I never know what to call them. Why do they have so many names? I like Noli a lot, and Miri." He laughed. "She's so funny."

"Who's Miri?" Kevighn pondered which piece to move. Already he had fewer pieces on the board than Aodhan.

Aodhan shrugged. "She's a sprite. She's Noli's nursemaid and friend."

"Noli's *nursemaid*?" Kevighn snorted as he moved a piece, rethought the move, and went a different way.

"Noli says handmaidens are nursemaids for grown-up girls." Aodhan moved his own piece, capturing the piece Kevighn just moved.

That sounded like something Noli might say.

"I think Miri's the sprite," Ciarán said from his perch on the settee behind him. "As in, when Magnolia was the sprite ... I still don't understand it." His hand rested on Kevighn's shoulder.

"I do." Kevighn nodded slowly, moving one of his pieces away from Aodhan's. "When Tiana made Magnolia a sprite there *was* a sprite inside her, two spirits sharing one body. The sprite would take over Noli's body, sometimes, when we were on the airship together. It was ... odd. But how did she get her own form?"

Ciarán shook his head. "As much as I pretend, I really don't know everything."

"Father, you won't let anyone kill me, will you?" Aodhan asked suddenly, looking up at Ciarán in earnest.

"Did someone say they would?" Outrage flashed in Ciarán's eyes, though his features remained carefully schooled.

Kevighn wasn't as politic. "Who said that? Tell me."

"No one. Noli had a book she was reading, and I ... I read it. I think ... " He chewed on his lower lip. "I think my father wrote it. It was a diary of a man married to a woman named Creideamh. She was my mother, wasn't she?"

Quinn kept a diary?

"Yes. Creideamh was your mother," Kevighn replied, mixed feelings rising inside him. "You look just like her—except for your hair. Who wrote the diary?"

"His name was Quinn. It said that the old earth king killed my mother because she had the wrong magic." Aodhan's eyes misted but he didn't cry. "I have the wrong magic. Will they kill me too? What about Elise? She has the wrong magic as well."

Kevighn sighed and looked at Ciarán. He didn't know what to say. At least, not things that could be said in front of children. Not to mention that he shouldn't disparage Aodhan's father in front of him.

"Quinn was your father, yes. He gave you to us to keep you safe. Kevighn and I won't allow *anyone* to harm you." Ciarán's voice went quiet. "Things are complicated. Technically, you're allowed to have your magic. This is hard to prove, but we will if necessary."

Kevighn looked at Ciarán, surprised. "What do you mean?"

"Think, Kevighn. Who's Quinn's half-brother?" Ciarán made a face.

Mathias. Who was of the high queen's house, where having multiple magic was allowed—to some extent. Quinn's father was high court, but Quinn was never officially accepted, just shunted off to the earth court. It was therefore easier to condemn Quinn's babe than prove that the child was allowed to possess multiple gifts through Quinn's lineage. Maybe. The law got touchy when it came to boys.

Not that any of this would have helped his sister.

"This is all too complicated for me," Kevighn said. "I'm just glad the monarchs don't understand how *many* people have multiple magics, especially in the high court. Mass executions are the last thing we need right now."

"Kevighn." Ciarán's voice went stern.

Kevighn saw the look on Aodhan's face and sighed. "I ... I'm sorry. Yes, your mother died because of her magic. But she wanted you to live. Quinn, too." That was the one thing that redeemed Quinn in his mind.

"Is Quinn dead? Was he the same Quinn that tutored Elise?" Aodhan asked.

"Yes," Kevighn said.

The boy didn't seem too concerned about Quinn's death. Good. He'd save the details of that event for another day. But then, he didn't *actually* kill Quinn ... the man would have died anyway. He'd just put him out of his misery.

"I know you'll protect me until I can protect myself." Aodhan smiled. "But ... " The smile faded. "What about Elise?"

"Elise will be fine. Magnolia will protect her," Kevighn assured him.

"They have a hound. May I have a hound?" Aodhan shot them a pleading look, changing the subject in the way only a child could.

"We'll see. You've heard a lot of things. Do you have

any questions for me?" Ciarán joined them around the table, game abandoned.

"Are you really a king? How can you be the king of darkness? You can't make things dark." Aodhan cocked his head as if pondering this. "You will have good relations with Noli's court, won't you, so that Elise and I can remain friends?"

"I am king, yes," Ciarán said slowly. "I never told you this because I wanted protect you."

Aodhan nodded. "Like Elise didn't know she was a princess, to protect her. I . . . I understand."

"You do? I'm glad." Ciarán smiled.

Sadness stabbed Kevighn in the chest. Yes, this was Creideamh's child. She, too, quietly understood such things, while he would have raged and yelled. Perhaps thrown a chair.

"As for what I'm king of . . . you understand how courts have opposites, don't you?" Ciarán asked. Aodhan nodded. "The dark court is the opposite of the high court. I don't control darkness any more than Queen Tiana controls light. While she was born to the position, I, being her opposite, had to *take* it. The high queen is always a woman; the dark king is always a man."

Aodhan thought for moment, then nodded. "Oh, good, so I don't have to be a king then. I'm not sure I want to. There are a lot of meetings. They make Noli cranky."

Kevighn couldn't help but laugh. Yes, Magnolia didn't like to sit still.

"We're still your family, Aodhan." Ciarán reached out and squeezed his shoulder.

"I know. I'm glad I'm home. I missed you." Aodhan gave

them a smile that lit up his entire face. "Uncle Kevighn, can we go hunting tomorrow?"

"Of course we can. Perhaps we'll bring your father...he was the one who taught me how to hunt." Kevighn looked over at Ciarán. "He taught me a lot of things. Much more than I give him credit for."

Like how to live again.

Kevighn's hand went to his sigil. Yes, this was where he belonged. With his family. With Aodhan and Ciarán, leading the dark court and the Otherworld into a new era. Ready or not.

"Aodhan, I...I have a present for you," Kevighn added. Yes, it was time to pass it on.

"You do?" Aodhan bounced up and down. "What is it?"

"It's very special. It belonged to your mother. But you must take good care of it."

"I will, I promise. What is it?"

"We need to go there." Kevighn stood and looked at Ciarán. "Can we go there now?"

Ciarán rose. "I think that's a great idea. I'll have Luce make us a picnic."

....

"What's this cabin, Uncle Kevighn?" Aodhan asked as they entered his lands.

"My house." He should get a few more things while they were here.

The boy frowned. "Won't you be staying with us?"

"He will. He and your mother lived here and sometimes he uses it as a base and a workshop," Ciarán assured him.

They walked past the cabin and entered the gardens, overgrown and wild, having no one to care for them.

"Your gardens need work, Uncle." Aodhan ran over to the roses. "Did you know Noli likes roses?"

"Yes, she does." Kevighn kept walking so he wouldn't think about Magnolia. That was the past, and he needed to live in the present because there was so much for him to live for. They walked through the gardens to Creideamh's grove.

"This was your mother's grove," Kevighn told him. "It's now yours. But you need to care for it." This grove held so many memories.

"Of course I will. But... how do I care for it?" Aodhan looked at the grove curiously.

"Let me show you." Kevighn took his hand and they crossed through the ring of trees. There sat her tree house, ringed by the star blooms Magnolia had planted.

Aodhan looked up at the tree house and gasped. "This... this is mine? All mine? Oh, Uncle Kevighn it's the best present ever!"

Tiny wood faeries appeared, looking at them curiously. A blue one sat on Aodhan's shoulder.

"This is Aodhan, Creideamh's son. This is his tree house now," Kevighn told the wood fairies who swarmed them, lighting up the grove.

A yellow one flew over and landed on Aodhan's nose. He went cross-eyed and laughed. "Hello. I'll take good care of it. I promise." Aodhan looked up. "May I go in?"

Kevighn gestured to it. "Go ahead."

He and Ciarán watched as Aodhan scrambled into the house and explored, the wood faeries giving him the tour.

"You're smiling." Ciarán stood close, their arms brushing.

Joy at hearing laughter once again coming from that tree house filled him with happiness. "I'm happy. I...I haven't been truly happy in a long time."

He hadn't realized that until this very moment.

Aodhan popped his head out the window and waved. "Hi!"

"Look at him." Ciarán put an arm around his waist. "Things aren't perfect—they never are. But you have a lot to be happy about. And contrary to whatever you might believe, you *do* deserve to be happy."

"I do, don't I?" For too long, he'd relied on vices to forget; too long had he shirked his duties, too long had he hurt the people he loved—and who loved him. Too long had he felt that being happy would be an affront to the memory of his sister; that he didn't deserve to be happy because he hadn't been able to protect her.

"You do," Ciarán said.

Kevighn turned and faced him. "Thank you," he said softly. "For showing me the error of my ways, for being patient, for welcoming me back after I left. I..."

Ciarán shook his head. "You owe me no debt. I have all I need. I hope that you've realized you have all you need, too."

Kevighn gazed at Ciarán, then looked over to the tree house and nodded. "Yes. It took me a while, but yes, I do."

He was ready to start his new life. After all these years of just existing, it was finally time for him to live.

· · · · · · · ·

Noli clutched V's hand as they all rode in a motorcab to Grandfather Montgomery's house. Ned and Etta had been returned to their homes.

Her father looked out the window and frowned. "This doesn't look like Los Angeles."

"No, Papa. We took the airship from Los Angeles to Boston because Mama's here," Noli reminded him. Ciarán had told her that her father would be a little disoriented from the forget-spell. As much as she hated lying to him, it was for the best.

"Oh, I see." He frowned, and rubbed his chin, which badly needed a shave. "The doctor said it would take a few days for my head to clear after being stuck in the aether, didn't he? I'm having trouble keeping everything straight."

"Yes, Papa." There'd been no doctor any more than there'd been an airship.

"I can't wait to see your mother." His eyes glowed, then he frowned. "It's nearly Christmas, isn't it? I don't have a present for her."

She patted his shoulder. "You're the best present she could ask for."

The car pulled up the drive at Grandfather Montgomery's, a grand house with columns and a large porch with a swing on it.

Papa frowned. "What about our home in Los Angeles?"

"It's Jeff's home now," she replied, giving his hand a squeeze.

He gave a little sigh. "I did love that house. I don't think the firm will have my job anymore. Your mother always did love Boston more; perhaps we'll just stay here."

"I think she'd like that." She squeezed her father's hand. If her parents stayed in Boston, that could make things a little easier for her and V. Maybe.

They climbed out of the motorcab, all in mortal dress. The driver got their bags. The motorcab drove off and they walked up the drive.

Taking a deep breath she knocked on the door. *Here goes nothing.*

The door cracked open and Jameson, Grandfather's ancient butler, peered out. He blinked. "Ah, Miss Noli. Please, come in."

Her insides bubbled with excitement. "Is Mama here?"

"Noli, you're here." The door flew all the way open, and Mama came out onto the porch in a pretty navy afternoon dress, a big smile on her face. She looked much more rested and more like the mother she remembered than when they'd lived in Los Angeles.

Yes, Jeff had been right. Letting Mama go had been the right choice.

And now . . . now she had Papa to keep her company.

"Are you all better now, Noli? You look pale still. I was so worried. But why did you return to Los Angeles to rest? You're welcome here." Mama hugged Noli to her.

"Well, Mama...you see... I had to get a special present and bring it here for you." Noli's heart thumped in her ears. "I got an aethergraph from San Francisco and so V and I went up and now..." She gestured to her father. "Merry Christmas, Mama."

Her mother's pale jaw dropped, blue eyes going wide as a pale hand flew to her delicate mouth. She began to tremble. "Henry?"

"I told you he'd come back, Mama. I told you." Noli wanted to jump up and down in happiness. She'd been *right*.

"Eady." Papa crossed the porch, gathered his wife in his arms, and spun her around while she squealed like a little girl. He pulled her to him and buried his face in her dark hair. "Oh, Eady, I missed you so much. You're as beautiful as ever."

"Henry." Mama cupped his face with her hand. "You... you look just as I remember."

"What's going on? Why are you all outside?" Jeff walked through the still-open front door out onto the porch and stopped short. "Father?" His voice shook a little.

"I told you he'd come back to us." Noli grinned at her brother. Even though she should be beyond such things, it felt good to say *I told you so*.

Jeff patted her on the shoulder. "Yes, you did. Father, I'm so glad to see you."

They embraced, and their father gave him a hearty clap on the back. "My, what a fine gentleman you've become, Jeff. I hear you have yourself a fiancée? I can't wait to meet her."

"I'd love for you to meet her," Jeff replied.

"Steven, it's nice to see you again, please, pardon my

manners. I...I'm a bit in shock here." Mrs. Braddock's eyes glistened, her smile wide. She looked around the porch. "Where's Elise and James? Is your father away on business?"

"It's understandable." V smiled back. "Elise and James are on their way, as for my father." His expression went grim. "My...my father passed right after Thanksgiving."

"He did?" Her hand went to her mouth in ladylike horror. "Oh dear, I'm so sorry to hear that. I respected Mr. Darrow immensely. Dear sweet Elise must be devastated."

"We all are," V said softly, shoulders slumping a little.

"But what will become of you three, you're so young." Her mother shook her head.

"Mother, why don't we all go *inside*," Jeff prompted. As usual he needed a shave.

"Oh, yes, yes," Mama blustered. "I..." Her gaze fell to Papa and she blushed.

Papa took Mama's hand and kissed it. "Yes, let's go inside."

Mama gave a girlish giggle and the two of them went inside.

Jeff rolled his eyes, then glanced at the doorway and lowered his voice. "How did you find him? Where was he?"

"The official story is that he and his team were stuck in the aether—but they were in the Otherworld. Kevighn found him, actually," Noli whispered, trying not to shiver from the cold. Yes, she was ready to go inside.

"Silver?" Jeff made a face. "That must be quite the story."

Noli nodded. "We have quite a lot to tell you and Vix. Is she here?"

"Yes, she is."

Her mother reappeared in the doorway. "Noli, come inside before you catch your death. Ellen's bringing tea to the parlor. Jameson will get your bags."

"Yes, Mama." Noli looked at V and her brother, who were still standing on the porch.

"We'll be right there." V smiled, but it was strained.

Noli gave Jeff a pointed look. "Don't hurt him. Papa already said *yes.*"

She went inside and shut the door, gazing at the grand entryway. A kissing ball hung in the archway. Christmas greenery decorated every available surface, from the banister to the doorways. How long had it been since she'd been to Grandfather Montgomery's? Although she'd been here at Thanksgiving, she'd been ill because of Brogan and didn't actually remember it.

Voices came from the parlor. Noli peeked inside and saw her mother and father sitting close together on the settee, speaking softly and holding hands. Her heart pattered happily. They were back together. A fire roared in the fireplace, a giant Christmas tree stood in the corner near the piano.

"Noli, why are you hovering in the doorway?" Grandfather Montgomery's voice dripped with disapproval from behind her.

"Hello, Grandfather. I . . . I brought Mama a present, and, well, it feels like intruding." She moved so her grandfather could see.

His hand went to his heart. "Is that . . . ."

"They found him. Isn't that grand?" Noli grinned so hard her face hurt. He was back!

"I ... I should tell your grandmamma, and send word to Winston Braddock. He'll find the news that his son is alive to be a wonderful present." Her grandfather squeezed her shoulder.

"Oh yes, he would." Sometimes she forgot about Grandpa Braddock, her father's father, who also lived in Boston.

"Noli, come warm yourself by the fire. I don't want you to catch cold," Mama called.

"Yes, Mama." She went into the parlor and warmed herself, stealing glances at her parents as they held hands, giddiness bubbling inside her.

Ellen brought tea and set it on the tea table. Grandfather Montgomery and Grandmamma joined them. So did Jeff, Vix, and V.

"Father." Jeff took Vix's hand and squeezed it. "This is Vix ... Victoria Adler, my fiancée."

"It's nice to meet you, sir." Vix's Southern drawl sounded more pronounced than usual. Today she wore a simple but elegant day dress. Noli had never seen the captain in a dress before. Probably her mother's work.

"Welcome to the family." Papa smiled at Vix. "Where did you two meet?"

"I'm a pilot on an airship, like I'd always wanted," Jeff said slowly. "Vix is the captain."

"Oh, what kind of ship?" His eyes lit up.

"Oh, Henry," Mama clucked. "You can talk about airships later."

"I...I...have something I'd like to say." V stood, looking paler than usual. "Noli and I have been accepted at a university in France, starting next semester. It's a very rigorous program and will keep us quite busy. We'll be leaving right after Christmas."

"That's an unusual program—have you even finished your schooling?" Grandfather frowned.

"It's... it's very special." V gulped. "It's no secret that we wanted to attend university together and well... before we leave... there's something I wanted to ask. I...I think this is something that should happen before we go to France. Um..." Shaking, he got down on one knee, pulling a box out of his pocket.

He opened the box, which held a beautiful ring. There were seven stones: a ruby, an emerald, a garnet, an amethyst, another ruby, a diamond, and a sapphire—which spelled *regards*. These rings were all the rage for engagements, but this one was like none that Noli had ever seen—the stones formed a flower.

Both her mother and Grandmamma gasped.

Noli's heart raced. She'd known this was coming, but it did nothing to lessen the excitement.

"Magnolia Montgomery Braddock? Will you... will you be my wife?" V's voice trembled as his eyes met hers.

Everyone watched them expectantly. Mama dabbed her eyes with a handkerchief.

Noli held out her hand as V slid the ring onto her finger. "Yes," she whispered. "The answer is *yes*."

TWENTY-NINE

Boston

Steven knocked softly on the door to the room Noli was staying in. He'd gotten used to sharing a room with her, but he could hardly expect that here.

"Come in," Noli called.

He entered. This wasn't the nursery where he'd found her so ill and pale from Uncle Brogan's magic. No, this was a cheery room, with a four-poster bed and a window seat.

Noli sat curled in the window seat, reading a novel. She looked over and smiled. "Hello."

"What are you reading?" He joined her.

She flashed him the cover. "Dickens."

Always with the fiction. Noli did love her novels, while he preferred practical things like history and philosophy.

"I think you should read Machiavelli. I read it while on

my quest. It would be quite enlightening, all things considered," he told her.

Noli stuck out her tongue at him in a very un-queenlike gesture. "I'm on vacation."

He was about to retort that monarchs didn't get vacations, but he closed his mouth. Instead he squeezed into the window seat with her.

"Haven't you read *Great Expectations* a million times?" he teased. That was her favorite, next to *Alice's Adventures in Wonderland.*

She shrugged. "What of it?"

He laughed, then caught hold of her left hand. "Do you like the ring?"

"It's wonderful. When did you have time to get it?" She reached out and ran her fingers along his jaw.

He liked it when she did that. It felt like love.

"I had James send Jeff an aethergraph asking for his permission, and wiring him money so that he could get it for you, since I wasn't sure I'd have time." Even though Steven had now secured Mr. Braddock's permission, he was grateful to have Jeff's blessing as well.

"It's perfect." Noli grinned. "I'm so glad I have my father back."

He pulled her onto his lap and they got comfortable. "I'm happy for you, though I'm a little jealous. There's so much I wish I could ask my father."

About ruling. About Quinn. About the staff. About Elise.

She gave a little sigh. "There's so much to do. I feel guilty being here."

He tightened his arms around her. "Me too. But let's enjoy the time we have."

There was a knock on the half-open door.

"Noli?" Jeff walked in, Vix behind him. "Good, you're both here." He closed the door behind them. "Darrow, are you marrying my sister because you've gotten her with child?"

Noli snorted. "What makes you think that?"

Steven was glad Noli replied, because he had no words.

"A couple of weeks ago, you mentioned nothing about moving to *France*, and the idea of a marriage between you two was a bit of a joke." Jeff's face flushed red.

Steven would hardly have called it a joke; it had been more of a far-off thing.

"Jeff, there's nothing wrong with rushing things a bit because you're with child," Vix said quietly, eyes downcast. "Not if you'd intended on being with him anyway."

Jeff turned to Vix. "Is *that* why you told my mother you didn't mind if there was a surprise wedding at Christmas?"

Vix nodded. "I...I didn't want to say anything until I was certain, and I'm still not completely sure. I'd marry you anyway, but I..."

"I love you." Jeff picked up Vix and swung her around, then planted a kiss on her still-flat belly. "We'll raise our own little crew."

It was everything Steven could do to not avert his eyes; it seemed to be such a personal moment.

"It can be the Braddock Finishing School for Air Pirates,"

Noli said with a laugh. "I'm so happy for you both. So, there *is* a surprise wedding?"

"It's not exactly a surprise anymore, but yes. Tomorrow, Christmas Eve. We've already been subjected to engagement dinners, meeting the family, and such. It's rather overwhelming." Vix looked a bit pale. "I think, since you're going to France, they intend to have you two married as well ... is that all right? Your mother, grandmother, and aunties tend to take over, so if you don't want this, you should tell them immediately."

"It's fine, as long as Papa walks me down the aisle." Noli beamed.

Steven was glad Noli would get her mortal wedding with her family.

"I don't object," he said when he noticed Jeff staring at him.

"Good." Jeff stood there, arms crossed, a stoic look on his face. "And France? What is this about *France*?"

Noli sighed. "Sit. We'll tell you the truth about everything ... including Papa. But you can't tell anyone."

They told Jeff and Vix everything that had happened since they'd left Los Angeles.

"Let me get this straight, Noli." Jeff frowned. "You killed Brogan. And by killing him, you became queen and you married Darrow? And now the two of you are king and queen of the faeries?" His face contorted in disbelief.

"Just the earth court," Steven assured him. "But we'll be spending a majority of our time there, so we were trying to explain why we won't be in close contact. France may not be the best explanation, but it was all I could think of."

"Especially since Mama hates airships and won't want to visit," Noli added. "But we'll visit as much as we can. After all..." She grinned. "I want to meet my niece."

"Niece?" Jeff's eyebrows rose.

"Why not?" Noli's grin widened. "Girls are just as good as boys, don't you think, Vix?"

Vix nodded. "Better. Maybe this one will be an engineer like Auntie Noli."

Jeff looked to Steven for support.

"I'm not getting involved, especially since Noli and I are now raising Elise," Steven said. An airship full of little Vixes and Nolies. Jeff was in for it.

"What about university?" Jeff prodded. "I thought your dream was to be a botanist?"

"We'll go to university there," Noli replied. "I'll still get to be a botanist and invent things. I have a tree house and a workshop. Sometimes dreams change—I'm all right with all this. It's a lot all at once, but I can do it. No." She tipped up her head and looked at Steven. "*We* can do it. Truly, Jeff, it'll be fine. Vix, do you have any idea how I might be able to get a hoverboard to work in the Otherworld?"

"I won't hold Noli back from her dreams," Steven told them. "And *she's* queen. I'm just her king." He didn't mind one bit.

"Just?" Noli laughed.

Jeff shook his head. "It's a lot. My baby sister, queen of the faeries."

"I'm going to need your help to make everything work, Jeff. Please?" she pleaded.

"Anything for you." Jeff smiled. His eyes narrowed. "I'm still watching you, Darrow."

Of course he was. At least they weren't aiming pistols at him. Right now.

"Are they in here?" Elise called. The door burst open and she ran in. She stopped short and looked around. "Oh, how do you do? I'm Elise."

James came in behind her. "Jeff, Vix, hello."

"Ooh, a window seat." Elise climbed into the window seat with them, making it quite crowded.

Noli did the introductions. "Elise, this is my big brother, Jeff—do you remember him?—and Vix, his fiancée."

"It's nice to meet you. Noli, this house is very grand. Have you seen the giant Christmas tree? Will there be presents for me under it?" Elise beamed with excitement.

Presents. Oops. He should get Elise and Noli presents.

"I'm sure there will be." Noli tickled her, making her laugh.

Vix turned to James. "James, Hattie says hello. She also says to tell you they're still in need of a gunner."

"They are?" James flashed a smile of true happiness, one they hadn't seen since Charlotte died. "I might need to find them. I'm getting a little tired of playing prince."

Was he now? Steven needed him. But now wasn't the time to pick a fight.

"Can I go on an adventure, too?" Elise's eyes pleaded.

"Not with Hittie and Hattie, but I'll take you for a ride

in my airship," Vix told her. "She's called the Vixen's Revenge. Should we go in a little while?"

"Can we?" Elise looked at Steven.

He squeezed her. "Of course we can. I've actually never been aboard, though Noli has."

"Ah, this is where everyone is hiding," a female voice said. Noli's mother and father filled the doorway, hands clasped.

Steven looked at Noli. Her eyes were on their hands, and her lips twitched with a silly grin.

"We're just talking, Mama," Noli said, leaning against Steven's shoulder. It was quite crowded in the window seat, but he wasn't about to eject either girl.

"We're going for a ride on Vix's airship. Would you like to come?" Elise bounced up and down in excitement.

Mrs. Braddock shook her head. "I'll pass. However, I need all ladies to come with me, please. Hello, Elise. For some reason I thought you were bigger."

Oops. Steven had forgotten that the spell that made Elise look older in the mortal realm would have worn off. Hopefully people wouldn't notice too much.

"Is it a surprise?" Elise tumbled off his lap and tugged at Noli's hand. "Come on."

"It's probably dress fittings," Noli whispered to Steven. "I'm sure I'll be back eventually."

Vix gave a little sigh and stood. "I suppose 'ladies' refers to me as well?" She shook her head. "Here I always considered myself a woman, not a lady," she muttered, giving Jeff a long look as Mrs. Braddock herded them off.

Mr. Braddock remained and gave them a sheepish

look. "I . . . I don't suppose anyone needs to go Christmas shopping?"

"I do." Steven sat up. "Do you think the shops are still open?"

"A few are," Jeff replied. "I've finished my shopping, but I'll go with you. James?"

James shrugged. "Sure. Elise is expecting presents."

Steven joined them. "I'm sure she is. Shall we be off? If it is a dress-fitting, they'll be busy for some time."

"It is; I heard Mother talk about it." Jeff grimaced. "Let's get far away before we're asked for our opinions. They say they want them, but they really don't."

James made a face as they walked down the hall. "Then why *do* they?"

"Women are different," Mr. Braddock replied.

"Oh." James' face lit up. "Tomorrow Jeff and V are to be married. That means tonight I get to take you two out for your last night of freedom. Jeff, do you think Vix will lend you the airship? There's this great place in New York City—"

Steven groaned. "We're *not* going to Mathias' Place." That was a recipe for disaster.

"I know a place." Mr. Braddock's look grew sly as they walked down the stairs. "It's a bit of a Braddock tradition. But we can't tell the women."

His belly dropped. *Uh oh.* Perhaps Mathias would be the better option.

Jeff nodded, then shot Steven a long glance. "That sounds great, Father. Especially since the women are throwing some sort of ladies only party tonight. Though I'm not sure Darrow can handle what you have in mind."

"I can handle it, Braddock," Steven retorted. If he could be king of the earth court, he could handle an evening out with Noli's father and brother. Perhaps.

• • • • • • • •

Elise couldn't sleep. Voices drifted up from downstairs, many voices, like they were having a party without her. Why did she have to go to bed so early? It wasn't fair. At least she got her airship ride.

As nice as Noli's family was, she missed her own father and Quinn. Most of all she missed Aodhan. If only Miri were here to tell her a story.

The door cracked open. "Are you asleep, Elise?"

"Will you tell me a story, Noli?" Elise sat up.

"Certainly." Noli sat down on the bed. "Can't sleep? I'm nervous about tomorrow, too."

Nervous? Elise was *excited*.

"The dresses are so pretty. Your mother is nearly as good a dressmaker as Miri," Elise told her. Now she'd get to be flower girl for two weddings at the same time.

"Don't tell my mother that," Noli laughed. "Here, let me read you a story."

She went over to the bookshelves and took down a book.

Noli read her a story. Closing the book, she said, "Now go to sleep. Tomorrow is Christmas Eve."

Elise sat up with a start. "I didn't get Aodhan a present."

"Tomorrow will be busy, but perhaps on Christmas Day my mother will help you make a present for him. The best presents come from the heart." Noli smiled and squeezed her hand. "We'll bring it to Aodhan when we return."

"Promise?" Elise settled back down in the bed. She hoped he wasn't disappointed that there wouldn't be one under the tree waiting for him.

"Promise. Oh, look, Elise." Noli flew to the window. "It's starting to snow!"

"Snow?" She'd never seen snow. Elise joined Noli at the window, faces pressed against the glass, breath forming little clouds on the cold panes. White snowflakes fluttered from the sky.

"Noli, dearest, where did you go?" Mrs. Braddock called. "You need to greet everyone."

Noli sighed and gave her a hug. "Good night, Elise. Coming, Mama."

Elise stood in the window, watching the snow and the moon. Was Aodhan watching the moon, too? She missed her friend. Never before had she had someone to have adventures with, someone who really understood her—what it was like to have no parents, to have strange magic, to feel lonely and misunderstood.

Putting her hand on the window, she gazed up at the moon. In her mind she could see him, standing in his room at the restaurant. She pictured him putting his hand on the window and saying *Good night, Elise.*

"Good night, Aodhan," Elise whispered. With a little sigh, she crawled into bed and went to sleep, dreaming of all the adventures they'd have together.

THIR+Y

Stag Party

"As long as your husband is gentle, you'll be all right," an older woman told Noli, nearly pressing her into the corner with her giant burgundy dress. "Just lie back and think of more pleasant things."

Noli's cheeks burned. Who was this woman, and was she speaking of what she thought she was?

"I...I appreciate the advice. Excuse me; I'm going to find my mother." Noli darted away, weaving through the parlor packed with well-dressed women her mother had invited to the party. Many were related to her—aunties, cousins, and such. The rest were friends of her mother and grandmother. Women she didn't know or care to know.

At least Missy Sassafras wasn't here. Though Noli wouldn't have minded if Jo could have been in attendance.

She wasn't actually looking for her mother, but this was

the *third* older woman dispensing vague advice. She found a spot near the wall and leaned against it, wishing she were invisible. All around her, women gossiped as they drank wine and ate tiny food passed around by Ellen and the other maids.

There were no men in the room. Not even Jameson. V, James, Jeff, her father, and both her grandfathers had left in search of more manly pursuits.

A few women giggled in a way that made her wince. Noli sighed as yet another woman entered the parlor, exchanging air kisses and high-pitched greetings with her mother while setting packages on the table overflowing with gifts.

"It feels so scandalous, having a gathering such as this at night," said a woman dressed like a cake to a woman who resembled a *sausage wearing a dress*, as Miri would say.

Miri. Noli actually missed the sprite. She would *adore* all of this.

"I think it's quite nice. After all, a ball or dinner party is this late; why not a ladies' party? It does seem sudden, though," the sausage replied. "Jeffrey and his bride only got engaged at Thanksgiving, and now the other is getting married as well. You don't think…" Her hand went to her mouth and Noli snatched a petit-four and popped it in her mouth so she wouldn't reply.

She'd heard some of *that* as well, though never to her face.

"No, no. The lucky girl is moving to *France* and she wanted to have a wedding before she moved. Also, apparently her groom is still in mourning, so a small affair is more appropriate." The cake shook her head. "Aside, she's Eady's *daughter* and proper-as-could-be, I'm sure. That other one, the one her son's marrying…" Her voice lowered and her nose wrinkled in distaste. "I hear she works on an airship." She made *airship* sound like a bad word.

"As captain," Noli put in, even though she should probably remain silent. "Vix is *captain* of an airship, and probably the most valiant person I know. Oh, by the way, both of your dresses are… *interesting*." She spun around and marched out of the room, taking refuge in the foyer.

Ugh. This was what she hated most about society. Someone knocked on the front door.

"Miss Noli, shouldn't you return to your party?" Jameson shuffled past her to answer it.

"I… I needed a breath of air." She fanned herself with her hand. "The perfume is threatening to choke me." Not to mention their fussy attitudes.

"Very good, miss." He opened the door and she could hear voices on the other side of the door. "No, I'm sorry, this is a private affair," Jameson told them.

Noli edged closer, trying to spy who was at the door. At this point she'd give nearly anything for Vix's crew to invade the party. Yes, what would they make of Asa, Thad, and Winky?

"We're good friends of Vix's, please, if we could speak to her…" one woman said.

"We should go, Hattie, I told you the likes of us wouldn't be welcome." This woman sounded sullen.

Hattie. Noli knew that name.

"Hittie, Hattie? Is that you?" She rushed to the door, worming her way past Jameson.

Two blond women stood at the door, wearing plain dresses. The older one had short hair. The pink didn't flatter her and she looked awkward, as if she wore dresses even less frequently than Vix. The younger one had long hair that had been put up, her blue gown decorated with a gold pin, a gift clutched in her hands.

"Do we know you?" the one with short hair cocked her head.

"You're Jeff's sister, aren't you?" the other said. "You look so much like him. I'm Hattie Hayden, and this is my sister Hittie."

"Yes, he's spoken so highly of you. Especially you and your engineering skills, Hittie. And Hattie…James isn't here right now but he was asking Vix about you." Noli couldn't help but grin. So these were the air pirate sisters.

"James has?" Hattie's hand went to her hair.

Hittie snorted. "Vix says it's a double wedding. Are you marrying the useless one?"

Useless? Oh yes; to an air pirate, V would be a bit useless.

"Yes. Please, come in." Noli turned to the butler. "It's fine, Jameson."

"Yes, Miss Noli." He frowned and shuffled off, probably to hide in the kitchen, far from the women and the party. Lucky.

Noli saw someone creeping up the stairs. "Vix, wait! The fun has arrived."

Vix turned, her eyes widening in surprise. "Hittie, Hattie, you're here!"

"Thad said you couldn't go to the stag party because you

had to go to some girly affair." Hittie leaned to the side, catching a glimpse of the soiree in the parlor. "I think I'd rather brave the stag party."

"Me too." Vix leaned against the railing. "How do you stand it, Noli?"

"At least we're getting the short version. Usually there are months and months of engagement dinners and teas and dances and calling on people." Noli wasn't sorry to miss all that, not to mention all the societal rules that bound engaged couples. "What's a stag party? I've never heard of one."

Vix grinned. "It's where the groom's friends take him out for a night of manly shenanigans. This one involves Steven and the rest of them."

"Oh dear." Noli laughed at the thought.

"It's why I sent Asa and Thad to join them," Vix told her. "I don't know your Steven well, but I have a feeling he might need rescuing. Not to mention that Jeff would want Asa and Thad to be there."

"Rescuing? It might be good for him," Hittie snorted.

"Probably, and Jeff needs a night with his father." Vix shook her head. "He sure didn't see that coming."

"Is Jeff all right with our father being here?" Noli's belly dipped. She never thought of the converse side of bringing her father home.

Vix waved her hand. "He's *fine.* Very happy, actually. If anything he feels bad because he'd given up all hope of your father ever being found."

"Jeff's father was missing?" Hattie frowned.

"It's a long story, but we found him." Noli glanced over

at the party and sighed. "At any moment my mother's going to appear and drag us inside. If one more woman gives me vague wedding night advice I think I'm going to scream. Or go hide in the kitchen and eat a lot of cake."

At the word *cake* Vix's face lit up. "Is there actual cake? All I see are tiny ones. I want a slice … or an entire cake. Why is all the food so small?"

"Because tiny food is ladylike." Noli grinned.

"Um, Noli…" Vix flushed slightly. "Do you need someone to explain to you what happens on the wedding night? I'm only asking since most society girls have no idea what happens—or what body parts are used."

"Or that it's supposed to be fun," Hittie tittered.

"I just don't want you to be surprised," Vix finished. "And if you do know, then Hittie should explain it anyway, because her version will have you snorting wine out of your nose."

Noli chuckled. "I … I actually know what happens, but I appreciate the offer."

"Oh." Vix's lips pursed as if keeping in her laugh. "Don't tell Jeff."

"He's the one who stormed into my room demanding to know if V was marrying me because I was with child." Noli couldn't stop laughing.

Mama walked into the foyer, looking radiant in a rose gown, her chestnut hair curled artfully. "There you are. Why are you all out here? I feel so terrible shorting you of all your parties, Noli dearest, but it's the best I could do given the time frame."

"It's lovely, Mama. You did a wonderful job. It's I who am

sorry for giving you such short notice. But as you were already throwing a wedding for Vix and Jeff, it made sense for us to be included."

Yes, her mother was having a good time playing mother to two grooms and two brides.

"Oh, Noli... I'm just happy you didn't elope. I don't know why that seems to be all the rage right now." Mama made a face at the notion.

"I have an inkling," Vix muttered to Hittie.

Mama put her hand to Noli's forehead. "Are you feeling poorly? I do worry about you. If you're not strong enough to go to France straight away, you can stay here with me until you're better."

"I'm fine, Mama," she gently brushed off. "Oh, these are Vix's friends, Hittie and Hattie. This is my mother, Edwina Braddock."

Her mother smiled. "Oh, hello. Welcome." She frowned. "Victoria, you also look a bit pale. It's all right; you two can go to bed after we open presents. After all, you need your sleep for tomorrow. Come along, ladies." Picking up her skirts, she sailed into the parlor.

Hattie looked at Vix. "I think after the presents we should sneak away and invade the stag party."

Now *that* sounded fun.

"I know where there are some hoverboards," Noli replied. She knew Vix didn't care about it being illegal for women to hoverboard. Hittie and Hattie probably didn't care either.

"Hoverboard in dresses?" Hittie's eyebrows rose. "Also, it's *snowing*."

"I do everything you do while in a dress and a corset, from fixing engines to hoverboarding." Noli shrugged, not understanding what the fuss was about. "I've never hoverboarded in snow. It might be fun."

"Or cold." Hittie shook her head.

"But James is there," Hattie added. "And Jeff…"

"Ladies." Mama appeared the doorway, wearing a stern expression.

"We better go. I know that tone," Noli said. "But after… I'm curious as to what they're up to." Hopefully *manly shenanigans* didn't mean *joy house*.

Vix nodded. "Yes, we should go."

In a flurry of laughter, the four of them piled into the parlor.

• • • • • • • •

Steven sat in the tall, ornate wooden chair, frozen. He was surrounded by men in suits and top hats, most of them somehow related to Noli. Jeff sat next to him, in an equally tall chair. They had drinks in their hands. On the table in front of them was a woman performing acrobatics while only wearing a corset and bloomers.

Well, he thought they were acrobatics.

In the background, other women swung on swings, or plied men with drinks and then danced with them. All around them, men drank, gambled, and smoked cigars, filling the room with a smoky halo.

"V isn't watching the show," James tattled. "Drink, drink, drink."

With a sigh, Steven took a drink of his whiskey. It seemed as if they'd been here forever. Somehow this entire night had turned into some sort of drinking game. Jeff called it a "stag party." Was it called such because the man of honor felt like a hunted deer?

Certainly the theme seemed to be *let's embarrass Steven.*

Could they leave already?

"Jeff, Jeff." A very large dark man in an ill-fitting suit came over to the table, a ruffian in an eye-patch and equally ill-fitting suit with him. They looked vaguely familiar.

"Asa, Thad." Jeff looked over and grinned. "You're here!" He drained his glass and stood.

"The Captain told us. Would've been here sooner, but we didn't realize there was a dress code," the one in the eye patch said. "Also, Asa had a little trouble getting in."

Ah, this would be Jeff's crew.

"Oh, is this one Noli's?" The dark one eyed him. "I'm Asa. You're Steven, I presume?"

Steven nodded, unsure if things had just gotten better or worse. "Yes, I am."

The other one, the one with the eye patch, stood there gaping at the woman on the table as she put her feet over her head.

"Oh, friends of yours, Jeff? I think we need more liquor," Mr. Braddock cheered. He was a bit tipsy…so were Noli's grandfathers, for that matter.

Asa scooted closer to them. "The Captain, Noli, Hittie,

and Hattie tried to come rescue you a short while ago, but they couldn't get in. I've never seen the Captain in a dress before. Hittie and Hattie either." He laughed.

"Noli was here?" Steven wasn't sure if he should be pleased or scandalized.

"Noli shouldn't be here, not with Father, Grandpa, *and* Grandfather present." Jeff shook his head. "Actually, none of them should be here, since my father and grandfathers wouldn't understand, though normally I'd find it quite amusing."

"We should have gone to Mathias' Place." James shook his head. "Wait, did you say Hattie was here?"

"Yes, she and Hittie came for the festivities. Said they wouldn't miss it." Thad's eye remained riveted on the girl on the table.

"I'll make sure they're invited to the ceremony," Jeff replied. "I think I might even be able to ensure you're seated next to each other at supper."

His father returned with more drinks and passed them out. Noli's grandfather gave everyone cigars.

Jeff clapped him on the shoulder. "You're doing fine, Darrow. We might just make a man of you yet."

Steven tried not to sigh as he glanced at the girl on the table. "Could we try something else? Gambling perhaps? Though James is lousy at cards."

Anything to get away from … this.

"Am not." James scowled.

"Yes, you are." Steven stood, the room swimming a

little. Already he'd had too much to drink. He had a feeling that was the point.

"Where are you all going?" Mr. Braddock asked.

Jeff raised his glass. "We're going to visit Lady Luck."

Mr. Braddock tipped his head. "Enjoy."

Not likely. Steven wished he was with Noli. Instead, he allowed Jeff to put a new drink in his hand and lead him off.

He wasn't sure what time it was when they piled back into a motorcab and returned to Noli's grandfather's house, reeking of alcohol and cigar smoke. At some point it had started to snow. Steven's head pounded as they walked inside, knocking snow off their shoes, and hanging up their hats.

"I hope you had a good time, son." Mr. Braddock clapped Steven on the shoulder. "I'm glad Noli has a nice chap like you to take care of her." He went up the stairs.

Jeff snorted from behind them. "I think Noli takes care of *you*."

"She does," he and James agreed in unison.

Everyone went upstairs to bed. Steven waited until all was quiet then snuck down the hall to Noli's room, a parcel in his hand. A light glimmered under the door.

"Noli?" he whispered, cracking open the door. She was in the window seat, asleep, *Great Expectations* on her lap. "Oh, Noli, you'll catch cold." He put her book and his parcel down, scooped her up, and tucked her into bed, pulling the covers up under her chin.

"V?" Her eyes fluttered open. She grimaced. "What do you smell like?"

"Cigars and whiskey." He sighed.

"Oh. So you went to—"

He held up a hand. "Not a joy house, but it was some sort of…gentleman's club. Like Mathias' only with gambling and mortals."

"And you didn't have to bring a kitten?" Noli sat up.

"No. No kittens." He couldn't help but smile. "I heard that you tried to rescue us. Didn't you have a party here?"

She made a face. "Yes, I now have more linens than I know what to do with. It was a present party, where all of Mama and Grandmamma's friends gave us advice and things for our new households. It's Vix I really felt sorry for."

"It sounds dreadful." Steven picked up the parcel. "I know it's not Christmas yet. But I got something for you."

"You didn't have to get me anything. Though I do have something for you as well." She opened the gift.

Steven sat down next to her. "I thought that we could read this together and discuss it, like we used to. It's not Machiavelli, though I still want you to read that."

"*The Art of War*, by Sun Tzu?" She traced the cover with her finger, then flipped it open to a random page. "*Can you imagine what I would do if I could do all I can?* I can't wait to read this with you. I appreciate it." Noli leaned in and kissed him. "I have something for you as well." She went to the dresser and pulled out a small box. Her cheeks pinked as she handed it to him and sat back down.

"What's this?" He opened the box and inside was a set of very fancy gold cuff links.

"They were Papa's, from when he married my mother. She'd had them put away for me to give to whomever I married." Her cheeks remained pink. "My father said it was all right, that he'd be pleased for you to have them. I ... I don't have anything else for you other than a kiss."

"That's all I need, and the cuff links are splendid." He tucked them in his pocket. It was such a thoughtful gift. "Now, about that kiss ..." Fumbling in his other pocket, he pulled out a bit of mistletoe. "I've wanted to kiss you under the mistletoe for some time."

"Have you?" Her eyes danced. "There's a kissing ball downstairs. Everyone's asleep."

"Us sneaking downstairs is asking to be caught." Steven held the mistletoe over them with one hand, then pulled her to him with the other. Their lips met and he kissed her gently, so happy that after all those years of loving her from the shadows, that he could now share his dreams with her without reservation. All this he poured into his kiss. He broke it off, heart beating quickly. If he continued ...

Instead, he kissed her forehead. There'd be time for everything else later. "Merry Christmas, Noli. I love you."

"Merry Christmas, V. I love you too." She grinned.

"Good night."

Uncertain times were coming. They had a staff to assemble, a queen to defeat, and a future queen to raise. He was grateful to have Noli at his side.

THIRTY-ONE

Wedding Bells

"Noli, dearest, it's time." Mama came into her room and straightened her veil, which was attached to a coronet of hothouse flowers. "You look beautiful. My baby girl is all grown up and getting married." Her fingers ran gently down Noli's cheek. "I hope this is enough for you—"

"Mama, I didn't want a giant society wedding, or a season, or any of that," Noli replied honestly. "All I really wanted was to have a wedding with my family...and Papa to walk me down the aisle." She sniffed, trying to keep back the tears. She never thought she'd be the kind of girl to get weepy at her wedding.

Mama gave her a kiss on the cheek and smoothed her hair. "Thank you for never giving up on your father. You have no idea how happy I am to have him back. Oh, that dress is so beautiful on you."

"I love it, Mama." Noli turned to look at herself. "You outdid yourself on the design." The dress wasn't poufy, nor was it a bustle gown, yet it had some body to it. It was made of white silk, swathed with white and gold brocade. The back was a swirl of ruffles that fanned out like a mermaid's tail, creating a small train. The brocade bodice laced up like a corset. Missy Sassafras would never approve—but Jo would. So would Miri … and Charlotte.

Mama beamed. "I just knew you would. It suits you perfectly."

She had never realized her mother had actually finished a wedding gown and a complete trousseau, and had them packed away, ready and waiting, along with other trifles and family trinkets.

"You and Papa are staying in Boston?" Noli asked. Her mother's dress was beautiful as well, as red as Christmas, with a slight gold accent around the neckline.

"Yes, he's going into business with my father for now." Mama beamed and picked up the bouquet of roses off the dresser. "There you are. You really do love Steven, don't you?" She handed her the flowers. "You always have. He's so young—and has so many responsibilities with his father gone. But…" A smile crossed her lips. "You two always have been able to accomplish anything when you worked together. I hope you remember that. Marriage is work for both parties. It takes patience, love, and compromise."

"It does, doesn't it?" Noli sniffed her bouquet of flowers. "I do love him. So much. I'm not marrying for duty; I'm marrying for love."

V made her a better person, and she'd like to think she did the same for him.

"I know, dearest, I know. Oh, before I forget." Mama opened a little pouch that had been hanging around her wrist. "Here." She fastened a necklace around Noli's neck. "Your grandmamma gave this to me when I married your father. It had been hers, then it was mine, and now...and now it's yours—it can be your something old *and* something blue."

"Oh, Mama." Noli's eyes teared up in gratitude as her hand went to the rather large sapphire and diamond pendant. She remembered her mother wearing it for fancy occasions before her father had disappeared.

Her mother's finger tapped her lips. "Something old, something new, something borrowed, something blue—and you have a penny in your shoe?"

"I do, Mama." A penny slid around in the bottom of her borrowed slippers. It was rather uncomfortable. "Are we ready?" All this fussing made her fidget.

"Yes." A sad look filled her mother's eyes. "Oh, I'll miss you. But now you have your chance to go to a university and see new and exciting places, just like you've always wanted."

If she only knew.

"I'll miss you as well, Mama." She'd miss her so much, but...

"It's a pity you must bring Elise with you. Are you certain you don't wish for me to care for her for a while so you can enjoy being a newlywed?" her mother offered. "I wouldn't mind."

"We'll bring her with us for now, but if it doesn't work out, you'll be the first person I aethergraph," Noli assured her.

She had a feeling her mother needed something to keep her occupied, with both children gone and no dress shop. They'd have to see how everything went, but Noli knew the offer was genuine, and she greatly appreciated it. It might end up being the best option for Elise; right now they didn't know. So much was uncertain.

"Noli." Her father stood in the doorway. "I ... you ... you ... " His voice choked. "And Eady ... you both look so beautiful. It's time, Noli." He offered her his arm.

Mama pulled the lace veil over Noli's face. "I'll take my seat. I love you."

"I love you too, Mama." Noli watched her mother hustle down the hall. Then, she took her father's arm as they walked down the stairs.

Vix stood in the downstairs hallway, trembling. Her lace dress wasn't nearly as fancy as Noli's, but its elegant simplicity was stunning. Then again, her mother probably started it at Thanksgiving when their engagement had been announced.

"Are you all right, Vix?" Noli left her father and gave Vix a hug.

"I'm fine." Vix smiled shyly and didn't shrug her off.

Noli looked around. "Are your parents here?" She hadn't heard any mention of Vix's parents, and she didn't see any man to walk Vix down the aisle.

"No. It's better this way," Vix said softly. "It ... I almost asked someone special to be here, but I'm not sure society is ready for the likes of him. I'm my own person, anyway. I don't need someone to give me away."

"I admire you for being such a strong woman." Noli had a feeling that the person who Vix spoke of was the fae air pirate who'd given her her start.

"You're stronger than you think," Vix replied. "And stronger than some men give you credit for." She grinned. "Keep in touch, all right?"

"We will." Noli returned to her father's side. They were to enter after Vix.

"Oh, you're both so pretty." Elise appeared, in a red and white ruffled dress, a basket of red rose petals in her hand.

"You look lovely, Elise. Are you ready?" Noli's heart thumped in her chest.

"Yes." Elise twirled around.

Jameson opened the great room doors. The music began to play and Noli's ears roared.

The crowd stood and Elise walked down the aisle scattering rose petals. Vix took a deep breath and followed. When Vix reached the altar, Noli and her father walked down the aisle, arm in arm. Noli looked into the sea of faces and almost froze.

She had to remind herself that she wasn't doing this for her mother or society. She was already married to V in the Otherworld. This … this was for herself and only herself.

Hattie waved at her. She caught sight of Thad and Winky and grinned. As usual, Winky wore his striped hat, glasses sliding down his nose. The great room at Grandfather Montgomery's had been decorated with greenery and ribbons.

Chairs were set up with an aisle in the middle, musicians in one corner, and an alter festooned with so many Christmas flowers it looked as if a garden had sprouted. The same pastor who'd married her parents had been found and he stood there, waiting, peering at a large book.

Next to him stood V, in a tuxedo, a nervous look on his face. James stood behind him. Opposite them were Vix and Jeff, Asa behind them as best man. All the men wore red accents. Someone had made Jeff shave.

Her father pulled her veil back over her hair and gave her a kiss on the cheek. "I love you, Noli," he whispered.

"I love you too, Papa," she whispered back, taking her place by V.

The pastor droned on about marriage and other boring things, and periodically read from the Bible. Her belly rumbled with hunger. There'd be a cake afterward for everyone in attendance, then an elaborate dinner for relations and close friends before they all went off to Christmas Eve services. It had already been a long day of preparations and it was difficult not to yawn.

Finally, the minister turned to Jeff and Vix. "Jeffery Cornelius Braddock, will you have this woman as your lawful wedded wife, to live together in the holy estate of matrimony? Will you love her, comfort her, honor her, and keep her in sickness as in health; and, forsaking all others, be true to her so long as you both shall live?"

Jeff gazed at Vix, who wore no veil, only a coronet of flowers, as he took her hands in his, bringing her close to him. "I will."

"Victoria Eleanor Adler, will you have this man as your lawful wedded husband, to live together in the holy estate of matrimony? Will you obey him, and serve him, and love, honor, and keep him in sickness as in health; and, forsaking all others, be true to him so long as you both shall live?"

"I will." She grinned. "Except for the 'obey' and 'serve' part. After all, *I'm* still the captain."

A scandalized look crossed the minister's face as a murmur ran through the crowd. Someone cheered, probably Hittie. Noli grinned.

The minister turned to them. Noli stepped closer to V.

"Steven Darrow, will you have this woman as your lawful wedded wife, to live together in the holy estate of matrimony? Will you love her, comfort her, honor her, and keep her in sickness as in health; and, forsaking all others, be true to her so long as you both shall live?" he asked.

"I will." V's eyes met hers. "By the Bright Lady I will." This last part was in a soft whisper as he took her hands in his and drew her close.

"Magnolia Montgomery Braddock, will you have this man as your lawful wedded husband, to live together in the holy estate of matrimony? Will you obey him, and serve him, and love, honor, and keep him in sickness as in health; and, forsaking all others, be true to him so long as you both shall live?"

"I will." She couldn't stop grinning. "However, I'm still the queen," she added in quiet Latin. V suppressed a laugh, his eyes dancing.

"The rings?" the minister asked.

Asa handed Jeff his rings, and James did the same for V.

V slid the thin gold ring onto her hand. "With this I thee wed."

The minister droned on again about boring things. Not that she listened. All she could do was hold V's hand and grin.

"Those whom God hath joined together, let no man put asunder," the minister announced. "Mr. and Mrs. Braddock, and Mr. and Mrs. Darrow, as witnessed before God and this company, having given and pledged their troth and declared the same; I now pronounce that they are man and wife. Gentlemen, you may now kiss your respective brides."

V leaned in and kissed her, so long and deep she could hear giggles and titters from the crowd.

The music played and Jeff led Vix down the aisle, then V led her out. Jeff and Vix disappeared and V led her into the parlor so they could steal a few moments alone until they were ushered back into the great room, which was quickly being converted into a reception hall.

With his foot, Steven pushed the door of the parlor closed and kissed her in a way that made her wonder how much time they had before they would be called back into the room.

Probably not that much.

"Why, Mr. Darrow, are you getting fresh with me?" She gazed into his eyes as he leaned her against the door, his face inches from hers, hat falling off his head.

"Why, Mrs. Darrow, I do believe I am." His lips captured hers as their bodies pressed together.

Mrs. Darrow. Oh. She was Mrs. Darrow, wasn't she?

"The day after tomorrow you're Your Grace again, but

for today and tomorrow, you're Mrs. Darrow." His grin widened as he leaned in for another kiss.

Someone knocked on the door and they jumped away from each other, startled.

"Five minutes until photographs," James called from the other side.

"That was *fast*." Steven shook his head. "Your mother and grandmother make things move at a speed that would make the seneschal's head spin."

"And we're not finished in the slightest. But yes, they're quite good, aren't they?" Even though the wedding had been quick and small, it was still an acceptably extravagant society affair.

"Oh, it's snowing again." Noli went over to the parlor window and gazed out at the piles of snowflakes. "I think tomorrow we need a snowball fight. Team Darrow versus Team Braddock."

"Why, Mrs. Darrow, I think that's an excellent idea." V came up behind her, wrapping his arms around her waist and bringing her close.

Noli traced the cuff links she'd given him last night, then turned to bury her face in his chest, breathing in the scent of him. He smelled like home.

"We did it, didn't we?" she said. "We took a kingdom, fell in love, and got married. Now we're going to university, ruling the kingdom, and doing our duty to your family. And they say you can't have it all."

V touched his forehead to hers. "No one can have it all. But we have what we need. At least, I have everything I need."

His fingers brushed her face, the movement as light as the touch of a feather. "Do you have everything you need, Noli?"

There was still so much to do, so much at stake, with Elise and the Staff of Eris and the state of the Otherworld. But it no longer seemed impossible. She looked into V's eyes and ran her fingers through his hair, which still wouldn't lie quite flat.

"Yes, Mr. Darrow, I believe I do." Noli reached up and kissed him, pouring everything into that single kiss as church bells rang in the distance, rejoicing with them.

EPIL⊕GUE

The Time is Near

Nearly all of the pieces of the staff were in the Otherworld now. She could feel it.

The time was drawing near.

The girl would assemble the staff, the small one would wield it, and the silly queen would be overthrown.

No longer would she need to rely on the sacrifice for nourishment. No longer would she be kept hungry.

Very soon, she would be free.

All she had to do was wait.

THE END

Author's Note

One of the things I enjoy about writing steampunk is the ability to move historical things back and forth, manipulating events, places, and history to suit my story. For example, Los Angeles didn't have an art museum in 1901; then again, they didn't have airships at all. In any case, robbing an art museum—even if you have magic—is probably not a very good idea.

Likewise, I'm not entirely sure there were "ladies' nights" such as the one Noli and company enjoyed at Mathias' Place, but it certainly sounds fun. Stag parties have been around in some way, shape, or form for some time, and this, of course, gave me one more way to torture V. Since I was torturing him, it seemed only fair to harass Vix and Noli with a bridal shower. Many wellborn girls of that era had no idea what happened on their wedding night, and the advice they'd get from their mothers, if they got any at all, would be vague at best, like what was given to Noli.

Mintonette was actually an early term for volleyball, although in the Otherworld they play it using no hands, just magic. I don't think there's a portal to Faerie in Central Park, but if you find one, please let me know.

—Suzanne Lazear

Acknowledgments

It takes a lot of people to make a book. I'd like to thank my awesome editor, who gave Noli a chance, and the Flux team who made her shine. My agent. The usual suspects, especially the Apocalypsies, the Class of 2k12, LARA, the Steamed Lolitas, and my ever-epic Airship Squadron.

Hugs and cupcakes to Rachel, Jenn, Julie, Harmony, Reina, Jenny, Susan, Robin, Sarah, and everyone else who helped me with this story.

I'd also like to thank all of you, because without readers there would be no books. Your tweets, emails, and messages mean a lot to me. *~launches cupcake cannon~*

Writing can be very solitary, and I'm quite grateful to Twitter, which not only cheered me on and gave me distractions when I needed it but has provided me with more crazy ideas than you will ever know. If you tweet it, it just might end up in a book. (Lauren is probably regretting inventing Missy Sassafras and her perfect scones right now.)

I also couldn't have done this without my husband and my daughter, who cheer me on and are patient when I'm on deadline. Last but not least, I'd like to thank my parents for buying me books and encouraging me to stick with my dreams.

Photo by John Lazear

About the Author

Suzanne Lazear (Los Angeles, CA) hopes to bring hats back into fashion. She's also fond of swords, cupcakes, and fairy tales. She's a regular blogger at *Steamed,* a group steampunk blog. *Fragile Destiny* is her third novel.

To learn more about the world of the Aether Chronicles, please go to www.aetherchronicles.com or visit the author at www.suzannelazear.com.